THE VICES

ALSO BY LAWRENCE DOUGLAS

The Catastrophist
The Memory of Judgment
Sense and Nonsensibility (with Alexander George)

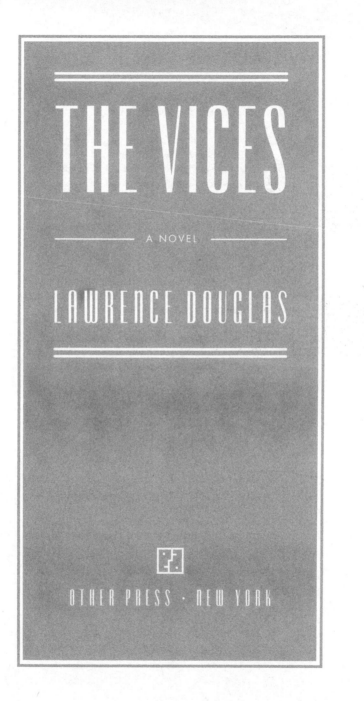

THE VICES

A NOVEL

LAWRENCE DOUGLAS

OTHER PRESS · NEW YORK

Production Editor: *Yvonne E. Cárdenas*
Text Designer: *Simon M. Sullivan*
This book was set in 12.25 pt Fairfield LH Light
by Alpha Design & Composition of Pittsfield, NH

10 9 8 7 6 5 4 3 2 1

Library of Congress Cataloging-in-Publication Data

Douglas, Lawrence.
The Vices / by Lawrence Douglas.
p. cm.
ISBN 978-1-59051-415-3 — ISBN 978-1-59051-416-0 (e-book)
1. Hungarian Americans—Fiction. 2. Jewish families—Fiction.
3. Art—Collectors and collecting—Fiction. 4. Domestic fiction.
5. Psychological fiction. I. Title.
PS3604.O928V53 2011
813'.6—dc22

2010054185

For Jacob and Milo

There was but one man who understood me, and he didn't understand me.

—HEGEL

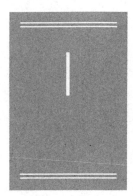

ONE

On July 18, 200–, at 18:00 GMT, the *Queen Mary 2* left Southampton with 2,912 passengers and roughly half as many crew. She arrived at the Brooklyn dockyards on the morning of July 24, with 2,911 passengers. In a brief wire service piece, the *New York Times* identified the missing passenger as "Oliver Vice, 41, a professor of philosophy at Harkness College in western Massachusetts." He was also my closest friend, and remained so, even after he ruined my marriage.

Officials for Cunard, owner and operator of the *QM2*, prepared a meticulous account of Oliver's last hours. On the night of July 22, the *QM2* passed seventeen nautical miles north of the point where, ninety years earlier, the *Titanic* had struck an iceberg. That placed her 150 miles south of Tilt Cove in Newfoundland, heading southwest at twenty-two knots. The evening's entertainment included a screening, in questionable taste, of the movie *Titanic* in the Queen's Room, and a performance of *Hamlet, Condensed*, in the Royal Court Theater on Deck 3, but apparently Oliver wasn't in the mood for either. He arrived promptly for the 20:30 seating in the Britannia dining room, joined by his mother, wearing the sapphire necklace that her second husband had

purchased in Zurich. The crossing was meant to cele-
brate her seventieth birthday, which technically wouldn't
fall until mid-August. Oliver wore a tux; I knew the
outfit well, for I was with him when he purchased it in
London's Jermyn Street several years before. According
to his mother, he was "a bit withdrawn," but that was
hardly news given their strained relations; she herself
was suffering a "withering atmospheric headache" as a
result of the storm. Shortly after dessert and a cigarette
in the Chart Room Bar, one of the two enclosed areas
that permitted smoking, Francizka retired to her Deck
12 suite, which had a connecting door to Oliver's room.

Oliver stayed in the Chart Room. Receipts show he
had a second gimlet, then crossed Level 3 to the ca-
sino, where he purchased two hundred dollars' worth of
chips and took a seat at a low-stakes blackjack table. He
played off and on for two hours, ordering a third gimlet. At 00:45 he cashed out with $280, that is, with win-
nings of $80, a tidy gain. Oliver always was a sensible
gambler. He made it a point to avoid unnecessary risk.

His next destination was the G32 Nightclub (named
for the QM2's shipyard hull number) on Deck 2. There
he met a German woman traveling with her brother, a
thirty-six-year-old journalist confined to a recumbent
wheelchair with late-stage amyotrophic lateral sclero-
sis. The brother and sister (accompanied by his round-
the-clock nurse) had boarded in Hamburg, the QM2's
original point of embarkation; half the passengers on
this crossing were German. Oliver and the Germans
conversed in a mix of languages—English, German,
French—and listened to a Caribbean band, St. Lucia,

play covers of popular reggae and soul classics. Oliver
and the German woman briefly danced together. As the
threesome prepared to leave G32, Oliver handed the
astonished lead singer of St. Lucia his eighty dollars
of blackjack winnings as a tip, certainly an impulsive
gesture, but a sign of a man shedding all worldly possessions? Not to my mind. If he was already planning
a plunge, why keep two hundred dollars in his pocket?

The brother's nurse, who also was suffering from a
headache, had been let off early, so Oliver helped the
German woman wheel her brother back to his state-
room on Deck 9. With the brother safely returned to
his medical suite, the woman invited Oliver for a drink
in the Terrace Bar, but he declined. It was now around
02:45, or rather 01:45, taking into account the one-hour
turn-back scheduled every night as the time zones were
crossed between England and New York. Oliver rode the
elevator or took the stairs to Deck 13, where he watched
four British teenagers playing Ping-Pong by the pavilion
pool. The three girls and one boy were surprised by the
unexpected appearance of a single man in tuxedo in the
otherwise empty pavilion. The boy, sixteen, responded to
my e-mail as follows: "Right, I remember him—he stood
there watching us for a time. We thought at first he was
drunk, but he didn't look wobbly. He simply watched
us, no smile or anything. Definitely a bit odd." Without
a word or gesture, Oliver then exited through the exte-
rior door to the boardwalk. The force of the wind from
the deck blew the Ping-Pong ball right off the table; the
game resumed only after the mysterious man had disappeared and managed, against the wind, to force the door

shut. A CCTV camera, one of nineteen that kept the ship under continuous but not complete surveillance, captured an image of Oliver on the aft deck of Level 13, holding fast to the guardrail, looking out to sea. The time was recorded at 02:32. In the grainy stutter of the CCTV, which I watch and rewatch on my laptop, Oliver can then be seen, back to viewer, walking toward the ship's stern. He never reached the area covered by the next camera, only twenty yards away.

Oliver and his mother usually had breakfast together. His failure to answer her knock didn't immediately alarm her. Twice on the crossing he'd risen early to perambulate the quarter-mile deck. It was only a half-hour later, when Francizka opened the unlocked door connecting their rooms and noticed his bed hadn't been slept in, that she contacted the QM2's security office. The officer on call initially resisted issuing a shipwide missing person announcement: experience had taught him that it was not unusual for singles to spend nights in cabins other than their own, and it was still early. Francizka, however, demanded to speak directly to the ship's chief security officer, who reluctantly commenced the full search procedure, a time-consuming combing of the entire ship. On a typical six-day crossing, the QM2 conducts perhaps two full-vessel searches; the missing person is usually located, inebriated or in an otherwise compromised state, within an hour of the first announcement. After an extensive search and an examination of the CCTV tapes, Oliver was officially listed as "presumed overboard" at 12:43 on July 23. Passengers swimming in the terrace pool, reading in deck chairs, or jogging on the promenade might have noticed three U.S. naval helicopters, scrambled from Pinchgut Point on Newfoundland, passing starboard of the ship en route toward the area where navigators had calculated the missing person would have entered the water. Briefly designated a search and rescue operation, this was changed at 16:00 to search and recovery. Oliver's body was never found.

Francizka always insisted it was an accident, and a preventable one at that. At the memorial service, conducted in the Harkness Club in Manhattan, she was dry-eyed but distraught, obscurely repeating, "Ollie, Ollie, Ollie— always so stubborn . . ." She sat flanked by her lawyer, who had already prepared a wrongful death complaint against Cunard, and by Bartholomew, Oliver's gargantuan fraternal twin, who surveyed the funeral and accepted condolences with the lethargic detachment of the clinically depressed. Depression explained Bartholomew's absence from the trip and also, I suppose, his failure to eulogize his brother. I'd intended to speak at the service—in fact, had stayed up the better part of the night preparing my eulogy—but in the end deferred to Oliver's colleagues in the philosophy department. It's a decision I'll always regret. Three professors made brief statements. The president of Harkness spoke of Oliver's philosophical accomplishments and political courage, of his well-publicized run-in with President Clinton at Oxford, and of his opposition to CIA recruitment on campus. But none of the eulogists showed any deeper appreciation or understanding of Oliver, the man. They ignored his suffering, when they should have extolled it. They described a thinker whose

gifts would have propelled him to the forefront of contemporary analytic philosophy, but their tone told of a
wunderkind who, after an early splash, had drifted into
premature irrelevance. They moved no one to tears, except maybe Oliver's "widows," five in all, drawn from
various spots on the globe, spread about the handsome
wood-paneled clubroom, and sobbing from beginning
to end. There was Jean Sommer, the so-called soul
mate, grief-stricken and jet-lagged after a flight from
London; Anna Strindberg, the stunning six-foot great-
granddaughter of the Swedish misogynist and play-
wright; Mary Gwon, the Korean-born museum curator;
Caroline Dworkin, the twenty-something bookstore
clerk who clutched a volume of Blake's poetry; and a
still younger woman I didn't recognize. Over the "widows" hovered the spirit of Sophia Baum, whose tragic
death a decade before preordained—so went the tidy
story that I've never accepted—Oliver's own. The "widows" cried openly, but not in competition. I doubt they
knew fully of each other. Like members of a terrorist
cell, each lover had knowledge limited to one degree of
separation, a blinkered picture of Oliver's complex romantic entanglements. They shed tears in memory of
their love for the deceased and of the futility of their
relationship with him.

The question of the manner of death was on everyone's mind, but no one spoke about it, at least not directly. Certainly accident couldn't be ruled out. Oliver
liked foul weather, and the weather on the night of
the twenty-second had been something worse than
that. The morning had begun with cheerful clouds

and bright sunshine, conditions that typically left Oliver glum. But the noon weather update, broadcast over the *QM2*'s public address system, warned of a North Atlantic storm moving in the ship's direction. By early afternoon the sky closed and the wind picked up. Passengers in deck chairs wrapped themselves in Cunard's woolen blankets, then escaped to the cabin as a thick, cold rain lashed the deck. The ship, which until then had plowed forward, subduing the Atlantic's swells, now yawed and pitched with the chop; the sick bay reported a run on Dramamine, freely dispensed at all elevator banks. A high-wind alert closed the passenger lookout and the forward decks; by midnight the aft decks should have been locked as well. By two in the morning, the time of Oliver's encounter with the teenage Ping-Pong players, the rain had yielded to curling ribbons of chilly fog that engulfed the ship. The wind had strengthened from gale to severe gale. In the silent footage from the CCTV, in the last moments of his life, Oliver looks almost Keatonesque: arm crooked around the guardrail, tuxedo whipping wildly, and his hair standing stiffly like a model Gibraltar. On a wet and slippery deck, on a night of violent winds—the strongest of which was clocked at fifty-six miles per hour by the Doppler radar on the bridge—the official report put it discreetly: "It cannot be ruled out that the overboard incident was the consequence of an accident and not of a deliberate act." In response to persistent inquiries from Francizka's attorney, Cunard acknowledged that given the weather conditions, *all* cabin doors should have been secured, both forward and aft. This admission all but invited the wrongful death suit, which was settled out of court for an undisclosed sum.

And this, too, is clear: that morning, on a computer in the Library, Oliver had confirmed an exam with a cardiologist for a month hence, to determine the cause of the "whooshing" noise his doctor had detected in his carotid artery during a recent checkup. Oliver's biological father, the "BF," had died of a heart attack at fifty-four, or so went the official story; the whooshing could have been an early sign of partial arterial blockage, and Oliver wasn't taking any chances. He was fastidious about his yearly checkups, and in an age of managed care, succeeded in extracting referrals on an annual basis for a whole battery of expensive procedures: colonoscopy, cardiac stress test, dermatological exam, calcification MRI. He took Lipitor for a cholesterol level that was only mildly elevated, and for years had been chewing a baby aspirin on a daily basis, although no doctor had recommended that he do so. Both his mother and brother smoked heavily, but Oliver never touched a cigarette and had last tasted meat as a teenager. He went to the gym regularly, running on a treadmill and doing light weights; earlier that day he'd spent an hour at the ship's health club. If he drank red wine and ate a square of dark chocolate every day, this was only because the science section of the *Times* had reported on the health benefits of doing so.

Professionally, things were going well, though maybe not as well as earlier in a career that brought precocious success. Writer's block had stalled work on *The Fake*, a book that promised to wed his philosophical and art historical interests. Still, *Paradoxes of Self,* his highly original, prize-winning contribution to the philosophy of identity, was scheduled to appear in Turkish and Japanese editions. He'd recently received an invitation to lecture that fall at Berlin's prestigious Wissenschaftskolleg. On the morning of his disappearance, after playing two games of chess with a British stage actor in the Chart Room, he'd penned himself a reminder found on his cabin desk: *schedule berlin flight.* He'd spent part of the afternoon reading and taking notes on David Hume's essay "On Miracles," writing in the margins of one page, *to believe in miracles is itself the most miraculous of things.* Hardly the behavior of a man planning suicide.

Only Oliver *was* suicidal. At the very least, he thought and talked about suicide a great deal. True, I'd never heard him describe a concrete plan, but he often discoursed at length on the general attractions of the idea. He continued to hold himself responsible for Sophia Baum's death, though, as I've said, I don't think this preordained anything. On a stand in his office, where you might expect to find a dictionary, Oliver kept the *Oxford Book of Death.* Tacked to a bulletin board were Wittgenstein's words: *Death is not an event in life: we do not live to experience death.* For years he'd collected the work of two artists—Jules Pascin and Ralph Barton—who shared little in common except that both had committed suicide. Oliver inherited his first "Pascin" from his biological father, the BF, a drawing of a naked prostitute pulling on, or maybe taking off, a black stocking. This was the work that he was to bequeath to me; it now hangs in the bedroom of the house I no longer share with my wife. Pascin never gained the fame he believed he deserved. A fixture of Montparnasse bohemianism in the 1920s, a spendthrift and an alcoholic, he remained largely unknown, long after his friends Modigliani and Soutine had achieved great success. On the eve of his first one-man show, he hanged himself after first slitting his wrists and writing a farewell note to his mistress in his own blood.

Barton was also an artist of the twenties, but in contrast to Pascin, successful and famous in his own lifetime. Oliver became interested in Barton's caricatures after reading a tribute written by John Updike for a retrospective at a gallery in New York. Before Peter Arno, Barton had been *The New Yorker*'s most influential and highest-paid illustrator. A close friend of Charlie Chaplin and George Gershwin, and graced with extraordinary good looks, Barton had killed himself shortly before his fortieth birthday. On the fateful morning, he changed into fresh pajamas, slipped on a silken robe, smoked a cigarette in the bedroom of his lavish apartment, opened a copy of *Gray's Anatomy* to a diagram of the heart, and then, perhaps on impulse, shot himself through the head. In a note pinned to his pillow, he had written, *Fed up inventing new devices for getting through 24 hours every day . . . If the gossips insist upon something more definite and thrilling as a reason, let them choose my impending appointment with my dentist, or the fact that I happen to be painfully short of cash at the moment.*

True, Oliver left no note, a striking omission given his devotion to courtesy and reasoned justification. But

like Barton he often complained about the wearying effort of trying to escape himself. On the afternoon of the
twenty-second, after logging on to a computer in the
QM2's library and confirming his cardiac exam, he sent
me an e-mail of two words: *Desperately depressed.*

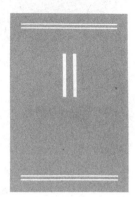

TWO

I'd met Oliver a dozen years earlier, and took an immediate dislike to him. It was my first year as writer-in-residence at Harkness College. Melissa—we were engaged at the time—was teaching at a private school two hours south in Connecticut, and on those weekends when I found myself alone, I would indulge my bibliomania, a passion for books not only as the most honest and intimate expressions of the lived experience of human beings, but as physical objects, specimens to be hefted and riffled through, held and appreciated for the texture and blush of their pages, the suppleness of their bindings, and the useful art of their typesetting. Financial necessity kept my purchases modest—no signed first editions by the titans of literary modernism, no leather-bound volumes from distant centuries; I mainly collected nice, tight hardback copies of books I'd loved or imagined one day loving. Harkness proved a blessing in this regard. What the Pilgrim Valley lacked by way of a rich and edgy cultural life, it made up for in the quality of its used bookstores.

On a cold, wet, muddy Saturday in early spring, I pulled to a stop before a sagging bungalow with unpainted, weather-beaten clapboards. A sign in Gothic script signaled the home of BROCH'S BOOKS: LITERARY, SCHOLARLY, WEIRD. A cowbell rattled my entrance, but the shop appeared untended until a short, overweight, and heavily bearded man emerged from the back room. "Welcome," he huffed. He wore thick glasses with dark blinders on the side, like those of a wayward racehorse; the lenses reduced his eyes to tiny pinpricks through which he appeared less to see me than to sense my presence. After moving papers about the counter for a few moments, he said, "Well, let me know if I can be of any help," and shuffled off.

Lit by a single gray dangling bulb, the back room was stacked from floor to ceiling with books, save for a constricted space in the middle, which accommodated a small table and two metal folding chairs. The owner had resettled himself before a game of chess; his opponent was staring intently at the board, though periodically he would, without the slightest movement of his head, cast his eyes in the direction of the time clock, evidently a source of concern. Only when he briefly lifted his gaze and scrutinized me with the same impassive expression he directed to the board did I see that it was a colleague from Harkness. I hadn't officially been introduced to Oliver Vice, but I knew some of the lore that surrounded him. A protégé of Willard Frech, the Harvard philosopher whose name couldn't be mentioned without the obligatory tagline "America's leading public intellectual," Vice had barely finished his Ph.D. when he received a Junior Research Fellowship to Oxford, a highly prestigious, nomination-only, three-year grant that came free of obligations. At Oxford, Vice reworked his dissertation on free will into a book that garnered attention not only in philosophical circles, but also in the pages of the *TLS*, the *New York Review of Books*, and *The Guardian*, publications that in short order were running *his* reviews. He shared, or adopted, his academic mentor's well-publicized political passions. Vice's agitations, in several well-placed op-ed picces about the unfolding human rights catastrophe in East Timor, led to an invitation to address a United Nations subcommittee on genocide. Vice left Oxford as a hot commodity. Harkness, eager to snatch him from the Ivies, hired him with tenure, an unheard-of arrangement. He had arrived at the college the year before, and during my first year on campus, I would see him walking about, the seeming embodiment of the young hip academic. With his thick chestnut hair swept back off his forehead, beaklike nose, and alert, dark, critical eyes, he suggested a young Bertrand Russell—a very young Russell, as his smooth chin appeared incapable of supporting a beard. He was tallish without being tall, trim in construction, though his neck was incongruously bullish and obstinate, and his ears—one was studded with a small diamond—were small and pinned close to his head, like those of a dog prone to sudden violence. He strode about campus in black jeans and meticulously pressed dress shirts with French cuffs. He never greeted me when our paths crossed—he would stare intently, his eyes wide in an expression of detached superciliousness—and he didn't greet me now. After a moment of silent clinical scrutiny, he returned his gaze to the board all the while fingering his earring as if adjusting the volume of a hearing aid.

I explored the narrow passages of the store. Bare wooden floorboards bowed under the weight of the books. A hidden fan cooed like a pigeon. Exposed bulbs lit crammed shelves organized along Borgesian principles, attractively idiosyncratic and obscure. After an hour or so, I carried a cairn of novels to the counter and peered into the back room. The chess set had been cleared, but the two were still seated in the folding metal chairs. The bookseller looked to be dozing, but then I realized that having removed his glasses, closed his eyes, and folded his hands across his expansive stomach, he was listening to Oliver Vice read aloud: *I see then I had attributed to myself certain objects no longer in my possession, as far as I can see. But might they not have rolled behind a piece of furniture? That would surprise me. A boot, for example, can a boot roll behind a piece of furniture? And yet I see only one boot. And behind what piece of furniture? In this room, to the best of my knowledge, there is only one piece of furniture capable of intervening between me and my possessions, I refer to the cupboard.* The bookseller listened intently, stroking his copious beard, as if weighing some abstruse Talmudic postulate. At some point Vice noticed my presence and broke off. "Your customer . . ."

I told him not to mind me, that I could wait until they reached a break.

"There are no breaks," Vice said. "That was a good resting point."

The bookseller regained his feet with a hand from Vice and shuffled toward the counter. He shifted his glasses to his forehead and held my books close, as if smelling rather than reading the titles. "Ah, it makes my day when someone buys Muriel Spark. No one's books look lonelier to me on the shelf. They're so slim and gregarious and eager to please." His voice was nasal, his enunciation nerdily precise. "Help yourself to some warm cider, there should be a thermos here somewhere . . ."

As I sipped the cider, the bookseller filled out the sales slip, a laborious process of shifting his thick eyeglasses up and down, like a welder inspecting his work. Oliver Vice remained in the backroom.

"That was Beckett?" I said.

"*Malone Dies.*" Vice appeared neither surprised nor impressed by what I inwardly considered a stupendous feat of literary recognition.

"We're colleagues," I said. "At Harkness."

He nodded expressionlessly, as if to show he knew this already or deemed it of no consequence.

"I'm in English."

"Yes," was his garrulous response.

"You read very well."

"Thank you." Glumly, Vice added, presumably not to me, "How'd I let that pawn go?"

"You played well today," said the bookseller. "Nothing like last week. You had that clever thing going with the rook."

"The pawn . . ."

"What of it? A miscalculation. Live to fight another day."

The bookseller finished the bill, then exclaimed, "Ninety-five fifty-nine, a numerical palindrome! I always find that exciting—that entitles you to a discount of ten dollars and one cent. And how about you, my friend—do you play?"

"I guess I once was pretty decent," I said. "In high school I nearly won the Long Island Championship before losing to some kid from Babylon."

"Well, it sounds like you were more than just decent," the bookseller said. "Feel free to join us one of these days. We play most weekends."

Vice glanced at me and frowned, without seconding the invitation.

"Thanks," I said, "but I really don't play much anymore."

When I first moved to Harkness—before the coming of Cineplex, Old Navy, Barnes & Noble, Target, Dick's Sporting Goods, Whole Foods, and, despite grassroots opposition, Wal-Mart—the Dead Mall was a huge cinderblock carcass of failed retail space. At the time, its sole tenant was Panda Garden, a Chinese restaurant that showed scant signs of life when I pulled up before its tattered awning a few minutes past noon on a bright spring day. By the entrance stood Oliver Vice, arms folded, a worn canvas rucksack slung over his shoulder. I expected him to say that the restaurant had died. Instead, he nodded by way of greeting and held the door open for me.

Inside, a lone waiter was flogging a tabletop with a towel. His face brightened when he saw us. "Good day, Vice!" he exclaimed. "Regular table?"

The waiter escorted us to a dark, undesirable booth by the flapping doors to the kitchen. I surveyed the menu while the philosopher gazed at an oversized fish tank in the middle of the restaurant that lacked both fish and water. Frankly, the invitation had surprised me. During our meeting at Broch's Books, Vice had appeared to take no interest in my existence and I hadn't exactly found warmth in his. And yet out of the blue he called a week later, inviting me to lunch.

"Do you recommend anything?" I asked.

"Not really. The food isn't particularly good."

"That's why you come here all the time?"

He didn't exactly smile, but his eyes, from behind black, heavy-framed glasses, the kind a newscaster in the sixties might have worn, registered a quiver of amusement. "When Wittgenstein lived in Dublin working on what became the *Philosophical Investigations*," Vice said, "he dined every night in Bewley's Café on Grafton Street. He told the waiter, 'I don't care what you serve me, as long as it's always the same thing' . . . Anyway the owner, that's him over there, uses an abacus. That alone makes it worth it." At the bar sat an elderly Chinese man with a comb-over, watching TV without the sound. "The steamed vegetable dumplings are plausible . . . If you'd like, we could split two dishes, though I don't eat meat . . . Sometimes I make an exception for fish, preferably one high in omega 3's."

This got us talking briefly about his vegetarianism. His voice, flat until that moment, jumped with animation. This was something I would come to know well: his pleasure in describing his boyhood, the one unconditionally happy period in his life. "I used to *adore* the taste of meat. My mother always shopped at Yorkville Meat, a Hungarian butcher shop on First Avenue, and she would take me along so I could breathe the odor of uncooked meat and organs. I loved watching the butcher slice Black Forest ham and hard garlic salami on the cutting wheel, how the threads of fat would separate and the meat would fall into a neat stack. When other children fantasized about becoming archaeologists or veterinarians or deep-sea divers, I longed to become a *butcher*. I wanted to chop meat, and slice it, and wrap it, and most of all, I wanted to *eat* it. My very favorite dish was steak tartare"—this was pronounced with a mild affectation—"which my mother used to prepare only twice a year—at Christmas and again at Easter. In high school I became a vegetarian. I haven't had meat in a dozen years, but I still often dream about it."

When the food arrived, conversation faltered. The windows of the restaurant were open to the mild spring breeze wafting over the weedy tarmac that once had been the Dead Mall's parking lot; still, sweat beaded on Oliver's upper lip. He was less dexterous with chopsticks than I might have expected. A cold sore glistened on the corner of his mouth; he must have noticed me glancing at it.

"Herpes," he said, adding, "simplex."

I asked about his work, but his answers came out clipped and unfocused. He fingered the cold sore as if pressure might heal it and not simply spread the germs. Food cleared away, he drank a cupful of tea into which he'd deposited two bags of sugar. Then, to my instant dismay, he retrieved from his daypack a rolled chessboard, a bag of tournament pieces, and a chess clock from the recently crumbled Soviet Union. He held a black pawn and a white pawn behind his back. "You choose," he directed.

"I wasn't kidding when I said that I hadn't played in ages."

"You were a high school champion. Of Lawn Guyland"—pronounced with mock derision.

"That was a million years ago."

He quickly set up his pieces and finished setting up mine. "Here, I'll let you play white."

Truth be told, I'd never exactly competed for the Long Island Championship. In high school, I'd played on a chess team that had placed third or fourth in Nassau County. But it was also true that since then I'd played only occasionally, never with much regret. Now before we even opened, I cursed the idiocy of my exaggerations and tried to bolster my confidence by telling myself that back then I really had been quite decent. The brown-on-beige vinyl board of the U.S. Chess Federation stirred a familiar and not particularly welcome somatic response: a sudden elevation of heartbeat, a spike in cranial pressure, a tightening of cheek muscles, a restlessness in extremities, and a discharge of adrenaline that set my left leg vibrating like a piston. It all came back in a Pavlovian rush.

Fifteen moves in, Oliver said, without looking up from the board, "See, I told you there are some things you never forget."

"I guess so," I said.

I always played best on the attack and, given my rustiness, figured an all-out assault was my only hope. My forces mobilized against his queen's knight, which anchored his defenses. An extraordinary tension accumulated and concentrated around a single square, and for a thrilling moment I envisioned his possible collapse. But Vice tenaciously weathered the onslaught. The demise of my king's pawn signaled the beginning of the end. All momentum leaked from my campaign and gathered on the other side. Oliver immediately pushed a series of exchanges that left me even in material, but with a weakened position. He exploited this weakness with precision; the board, as it emptied of pieces, looked deforested: there was no place to hide.

"See, you did just fine," he said, after I'd tipped my king.

"Thanks," I said. "I didn't embarrass myself."

"Far from it. You could have done better toward the end, but you still have a feel for the board. It wouldn't take you long to get your game back up to speed."

"Yeah, maybe." And yet improbably, I had mustered a game as strong as any I had ever played. "What about that bookseller—how good is he?"

"Sam? He's in a different league. He was a prodigy. He could have been a grand master, but his health failed him."

Vice said that the bookseller suffered from diabetes and a degenerative retinal condition that was slowly destroying his eyesight. Their chess playing involved an ongoing wager. For every loss, Vice had to read aloud for an hour. For each victory, he got a free book of his choosing.

"And?"

"Recently we finished *Middlemarch*. Before that was *Bleak House*. My library hasn't expanded."

"You've never beaten him?"

"Never will." He said this with great certainty.

The chess appeared to have relaxed Oliver. Board cleared, he insisted on picking up the check. He cracked open his fortune cookie and read: *A great romance waits you.* "'Waits,'" he repeated, bemused. He rolled the fortune into a tight coil and pocketed it. Evidently he kept a collection of malapropisms and solecisms. The cookie he didn't touch. In silence we walked to our cars on the weedy tarmac. "Well, thanks for the lunch," I said. "Next time it's my treat."

He offered no response. But as he unlocked his car, he said, almost under his breath, "Have you ever fallen in love with someone you're not attracted to?" Then he climbed in and drove off.

Over the years, I've often thought about that line. More than once it crossed my mind that he might have been talking about *me*. But even after I met and came to know Jean, the comment's intended subject, I never understood the emotional weight of Oliver's words. I could imagine being attracted to someone without being in love, and could also understand falling in love with someone you might consider fundamentally unattractive as a person—someone selfish or lacking a generosity of spirit. I could also, of course, understand falling in love with a person you don't *originally* find attractive. But falling in love with someone you're not attracted to? It never made sense to me.

I never doubted, though, that it made sense to Oliver. As we came to be the closest of friends, I often would chastise myself for failing to understand his suffering, for lacking the imaginative depths to make sense of his pain. In his memoir, *Montauk*, Max Frisch offers a lovely description of a friend's suffering: "His was always exemplary, mine only personal." So it was with Oliver. Perhaps it was the connection to the melancholies of the philosophical spirit, to the generational woes of Middle Europeans, or to the peculiar afflictions of fallen aristocrats, but Oliver's suffering had volume and depth. It was large, relevant, and ramifying, not merely suburban, Jewish, and neurotic. I knew the latter world intimately; I came from it, had written a novel about it, and would never fully escape its orbit. The former, the old world of titled wealth, doomed romance, and congenital sorrows, was largely unknown. It was the world whose heavy ornate doors Oliver would open for me, and I would enter gratefully.

At the time, I felt simply flattered by the overture the young philosopher had extended at our first lunch in the Dead Mall. The fact that most everyone at Harkness found him aloof, if not arrogant, the fact that he'd shown so little interest in me at Broch's Books, only strengthened my curious sense of election. His words may have been cryptic, but they signaled an unexpected and welcome desire to reach out, a willingness to expose private feelings. Unsure whether I wanted to be his friend, I was glad that he appeared to want to be mine.

A week or so later, we found ourselves back in the Naugahyde booth by the swinging doors to the kitchen, sharing an order of rubbery steamed vegetable dumplings. Again playing white, I used my favorite gambit from years back, but Oliver declined it. He picked off a bishop I'd left badly exposed. Sun poured through the dirty windows and my concentration wandered. I hurried my moves; the end came quickly.

"Why play King's Gambit?" Oliver said. "It's too easy to parry. No one plays King's Gambit at the competitive level anymore."

"I thought it was worth a try."

He shook his head emphatically. "Don't use it. Let's play again."

I reassembled my pieces with dread. A few moves in and the board already posed vague menace, threats I was too dull to perceive. The first time out, I'd surprised myself, playing boldly and well. Now I was expected to play to a level beyond my reach. The pressure left me tentative and error-prone. I tried to force exchanges in the hope of eking out a draw, but was slow in castling and left my pawns vulnerable. I apologized for my dismal performance.

"You're not focusing," Oliver said. He adjusted the clock. "Let's try some speed chess. Five minutes each."

"I hate speed chess. I'm sorry. We shouldn't have played today. I'm just not in the right mood."

"You're really not all that passionate about chess, are you?" He sounded perplexed, reluctant to accept this unwelcome fact. "I find chess one of life's few unalloyed pleasures. I'm always in the mood."

"Maybe I fell in love with chess," I said, "without ever being attracted to it."

He packed away the pieces. Had he asked me to parse my words, I don't know what I'd have said. Having disappointed him with my chess, I suppose I was trying to be witty, though I'm not sure where the wit was. It appeared I had only succeeded in angering him. I felt slight and inferior, but then he said, with strange formality, "I'm sorry if my parting words sounded obscure. There'd been a decision weighing on my mind, and making decisions isn't exactly my forte."

In the twelve years of our friendship I would come to appreciate the profundity of that understatement.

He said that he had been offered a position at Oxford, or rather, as he put it, at "St. John's," and had had to decide whether to take it.

"And?"

Instead of simply telling me his decision, he produced from the breast pocket of his immaculately tailored lilac shirt a piece of lined paper, which he unfolded and spread before me. On it he had sketched an old-fashioned beam balance, a scale of justice, the base of which had been obsessively shadowed with cross-hatching. The left side was labeled STAY; the right, GO. Beneath the respective headings, in an elegant, minute script, stood perhaps a dozen separate considerations, the identical number on each side. The scales stood in perfect equipoise. Under STAY, I could decipher *New York—the city itself + Mamy, Pappy, Mew*. Under GO, *Oxford—general fondness for + London—proximity of*. Countervailing on the side of STAY was a name in capitals, *JEAN*. But *JEAN* also appeared under GO.

"Jean—" I said.

"—Yes—"

"—appears to be a complicating factor."

"True."

"Jean is a he—"

"A she. Like everyone, you assume that I'm gay."

"I'm not assuming anything. I was just asking about the name."

"Well, I'm not gay. Alas."

It wasn't clear what he meant by this. "So Jean, I take it, is a romantic interest."

He removed his glasses and rubbed his eyes. The question appeared to pain or otherwise weary him, to exhaust his reserves of explanation. Without the heavy frames, his eyes looked unexpectedly soft and defenseless. "I'm not sure I can answer that . . ."

"Well, let me try an easier question. Is Jean here or at Oxford?"

"She lives in London."

He was willing to confirm some complex involvement going back to his fellowship at Oxford. But whether she had contributed more to staying or going, he wouldn't— or couldn't—say.

"Would you like to see another diagram of my thought process?" he asked.

"I think I have a grasp on your method. So how did you decide—by flipping a coin?"

Glasses back in place, his eyes turned a warm happy autumnal color. "How did you know?"

"You didn't really."

"And even that didn't end matters. Because then I asked myself whether a single toss should be dispositive or whether it should be best of two out of three, or three out of five. I finally settled on four out of seven."

"And?"

"I'm still here, aren't I?"

THREE

We discovered, as friends do, that we shared many interests, though asymmetries persisted. I never became the chess partner he'd hoped for after our promising first encounter, and at some point he stopped challenging me to regular play. I liked looking at art, particularly modernist painting, but I lacked the deeper knowledge and resources of a collector. As for philosophy, in college I gave serious, if only brief, thought to pursuing it in grad school. Oliver, by contrast, had felt *called* to philosophy, and remained gripped by even the most recondite and bewildering questions until the end. He once tried to draw me into a debate about "unicornicity," which left him obviously disappointed with my refusal or inability to take the issue seriously; for me, the conversation brought to mind all the reasons why, in my junior year of college, I suddenly switched my major to history. Even then I struggled to shape a vision of my life, and it wasn't until I arrived at Yale Law, where I spent three desultory years trying to ignore the creeping certainty that I was willing for myself a future I couldn't stomach, that I began writing in earnest.

I was several years out of Yale and doing legal temp work when my first novel came out. *Exit 33* was loosely based on the story of a childhood friend, whose gifted brother, a double major at Brown in physics and religion, suffered a severe breakdown on the eve of his departure to England on a Rhodes, precipitating the collapse of his entire family. The novel got a number of strong notices and I got hired at Harkness on a three-year appointment as the "visiting writer." In the past, the position had attracted some big-name writers with some big books behind them. I arrived on the picture-book New England campus on Labor Day, 1992, younger than most of my predecessors and with a far more modest reputation. During my first week, a colleague in English cheerfully informed me that the department's first *two* choices had accepted offers elsewhere. Another colleague made it abundantly clear that she considered my suburban Jewish novel—the title came from the exit on the Long Island Expressway for Great Neck, where I grew up and where my fictional family unraveled—a contribution to an exhausted and clichéd form. Dizzying feelings of fraudulence periodically took hold of me that first term, but soon enough I came to feel comfortable, if not entirely welcome, at Harkness. A steady diet of academic farces had prepared me to encounter a strange mix of boozing, blustering pedants in stained tweed and spiky-haired feminazis spouting a politics of preemptive castration, but I got to know a handful of friendly young academics, working to balance the demands of classroom, scholarship, and life on a junior professor's salary.

The summer after my first year, Melissa and I married. We had met at Yale; Mel had started a doctorate in comparative literature but her true passion was writing poetry, and had abandoned the program after her course work. That summer, she found a job teaching eleventh-grade English at the Inverness Academy, a nearby boarding school located on the site of one of the great Indian massacres of colonial America. The town surrounding the school had been painstakingly reconstructed to look as it had two centuries earlier, supplying the stage for an "immersive" experience for tourists: historical reenactments of candlemaking, wool dying, blacksmithing. Once a month, Mel, in a colonial calico dress with flounced sleeves and a pinner cap, would demonstrate the art of spinning hand-carded wool to weekending New Yorkers. None of her forebearers, or mine, for that matter, had set foot in America before the first decade of the twentieth century, but Mel was good at playacting, and came to enjoy the smell and feel of the wool and the meditative monotony of the spinning itself.

We honeymooned in Sweden, a week in Stockholm and a week on the Baltic island of Gotland. We stayed in the medieval town of Visby and ate fermented herring in brine. On Midsummer night, we danced with locals around a pole, hopping like frogs and oinking like pigs. We cycled to what we had been told was the summerhouse of Ingmar Bergman, an isolated, weather-beaten cabin on a wind-buffeted cliff overlooking the sea. We got within a hundred yards of the front door before being chased away by a pair of enormous slobbering dogs. We camped on a beach stacked with limestone columns that looked like the ruins of a pagan temple. We drank elderberry schnapps and read lots of Knut Hamsun, figuring that all Scandinavians shared a like derangement.

And we believed we had attained a purity of love and happiness that few humans had ever known. As Melissa put it, "I don't understand why I deserve to be this lucky, but I'm not about to complain."

The remainder of the summer was spent moving. Before our honeymoon, in a rash gesture, we bought a two-hundred-year-old five-bay colonial farmhouse with a central chimney and a slate roof, high on charm and low on everything else. We closed in July, and then came two months of painting walls, sanding floors, replacing switch-plate covers, and building bookcases. I went into my Harkness office only to go through mail, and there, in a slender stack, I found a postcard of a dour, tousled-haired August Strindberg. A single sentence in elegant, minuscule script occupied the center of an otherwise blank flipside, *Greetings from Stockholm*. It was signed with a flourish, *O*. Apparently we weren't the only travelers to Sweden that summer. I registered a mild regret that we hadn't met up there; I would have liked to introduce Melissa to him, though, as things turned out, I didn't have to wait long. A couple of weeks into the fall semester, we received a formal invitation on Smythson stationery—*Please join me in a celebration of the 25th anniversary of the Rolling Stones' Beggars Banquet*.

The Party, as I would refer to it afterward. The scene of my initiation into the Oliverian universe. Of my seduction.

On a cool Saturday night at the peak of leaf season, we drove to a converted mill that straddled an estuary of the Connecticut River. A freight elevator, with doors that clanged shut horizontally, lurched and shuddered upward for three floors before disgorging us onto a gloomy corridor where floor candles led the way to a loft with towering ceilings. The loft had no overhead lighting; discrete spots and sconces offered warm island sanctuaries in a sea of dark. Oliver, dressed in an outrageous burgundy smoking jacket over a paisley dress shirt, greeted us and introduced us to the other guests, maybe twenty in all. I recognized only two: the chess-playing bookseller with failing eyesight and an art historian from Harkness who specialized in the aesthetics of war memorials. Standing at Oliver's side was a woman, her thumbs hitched through the belt loops of a pair of low-slung sixties-style bell-bottoms, tight across a voluptuous butt. Her inky eyes were heavily made up, and fastened around her long beautiful pale neck was a choker, an article that reliably conjured in my mind images of erotic submission, the very word a source of guilty thrills.

After a round of cocktails, we were ushered to a long table for a sit-down dinner. A dozen tapers burned in a candelabra draped in gothic piles of accumulated wax; around this centerpiece, piles of fruit and goblets of wine mimicked the "beggars banquet" on the inside cover of the Rolling Stones' 1969 album. Several signed and framed photos of the band in recording sessions flanked a mission-style bookcase. A candid of Mick Jagger wearing headphones and strumming an acoustic guitar bore a dedication in a neat schoolboy's script, *To Jack Epstein, who casts us in a better light, your mate, Mick.* As we dined on vegetarian tea rolls and coconut curry with seitan, Oliver told us about Epstein, his stepfather.

"He basically revolutionized the lighting of rock concerts," Oliver said. "Even as a boy, my stepfather was obsessed with *lightbulbs*: when other boys collected rocks or bottle caps, Pappy collected early Edison incandescents. He still has the collection, hundreds of bulbs with every kind of filament—carbon, platinum, bamboo, iridium. He spent one term at City College studying engineering before dropping out to start his own company that specialized in stage lighting. He began doing theater, but then in the late sixties he switched to concert lighting. His big innovation was designing beam-weaving techniques that made huge stadium concerts possible. He's worked with all the big groups, Led Zeppelin, The Who, The Grateful Dead, the Stones. Only thing is, to this day he *despises* rock music. The sole rock musicians he can abide are Jimmy Page and Charlie Watts, the Stones' drummer—he says they're really both jazz artists at heart."

"Tell the story about playing Ping-Pong with Keith Richards," said the woman with the bell-bottoms and choker.

"That was in 1972, during their summer American tour, the so-called Cocksuckers' Tour. That's *really* what Stones historians call it. Before the tour officially kicked off, the band spent a night at our country house. I was eight and a Ping-Pong *fanatic*. I've probably never been as good at any sport as I was at Ping-Pong at eight. I dreamed of traveling with Nixon to Peking to play the Chinese eight-and-under national champion on the Great Wall. Anyway, Keith"—the first-name basis wasn't lost on me—"and I played maybe six games or so. I destroyed him every time."

"He was probably hopped on smack," I said. "Probably couldn't see the table."

"Actually, I remember him being *quite* focused and competitive, and not at all happy about losing to an eight-year-old."

"That must have been when *Goats Head Soup* came out," I said. Something powerfully juvenile and regressive made me want to demonstrate my Stones knowledge.

"*Goats Head Soup* was '73," Oliver corrected.

"'72," I insisted.

"Wrong," he said decisively. "'72 was *Exile on Main Street*, their best album. Arguably the greatest rock album of all time. *Goats Head Soup* was '73 and garbage."

"What about 'Angie' and Billy Preston's guitar work on 'Heartbreaker'?"

"Oh, my God," said the woman with the choker, "Is this a game show?"

"The song's title is 'Doo Doo Doo Doo Doo,'" Oliver said dismissively, "and Preston's playing the clavinet, *not* the guitar. Do you even know what a clavinet is?" He cast a withering look my way. The rapid descent to alpha male adolescent competition was complete.

"Of course." I felt myself redden, though maybe the candles saved me.

"Really? What is it?"

"Hey, even I know that," exclaimed Melissa. "It's an electronic clavichord."

"Keith Richards hit on Ollie's mother," declared the woman with the choker.

"That was a later tour," said Oliver, still smiling at me wryly.

"Ollie's mother never tires of telling the story." In a passable imitation of a thick, geographically uncertain European accent, the girlfriend said, "Keif vaz vezy vezy handtsum. I *luved* de vay he vood stwum ze geetar. I only vish he had vashed!"

After the curry, Oliver served us a lentil version of Fidget Pie, a recipe from his Oxford days. Handing me a slice, he whispered in my ear, "You had *no* fucking idea what a clavinet is."

Conversation continued, but now fragmented from pan-table storytelling to adjacent-eater dialogue. "You really know your Stones." This came from the guy to my left. He had a friendly face with innocuous features arranged in a helpless smile. "You and Oliver, both."

"I listened to them a lot in college," I said, "but not so much now. How about you?"

"What about me?" he asked.

"Were you also into the Stones?"

"Oh. Sort of. Not really. They were never really my thing."

I excused myself to get something to drink, but the man followed me to the bar. At a loss for words, we found ourselves examining the art in Oliver's loft. An over-sized placard of Joy Division's *Love Will Tear Us Apart* hung over the door to Oliver's bedroom, but everything else appeared original: etchings and prints by Thomas Hart Benton, Mardsen Hartley, George Grosz, and Max Beckmann. The works hung bunched together, as in a nineteenth-century salon. Other artists I couldn't identify, though I later learned these were the Pascins and Bartons that connected Oliver to his family's obscure past and presaged his tragic future. This latter work didn't exactly speak to me, but I absorbed the fact that one of us had the resources for something other than museum posters mounted with thumbtacks. If the huge loft and casual reminiscences about rock legends left any room for doubt, the art collection made it obvious that Oliver came from serious money. I stopped before a vitrine containing what appeared to be nothing more than a white aspirin tablet. On closer examination the tablet revealed human features.

In alarm, I turned to the smiling guy. "Am I hallucinating, or does that look exactly like a minuscule bust of Oliver?"

"It is Oliver."

"How do you know?"

"I made it."

"*You* made *that*?"

"Yeah."

"How on earth did you do that?"

"I sculpted it . . ."

"Yes, but *how*?"

"Small tools. Dental equipment is real good for detail work."

"And the tablet?"

"Excedrin. Oliver gets lots of headaches—the piece is kind of an homage . . ."

"It's incredible."

"Oh. Thanks."

I was reminded of the story about Giacometti, who, after suffering a serious breakdown early in his career, went through a phase of only making extraordinarily tiny sculptures. He said he found comfort in being able to carry around a full body of work in his coat pocket. But when I told the story to the artist, he nodded vaguely and said, "Is that a friend of yours?"

"Not directly . . . Does Oliver have any more of your work?"

He showed me a second piece, a framed rectangular sheet of undulating blue, maybe two feet by four, that looked like a drawing of a lake, as seen from above, nudged by a slight breeze. But here again, all was not as it seemed. As I leaned closer, the blue became a marvelous dense sea of words.

"What *is* this?" I asked.

"*The American Heritage Dictionary.*"

"What do you mean?"

"*American Heritage* is a dictionary. Like *Webster's.*"

"Yes, I'm familiar with it. But what am I *looking* at?"

"Oh. All the words. Well, not all—just the entries."

"You copied out every word in the dictionary?"

"I have a reading problem, kind of like dyslexia, so I thought if I dealt with the words on their own, you know, one at a time, I could understand them better."

"And did you?"

"I think so. It really built my vocabulary. I learned that 'purblind' means blind. That 'nonplussed' doesn't mean what it sounds like."

"How long did it take?"

"Around three years. But I was working on other stuff, too. I was also hospitalized a couple of times."

As I studied the work, from close up and then from afar, I had to acknowledge that it was more than the product of a deranged expenditure of patience. From every angle it revealed unexpected beauty, the breathless clutter and tumult of words transforming, with distance, into gentle harmonies and tranquil waves.

Just then the choker woman joined us; she gave the artist a kiss on the cheek. "That's for being a genius," she said, before turning to me. "Max is our resident genius. Did he tell you that he just had five pieces accepted for a show at the Guggenheim?"

The artist named Max smiled disarmingly. He seemed incapable of doing anything but.

The woman tugged on the sleeve of his T-shirt. "Come, let's go outside and have a smoke. Oliver would kill me if I lit up in here."

"Nah, I'm trying to quit."

"Booo. You're supposed to be my smoking buddy."

Max shrugged.

"Then, you keep me company." She turned to me. "First I've got to fetch some matches."

Obediently I followed her to a corner of the loft that served as Oliver's study. There a frightening order reigned. A tall bookcase displayed its volumes rigorously segregated by height. On his desk reposed a dozen fountain pens in a wooden case with a beveled glass top. A pool of blue-black ink glistened in an antique inkwell. Groups of papers formed overlapping bundles, like steps leading down to a meticulous garden. On a side table, a chess set showed a game in progress. In a spontaneous act of mischief, I switched the places of the knight and the rook. Over the desk hung several photographs. As the search for matches continued, I studied a black-and-white print of a handsome woman voguing like Greta Garbo. In profile the woman's nose cut a haughty angle, while her visible eye, outlined like Nefertiti's, gazed downward. Bare shoulders looked as if a negligee had just slipped from them.

"The mother," said the woman.

"That's Oliver's *mother* . . . ?"

"From her modeling days."

It was an extraordinary picture, made all the more so by its spot over his desk. The former model, no older in the photo than Oliver was now, watched over her son with an expression far from maternal. Her lips, ever so slightly parted, seemed to whisper impulsive abstractions and passionate half-sentences.

"It explains a lot," added the woman, gnomically.

Next to mom hung another remarkable photo. A pair of boys, flanking a man with an elongated aristocratic head, sat on a prone *cow*. The man, trim in a three-piece suit of tweed, smoked a pipe. The boys, seemingly plucked straight from the Eton preschool, wore corduroy shorts and matching caps. It was easy to identify Oliver, the smaller of the two, hands raised in remonstrance, a four-year-old already training for his first lecture. His eyes looked puffy, as if tears had punctuated his talk. In the background stretched a fog-shrouded meadow dotted with brethren of the bench. I took this to be the Lake District, a name that in my mind referred to no locale in particular, but was a generic placeholder for the mythic English Countryside.

"The older boy is Oliver's brother?" I asked.

"No—I mean, yes, but not *older*. They're twins, fraternal."

"But the kid's twice Oliver's size."

"Poor Bartholomew—even then he was enormous. He still lives with mom. He's not entirely well, but no one will admit it. The family is in denial."

"And the man?"

"That's Victor Vice, Oliver's 'biological father.' Oliver calls him the BF."

"Victor Vice," I repeated. "Sounds straight out of Dickens."

"Apparently he was a real bastard. He abandoned the family when Ollie and Bart were just boys—probably not long after this picture was taken. Poor Ollie. That's why he turned out the way he is."

"What way is that?"

She shrugged. "Like his hero, Wittgenstein. Brilliant but incapable of some pretty basic stuff. You know."

The woman had smoked down an entire cigarette and now lit a second with the stub of the first. What was a choker supposed to signal, I wondered, besides a willingness to be mounted from the rear? I wasn't proud of my thoughts, but the martini in my hand was my third. "We haven't really been introduced," I said, without adequate reflection. "You must be Jean."

Her shrill laugh exposed a colossal mistake. Just then Oliver sidled up from behind and wrapped his arms around the woman's slender waist. "Hello," he said. "Bonding ethnically?"

So she was Jewish. It wouldn't have occurred to me, but Melissa always faulted my Jewdar.

The woman directed smoky words to me. "Oliver's just like his mother—a latent anti-Semite. The family surrounds themselves with Jews and secretly hates them all."

Oliver ignored this. "What did I say about smoking in the apartment, Soap?"

Perfunctorily she apologized. "Ollie has nicknames for all his girlfriends. Jean is 'Welpe.' It's German for little fox."

"Little *wolf*," he corrected through a tight smile.

"Now, beat it," she said. "We were having fun. I like your new friend, he's cute." All at once she pressed a moist, rather sloppy kiss directly on my lips.

"You have some amazing art," I said, aiming for nonchalance.

"Maybe," he said, "we've had enough to drink for one night."

"Oh, don't be an old fart," she said. "Seriously. Go away."

A guest tugged Oliver toward the bar, but not before his fingers did something punitive to her behind.

Later, joints were lit and passed around; the ban on cigarettes apparently tolerated exceptions. Melissa and I exchanged tired glances. "Shall we?" But as we prepared to leave, the bookseller called out, "Card tricks!" Other guests joined in a chorus, "Card tricks! Card tricks!" Oliver briefly demurred, then returned from his study scissor-shuffling a deck and wearing a pair of gold-tasseled slippers, seemingly plucked from *The King and I*. He said that he had learned most of his tricks in a tutorial with Michael Dummett, the Oxford logician, and showed us copies of Dummett's two classic books about magic and tricks, *Game of Tarot* and *A Wicked Pack of Cards*.

"Dummet taught me how to do a number of nice tricks. He's a very skilled conjurer, but dexterity is only half the art. The real key to success is mastering the art of misdirection, drawing the audience's attention one way while you do something else. Now this deck, because of the four Fools, actually has fifty-six cards, not the usual fifty-two. Let's make sure it's full, and then I'll do a couple of tricks if you'd like."

Oliver slipped off his jacket, removed his monogrammed cuff links, theatrically folded up the sleeves of his paisley shirt, and began counting the cards with great deliberation.

". . . fifty-one, fifty-two, fifty-three, fifty-four . . . Hmm, only fifty-five. That's bad. We're missing one. I suspect the missing card is the knave of spades—he's known as the Wanderer, he's notorious for going off on his own."

He sighed in exasperation and scanned the apartment for the missing card like a ship's captain squinting at the dark sea. Then he asked Melissa to stand up and turn around.

"What do you want me to do?" Mel asked.

"Nothing at all. Just stand up and turn around, if you don't mind."

Perplexed, Mel obeyed. Oliver slid his hand deep into the back pocket of her snug jeans and slowly removed a card. It was the errant knave.

"Just as I suspected . . ."

The night offered one final surprise. As the guests prepared to go, Oliver handed me a book wrapped in elegant Florentine paper. "I never got around to giving you this earlier. It's a wedding gift, a bit belated."

"That's very kind."

I gently removed the wrapping from a pristine copy of Muriel Spark's *Memento Mori*. I glanced at the copyright page: the British first edition. And the title page bore an inscription addressed to us from Dame Muriel. *A work from my past bestowed with warmest wishes for your future happiness and writerly success. With kind regards . . .*

"You do like Spark, don't you?" Oliver asked.

"I *love* Spark. And this one is my favorite. Mel loves it, too. How did you get her to sign this? Do you know her?"

"Not well. She's a close friend of a close friend."

Melissa kissed him. "It's an *incredibly* generous, thoughtful gift," she said. "Thank you *so* much."

By the time we got home, pale light skimmed the eastern sky. I wanted to jump straight into bed, but Mel had to floss. She stood in bra and nothing else, staring at herself in the mirror, cleaning her teeth. "That was one of the more unusual evenings in recent memory," she said.

"I told you you'd like him."

"He can be very charming. He tells interesting stories."

"You think all the money comes from his stepfather?"

"I liked the story about playing Ping-Pong with Keith Richards."

"I could have sworn *Goats Head Soup* was from '72. I'm going to check that tomorrow."

"You haven't thanked me for saving your ass with the clavinet."

"Thank you, love." I kissed Mel and tried to obstruct her effort to slip on a nightgown. It occurred to me I didn't even know the name of Oliver's girlfriend, the woman in the choker he called "Soap."

Mel fended me off and climbed into bed. The windows in our bedroom were old, drafty, hand-blown crown panes. They magnified the fading stars, made them round and liquid.

"He's got nice hair," Mel said, as if searching for a summation. "His eyes are *very* intense."

I thought of the sculpture in the Excedrin tablet, the tiny bust of the philosopher prone to headaches. "What about my eyes? Aren't they intense?"

"Of course, they are, you little beast. Your eyes are the best and the intensest. It's just something about the way he would stare—at moments it was like he was *too* attentive. And that business with the card and my jeans. I wouldn't call that entirely kosher . . ."

Mel took hold of my importunate fingers and brought them to rest on her tummy. "Come, it's late. Let's wait till tomorrow." But she didn't curl up for sleep. "And what do you make of that present?"

"I wonder how well he knows Spark. He seems to travel in pretty rarefied circles."

"I meant more the book," Mel said. "I love *Memento Mori*, but as a *wedding* gift? Don't you find that a bit odd?"

Melissa, the poet, communed with a grim muse, though years would pass before I'd come to appreciate her apprehensions. That night I thought no more about Oliver. Instead, my mind traveled back to the startling and beautiful image I had seen hanging in his apartment: the sea of words, swimming together, collecting in ways no one could anticipate or intend. The words surrounded me like schooling fish, lovely and unthreatening, the water warm and clear.

We fell asleep shortly before dawn, only to be awakened at eight by an invasion of fall sunlight. The moon lingered in the north. I nuzzled toward Mel, draped an arm across her waist. She read to me from the Spark until the sun climbed above our bedroom window and we fell back asleep.

FOUR

What made Oliver extraordinary wasn't his wealth or ancestry or political courage or even his philosophical gifts. His most outstanding trait was his loyalty, both to others and to himself. For some "great minds," suffering delivers an excuse for the most outrageously self-indulgent behavior, as if unhappiness mixed with brilliance supplied a release from the normal constraints of morality. In Oliver's case, suffering made humble. A creature of courtesy and old-world formality, he never let a birthday or anniversary pass without posting a thoughtful card or penning a kind word. He took teaching seriously, demanding much from his students and rewarding them with fairness and respect. You could trust him with secrets, with your children. I can't even blame him for what he did to my marriage. It wasn't his fault; grief makes us act in peculiar ways, and once the damage had been done, he tried hard to undo it. He always tried hard. After he renounced his inheritance, he never missed his morning shave at Paul's Barbershop, not because he always needed one, but because Paul's, like Panda Garden, was one of his projects, a failing establishment that he refused to abandon. Charity for Oliver was a matter of duty. But even this doesn't begin to capture his steadfastness, his *greatness*. Highly regarded for his scholarly work on the instabilities and slippages of identity, Oliver was the most *constant* person I've ever met. Spinoza observed that people persist in being themselves. Oliver showcased this simple but elusive truth.

This, of course, was his tragedy. Oliver didn't despise himself. His problem was more acute and exemplary: he despised *being* himself. He longed to jump over his own shadow, to escape the stifling confines of Oliverhood. It was this, above all else, that made his problems insoluble and resonant—and so much more interesting than, say, my own.

That term, he learned that his stepfather was suffering from Pick's disease, a rare and devastating form of dementia. The previous spring, he'd received complaints that his stepfather had groped his two secretaries, both in his employ for decades. Oliver's mother refused to become involved—I learned that she'd divorced the stepfather several years earlier. In arranging for his stepfather's diagnosis and care, a process which required contacting the estranged sons from Epstein's first marriage, Oliver made the unwelcome discovery that Epstein's company, Lime Light, was also in failing health. Once the industry leader, Lime Light evidently hadn't kept up as computers replaced wiring and circuitry for the control of stage effects. Barely able to understand, much less guide the business, Epstein nevertheless refused to relinquish his position as CEO, effectively paralyzing the company. It fell to Oliver to convince Epstein to delegate responsibility to others in the organization.

Every week, after his Thursday class, Oliver would drive down to New York and stay in the city until early Monday, when he'd returned to Harkness to teach and work on the manuscript of *Paradoxes of Self*. He'd been scheduled to speak at a number of conferences, but canceled to attend to his family. He'd spend one night each weekend at his mother's apartment on the East Side, and the other two with Sophia Baum, which happened to be the name of the woman we'd met at the party. Sophia, we learned, lived near Columbia and worked as a fund-raiser at the Brooklyn Academy of Music. On Sundays, Oliver and she would arrive at the stepfather's apartment on Central Park West to take him to Barney Greengrass's for a whitefish sandwich and a side of German potato salad. We learned this all courtesy of Sophia. It was the pioneering days of e-mail, and she was our first regular correspondent:

jack's slipping fast. it's gotten to the point that oh
has to feed him, but he does it so delicately &
straightforwardly—it's not like he's patronizing or nursing. he makes it look absolutely natural. oh always talks
to jack, tells him stories, reads to him from the paper.
& you can tell he's reaching him; even when jack's not
speaking, you can see it in his eyes, he's following and
listening, and you can tell he knows oh is doing this
for him. the hardest part is when jack gets explosive or
lewd, like yesterday out of the blue he reached over and
grabbed my tit and squeezed really hard. we were in
a deli & i screamed because of the shock & because it
also hurt like a bitch. oh grabbed jack's hand, looked

jack straight in the eyes & said, 'not that. you *know*
that's wrong.' jack was so remorseful, it broke my heart;
he even cried a little. it's truly an awful disease. every
week, a little bit more of him is just gone. it's like watching this lovely beach sculpture being worn away by a
wind that comes at night when no one's around. you
can't see the change happening, but every time you
look, there's just less there. i'd end things *long* before
it ever came to that.

My problems that term were minor by comparison. They
centered on a student I'll call "Disturbed." Early in the
semester, Disturbed wrote a first draft of a story of great
promise, full of black humor and audacity. The story,
about a nerdy tenth grader who terrorizes his mother by
falsifying entries in a diary that he knows she's secretly
reading, put me in mind of the young Ian McEwan. I
told Disturbed that I believed it to be, with some re-
working, a publishable piece of fiction. Weeks passed
without Disturbed submitting the redraft—or anything,
for that matter. I asked him to come to my office hours;
he arrived early and excitedly told me that in the last
few days he'd been writing in a frenzy. Not only had he
finished the story, but he'd also written drafts of two
more, by far the best things he'd ever written. They just
needed a bit more work before he'd submit them, and at
the very latest, I'd get the entire packet of work after the
weekend. Days passed and still nothing; he was absent
from our seminar that week, and ignored my e-mails.
The next week he showed up to class, but didn't utter a

word, just sat with his arms folded, his face creased in what I can only describe as a smirk. When I spoke to him after class, he expressed astonishment that I hadn't received his stories. He swore he'd sent them days before; in fact, he'd been surprised that he hadn't heard anything from *me*; in any case, he promised to resubmit them. Again, nothing. When I summoned him back to my office, he emailed to say he was too busy to meet, maybe next week might work. Furious, I wrote back ordering him to come see me posthaste; he ignored this note altogether and again missed class. The next week he arrived at my office unannounced, and before I could say a word, shut the door and burst into tears. When I gently asked after the promised materials, he shouted between sobs, "You take *pleasure* in humiliating me!" I assured him that this was most emphatically not the case, but without another word, he bolted from my office, trailing curses and tears. I followed Disturbed into the hallway, only to find myself strafed by the puzzled looks of my colleagues who, startled by the ruckus, had emerged from their offices. Disturbed didn't return to our seminar, and shortly before the end of the fall semester, I received a long handwritten note:

> *Early in the term, I came to the reluctant conclusion that I could learn <u>nothing</u> from you as a writer. This is not meant as a general indictment —I'm certain many Harkness students will benefit from your conventional ideas about what makes a piece of fiction successful. I, for one, reject these conventions in my person and art. Still, I was*

prepared to respect your pedagogy. Unfortunately,
this respect was not mutual. In the course of the
term, it has become obvious that you cannot accept
<u>any</u> challenges to your safe way of doing things.
Your hostility to me personally and to my writ-
ing has made this semester unendurably painful.
Even after it became abundantly clear that you
were unable to read my work in an open-minded
fashion, you kept demanding more from me. Oth-
ers had warned me about professors who are so
insecure and so controlling that they punish those
who dare to break new ground. Maybe I was naive,
but I never expected to encounter them at Hark-
ness, least of all in a CREATIVE writing course.
I tried to play your game but no more. DO NOT
BADGER ME ANYMORE. I will protect myself
against any further humiliation and hurt.

PS. I thought the first fifty pages of your novel
showed promise before you succumbed to banality
and cliché.

Oliver read the note and handed it back to me. "Quite remarkable," he said. We sat in our familiar booth, sharing the familiar dumplings. "Have you contacted the dean of students?"

"I thought about it."

"But you haven't."

"No." Feelings of dread percolated in my bowels.

"Why not?"

"I'm not sure. I guess I feel bad for the kid."

"For someone trained as a lawyer, you don't have very lawyerly instincts. Why did you go to law school?"

"I don't know. I did well on the LSAT."

Oliver removed his glasses and cleaned the lenses, as if to begin a tutorial. "You need to contact the dean. His name is Lieber, a smart, grounded guy. And he's seen it all before. You'd be surprised how common this kind of thing is. Last year I had a student who said he was Nietzsche's great-grandson. He really knew a great deal about Nietzsche and was quite imaginative in making up the things he didn't know. He was crestfallen when I told him that Nietzsche never had any children. And when I failed him."

"You flunked him for saying he was Nietzsche's grandson?"

"I failed him because he didn't do required work and then lied about the reasons. What are you going to do, give your student here a B-plus for above average paranoia? Or maybe an A-minus? After all, that threat was pretty well written . . ."

This was still in the early days of our friendship. I'd assumed that someone who consigned his future to a flip of a coin would be sympathetic to all forms of struggle. But far from it. Here was Oliver's moral self, a creature of Kantian firmness, intolerant of excuses or embellishments or missed deadlines. That wasn't my way of dealing with students. I myself remembered college as a time of uncertainty, a time for discarding old identities and trying on new ones. I didn't want my students to arrive fully formed or altogether normal; I liked messy works in progress. But what had that gotten me? A belligerent note from Disturbed.

The Kantian self propped its elbows on the Formica table. The ancient owner craned over his abacus. The fish tank stood empty, its glass fogged luridly by dried algae. We divided the last of the vegetable dumplings.

Oliver leaned back and exhaled. "You spoke of problems. Plural. What else?"

"Nothing really, just a little matter that came up with Mel."

Oliver signaled to the waiter, who bounded toward us energetically. "I'd like a gimlet, Bombay Sapphire, straight up."

"Of course, Vice!"

The waiter bounded back a moment later. "No Bombay Sapphire!"

"Then whatever you have."

"Yes, Vice!"

"And I'll have a vodka martini," I called after him.

It wasn't a problem per se, more a point of controversy, a ripple of discord. It involved a former boyfriend of Melissa's, someone she'd gone out with in college and who now worked in a New York gallery.

"Which gallery?" Oliver asked.

"It doesn't matter. I think OK Harris."

"In Soho?"

"I don't know. What on earth difference does that make?"

"All right, go on."

It had recently come out—I couldn't recall how—that

the ex-boyfriend had passed through Harkness and that he and Melissa had met for lunch. I hadn't been apprised of the plans and certainly had not been asked to join them. I only learned of their lunch after the fact, and fortuitously.

"Do you think she stills loves him?"

"No."

"Did you *want* to have lunch with them?"

"Not particularly."

"So what's the problem?"

He was playing devil's advocate. His challenging tone reminded me of a law school professor prodding his student to distill a shapeless dilemma into precise speech. But before I could formulate a response, he continued: "You mean you don't like the fact that your wife is trying to maintain an intimacy with an ex-lover predicated on your exclusion? That she neglected to invite you in deference to his wishes, either explicit or implied, thereby placing his desires before yours? Or else because she wanted to be alone with him, in which case she hoped to send the message to him—and possibly to herself— that her recent marriage had in no way changed the terms of her past intimacies?"

If at times inflexible, Oliver was no slouch when it came to reading motive and psychology. A second gimlet had only sharpened his insight. Nursing my martini, I reveled in grim satisfaction. My displeasure had been validated. I would have to remind myself to resist the impulse to enlist his words as support against Mel.

He handed me a vial of eyedrops. "Your eyes are bloodshot."

"Okay, thanks." I administered the drops and blinked, dabbed at the excess fluid like tears.

"Are you happy you got married?" he asked.

"Yes, of course."

"Don't get defensive. I wasn't trying to suggest otherwise."

"I wasn't being defensive," I answered.

"Soap would like to get married." The hint of weariness in his voice put me on alert. The Kantian Oliver was slipping away. Across from me I recognized the Oliver of our first lunch, the entangled Oliver.

"That's great."

"Is it? Do you think we'd be happy together?"

"I can't believe my opinion would be dispositive."

"Not dispositive. Just . . . probative."

I struggled to put into words everything I found wrong with the question. "Oliver, I don't know Sophia well. She's extremely attractive and seems bright and personable. But I've hardly seen you two together. How can I possibly—let me put it this way, I don't think it's a great sign that you're asking for my input."

"Why? What's wrong with that?"

"I think you more than understand," I said.

"No, I don't. I'm being perfectly serious. I need to learn from people who have a clear understanding of the meaning of things like love and marriage. Sophia's always telling me that she loves me. I tell her that I *think* I love her, but that she's in the best position to know.

She's confident about what love means, *I'm* not. So she's in a better position to tell *me* whether I love her. I say, 'You see how I act toward you, is this the behavior of someone in love?'"

I imagined Melissa's response if I had ever said, *Mel, do I love you?—because I have* no *idea.* She would have ended our relationship on the spot.

"Sophia says I'm incapable of love—I only know how to pity. She says I pity beautifully but love not at all."

I couldn't recall having seen Oliver drink at his party, but he now made quick work of his second gimlet and promptly tucked into a third. I ordered a second martini. I reminded him that the first time we met, his internal debate had involved a completely different woman.

"Jean."

"Is she now out of the picture?"

He shook his head. "What gave you that idea?"

Irritation flared inside me. "Why don't you start by telling me exactly what's going on with these two women."

"One day, I promise. But for now you just have to trust that my *arrangement*"—a word he pronounced with peculiar emphasis, as if it were the proper name of a secret society—"with Jean has no bearing on the question of whether to live with Sophia."

"How can that be?"

"Please, *trust* me." Only to add, flatly, "You see, it's all pretty simple. I'm a sick person."

It would be years before I would be prepared to accept his self-assessment, and even then, not fully. In the moment I pointed out that he was handsome, wealthy, the youngest tenured professor at one of the nation's most prestigious colleges, and already internationally known for his work; many people would have happily traded up to that level of sickness.

"Wittgenstein's sister often used the same argument on him," Oliver said. "His response was, 'You look at my life like someone watching a man caught in a storm from the safe confines of a house. From your perspective, you think, "Why on earth is that man struggling so?" You can't see the fierce wind blowing against him.'"

He folded his fingers around the base of his cocktail glass. "I desire her more than I've ever desired another woman."

"Jean?"

He shook his head. "Sophia." His voice suddenly jumped in volume, like a dial jostled. "I've recently made a very interesting observation. It has to do with sex. Have I already told you?"

"I don't think so."

I glanced around; the owner and lone waiter were sitting at a vacant booth in stony silence. Otherwise the restaurant was empty. The only sound was Oliver's voice. Which I indicated he might want to lower.

"I've noticed that when we have sex after a considerable absence, my thrusts are always deeper, almost violent. Do you know *why*?"

"Because you're excited to see her? You might want to keep it down."

"No! That's not it at all! It's because I'm in the grips of an evolutionary *imperative*. Those deep, violent thrusts are meant to expunge the cum of my competitor. You see, as an evolutionary matter, I have no idea how Sophia has spent the time while I, so to speak, have been away hunting, so when I come back to the cave, I have to use the only tool at my disposal to *expunge*"—and now he was very loud—"the competitor's cum. First I have to *expunge* his cum before I replace it with my own."

Maybe it made sense evolutionarily, but I confessed I didn't see the mechanism. "How do the deeper thrusts expunge? Don't they just drive the competitor's cum deeper?"

"No. They clean and vacate."

"I don't see it. They'd push the competitor's cum toward the egg."

"*No!* They *expunge!*"

"I just don't see it."

By the time we made it to the parking lot, we'd taken tentative strides toward sobriety. In the past day, winter had sneaked up on us. I squinted into the sunlight, dagger sharp and devoid of heat. A wicked wind made swirls and eddies of dust and cigarette butts. Oliver thrust his hands deeper into his pockets and bunched his shoulders. His coat, though, remained unzipped. He looked at me; his eyes, behind the formidable newscaster's glasses, were tearing from the cold. A blast of wind made him nearly swallow his words. "Did I tell you that I was dumped by my therapist?"

I shook my head, suppressing a shiver.

"I started seeing him about two years ago, when Sophia and I got involved. He's really an excellent therapist, smart and insightful. A dead ringer for Gene Wilder. But gradually he became so fed up with my endless frantic rehashing of the same problems, so dispirited by my compulsive tendency to seek advice which I then ignore or declare myself incapable of implementing, so perplexed by my penchant for self-examination without profitable end, and so alarmed by my inability or refusal to restrain my thoughts, which overheat and go nowhere, like bats flapping around a closed attic, that he began last week's session with the simple declaration, 'I don't think I'm helping you. I don't think I'm *capable* of helping you.' He apologized and we shook hands; I even tried to cheer *him* up—he did as good a job as anybody could have . . ."

Oliver smiled wanly and pointed a finger toward his temple, not pistol-like, but as one might to a curious artifact in a museum: "Sick."

FIVE

The last glow of a sky ribbed with coppery clouds was fading over Manhattan when we arrived at Oliver's mother's building, a prewar Tudor between Lexington and Park. A liveried doorman ushered us into a lobby festooned with Christmas wreaths and relieved us of our umbrella; a second doorman called up to announce our arrival. "I'll send them right up. And have a very merry Christmas, Mrs. Nagy!"

The surprising invitation to spend Christmas with Oliver's family had come during a phone call with Sophia.

"That's very kind," I said. "Will you be there?"

"I got my fill last year. I don't need to spend another Christmas with an anti-Semite. But I'm sorry I'll miss you and your delicious wife."

From the background came a muffled shout: "She's not an anti-Semite."

"She doesn't want me there anyway. There's only one woman in the world good enough for her boys. Be nice to Bartholomew, the poor sweetie."

A day or so later, Oliver called, the irritation in his voice clear from his first words. "Didn't Sophia extend an invitation?"

"Yes . . ."

"Don't you think it's *exceptionally* ill-mannered not to have RSVP'd?" It was the first time I had heard him genuinely angry.

"I didn't realize that you needed an immediate answer. I haven't even discussed it with Melissa."

He appeared to find this deeply insulting. "So when were you planning on letting me know? My mother needs time to plan."

It was still three weeks before Thanksgiving.

"Oliver, I'm sorry about the confusion. I'll let you know tomorrow at the latest."

Melissa was enthusiastic. "We won't have to rent *Zelig* again."

When I called to accept, Oliver carefully laid out the protocol. "You're welcome to stay over at the apartment. There's more than enough space, and the guest room has its own bathroom. You should plan on getting presents for my mother and brother and a few old friends who will be there—nothing elaborate, but opening presents on Christmas Eve *before* dinner is our tradition, so it would be nice for you to partake. And *please*—don't be late."

We rang the bell at precisely four p.m., the agreed-upon time. Oliver, in a gray cardigan vest and flannel slacks, answered the door and ushered us into the center hall. What I noticed first—before the hand-painted Tuscan murals in the kitchen, before the Dufy and the Pascin and the Kokoschka in the living room, before the Dresden figurines on the dining room table—was atmospheric, a dizzying, heavy mix of perfume and cigarette smoke.

In all the years of our friendship, Oliver and I rarely touched, and now, by way of greeting, he simply took my coat. He and Melissa exchanged an awkward hug that resulted in a near collision of heads and shy smiles. Behind him stood a tall, thin, and very handsome woman whom I immediately recognized as the sixty-year-old incarnation of the thirty-year-old model who cast a watchful eye over Oliver at his desk. "I am Francizka Nagy. It is so good for you to come." She extended her hand for a firm, bony handshake, but also pulled me closer for a series of kisses on the cheek, left, right, then left again, "the Hungarian way," she explained. She wore a blouse of cream-colored silk over a dress that shimmered expensively and draped to an end at her knees, flattering a pair of shapely legs. Her thin wrists were cluttered with bracelets and around her neck she wore two Phi Beta Kappa keys, a mother's pride in her sons' achievements. "I hope the drive down was copacetic. Tell me, has it begun to snow . . . ? No? Thank goodness for that! Now you'll have to excuse me, I must toil in the kitchen. Make yourselves comfortable. Oliver, why don't you offer your friends a drink?" The mother's accent was throaty, smoke-pebbled, and Middle European, pleasingly seductive.

Oliver showed us into the living room, where the others sat drinking. The room was spacious but densely arranged, the reigning design principle old-world, high-bourgeois, eclectic. Paintings hung on the salmon-colored walls one atop the other, salon style, as in Oliver's loft. Dried hydrangeas were collected in Chinese vases. On a side table sat a collection of porcelain cats, carved boxes of amber and jade, and silver teaspoons with hand-painted handles. There was a tasseled dinner bell of bronze enameled in lapis with a design of dragons, and another with a pattern of warriors riding costumed elephants. Manhattan must have had hundreds, maybe thousands, of such apartments, but for me, the son of Long Island, it was something new, intimidating in its casual opulence and suggestive of self-sustaining and inexhaustible wealth.

Oliver made short work of the introductions. "This is my brother . . . This is Bernie, whom we've known forever . . . This is Nora and Jeffrey Ferris, family friends. So what can I get you to drink—a vodka martini? And for you, Melissa?" He hurried off to the bar.

Evidently we had intruded upon a conversation about city politics.

"They're not going to strike," said Jeffrey Ferris. I gathered they were talking about the New York transit workers. "They'll reach an agreement at the last minute. They always do."

"Not in 1980," muttered Bartholomew. After rising to proffer a moist handshake, Bartholomew settled back into an armchair with a tumbler of Scotch and a cigarette. He was an enormous man, half a head taller than his fraternal twin and easily a hundred pounds heavier. Like Oliver, he wore a woolen vest—in fact, they appeared to match—but the buttons of his strained to contain his girth. He had a carefully groomed walrus-like mustache and brown hair slicked straight back over the crown of his head. Around his thick, creased neck hung a silver crucifix.

"That was then," said Jeffrey Ferris. "This is now. They'll settle."

A silence ensued. Was it odd, I asked myself, that we had been invited to such an intimate family gathering?

A spread of sturgeon and slices of pumpernickel quarter-breads had been arranged on a walnut side table with scrolled legs. On a matching table were bowls of caviar, chopped egg, and diced onion, and a plate of toast points.

I helped myself to the sturgeon.

"Hey, take it easy there," Bartholomew exclaimed. "Leave some for others."

I wasn't sure whether this was intended as a joke. There was enough sturgeon for a wedding party. He wasn't smiling. Oliver had not returned with the drinks.

"Don't listen to him," said Bernie. "Bart is all bark and no bite."

The mother's friend, in his mid-sixties, was tanned and smooth-skinned but with a lopsided gait, the aftermath of a recent hip replacement. Closer inspection revealed additional signs of small, unexpected dishevelment: an ink stain by the breast pocket of his colorful plaid shirt, a belt loop missed, a fraying shoelace.

The brother poured himself another Scotch from a bottle he kept by his side. Grudgingly he offered me a tumbler.

"Thanks, but Oliver's bringing me a drink. I don't know what's taking him."

Oliver finally appeared, bearing a silver tray. "One vodka martini and one gin and tonic."

"I asked for a Gibson," said Melissa.

"My mistake." Oliver promptly took the drink and disappeared back to the bar.

"Oliver says you're a writer of fiction." Bernie's voice was pleasingly deep, with vestigial traces of Brooklyn. "Would I know your books?"

I mentioned the title of my novel.

Bernie smiled politely.

"I once met Borges," Nora Ferris volunteered.

"I don't read fiction," declared Bartholomew. "Life's too short." And yet we knew from Sophia that Oliver's twin had no career or even steady job. Living with his mother, he worked as a substitute seventh-grade history teacher in the city public schools.

"Bart collects books on Churchill," said Bernie.

"A man of true format," commented Bartholomew.

"May I see your library?" I asked.

Without directly responding, Bartholomew rose from his chair and signaled for me to follow him down a long hallway. The apartment was clearly vast. Through an open doorway I caught a glimpse of what must have been Francizka's bedroom. On an enormous bed with a quilted sham and scrolled Napoleonic headboard lay a plump, yawning cat. Farther down the hallway, we entered a cozy room that looked as if lifted in its entirety from an English manor house. A standing globe showed a fanciful outline of Africa, still half unexplored. A Persian rug the color of plums was spread before bookcases of carved teak.

"I have roughly fifteen hundred Churchill books split into two sections, those by him and those about him," Bartholomew explained. "Most are the latter, obviously."

But you know Churchill himself was a prolific and superb writer. He actually won the Nobel Prize for peace *and* for literature. Two Nobels, not too shabby. And you'll be pleased to know that he even wrote a novel."

Bartholomew handed me a clothbound book in wrappers called *Savrola*. "Published when he was twenty-six. He never wrote another but he continued to write the occasional short story. 'Man Overboard' is probably his most famous—a man falls overboard on a cruise liner and gets eaten by sharks. All in three or so pages, a model of compression . . . For my money, this book is his best."

He placed his Scotch on a coaster of a World War II battleship, dried his hands on a pocket handkerchief, and removed from a glass-enclosed case a tidy volume, *My Early Life*.

"Yes, I've read it," I said. "It's wonderful."

Bartholomew glanced at me skeptically, as if unsure how to process this unexpected response, then his expression softened as we experienced the power of books to establish secret and enduring fraternities.

"Here." He thrust the volume at me. "Try not to soil it, it's a first edition, Butterworth. Worth a pretty penny."

I admired the lovely frontispiece of a young, trim, haughty Churchill, hair neatly parted on the side, dressed dapperly in the uniform of the Hussars.

Bartholomew plopped himself into a leather armchair and took a long bracing sip of Scotch. Watching us from several corners of the room were reproduction busts of Churchill in unsmiling poses of cigar-chomping, indomitable steadfastness. Several die-cast models of Wehrmacht tanks trained their gun turrets on me.

"I also collect toy military vehicles and some figures, too. I have some original G.I. Joes I could show you. The critical part is the box. Even if the toy is pristine, without the box it's not nearly as valuable."

On a bookshelf, next to a half-track from Rommel's desert campaign, I noticed the same photograph I had seen in Oliver's apartment—of the two little brothers, the father, and the cow. Or rather, it was *almost* the same shot. It must have been taken either seconds before or after, as here the man's arms were folded across his chest, and the bald intelligent egg-shaped head was foreshortened by a chin thrust forward in a broad smile.

"Is that your father?" I asked.

"My biological father." The same locution Oliver used.

"He looks like Nabokov."

"Does he? Never read him. Never tempted."

"Do you know where this picture was taken?"

"Cornwall, maybe. We used to spend summers there."

"Where does he live now?"

"My biological father? Somewhere in hell, I suppose."

"Why do you say that?"

Bartholomew gazed at me, his jowls lifted in a half-smile. "Accumulating material for your next novel?"

"No. I'm just curious."

"Then I suggest you ask my brother."

"But you're the one who made the comment."

"He would say the same thing." Bartholomew fingered his silver crucifix. His eyes were like his twin's, the same chestnut brown, only more almond-shaped, feminine. "If he believed in hell."

"Do you?"

"Believe in hell? Of course. Only an apostate wouldn't, like my brother."

"I don't believe in hell and I wouldn't call myself an apostate."

"You're Jewish, that's different"—presumably Oliver had shared this with his family—"but that doesn't mean you shouldn't come to Midnight Mass. My stepfather is Jewish, and he never missed a Midnight Mass. Until he got ill."

"How's he doing?"

"I'd prefer not to talk about it."

The light in the study appeared to dim. Bartholomew gazed into the ice cubes of his tumbler. The clock scratched out the time. I glanced at the statues of Churchill and the toy Wehrmacht tanks. I wasn't sure what was going on with Bartholomew, whether he was lost in thought or wrestling with some strong emotion. Finally, he pitched himself from his reading chair. "Come," he said. "High time for another drink."

We rejoined the others in the living room, where we found my wife changed.

"What do you think?" she said.

She was wearing an apricot-colored cardigan that lovingly followed her form.

"It's beautiful."

"Feel," she said. "Cashmere."

"I always adored the cashmeres from Chanel," said Francizka. A lit cigarette dangled from the corner of her mouth, and squinting into the smoke, she looked like Marlene Dietrich, a CD of whose cabaret songs was playing. "It fits you perfectly, like a glove. As soon as you walked in the door, I said to myself, such a splendid figure, we must go through my closet together. It is the rare woman who can fit into my outfits."

On a chair was folded a pile of clothing for Mel.

"Wow," I said, "that's incredibly generous."

"It's my pleasure," said Francizka. "Many of these pieces I haven't worn in years. They're all in perfect condition, and they look absolutely lovely on your wife. Now, Melissa, why don't you help yourself to a blini while I start a fire."

Francizka squatted, dress drawn to mid-thigh, to light a Duraflame log in the fireplace. "Alas, the building does not allow anything else."

"Let me help you," said Jeffrey Ferris.

"A true gentleman."

As they arranged the logs, Francizka's dress inched up to reveal that her dark stockings were held up by garters. The glimpse of garters was so unexpected that it took a moment for any feeling to register other than surprise. Then I found myself gallantly joining the effort to assist Francizka, hoping to catch another glimpse of those mature, smooth, shapely thighs. Was it typical, I wondered, for European women of her generation to wear stockings, or was this a special holiday gift for her friend Bernie? To my regret, her dress crept down as if of its own accord. I would mark it as the first time that I had been licked by desire for an older woman.

It was traditional to open presents before the Christmas dinner. The gifts we had brought along had disappeared into the hillscape of boxes spread around the tree, which was decorated with hand-painted glass balls and antique ornaments of tin. A die-cut monkey blared at a contrabass, a wolf bore an armful of flowers, and a pig blew a horn. A banner of handcut letters draped across the tree: *Boldog Karácsonyt.* Merry Christmas in Hungarian, presumably.

Oliver distributed the presents. Melissa and I had gotten everyone a gift, but not each other. Hanukkah had already come and passed.

Francizka unwrapped my gift, an inscribed copy of my novel. "I hope that doesn't seem too narcissistic," I said.

"I am flattered and look forward to reading it. Do you know, I read every word that Ollie writes, even when it goes directly over my head?"

From Bartholomew I received an Hermès tie patterned with curlews, a strangely lavish gift; and from Oliver, a bottle of Arpège Pour Homme cologne and a monograph on the artist Pascin. He drew my attention to the fact that the painting reproduced on the cover hung over the mantelpiece.

Bartholomew appeared pleased with our offering, a book on the battle of Stalingrad.

Sophia, on the West Coast with family, had sent along presents, presumably something for everyone, though memory has preserved only the gift to Oliver's mother. The box was elaborately tied with ribbons and packing string; inside, the gift had been carefully cushioned with bubble wrap and layers of tissue paper. Oliver fetched a pair of scissors and we watched Francizka make several surgical snips before pulling free the present: a tiny bird's nest, like that of a hummingbird. It wasn't a real nest, though, but a sculpture, unmistakably the work of the artistic savant I had met at Oliver's party. Max had modeled a mother bird feeding her two chicks in a macabre tour de force of expressive miniaturization.

"My heavens," exclaimed Francizka. "Vultures!"

"They're not vultures—they're birds," Oliver protested.

"Since when is a vulture not a bird?" said Bernie.

"Tell me,"—Francizka held up the bizarre little sculpture for inspection—"are these not vultures?"

The minuscule, featherless, weak-necked chicks may have supported any number of plausible ornithological identifications, but the mother bird, with her dark blue tail feathers, malignant red wattle, and hideous talons for shredding, left little room for disagreement.

"Look like vultures to me," said Bartholomew matter-of-factly.

"Take it away!" Francizka cried. "It's the most *horrible* gift I've ever received in all my life!"

"It's the work of a friend of ours," Oliver protested. "He shows all over the world. She commissioned it just for you."

"That makes it even worse. Remove it *immediately.*"

Oliver meekly carried Max's sculpture from the room.

The exchange of gifts proceeded: slippers and soaps and shirts; books and belts and money clips and monogrammed silver collar stays. But the nest lingered in Francizka's mind, for all at once, as if in the grips of flashback, she exclaimed, "Horrible!"

After all the other presents had been opened, what remained were the sons' gifts to the mother. Withholding these until the very end appeared to be a well-rehearsed part of the Christmas ritual. Oliver gave his mother a

CD that he had digitized to hold her old photos. "I've transferred all the pictures and descriptions to your computer, so not only are they preserved, but they're fully searchable."

"Ollie, what a wonderful and thoughtful gift. And the time it must have taken! After dinner we must look at the pictures. It's been aeons . . ."

Then came Bartholomew's turn. From a small Tiffany box the mother removed a platinum necklace with a single tear-shaped diamond pendant.

"Oh, Mew, it is magnificent!"

"Do you really like it, Twigs? Let me give you a hand."

Bartholomew took the necklace from his mother, and standing behind her, fastened it around her neck. His sausage fingers handled the clasp with surprising dexterity. Francizka examined herself in an antique pocket mirror with the confidence of a woman well accustomed to the flattery of her own reflection.

"What do you think, Twigs?"

"Mew, it's a thing of beauty!"

The massive son absorbed his slender handsome mother in a tender hug and they kissed. It might have been my imagination, but it seemed their lips grazed. The rest of us remained silent. Only Oliver hazarded an observation. "It reminds me of the one you gave her last year."

Dinner followed, a lavish Hungarian Christmas meal.

We started with three appetizers: slices of cold goose liver cooked in its own fat, paprika-spiced goat cheese, and biscuits made with pork cracklings. Two main courses then followed: beef goulash simmered with smoked bacon and caraway seeds, accompanied by buttery dumplings; and rolled cabbage leaves stuffed with minced pork and garlic. Stewed fruit and fresh-baked loaves of crusty potato bread made the rounds. Wine was plentiful—Bull's Blood—as was champagne. Dessert brought thick slices of walnut and poppy-seed strudel, and Hungarian apricot schnapps served in crystal glasses. Stupendously delicious and filling, the orgy of food weighed down conversation, rendering it intermittent and framed by short, winded sentences.

Unfortunately, we had failed to anticipate that the dinner would showcase pig in such prominence and variety. Melissa's best efforts to shift the proscribed meat to the edges of her plate did not escape Francizka's notice.

"Is there a problem?"

"Everything is absolutely delicious," Melissa said. "It's just—I'm terribly sorry, but I don't eat pork."

"You're on a diet?"

"No, no. It's religious."

"Well, then, I should have been told." She glared at Oliver, who, in turn, glared at us. Melissa came from a secular home that had never kept kosher. But for some years she had avoided pork as a symbolic gesture, a minor concession to a way of life she didn't fully accept or understand but felt was owed its due. I wondered which obligation should have superior claim: to one's religion or one's host.

"Come," said Francizka. "Hand me your plate and I'll discard what's there."

"No, I love it, really. I just hope you don't mind if I leave a little bit over."

"As you please. But really, it's a shame. All the flavor is in the bacon. It is smoked in the only true Hungarian delicatessen left in the city. It's like listening to an orchestra without the violins, a waste. You must at least try some of what I've made for Ollie."

As the lone vegetarian at the table, Oliver presided over a plateful of bread, stewed fruit, and boiled spinach that Francizka evidently prepared for him every year.

Francizka passed Melissa the bowl of spinach, but as Melissa dished herself an obligatory spoonful, the serving spoon slipped from her grasp and fell to the floor.

"My God, my God!" the mother exclaimed. "Look! My spoon!"

The rounded porcelain handle of the serving spoon had cracked off, shattering into a dozen pieces.

"It's all my clumsiness," said Melissa, contritely. "I'm *so* sorry. We'll get you new one, I promise."

"My dear, this is a piece of antique Zsolnay! Where could you possibly find another? It is irreplaceable!"

"I feel awful, really. Maybe we can get it repaired."

"Repaired? Look at it—it's finished, destroyed!"

"We'll at least try. Please. We'll try."

Shaking her head at the futility of it all, the mother watched us painstakingly collect the tiny porcelain shards from the handle and place them into a Ziploc bag.

Desperate to deflect attention from Melissa's crime, I asked, "Did you do all the cooking by yourself?"

"Have you seen any hidden servants lurking about?"

"And did you learn these recipes from your mother?"

"My mother?" Francizka laughed, but her lips turned down in a frown. "My dear, the only times my mother set foot in the kitchen were to make sure that the cooks weren't stealing meat."

I glanced at Melissa. She secretly made a gesture of shooting herself in the temple, her left hand pantomiming the exit wound.

The spirit of the disaster threatened to darken Francizka's mood for the remainder of the meal. A heavy silence descended upon the table. Oliver barely lifted his gaze from his plate. Ever since we'd arrived, my friend, the formidable young philosopher, had been a thing diminished; now the pork and spoon calamities left him withdrawn, virtually catatonic. Bernie smiled at us helplessly. A feeling of embarrassment gripped me as well, as my mind failed to locate a reliable topic of conversation. All at once, though, Francizka exclaimed, as if everyone but herself needed cheering up, "Come, let's not lose our appetites over a silly spoon! Not after what I've been through in my life. Let's raise our glasses to old friends and new, and drink to peace and to health." She repeated the toast in Hungarian. "Now, who can I interest in seconds?"

It was a crucial intervention. Talk didn't exactly revive, but we all shared in the restored cheer, even Oliver, who suddenly said to Melissa, "I remember when my mother used to wear that sweater, the one you have on."

"So do I," chimed in Bartholomew. "Twigs liked to wear it to the Met."

"My boys have such marvelous memories," boasted Francizka.

But it seemed like the power of something other than memory was on display. Mel looked beautiful in the Chanel top, and in their pleased glances, it was as if the brothers saw in my wife a younger version of their own glamorous mother. I couldn't suppress the feeling that this transposition pleased Francizka, perhaps had been her aim.

Our eating slowed, though not Bartholomew's. He cut himself thick pieces of potato bread, speared wedges of butter, and, breaking up the bread, used the buttery chunks to mop up the bacon grease and the juices from the pork, venison, and stewed fruits. His aggressive bloated chewing was punctuated with gasps of satisfaction. Sauce beaded his mustache; he dabbed it away with his napkin, masticating continuously. Far from concerned, Francizka watched her son with an expression of maternal pride. She herself had made do with a birdlike portion. A story idea presented itself to me: a wonderful cook, who dies of anorexia.

At last came the digestifs—a thirty-year-old port—and the night's entertainment. Oliver shepherded us back to the living room, where we clustered around a computer monitor to look at the photos he'd transferred to CD. Now such a display is humdrum; at the time, it seemed like a small miracle of recovery. In the place of yellowed albums, boxes of loose snapshots, and trays of dusty slides, here was a technology that promised effortless retrieval, a past transformed into an ever-accessible, indexical present. But there was something peculiar about Oliver's digital project. Instead of hewing to a neat chronology, the pictures skipped around in time, following unknown or unknowable byways of familial memory.

The first shot was of an almost unrecognizable Bartholomew from perhaps a decade earlier. Dressed in an elegant dark suit, he was trim and broodingly handsome.

"Mew, on his graduation from Princeton," Francizka said.

Next came a photo of Oliver standing, arms folded, before the British Museum in the company of a woman.

"Ah, dear Jean," exclaimed the mother. "Here she looks so cheerful and confident—they make such a nice couple, no?"

She turned to her son as if for confirmation, but Oliver only fidgeted with the mouse. In the moments it lingered on the screen, I closely studied the picture of the London woman, the self-canceling weight on Oliver's decisional scale. Her hair, cut in a pageboy, was dyed something purplish, an exotic touch for sure, but otherwise she looked happily conventional: eyes enlarged by wire-rim glasses, shy chin, plump cheeks lifted in a pleasant smile. And yet behind the woman loomed a tower crane, which, by compositional accident or design, appeared about to dump a load of cinderblocks directly on her head.

"Such an intelligent and cultured girl," Francizka said. "I fear, though, that sometimes it is a curse when a woman is too good up here"—she pointed to her platinum bangs. "A woman must also know how to be . . . a woman."

Nobody asked for amplification. Oliver's ears reddened. Immediately he switched to the next picture.

"Ah, here I am with my second husband." Francizka, in a halter top and large oval sunglasses, arm hooked in Jacob Epstein's, smiling before a fountain of water-spouting dolphins dappled in sunlight. "Poor Jake, you know of his terrible illness. We are in Rome, of course. During this trip I found him in our bed in the Hassler with a floozy."

Oliver's ears remained the same florid color. Promptly he advanced to a black-and-white studio portrait of the handsome imperious man whom I recognized from the twins' nearly matching photos.

"And this is my father," said Francizka.

I thought I must have misheard. "Oliver and Bartholomew's father?"

Francizka flashed me a worldly smile. "No, my dear, *my* father. But I can certainly understand the error—they did share many things in common. They both were great lovers of art. Victor, the boys' father, was a professional dealer, you know. To him we owe all the paintings you see on these walls, though little else, I'm afraid. He was terribly successful in his career, but not suited to family life. My father was altogether different. He was a great man."

Francizka allowed that her father was a direct descendent of one Miklós Nagy, a famous sixteenth-century count who presided over the Diet of Transylvania. "The Nagy family was one of the wealthiest and most decorated in all of Hungary. Yet to be truthful, it was a curse for my father, to come from such privilege. It was expected that sons of the aristocracy would pursue a career either in the military or in government. But my

father abhorred war and violence and had the tempera-
ment of an anarchist. He was fascinated with natural
science and longed to be a doctor, a profession considered undignified for a gentleman. So he broke with his
family, studied medicine, and became one of the most
prominent physicians in all of Budapest, conducting
important experiments on glands and secretions at the
Forensic Medical Institute. He was also a passionate
reader of literature—he knew German intimately and
adored Kleist and Hölderlin above all others. He also
loved to garden, but had few chances at our apartment
in Budapest, so he bought a beautiful country estate in
Visegrad, not far from the former royal residence. There
he pursued his passion for gardening. Most of the year
we lived in Budapest, where he lectured, conducted his
research, and maintained a clinical practice—a 'surgery,'
as it was called."

"When did your family move to the States?"

"I came in 1947—I was barely fourteen. But by then,
of course, I was an orphan. My parents died in the war."

"I'm very sorry, I had no idea."

"It was in the summer of 1944. I was away at a day
camp, learning to ride 'English' saddle. How can I forget?
It was a terribly hot day, very dusty, and my horse was
very badly behaved. My mother, who typically spent her
days in shops and cafes, had stayed in our Buda apartment to assist my father—his receptionist had called
in sick that morning. Shortly after noon, the sky filled
with Soviet bombers. From my camp we could hear the
explosions in the city, but I thought nothing of it. That
evening I returned home eager to complain about my

difficult horse and found our building completely destroyed. My parents' bodies were never recovered."

"Horrible. And you were eleven at the time?"

"Yes, just a girl."

"How did you live after that?"

"One learned. It was not a happy education."

"That's enough questions," Bartholomew snapped.

"You must excuse Mew. He's very protective of his mother, just as I am of my boys. There is nothing more tragic in life than being powerless to protect your loved ones. That is a tragedy I wish on no one, not my worst enemy. May we all know nothing but the blessings of peace. This is why I hate all these foolish, foolish politicians who send armies here and there to fight—for what? Nothing!"

Just then we heard a light snore from the recliner. Bernie had settled back and dozed off, his head tilted to the side, mouth slightly agape. The mother eyed him with fondness. "Dear Bernie—but look, don't his ankles look swollen? I can't bear to wake him—he looks so comfortable. I think this is a sign that a long happy day has come to a close."

Only the day wasn't quite over. Melissa and I were shown to the guest room. A radiator clanked riotously. We cracked open a window to release the room's oppressive heat, and I went to get us both a glass of water.

The kitchen had been scrubbed clean, betraying no traces of the day's cooking. One certainly could not gainsay Francizka's industriousness. An odor lingered, though, an old-world mixture of garlic, paprika, and cigarettes. The apartment was quiet. Bartholomew and Francizka had left for Midnight Mass. In semidarkness, I drank a glass of water and helped myself to a tangerine, as if only more food could conquer the unpleasantness roiling in my stomach. When I disposed of the rind, I noticed the battered remains of Sophia's present in the garbage. The tiny nest had been flattened, as if stomped underfoot, leaving no trace of the mother vulture and her two chicks. I couldn't resist foraging, and to my astonishment, discovered that Max's sculpture wasn't the only gift to find its way into the trash. Below a pile of discarded wrapping paper and food scraps, I caught a glimpse of something familiar. It was my novel, *Exit 33*, the inscribed copy I'd given to Francizka.

Just then, Oliver shuffled into the kitchen in monogrammed pajamas and slippers. "Oh, hello." He poured himself a glass of mineral water. I drew his attention to the garbage, but he already knew. "To be honest, I've always found vultures to be quite beautiful," he said. "They look like eagles, the way they wheel in the sky, wings fully spread and turned up in a shallow V. And they're such thrifty creatures, picking bones perfectly clean, leaving nothing to waste. Still." He shook his head sadly. "What was Sophia *thinking*? She'll never live this down with my mother. That relationship is over."

He sounded exceptionally fatigued. I mentioned that his mother had also thrown away my novel.

"That was me."

In a whisper, he explained: "The scene where the protagonist gags on a pubic hair during oral sex—I can't have my mother read that. It would completely disgust her."

I reminded him that the character also reacts with disgust.

"Immaterial. You don't know my mother."

"So you threw out my novel?"

"Trust me, it's for the best. You really don't have any idea of how that type of thing revolts her."

I observed that his mother appeared quite comfortable with sex. Without mentioning the stockings, I reminded him that she was the one who'd spoken with candor about Jean and of the importance of a woman being good in bed.

"Impossible. You must have misheard her."

Back in the guest room, I found Mel propped up in bed, wearing a pale beige silken camisole, a color once called "flesh tone."

"Nice," I said. "Where did that come from?"

"Guess."

The silk was sheer, virtually see-through. Mel clasped her bare arms over her head. She was never shy about showing off what she called her "two best features." I climbed into bed, in a confused state of arousal. I imagined a younger Francizka in the camisole and black stockings, lying atop her comforter, languidly reading while her sons tumbled about the floor.

We left in the morning. The plan was to stay through the afternoon, but we used the news of an approaching storm as an excuse for an earlier departure. Bernie, comfortably ensconced in his recliner and the *Times*, appeared never to have stirred from the night before.

Bartholomew and Francizka were smoking. A Christmas Eve deal had averted the transit strike, but the weather posed a fresh menace. In two days the family was to leave for Switzerland. They were scheduled to fly to Zurich, and then would drive to Bad Ragaz, staying through New Year's to ski and "take the waters." Evidently it was an annual tradition. Only now the forecast was predicting heavy snow for the evening of their flight, and Francizka, certain that Kennedy would close, was glued to the Weather Channel. We said our goodbyes in the TV room, while Francizka nervously echoed the newscaster's dire prognostications: "Possible accumulations of six to ten inches! Did you hear that? But truly, you must come again, it was a pleasure. Next time we will make another visit to my closet, yes? Wind gusts of twenty to thirty miles an hour, this is truly too much! And don't worry about the spoon, my dear, I mean that seriously. Have a safe drive back; I have already written you in for next Christmas. Possible blizzard conditions! My God, can you believe it?"

In the car, Melissa reclined her seat as far back as it would go. She pulled a knit cap over her eyes and crooked her head against her shoulder. She had slept poorly and now was determined to nap.

Snow may have been in the forecast, but though the sky darkened and glowered, only the isolated flake spun down. The highway was empty, even the exits to the malls, which I'd expected to find clogged with cars loaded with gifts to be returned. Then I realized that this was Christmas Day; everything was closed except for the Chinese restaurants and kosher delis that my parents used to take me to on the holiday. In the rearview mirror I could see a large bag of Francizka's hand-me-downs. Back home, we'd discover that not all the articles were in pristine condition. Some had small stains, snags in the fabric, a bulge in a seam, and Mel would carry an armful to Goodwill. But Mel looked lovely in the cashmere sweater; I tucked my right hand under her thigh and drove with my left. My mind wandered freely without quite escaping Francizka's large apartment. I thought about the crushed baby vultures and my novel consigned to the trash for smuttiness. I thought about how unrecognizably small and guarded Oliver had behaved in his mother's presence. I saw Francizka's shapely legs and stockings and her father who looked exactly like her first husband. And I couldn't shake the image of Bartholomew, in all his gargantuan fleshiness, fastening a diamond pendant around his mother's neck, and then taking her, the platinum-haired former model he called Twigs, in his arms. It all kept returning with stubborn persistence. Whether I'd enjoyed myself was entirely irrelevant. I'd been drawn in. That was the point.

As if agitated by my thoughts, Mel woke with a start. "He wanted you to see it. He wanted you to bear witness."

"Why?"

"Maybe he's a little in love with you. Or maybe he wants you to write about it. Who knows?"

SIX

Years later, after her death, Sophia Baum installed herself as a regular in my dream life. She was the casual walk-on, carrying a potted plant across a stage that had me performing an absurd gymnastics routine in my underwear. She was my spirited interlocutor in an Albee-esque drama in which we argued vociferously over the proper spelling of the word "referral." She pulled off neat tricks of disguise, appearing with wavy cascades of blond hair, or in the tight-fitting, front-zippered, one-piece outfit of a sixties spy. I wasn't fooled for a moment—I knew the real identity of the voluptuous KGB mole.

Why she came to play such a role is anybody's guess. Even as she continued to pass in and out of Oliver's life, I never got to know her well. She was like a celestial body, an object of attractions and collisions, something on the horizon that suddenly tugged at your attention.

On New Year's Day, an innocuous but picturesque inch or two of light feathery snow fell windlessly from New York to Vermont, leaving a bib of white on mailboxes, shutters, and fence posts. That night Sophia called from San Francisco to announce that she had broken up with Oliver. It was not a tearful declaration.

"I couldn't take it any longer. I mean, nothing ever changes with Ollie. It's always the same."

"I can imagine."

"No, sweetie, I don't think you can. I'm sure you haven't heard the half of it."

"Like what?"

"Like . . . Do you know who's with him and Bart and Mom in little Swiss curetown?"

I confessed I didn't.

"Of course, you don't. Because you haven't been introduced to all the wonderful Vice traditions. Like meeting Jean in Zurich before they all head off to the grand hotel in the Alps."

"The London woman is with him?"

"See what I mean? Every year it's the same. They always stay in adjoining rooms, Bart and Mom in one, and Oliver and Jean in the other. They take thermal baths and get massages and then at night they get all gussied up and have dinner like characters straight out of *The Magic* fucking *Mountain*. And he wonders why I dumped him, the bastard." She laughed shrilly. "You probably have no idea about the smuggling, either."

"The smuggling?"

"The great thing about these incredibly expensive trips is that they always return with more money than they left with, *a lot* more money. They spend a week skiing and steaming and eating—poor Bart!—and then they drive back to Zurich and make a beeline to the proverbial Swiss bank. The next day they fly home with like a hundred thousand bucks stashed in their suitcases."

"You're kidding."

"May God turn my ass to dust, I swear to every word. It's like something straight out of who-knows-what. They smuggle the money in Mom's lacy apparel, and Mom just sweet-talks her way through customs. An agent once asked them to open the suitcase where all the cash was stashed. Ollie said he nearly dropped dead on the spot, but Mom didn't bat an eye—she remained cool as a cucumber, and said to the customs guy, 'Dahling, I vill blush to open my suitcase in fwont of my sons,' and incredibly he just waved her through."

"Where does the money come from?"

"Fuck knows—it's a family secret. I'm not even sure Ollie knows. Or if he does, Mom has sworn him to se-crecy, and Ollie would never disobey his mother."

That was all Sophia could say about the Swiss ac-counts. The conversation followed other turns. She talked about relocating to the West Coast, finding work there. I heard her sigh, not a world-weary sigh, but a disagreeable task-completed sigh, the sigh of someone peeling off the rubber gloves after cleaning a filthy stove.

"You think the break is final?" I asked.

"Sweetie, I'm not sure we were ever *together*. Do you know that a couple of weeks after we first started going out, Oliver flew to London to see Jean? And I was stupid enough to put up with it. For three years I put up with his shit. For three years, every summer and every winter he'd go off with Jean. 'What about a trip with me?' I'd say. 'Sure, we can do that.' So what'd we do? The *three* of us traveled together. Even now I can't believe I did that.

It was completely insane. But did it bother Ollie? Are you kidding? He was in fucking paradise. I remember the three of us watching a movie in Paris, Ollie in the middle and Jean and me on either side of him. It was some stupid old French classic that Jean wanted to see, and Ollie *always* does what Jean wants. As soon as the movie started, I realized, shit, no subtitles. Of course, both of them speak *perfect* French, so it didn't matter to them, but I had no idea what was going on and *still* I sat through the entire thing, only because I didn't want to admit that after a million years in high school and college my French still sucks. Oliver kept glancing at me, but not with sympathy, not with a look of 'Hey—you able to follow this?' No, he had this incredibly obnoxious supercilious smirk on his face, like he was saying, 'You can't fool me, you little dope.' He and Jean kept laughing in this quiet totally repulsive way at all the supposed funny parts. Finally I just lost it. A character in the flick was staring at himself in the mirror, his face all angst-y, and I laughed as loud as I could, like I'd just heard the funniest thing in my life. Then I got up and walked out. And guess what happened afterward? Later, when we were alone, Oliver went completely nuts—he accused *me* of ruining the film for *everybody*. You've probably never seen it, but Ollie can have a really ugly temper. And you know what I did? I *apologized* to Jean; I told her that I was sorry for *ruining the film for everybody*, and she accepted it all so graciously, like 'No really, don't say another word, *please*.' If there's one thing in my *entire* life I wish I could undo, and I've done *a lot* of pretty dodgy things, it's that apology. I mean, I still love him, I really do, but I never should have let myself get dragged into his world."

Some days later I got a letter from Oliver, bearing no salutation and written in his elegant, minuscule, barely decipherable script on stationery from the Grand Hotel Quellenhof:

> By now you've heard that Sophia and I have de-
> cided on a trial separation. In a way, I'm happy for
> her. At least she has the advantage of being able to
> maintain distance from me; I have no such option
> with myself. I know you think I exaggerate my rea-
> sons for self-loathing—though I can't imagine why
> I would—but let me give you a small example. One
> of the many things Soap & I recently fought about
> was her smoking. Soap isn't a heavy smoker and usu-
> ally respects my insistence that she not smoke in my
> apartment. But her apartment stinks of cigarettes,
> and I can't stand being there—the odor is so vile, it
> makes me physically ill. But here's the catch. The
> cigarette odor in S.'s studio is no different from the
> smell in my mother's apartment, which has never
> bothered me. In fact, I would go so far as to say that
> I find the smell in my mother's apartment pleasing.

The letter continued, now in darker ink:

> Just returned from dinner: four-course meal of cui-
> sine équilibrée. Incredible. Can't move. Stuffed.

Hate overeating. Anyway, it now looks like I'll be staying in Europe next term and through the end of the summer. I've received a fellowship from the David Hume Society. At first I thought there must have been a mistake—I'd never even heard of the David Hume Society much less applied for one of their fellowships—but then I found out that it's another of these nomination-only things. Now I'm feeling very grateful to the Society & very warm toward Hume himself. I'll be living with Jean in her place in London. I'll probably go to New York a couple of times in the spring to visit my mother and stepfather, who's not doing well at all. I doubt I'll make it up to Harkness, but let me know if you're interested in meeting in the city. Otherwise, if you don't already have plans for the summer, why don't you visit us in London? Jean's apartment has a small but comfortable guest room, and we both know the city well and would enjoy showing you and Mel around. & it would be nice for you to meet Jean; I think you'd like each other very much. (She says hi.)

O

PS. Forgot to mention yesterday's near-death experience. Jean and I got up early and rode the cog railway up the Jungfrau. The line usually closes down for the winter months, but this winter has been unusually mild, so it's still running. During the ride, the sun was shining brightly and *the peak was clearly visible, but by the time we reached the terminus, only five hundred meters below the summit, an impenetrable alpine fog had settled over the entire area. We wandered out onto a glacial field, which, because of the weather conditions, had been declared off-limits. You couldn't see ahead more than a couple of feet, and because the glacial snow was indistinguishable from the fog, you had the uncanny sense of being suspended in space. It seemed impossible <u>not</u> to get lost, and the danger of falling into a crevasse was all too real. The only thing we had to mark our movements was an orange that I'd brought along as a snack. So we adopted the following strategy: we would roll the orange a few feet, then walk to it and pick it up, and then repeat the procedure. This worked well to avoid crevasses, but not as a hedge against getting lost, which should have been clear to us but somehow wasn't. We kept rolling the orange and advancing, until we realized that we didn't have the slightest idea which direction we'd come or how to get back. It occurred to us that we should have marked our trail, Theseus-like, with pieces of orange peel, but it was too late for that. Jean was wearing a heavy woolen sweater and proper boots, but I'd dressed in line with the bright sunshine and moderate temperatures of the morning, and in no time was completely chilled to the bone. Then Jean forced me to <u>eat</u> the orange because I was showing signs of hypothermia. My teeth were*

*chattering violently and I was starting to feel
very lazy. Meanwhile, the conditions had reached
total whiteout. I was so completely numb with
dampness and cold that I decided to sit down. I
felt such profound peace sitting on the ice that
I couldn't bring myself to move. Jean was very
dismayed with the entire situation and started
screaming for help, though her voice seemed to
come from far off. Then, all at once, the fog lifted.
The sun was dazzlingly bright and we had a magnificent view of the summit overhead. But more
incredible still, we were able to see that in the
hours of our wandering, we had managed only to
walk in a tight circle: we were no more than fifty
yards from where we'd set out. Back in the terminus, Swiss Alpine Guides wrapped me in woolen
blankets and forced me to drinks lots of hot tea
and eat lots of chocolate (Swiss, of course) and
scolded us for ignoring the warnings. All said and
done, it was a very satisfactory day . . .*

Oddly, I've never been able to corroborate the story of
hypothermia on the Jungfrau. After Oliver's disappearance, when I talked to Jean, she insisted that she had
absolutely no memories of the incident. She agreed it
was unlikely that Oliver would simply have invented it,
but found it even less likely that she would have no recollections of the episode had it happened. I like, then, to
think that maybe this one time Oliver decided to swap
places with me, to write a short chapter straight from his

imagination, to commit the victimless crime of creative self-fashioning.

That spring, I had little contact with what Melissa dubbed "the circle of Vice." Sophia took a job with an arts nonprofit in San Francisco, and within weeks was dating a computer animator from Berkeley. She sent us a postcard of a craggy Yosemite peak: *Picture me on the top of this baby. I've taken up climbing! And I'm pretty good at it, too . . .* A few weeks later came a photo in the mail of a puppy sitting on a man's lap. *Meet Rex, the newest member of our household.* The puppy suggested mutt and the man appeared only as a pair of crossed tanned legs in hiking shorts and Birkenstocks. *Our*: they were living together.

Oliver flew to New York twice, but I didn't make it down to see him. His stepfather continued to ail. Doctors discovered that in addition to Pick's disease, he was suffering from pancreatic cancer, which at least promised a quick end to his suffering. Unfortunately Oliver's stepbrothers, whom he barely knew and who'd long been estranged from their father, wanted the cancer treated aggressively, a course that Oliver and Bartholomew considered foolish and cruel. Epstein had never assigned a power of attorney, and the doctors, caught between the warring pairs of brothers, found themselves legally obligated to defer to the biological sons. Oliver contacted his stepfather's lawyer, but the lawyer was powerless to effect a change.

Our most substantial contact was with Francizka, and it involved the ill-fated Christmas spoon. With some research, Melissa was able to locate a craftsman, formerly with the German firm of Meissen, who now ran a small business outside of Philadelphia specializing in the repair of antique porcelain. After mailing him the spoon, chips and all, mummified in bubble wrap, she received a call from his workshop asking whether she really wanted to go forward with the repair.

"It can't be fixed?" she said, suspecting the worse.

"Of course, it can!" insisted the craftsman. "It's just a lot of money to spend on a piece of imitation Zsolnay."

"The spoon's not real?"

"It's a real spoon," he said. "Just not real Zsolnay."

He told Mel that the majority of "Zsolnay" in circulation was imitation. Most of the knockoffs had been produced in Eastern Europe during the Cold War and were typically of good quality; only an experienced dealer would have the knowledge—and the motivation—to distinguish the bona fide from the fakes. In any case, the cost of repairing the spoon far exceeded its actual value. Francizka's Christmas table had featured eight complete settings of "Zsolnay," and Melissa didn't relish the prospect of breaking the news to Oliver's mother. So we swallowed the cost, and the spoon was mailed directly to Francizka from the craftsman's studio.

Several days later, Melissa received a note of exuberant thanks.

I would never have thought such a repair possible, especially here in America where all anyone cares about is glitter and junk! So thank you! Now tell me: what do you make of this business about Ollie and our President? Can you imagine? Sometimes I truly must question my son's judgment. But that's another day's discussion. Remember, I've already penned you in for X-mas.

Fondest Regards,
Francizka

SEVEN

Oliver never liked talking about the run-in with Clinton, not that summer when Mel and I visited him in London, not ever. He said his point had been to make a personal statement, not to cause a ruckus. He'd been excited to receive a coveted invitation to the degree ceremony at Oxford to honor the president, who'd studied at University College on a Rhodes (the same college where Oliver had been a Junior Research Fellow); he was eager to see the man he'd canvassed and voted for. The protest came as an afterthought.

It's hardly surprising that the moment was captured on video; what's remarkable is the fact that, after moldering in someone's home video library for more than a decade, the footage would surface on YouTube. Admittedly it's yet to go viral; my obsessive spectatorship probably accounts for 53 of its 491 views. The search parameters, "Clinton, Oxford, Vice," generate seemingly random results on You-Tube's site: "President Sings Beatles 'Imagine,'" "I did not have sexual relations with that woman," "Hillary Snaps at Student," "Bosnia gunfire footage," in addition to "Presidential heckler," itself a misleading tag.

The video, running time 3:36, makes for cherished viewing—together with the CCTV footage of Oliver on

the wind-whipped deck of the QM2, it is the only ex-
tant footage of my friend. The images are grainy and
the sound quality poor. The handheld camera moves
herky-jerky. Yet the amateurishness, the abruptness of
its end, makes it all the more essential, a reminder of
the unsettling connection between film and mortality.
At the altar of University's gothic chapel, Clinton stands
in robe and mortarboard. He's flanked by Oxford's chancellor, intoning indistinct words in Latin, and by the
college's master, ready to slip a scarlet and blue hood
over the president's head. A murmur erupts from a spot
off camera; we sweep to the chapel's crowded pews. In
the second row stands a man in a dark suit and familiar rectangular glasses. He holds a small sign before his
chest, partially concealing his tie—an Hermès is my
guess. The camera first zooms out before self-correcting
to focus on the sign. The chapel's lighting is dim, but the
neat letters can be readily discerned:

THE WORD IS GENOCIDE.

The murmur builds, and it doesn't sound friendly. A
hand grabs at the sign, but abruptly we're on a picnic:
willow trees massaged by a breeze, a woman in skirt
and tank top. Someone hasn't read the Sony instruction
manual carefully. The woman sticks out her tongue and
tosses a peanut or an olive at the camera. She crosses
her arms; pouting lips come to occupy the screen, dark
and blurry. Then it's back to the chapel. The chancellor
and master look shaken by the disruption—to the ceremony, not the film. Clinton's mouth is set in trademark

overbite. The camera swings to the pews. A phalanx of men in matching gray suits surrounds the protester, ready to bustle him away; in the next moment, they magically disband. Back to the altar. Clinton holding out his arms in a calming gesture, *Stand back, let him be.* Smiling—has any world leader ever managed to smile so disarmingly? Pan to Oliver, still holding his sign, still impassive. A venerable Oxford don in bow tie flashes him the finger. Then the willows, the girl, and the picnic— but just for an instant. Then blackness.

Share? YouTube asks. *Replay?*

Oliver was hardly the first to call the atrocities unfolding in Rwanda that spring genocide. Amnesty International and Human Rights Watch had already rebuked the Clinton administration. Still, Oliver's protest created a stir. Interviewed on the BBC, profiled in *The Guardian*, and vilified in the *Daily Mail*, Oliver became an instant, if short-lived, media hit. Whether he played any role in Clinton's volte-face is hard to say. In any case, on May 25, 1994, the State Department finally called the killings "acts of genocide." By then eight hundred thousand Tutsis were dead.

Back at Harkness, where students protested even the suspension of soft-serve ice cream, an acrimonious debate was triggered. An organization of conservative alumni, the Harkness Federalists, whose members had despised Clinton from the get-go and were later to disgorge huge sums in an effort to remove him from office, now rallied to Clinton's defense, distributing an open letter that accused Oliver of besmirching the college's honor. A motion, submitted to Harkness's president and the Board of Trustees, requested that Professor Vice receive an administrative censure, a punishment typically reserved for professors guilty of plagiarism or sexual harassment.

Professors on the left—the vast majority of the faculty—failed to come to Oliver's defense. Perhaps they didn't take the motion seriously. Or maybe their silence had more to do with Oliver's reputation at Harkness. Hired with tenure, independently wealthy, judgmental and supercilious, Oliver wasn't exactly a beloved figure on campus. He had nothing but contempt for continental philosophy, deriding Derrida as an obscurantist, Foucault as a charlatan, Lacan as a fraud, and Heidegger as a hack. A "traditionalist" in matters of philosophy, he was assumed to be politically conservative as well—a terrible stigma at Harkness, where the head of the college's black studies department called his homeland AmeriKKKa.

And yet Oliver remained a far more radical and vocal critic of American policy than most of our colleagues. Every year he'd stage a one-man protest against the CIA's on-campus recruitment, planting himself by the entrance to the career development office and holding a small placard lettered in the same elegant hand as the Oxford sign: THE CIA TORTURES. That the motion of censure also raised larger issues—of freedom of thought and speech, values not irrelevant to the mission of the college and the liberal arts—appears to have been lost on many in the Harkness administration.

The censure motion threatened to pass until a member of the Board of Trustees, a billionaire software engineer, issued a private statement condemning the Federalists and praising Oliver, a point he drove home by announcing a gift to alma mater of ten million dollars. Abruptly, the motion was tabled.

While the issue was still raging, I drafted a letter to Harkness's president, drawing hesitantly on my legal education. I invoked Alexander Meiklejohn's famous defense of free speech, quoted Judge Woolsey's decision in the *Ulysses* obscenity case, and appealed to the Supreme Court's *Skokie* decision. Why I never sent the letter is hard to say. I don't think it was cowardice, though prudence no doubt played a role. Oliver had instructed me to treat Disturbed, my wayward student, with caution. Didn't that also apply to Harkness's administration? I was on a renewable contract; Oliver was tenured. Mel and I had to support ourselves; Oliver's acts of protest were cushioned by vast family wealth, augmented by secret Swiss bank accounts. Mel read the letter, urged me to send it, but added, "Don't feel like you have to play the hero."

Around this time I also came to realize that several people on the Harkness campus routinely mistook me for Oliver. How this confusion took root has never been clear to me. True: we were the same height and had similar builds; when Oliver stayed with us after Sophia's death, he was able comfortably to wear my clothes, and after Oliver's disappearance, I was startled to discover that his shoes were a perfect fit. (The Church wingtips, consigned to the bag for charity, I opted to bring home.) It was also true that I'd recently bought a couple of shirts with French cuffs, not because I was trying to imitate Oliver, but simply because I liked the look. Still, there was no deeper resemblance: his eyes were brown, mine are hazel; his hair chestnut, mine dishwater blond; I could go on.

All the same, a cashier in the faculty cafeteria, a reference librarian, and a custodian greeted me with a nod, saying, "Hi, Professor Vice," or "Hey, Oliver." If Oliver and I had been locked at the hip, I might have understood the confusion, but we weren't. After all, at the time *he wasn't even in the country.* The misidentification happened no more than a handful of times—just enough not to be a random mistake. When it did, I merely nodded and continued on my way, too puzzled to respond, vaguely concerned that any correction would be dismissed as a joke. *Oh, Professor Vice, you have such a wicked sense of humor! Enough of the funny business!* How this contributed to my temporizing over the letter is difficult to articulate, but I'm certain it did. In the end, the trustee announced his vast gift, and that was that.

EIGHT

We arrived in London to brilliant cloudless July skies and temperatures in the mid-eighties, an intolerable heat wave for the locals. LONDON BURNING, screamed the headlines. ZOO PANDAS BUSSED NORTH. MAYOR TO CITY: REMOVE YOUR TIE! CHELSEA MUM COLLAPSES ON TUBE. Jean's Hampstead apartment occupied two floors of a narrow yellow-brick walk-up on a steep street of adjoining houses, their rooflines ascending like a staircase. Across the street, a tree-lined path led into the Heath, the great untamed park. The apartment's interior was cozy enough, though hardly up to Oliverian standards—brown floral wallpaper throughout and a windowless bathroom with sensitive plumbing. A minuscule study doubled as a guest room where Mel and I slept, somewhat fitfully. It wasn't just the weather; Mel was four months pregnant with twins. I suggested we cancel our trip, but she strongly insisted on going. "This is my last chance to travel. I don't care if your mother worries."

Jean, an awkward hostess, was more attractive than in my memory of the Christmas photo. She had a full figure, plump elbows, and a vanishing chin beneath a shy, pretty smile. Her hair, still colored a lurid shade of

pomegranate, stood out as her sole point of flamboy-
ance. She worked quietly as an editor for Harvill, a pub-
lisher of literary fiction. Harvill had rejected bringing
out *Exit 33* in a British edition, and I wondered, never
daring to ask, if that decision had been hers.

This was my first trip to London and Melissa's first
since college, but we didn't do much sightseeing. Desire notwithstanding, Mel tired easily. We knew both
tiny beings inside her were boys; only later would we
learn they were identical. I had told Oliver shortly after
we found out, and within days Mel had received a note
from Francizka:

*My Dear, what wonderful news. I knew from the
moment we met that you and I would have so much
in common. Children are the greatest blessings in
life, and as a woman, I must say that I always only
wanted boys. And do not fear about having two at
once. Do you know, my belly was absolutely con-
cave until the fifth month and even at the end of my
confinement I gained no more than twenty pounds!
These pounds melted off just like butter when the
boys began to feed. At the time, all the mothers were
giving their babies horrid formula, but I insisted on
using the little contraptions that nature had given
me. My father, a medical doctor famous throughout Budapest, instilled in me his progressive ideas
about homeopathy and natural medicine. You'll be
surprised to learn that although Mew was always
the larger, it was Ollie who was the more energetic
at the breast. Of course, two can be a handful, and*

I had the added hardship of being abandoned by my
husband when my boys were still little, a devastation
I trust you'll never know. My one recommendation
is that you hire a live-in nanny and cook. The cost
is less than you might think, and it will do much to
preserve your sanity.

With warmest regards,
Francizka

We were content to spend our days in Hampstead. We took long, slow strolls in the Heath, often in the company of Ulysses, Jean's delinquent mutt. Let off his "lead," Ulysses upset toddlers, disrupted picnics, and ran threateningly at strangers, his stumpy legs propelling a muscular body of colorless fur. Once he collapsed onto his side, twitching pathetically and urinating profusely. He'd failed out of obedience school twice; his last instructor confided to Jean, "If it was my mutt, I'd put him down."

But Oliver and Jean doted on Ulysses. Every morning Oliver would grab the dog by the scruff, prize open his mouth with pressure to the hinge of his jaw, insert anti-seizure pills to the back of his throat, and clamp down on his muzzle, forcing him to chew, all the while staring into his eyes with tender insistence.

We all got along nicely. Oliver showed us the local sights: the house of Keats, the graves of Constable and Marx, and the church where Coleridge, addled by opium, had sought salvation. Still, there was something disappointing about our visit. Though perfectly gracious,

Oliver made it clear that he wasn't about to alter his routine with Jean. When I suggested one evening that we play chess, he shook his head, saying it would be rude.

And so I became an observer of their life together. Mornings, Oliver would grind the coffee and set Jean's two slices of oatmeal toast, unbuttered, in a metallic toast rack. She preferred to edit from home, waiting until early afternoon to take the Northern Line to Harvill's Islington office. Morning was also Oliver's time to write. He was completing the manuscript of *Paradoxes of Self*, the book that would gain him renown and notoriety in the constricted world of contemporary philosophy. He also read newspapers compulsively—*The Guardian*, *The Independent*, *Le Monde*, and the *Herald Tribune*— and when so moved, would churn out an op-ed or a letter to the editor denouncing human rights abuses in some hot spot—East Timor, Israel, Serbia, Somalia. I marveled at his speed in composing such pieces and, frankly, envied his success at placing them.

Nights were spent watching the tiny television. Although no athlete herself, Jean passionately followed tennis, and so we dutifully watched each day's hour-long BBC recap of Wimbledon. They also never missed a rerun of *The Benny Hill Show*, thirty minutes of preposterously politically incorrect comedy. After they retired to their bedroom with Ulysses, I'd hear the murmur of quiet conversation from behind their closed door. I couldn't help reflecting that Mel and I no longer talked like that in bed.

Their relationship had its odd aspects, though. At some point it occurred to me that I had never seen them *touch*. Books were handed over, doors held open, plates proffered, but without bodily contact. It was as if all physical interaction passed through the intermediary of Ulysses, whom they both lavished affection on, scritching and stroking, often at the same time.

One night I got up to use the bathroom and noticed their door ajar. Jean was curled on her side, a sheet drawn lazily across her breasts, a plump naked arm furled around her pillow. Free of all bedding, Oliver lay on his back in long-sleeved pajamas, hands solemnly folded across his chest, as if lying in state. Between them slumbered Ulysses.

Two nights later, I made the same observation: Jean seemingly naked under the sheet, Oliver pajamaed atop it, and Ulysses between them, the canine bed divider.

Then there was the Thin Man. Twice a week a brownish Austin Mini would pull up in front of the apartment and an exceptionally tall, skinny man would extricate himself from the car and stride to the front bell in oversized styleless English walking shoes. I later learned that the Thin Man was a well-known journalist with his own radio show, so presumably he had a voice, though I never heard it. The front bell would ring and Jean would leave without word. The two exchanged no greeting. The man would hold the passenger's door open for her, then pretzel himself into the driver's seat; knees pinned around the steering wheel, head craned forward, he'd shudder the car into first gear and putter off.

"Who's that?" I asked.

"Alastair," said Oliver, as if no further explanation were needed.

Three or so hours later, the Mini would grind to a halt in front of the apartment and out would spring Jean, hair still wet from a fresh washing. And the happy domestic routine would continue.

On the first day of cooler weather, Oliver took us to the British Museum to see the Lewis chessmen, the strange figurines whose frantic bulging eyes and thin worried mouths suggested they took no pleasure in the role fate had assigned them in the martial game. Then it was off to the National Gallery, where Oliver made sure we paid homage to the Arnolfini portrait by Van Eyck, his favorite painting of all time. ("Why all this technical wizardry to paint this hideous, cadaverous little Nosferatu? Why, why, *why* such a beautiful, intricate, and loving portrait of someone so fundamentally repulsive?")

After lunch and assured that Melissa wasn't flagging, Oliver took us to Chapman's auction house on New Bond Street. There he showed us a Pascin drawing, no larger than a sheet of loose-leaf paper, of a pair of prostitutes languidly reclining on a divan, their negligees and legs parted. They looked bored and dreamy, as if lost in thoughts of chocolate, coffee, and cigarettes.

"So, what do you think?" Oliver asked. He stood before the drawing, admiringly.

"It's very . . . louche," Melissa observed.

"The reserve is set at twenty-five hundred pounds. Seems a bit high . . ."

"Are you thinking of bidding?" I asked.

He nodded and continued to consider the sketch. "You don't love it," he said.

"It's not exactly my thing. I'm not really all that familiar with Pascin."

"I gave you a book about him for Christmas," he said. "You never looked at it." Before I could respond he added that Pascin had spent most of his life in the company of prostitutes before killing himself.

"You told me that once before."

He asked for the drawing to be taken down and removed from its frame. Wearing white cotton gloves supplied by a Chapman's sales rep, he lifted the hinged matte board and examined the drawing from the back. Eyeglasses pushed up on his brow, he continued his examination, searching for who knows what.

Mel let it be known that she was ravenous. Oliver brought us to a restaurant tucked darkly in the crypt of St. Martin in the Fields. There he said, "I may have forgotten to tell you its provenance." He was back to talking about the Pascin. "In the early seventies it was sold to a London banker by my father."

"Victor Vice?"

"Well, yes, that was his name. My biological father was a trader of fine art. Maybe I've mentioned that already." We knew this from Francizka, but Oliver had never before uttered a word about his father. "He traveled around Europe purchasing works and then selling them to interested clients. On rare occasions, he worked on consignment. His specialty was European modernism."

We pressed him with questions, but he insisted that there was not much to tell. "What can I say? My biological father"—Oliver insisted on this locution—"left my mother when Bart and I were still boys. He was English by birth, and after the divorce moved back to Europe, where he continued to work in the art trade, pretty successfully, it appears. In any case, he severed all connections with us. I think he might have sent me a birthday card for my tenth birthday, but I was under strict orders from my mother not to communicate with him, and to be honest, I didn't want to, not after what he'd done to us. In college I wrote him a rather long involved letter, but never heard back—I assumed that what I wrote upset or irritated him, or that he simply didn't want to hear from me. Around five years ago, my mother received a copy of a death certificate in the mail from his second wife—we had no idea that he'd even remarried. But the remarkable thing was that the death certificate was already several years old. He'd died of a heart attack back in 1984, around the time I'd written to him in college. Which is maybe why I never got a response."

"Why did his wife wait all that time before contacting you?"

"Our address was certainly easy enough to find. My mother thinks it all has to do with his estate. She's convinced that his second wife didn't want to share his money with us."

"Then why contact you at all?"

"That's the more interesting part. Maybe she felt guilty. Maybe it preyed on her. Maybe she had a disturbing dream, who knows?"

"And you've never tried to contact her yourself?"

Oliver offered no response, his characteristic way of saying no.

"What about the will?"

"No will."

"You mean he died intestate or you don't know if he had a will?"

"I mean, I'm not interested. My family has enough money as it is. Too much." Smuggled, as I recalled, in his mother's lingerie.

"Aren't you just the least bit curious to meet his second wife, to find out what happened to him?"

"Why should I be?"

"He *was* your father."

"You know, Max, my artist friend—he was adopted. I've met his adoptive parents a couple of times, and what's extraordinary is how much he looks like a *perfect* genetic cross between them, mother's eyes, father's nose, to a tee. I once asked Max whether he'd ever tried to contact his birth parents and he said no, he had no interest. Not because he was scared to find out that they were insane or had died by lethal injection, but because he had *no interest*. That made perfect sense to me. You probably find it odd. But I find *your* questions odd. And I think the burden of proof is on you to explain why I should be interested in a man who showed no interest in me."

"Then why are you interested in his art?" I asked.

He hesitated, as if weighing an adequate response only to head off in another direction. "I *do* have a very vivid memory of riding in a car next to him. He's wearing a forest green Windbreaker and sunglasses and whistling. Looking out the window of the car I can *clearly* see the entire profile of the Matterhorn majestically framed against a very blue sky. Only my mother says that the memory is impossible—we didn't start going to Switzerland until years later, after my mother remarried, and we never traveled to Zermatt. The BF did, though, take us on a trip to Los Angeles when Bart and I were three, so my mother thinks the memory is from Disneyland. The mountain must be the Matterhorn roller coaster."

"You have that wonderful photo in your apartment of you, your brother, your father, and a cow."

"Oh, the one from Scotland, the Caledonian Forest. My only memory of that was Bart crying his head off right before the picture was taken."

"From what I recall of the picture, it looks like you were the one crying."

"Really? Well, maybe it *was* me. I didn't realize you had studied the picture that closely . . ."

"Well, I was struck that Bart has virtually the same shot in his study at your mother's apartment."

"Does he? I should take a look . . ."

"I love the family name," said Mel. Regal and sinister, it certainly had a richer ring than Dlasnowicz, Dumbrowski, Farbstein, and Weintraub, the names of my shtetl forebears that happily had been cast off for more suitable American accents.

"It's actually not that uncommon in England. There are a number of spellings. *V-i-c-e; V-i-s-e; V-i-z-e.* Next time you come to my place, I'll show you this wonderful set of antique coasters that I have with the family crest, 'The Ancient Arms of Vice.' According to my mother, the BF could trace his family tree all the way back to some prince born in Sussex in 1327. My mother won't talk about the BF, but she loves that kind of thing, the ancestry, the royal blood."

"Do you still have family in England?"

"Not that I know of."

"And where does the second wife live?"

"I don't know. Maybe Portugal. I think that's where the death certificate was mailed from."

"Is that where he's buried?"

"I think so—but I could be wrong. Again, I hate to disappoint you, but I really don't care."

The crypt supplied a suitably gloomy space for talk about Oliver's family. Electric sconces effectively imitated guttering candles. Chords of organ music from the evening concert in the church overhead dully reverberated in the vaulted ceiling. A group of American college students were absorbed in making wax rubbings of the tomb of Thomas Chippendale, whose flat stone grave in the floor had been worn smooth but not completely effaced by generations of pious or indifferent feet. I bent down to retrieve a napkin that had slipped from my lap and noticed to my mild consternation that we were dining atop the earthly remains of Rector Charles Simmons, dec'd 1626. And when we finally quit the crypt, strolling to Charing Cross to catch the Northern Line back to Hampstead, the weather submitted to the pathetic fallacy: it had begun to drizzle, our first London rain.

Melissa awoke the next morning with hives on her elbow and knees. An hour later they'd spread to her belly, thighs, and neck. We inventoried the possible triggers:

the almond-dusted *pain au chocolat* in New Bond Street, the Japanese bean paste snack in Picadilly, the lamb chops in St. Martin's, the noxious belchings of the buses in Trafalgar Square. By midafternoon the hives ribboned Mel's body and covered her face. Her eyes were swollen; welts ballooned on the soles of her feet. She itched everywhere. Jean's personal physician was on holiday, so we scheduled an appointment at a local walk-in clinic. A dingy waiting room greeted us with dire warnings. OBESITY KILLS. CIGARETTES ARE KILLERS. ALCOHOL: IT WILL DESTROY YOU. The room was clogged with persons who appeared not to have taken these warnings to heart. Mel sat on a bench outside while I waited in a room full of hacking, sniffling, rumbling, and otherwise leaking bodies for her assigned number to flash, deli style, on a digital display that hung beside a poster of a healthy blond couple cycling with child through a leafy countryside. VISIT WALES!

A doctor, upper lip hidden by a suspiciously bushy mustache, ushered us into a crepuscular office. He examined Melissa in semidarkness, his features screwed in concentration and puzzlement, the very expression of incompetence, only then to declare with finality the hives to be mosquito bites. He asked us if, during the heat wave, we'd slept before open windows, and took our "yes" as definitive confirmation of his diagnosis. I pointed out that we'd seen and heard no mosquitoes, that I remained curiously free of any "bites," that the hives had spread during the morning hours, but he simply shook his head condescendingly. He recommended a mild antihistamine and cool oatmeal baths.

Appalled by the moron's actionable ignorance, we took a cab straight to the emergency room of the Royal Free Hospital, where a lovely, gap-toothed nurse tittered at the mosquito story and explained that it was not uncommon for pregnant women to suffer a variety of auto-immune reactions, including hives. She recommended a mild antihistamine and cool oatmeal baths.

It turned out that Jean had suffered from eczema as a child, and was familiar with these treatments. She prepared a slurry of oatmeal, buttermilk, olive oil, and Epsom salt in her bathtub. Oliver added a touch of lavender buds.

While Melissa rested in what looked like a trough of warm breakfast cereal, Jean and I took Ulysses on a long walk. The rain had given way to another day of what Oliver called "unconscionable sunshine." In the Heath, Jean and I followed a path lined by towering plane trees to Kenwood House, a neoclassical homestead that serenely surveyed a rolling field that might have served as a backdrop for a Masterpiece Theater adaptation of *Middlemarch*, except for the young Pakistanis playing pickup soccer with a group of Hassidim from Golders Green.

As we strolled, Jean turned to me. "So what kind of philosophy do you do?"

"I'm not a philosopher. I'm a writer."

"Oh, really!"

Having spent nearly two weeks in each other's company, we still knew nothing about each other. I liked her, but as one might come to like any solid familiar object in one's direct environment. Our previous efforts at conversation had not gone far. Once I asked her if she enjoyed working at Harvill, and she answered, "After a manner." She only became a bit more loquacious on the topic of Wimbledon, now entering the quarterfinals, and about Ulysses, specifically his long list of behavioral and neurological woes.

Trying now to sustain conversation, I noted that Ulysses had not been the name of Ulysses' own dog.

"True," she said. "That would be Argos."

Just then a gust of wind swept her pomegranate bangs off her brow, and the sun smiled on her face, turning her eyes the color of agate. She didn't say any more, yet her face lifted toward mine in an expression of welcome and openness. In silence we looked in each other's eyes, unsure how we had stumbled upon this moment of intimacy, and unsure what to do with it.

"Did you . . ."

"Yes," she said.

But I'd started the sentence ahead of any thought or question. ". . . did you know that my mother once played at Forest Hills?"

"Really? How remarkable!"

Just then Ulysses tugged on his lead. He had caught a glimpse of kites on Parliament Hill.

When we got back, the flat showed all the signs of a thorough Oliverian cleaning. The kitchen's gold-speckled Formica countertop and tan vinyl floor gleamed. The cooking grates of the gas range had been freed of stubborn stains. The recycling was neatly stacked. A bifocaled eye had even been completed in Jean's thousand-piece jigsaw puzzle of a Chuck Close self-portrait.

From the second floor came the sound of Oliver's voice. He was reading aloud, just as when we'd first met. Treading the steps softly, I picked up on an odd trail of fragments: *She also felt very sweet towards me . . . little button nipples . . . she would mount my leg, standing up like a kangaroo to clasp me around the thigh and try to work herself against me.*

"That doesn't sound like Beckett," I said, nudging open the partially closed door to the bathroom.

Color rushed to Oliver's cheeks. "No, not Beckett . . ." Without moving from his spot on the floor, he handed me a book called *My Dog Tulip.* "It's Ackerley's paean to his German shepherd. It has the most remarkable descriptions of bitch genitalia."

Mel confirmed this.

I felt grateful that Oliver's patient reading had helped take Melissa's mind off the hives. But I should add that the reading had taken place in the bathroom while Mel soaked in oatmeal. The oatmeal provided a more consistent cover than, say, bubble bath, and a drawn shower curtain separated them. For his part, Oliver sat on the bathroom floor, back against the wall, knees bent, and feet pressed against the foot of the tub. I noted, not with alarm, but in a spirit of cautious observation, that the shower curtain, with its beach motif of seashells and starfish, was far from opaque. Diaphanous would better describe it. The atmosphere in the bathroom was heavy for reasons other than the smell of steamed oats.

"Why don't you take over the reading," Oliver suggested.

"No, no. You go ahead. You do such a great job. I'll make us some lunch."

"Thanks, but I already ate."

"How about you, Mel? What can I get you?"

"Oliver already brought me a bite."

Sure enough, there was a plate with some crumbs by the foot of the tub.

So the question arises: Did I trust Oliver with Melissa? I have my problems, but I'm not a dunce. No doubt Oliver was attracted to Mel. Many men were. And it's true that I had occasion to witness some questionable behavior on his part toward her, a pattern that announced itself as early as the *Beggars Banquet* party, when, as I've mentioned, he raised the knave of spades from her snug jeans. On another occasion, shortly before her period, Mel complained, "My boobs are swollen," which might sound like an odd thing to announce in Oliver's presence, except that Mel always talked openly about such matters. In any case, Oliver took this as an invitation to pull at the neckline of her blouse in order independently to corroborate her claim. Mel (she was wearing a bra) exclaimed something like *Excuse me!*, but I couldn't get angry. The act was so transparently sophomoric, so the product of arrested development, and so patently overt that I had to laugh. Do I regret that in retrospect? The answer is no, emphatically no. It is, of course, tempting to draw a line between these points of misbehavior and what happened later. Mel long ago succumbed to this temptation. But it's always easy to find harbingers after the fact. Put another way, I wasn't wrong to trust Oliver. If he wronged me, it wasn't by betraying that trust.

Two days of oatmeal baths, half-doses of Benadryl, and *My Dog Tulip* largely cured Melissa's hives. A few malingering welts dotted her neck and arms, but the torment was over. It was our last day in London and she insisted that I go to the auction with Oliver; she was content to stay home with Jean and Ulysses.

Oliver and I arrived at Chapman's well before the Pascin was scheduled to be cried. Paddle in hand, dressed in his standard outfit of black jeans and pressed Turnbull & Asser shirt with French cuffs, Oliver blended in nicely with the other posh clients. He steered us to seats in the back, "where you can better follow the action." In a hushed voice, he explained: "The classic mistake of the novice is to get caught in a bidding war. In the heat of the moment, you suddenly find yourself making bids you'd never have been prepared to make before the auction. The first rule is to settle on a maximum bid in advance and not to waver from it, no matter *what*. That way, at the end of the day, you might feel a little regret should you get outbidded, but you're spared the *horrendous* feeling that comes from overbidding."

As the auction proceeded, Oliver detailed his strategy. "The reserve is usually set between sixty and eighty percent of the low estimate, which for this Pascin would put it around twenty-five hundred. Usually, I like to stay as close to the reserve as possible. So maybe I'll go to twenty-seven hundred. It's an erotic drawing, so that usually keeps the price down because it can't easily be displayed. On the other hand, collectors of erotica tend to be pretty devoted, so that could drive the price up. Maybe three thousand two hundred should be my limit. What do you think?"

"That sounds good."

"Of course, there's the matter of the provenance, the connection to my biological father. So maybe I should be prepared to go to thirty-five hundred. On the other hand, the BF handled lots of Pascin, so it's not that unusual to find work that he traded coming up for auction. I'll go to thirty-five hundred."

"That makes sense."

By the time the Pascin was called, the crowd had thinned. A Chapman assistant placed the drawing on a display easel beside the auctioneer, an attractive, immaculately assembled young British woman with an imperious sail-like nose.

"Our next piece is *Deux nus couchés*, by Jules Pascin, born Julius Pincas. It measures fifteen by twenty-two centimeters, charcoal on gray cardstock. Signed bottom left, it also bears Pascin's atelier stamp. Marked verso, Galerie Berthe-Weill. Year, 1929, possibly 1930. Condition, excellent. A splendid example of Pascin's casual École de Paris style. Bidding will commence at two thousand pounds. Two thousand I have. On the phone at twenty-two hundred."

"I usually wait til there's no more bidding in the room before I enter the fray," Oliver whispered.

"At twenty-five hundred here. Any advance? I have three thousand."

"Decent interest—could be a problem."

"Thirty-five hundred I have. Four thousand on the phone. Any advance?"

"Much more interest than I anticipated."

"I have forty-five hundred. Forewarning at forty-five hundred. Five thousand I have."

The bid belonged to Oliver. He shook his head in alarm. "Too high, too high," he muttered.

"On the phone at fifty-five hundred."

"Impossible!" he whispered.

A minute later she hammered the final price. "Sold for seven thousand pounds. Congratulations, sir. Paddle number, please."

Oliver dutifully raised his paddle so the auctioneers could record the number.

His face was blank, coolly without expression, though sweat beaded his upper lip. With a Chapman's clerk he emotionlessly arranged the terms of payment and shipment, but no sooner had we reached the street than he exploded, "Why did you let me *do* that? The buyer's premium is another *twenty* percent. I just spent *eight thousand* pounds. More! That was an act of *total* insanity . . ."

I followed him into a boutique hotel off New Bond Street. He made a beeline to the bar, where he promptly drained a gimlet.

"It was the auctioneer," he lamented. "Did you see her *neck*?"

"I noticed her nose."

"The nose was okay, but the neck was *outstanding*. I've never seen such a neck in my life. Think of the *millions* of pounds overbid each year because of that neck."

A second gimlet put an end to the sweating, but not to his agitation. "So what do you think I should do?"

"I'm sure it's a good investment," I said.

"If you're buying art for investment purposes, you don't buy Pascin. Anyway, I didn't mean the Pascin. I meant about Sophia."

"Sophia?"

"Is there an echo in the room? I think the breakup was a dreadful mistake. What do you think?"

"Have you been in contact with her?"

He didn't answer. As I've mentioned, silence in Oliverese typically meant no. On other occasions, though, it could mean yes.

"How often?"

"Often enough."

"What does that mean?"

"We e-mail. Two, maybe three times a day. No more than that."

"You've got to be kidding."

"Why would I kid you? I'm asking for your *advice*."

"What does Jean have to say about all this?"

"Nothing."

"Does she even know about Sophia?"

"Of course."

I felt a stab of irritation, less toward Oliver than toward what he called the *arrangement*. People will behave as badly as they are permitted to, particularly men in relationships. History and the novel have amply demonstrated this. At least Oliver punished himself for his ambivalence and irresolution. But why would any self-respecting woman put up with such behavior? My anger turned on Jean, for tolerating the reassertion of Sophia, and on Sophia, for having tolerated the immovability of Jean. Where did Oliver find such women?

"What are you getting so worked up about?" he asked. "You know Jean and I don't have a conventional relationship."

"I know nothing about your relationship with Jean. Nothing."

"No?" He appeared to think this over. "You have eyes, don't you?"

As proof I glared at him. He fell silent, as if awaiting my next question. But I refused to play Grand Inquisitor. Finally he allowed, "Our relationship—it's not . . . amorous."

Three years hence, Harkness College would amend the faculty handbook to express formal disapproval of "amorous" relationships between professors and students, language that Oliver would draft as chair of the College Council, only later to fall afoul of. His admission confirmed what I'd suspected, but still packed a minor surprise. He and Jean had often put me in mind of an older couple brought together via a wry ad in the *London Review of Books*, who now shared their twilight years in quietude and companionable friendship. Except that even septuagenarians had sex.

"During my Junior Research Fellowship at Oxford we lived together for three years. We were incredibly happy, and you know how rarely I use that word. And you see how well we get along. I can't imagine *ever* getting along with another woman like that. We were close to becoming engaged. But there was never any *intimate* contact, ever. We read a lot about couples with unorthodox unions—Virginia and Leonard Woolf, Vita Sackville-West and Harold Nicholson. We thought that maybe we could be like them. But it didn't work. When I took the job at Harkness, we broke up."

"What was the problem?"

"I told you, I fell in love with Jean without ever being attracted to her."

I thought back to the moment two days before when the sun had played in Jean's eyes, and her gaze had lifted to mine. As if privy to my thoughts, Oliver said, "It has nothing to do with looks or appearance or matters of beauty. I know she's attractive, just as I know the plant in the corner to be green, because I trust what others tell me. But for me it just doesn't register."

"I don't follow the plant connection. It's a hydrangea, by the way."

"I'm color-blind."

"I didn't know that."

"So I'd never deny that the plant is green, even if I don't see it. It's a bit like that with Jean. Somehow I can only see her as Jean, not as a woman."

"The two aren't mutually exclusive."

"I realize that. It's very hard to explain . . ."

I observed that in the case of the couples he'd given as examples, the Woolfs and the Nicholsons, one or both or all of them had been gay.

"I think I told you the very first time we had lunch, I'm straight. But you insist on expounding this popular, reductionist, *dull* theory that all sexual ambivalence signals some unresolved latent homosexuality. That coming out of the closet is the necessary and sufficient response to all forms of erotic ambiguity. If only things were that . . . simple."

I didn't realize it at the time, but our destination that evening had something to do with proving his point. We left the pub and headed south or maybe west; I remained in awe of the city's power to disorient. The streets appeared designed by a seventeenth-century weaver clumsy with a spool of yarn. Oliver also struggled, pausing by street signs and scrutinizing the facades of buildings.

"I've been once before . . ." His voice trailed off. "Ordinarily I have an excellent sense of a direction."

"Why don't we ask? And where exactly *are* we going?"

We strayed into an odd, run-down part of town. Next to a trashed motorcycle, its stripped carcass irrelevantly chained to a streetlamp, idled a shiny canary yellow Bentley. A rat, black with soot, emerged from a grate, unhurriedly made its way across the street, and disappeared into an alleyway. The narrow twisting streets bore names like Haunch of Venison, Blood Basin, and Foul Mews. We continued our inconclusive search, and then all at once the signage of butchery began magically to repeat. Next, the motorcycle and the Bentley, presumably left behind for good, came back into view, suggesting that either we'd stumbled into a parallel universe or our steps had unwittingly described a circle. The driver-side window of the Bentley silently lowered. An elbow in white starched livery emerged.

"You gents looking for The Leash?"

Oliver nodded.

"Fancied as much. Entrance doesn't exactly sport a big flashy grin, if you catch my meaning. Once drove Ron Jeremy there—he likes a good turn, he does, but left without a tip, the old wanker. The Lords and whatnots don't fancy their cars parked in front, not the best publicity, that's why I'm a couple of blocks off. You gents will want to continue straight and take your second left, then about halfway down the block, you'll come to a black awning . . ."

We followed the chauffeur's directions.

"Who's Ron Jeremy?" I asked.

"An actor. You might not know his work."

"The name sounds familiar. Was he in *Raising Arizona*?"

"I don't think so . . ."

We made our way down uneven steps into a damp subterranean corridor. A hooded bouncer, scowling, steroid-inflated, and seemingly Slavic, measured us out of the corner of an evil walleye, then nodded imperceptibly before slipping on a pair of wraparound shades. A warehouse door groaned along an ancient iron track, opening just enough to admit us into a black cavernous space. Oliver paid the cover with cash. I followed him to the bar. A crudely stenciled sign announced No Alcohol. The bar was crowded with people sipping colorful kiddy concoctions through straws. A chalkboard menu listed the puerile offerings: Egg Creamed. Penis Colada. Screwed Driver.

There was a dance floor absent of dancers. Whether music was playing, I can't remember. A solitary man occupied the center of the floor. He wore a pair of Tretorn sneakers, the kind I'd proudly sported in tennis camp as a twelve-year-old, over gray Argyle socks. Otherwise he was naked. Lanky and pale, the odd tuft of ginger-colored hair sprouting from chest and shoulders, the man reminded me of Jean's Alastair, the mysterious visitor in the Austin Mini. How far the similarities stretched was impossible to say. His penis, the man in the Tretorns, was long and canine pink. Stroked with the mindless persistence of a metronome set to adagio, it stuck out like a half-raised drawbridge.

"I'm going to have a look around," Oliver said, drifting off without waiting for a response.

I found an empty stool at the far end of the bar, ordered a drink, and clamped my lips around the straw of a fruity punch, my features imperfectly arranged into an expression of nonchalance. Oliver had brought me here without consultation, only to abandon me without a thought. This was not Oliverian behavior. I didn't want to stay, but also didn't want to leave, mainly because I had no idea where we were or how to get back to Hampstead. So I sucked at my fruity punch and shunned eye contact, especially whatever was coming my way from across the bar. Furtive glances on my part took in a figure in a black cocktail dress, legs crossed. Dress and legs suggested woman, everything else raised doubts, in particular, the sheer size of it all: the linebacker shoulders, the round paws and square elbows. As for the face, there was none—just a curtain of feathers, hair, and leaves, primitively quilted together into an outsized tribal mask. It sipped its drink through a straw passed through an opening in the mask. Dark pupils through jagged eyeholes continued to pin me in a gorilla stare.

I was just starting to feel a semblance of composure when a terrifying sound, like a gunshot, made me spring from my stool. I turned to the woman next to me, expecting to find her sliding to the floor, blood streaming from mouth and nostrils. She was maybe thirty, my age, and wore a black latex bodysuit. Scoops of flesh bunched by her armpits, pale breasts swelling from a tight bodice. She ran a leather riding crop with the trembling delicacy of a feather over the cheek of an older gentleman in a tuxedo. Suddenly she brought the riding crop down; it cracked across the countertop like a rifle report. Again I sprung. The gentleman in the tuxedo bowed submissively.

"First time?" A guy across the bar flashed a sympathetic smile.

I nodded.

He came around and pulled up a stool.

"Takes a bit of getting used to." He wore a navy pinstripe suit, a purple banker's tie, and modish rectangular glasses. "Madonna—she's a regular, you know."

"I didn't know that."

"Absolutely. Have you seen her book, *Sex*? All the domination shots were taken here. But what with all my travels, I rarely find the time to come down. It's really quite the scene. Christopher."

I accepted his friendly handshake. "I'm . . ."—I hesitated no more than a moment—"Oliver."

"Nice to meet you, Oliver. From the States, are you? Here for a little R and R?"

"Actually, I used to live in London. I'm just back for a few months."

"So you must know the city well, that's splendid. Wouldn't trade London for anywhere else in the world, but you have to have the quids. Of course, it's all you Yanks who are driving up the prices."

"That's true."

"So what brings you back? Hope you don't mind my asking. I've always been a nosy sort. Not exactly a standard trait of my compatriots."

"I'm a professor. I'm on sabbatical."

"And what do you profess?"

"Philosophy."

"Brilliant! I never had a mind for those abstractions—I've always been more a results-oriented chappie. But I've always respected the university types—they come up with the ideas that we blokes put into practice. Whereabouts do you teach?"

For simplicity's sake I said Harvard.

"Ah, I should have guessed. Very impressive, indeed. Boston, now that's a great town, isn't it?"

"It's very nice, but to be honest, I like London more. I love that old-world sensibility."

"Ah, not me. I prefer that American intensity—it fits my personality to a tee. Bonds by day, bondage by night, so to speak."

Our attention was drawn to a stunning young woman in a chartreuse dress, who had taken a seat a few stools down. As she chatted with the bartender, a bald homunculus crawled toward her on the concrete floor, tremblingly undid the clasp of her stiletto-heeled pump, eased her foot from the shoe, and, curled nautiluslike at her feet, set to work sucking on her toes. We could hear his soft moans of satisfaction.

"I'd suck those feet," Christopher observed.

I didn't go off in search of Oliver, but I found him in a group gathered around a bare female ass. Presiding was an elderly man, clad in black leather briefs and matching vest, a wooden paddle in hand. The ass, hoisted into the air by a pulley, bore a cherubic expression: each cheek glowed a healthy red. The cheeks belonged to a pretty woman whose face shone with perspiration, eyes pressed shut in intense private concentration. Sweat matted her hair. Around her neck had been fastened a studded dog collar. The old man tugged fast on the leash, and the slave's eyes, smudged with mascara, opened wide and lifted toward her master. In that moment, the paddle crashed down.

Oliver glanced at me. I signaled my revulsion with a frown, but apparently I'd missed a crucial detail. "Did you see the look in her eyes?" he whispered, as if to help me better understand an obscure piece of art. "Absolute trust. I wonder if I've ever evoked that measure of trust in anyone." Then he disappeared off into another dark chamber.

I lingered before a table that looked like a butcher's block. A woman, lying on her back, knees bent, legs open, dress drawn to up to her hips, was displaying herself to a group of three men, who had drawn up chairs and were sitting scant inches away from her shaven sex. Hands folded behind her neck, the woman had partially lifted her head, as if to start a sit-up, to better watch the men watch her. Watching her watch them watch her, I felt I had passed into the realm of pure allegory. The first man was grinning helplessly, as if the woman's sex were not a flower, or maw, or any other of the clichéd metaphors it had sponsored over the ages, but was a quick-talking mouth that had just jabbered a joke that had gone straight over his head. The second guy sat expressionless and unblinking, as if dazed. The third, channeling Rodin's *Thinker*, studied the sex with the vexed expression one might direct toward a refractory problem that should have been solved long ago.

The woman climbed down from the table and smoothed her dress. The group dispersed. I drifted along, pulled by the force of the small erotic dramas that materialized like dark whirlpools, gained strength, then dissipated, with or without resolution.

I watched a cloud of red hair settle into a neighbor's lap. Arms cradled denimed thighs, while the red curls bobbed as if signaling agreement with some unvoiced proposition. All at once, a bouncer, a miniature porkpie hat Velcroed to an outsized head, tugged the red fleece from the adjacent lap. "Okay, mates, that's enough!"

The woman's mouth, rouged, formed a vacant O, while the exposed member of her neighbor settled on the denims like a fish weakly flopping on a dry dock.

"No pissing with the rules," said the bouncer. "Wank all you want, jerk to your heart's content, but no direct exchange of bodily fluids. Up and out you go."

The redhead lodged a dazed protest, as the bouncer pulled her to her feet. "But, he's my *husband*. Look, our wedding bands. We've been married three years."

"Couldn't give a bloody toss. Rules are rules."

Humbled, the married couple followed him out.

The figure in the Tretorns remained anchored to the center of the empty dance floor. The metronome moved in its relaxed rhythm; the drawbridge drew incrementally higher.

There were no clocks, no windows. For a period I lost track of Oliver altogether. I wondered how many chambers, darkened vaults, and secret sanctuaries were available only for the initiated. How much eluded me.

I understood the logic of the kiddy cocktails. Alcohol would have been redundant. I moved in a parallel reality. It wasn't a state of arousal, exactly—more a cumulative assault on my senses that made everything unexpectedly plausible, even necessary. The initial feeling of menace had worn off, as had the vague thrill that supplanted it; now I traveled in an eerie calm. I yawned impressively but wasn't bored. Nothing long held my interest, but I wanted to see more, see it all, lest I miss something crucial.

I opened doors off a darkened corridor onto scenes of molten wax, diapers, human dressage. Barking issued from one chamber. I tried the door: locked.

Was this what I was searching for? I nudged open another door, and there before me stood the stunning blonde in the chartreuse dress. Commandingly tall in five-inch heels, thick piles of hair scalloped like the Sydney Opera House, hips canted, she stared straight through me with cool blue eyes. It was only when I followed her gaze did I realize that she wasn't alone. In the near corner stood my friend. They appeared locked in a battle of wills, who would blink first. Oliver was a master of blank stares, and this was the blankest I'd seen, a triumph over the distracting work of her hands, which had dipped under her dress. Her lips traced a smirk, as if to say, "Gotcha." A single exposed red bulb lit the space like a darkroom. Given the shadows, I could only account for Oliver's left hand, casually tucked in a pant pocket. Where was the right? I didn't look hard but my heart rapped sympathetically. I thought of Oliver's color blindness. What could he see? Clearly not me. Their expressions didn't waver, though her lips parted ever so slightly. I remained hidden in the black doorway. Her fingers were long, nails done in matching chartreuse polish, but this was pure conjecture. Her hands rummaged under her dress, as if preparing a magic trick. Oliver's right remained unaccounted for. A feeling of exclusion clawed at me. They were oblivious of my vigil. Their stare admitted no one else yet seemed to absorb the entire room, drawing in the reddish light. I could move freely and still remain invisible to them, so pitched was their struggle. I took a single step forward, to put my invisibility to the test. Their expressions didn't immediately change, but two pairs of eyes met mine. Hers were defiant, beckoning. Come, they said. Join in. The more the merrier. Oliver's narrowed and warned. No further, they said. Leave now. *You're not like me.*

It was then that I understood why he'd brought me to The Leash—for the same reason that he'd invited me to his mother's for Christmas, so that I might feel the strong invisible winds he fought against. But in this case, the attractions of watching went only so far. I rebelled against my assigned role, the chronicler, the witness.

That step I took: it wasn't an expression of intention, more an attempt to learn for myself how far I'd go. What happened next remains confused in my mind. Oliver's eyes closed in pain, as if to say, *No!* The woman laughed from across the room. Where the napkin came from I can't say.

A minute later Oliver found me on the street.

The Tube was no longer running. As I raised my arm to hail a cab, our elbows collided. Startled, we glowered at each other.

We rode in silence, each looking out the opposite rear window, our reflections splintered in the beaded rain. As we approached Hampstead, Oliver quietly said the words that, I confess, made me clamp my mouth shut in envy. "She's Swedish, the great-granddaughter of Strindberg."

A day later Mel and I left London for Budapest.

NINE

The M1 metro line, the oldest in continental Europe, runs diagonally under Pest like a bend sinister. Its beautiful unrestored boxy cars have grooved wooden seats, leather hand straps, and hinged windows that open to the subterranean air. Art Deco mosaics announce the stations, time capsules from the fin de siècle: tidy spaces constructed of cast-iron beams painted the color of matte copper. Mel, free of hives and full of energy, studied the map. We got off at the Oktogon, a grassy roundabout where the heavily trafficked Teréz Körút intersected Andrássy út. Our local guidebook, heavy on historical anecdote, noted that the tree-lined boulevard had been named after Count Gyula Andrássy, Hungary's first constitutional premier, known for his "firmness, amiability, and dexterity as a debater." After World War II, the boulevard was renamed Sztálin (Stalin) út, and after the uprising of 1956, Népköztársaság út (People's Republic Avenue), only to be changed back to Andrássy út with the collapse of the Soviet empire.

We had come to the city for a conference, "Minority Voices in American Letters," hosted at the Central European University, whose principal benefactor, George Soros, greeted us—though not in person. In what seemed at the time an astonishing display of futuristic and vaguely dystopic technology, Soros hovered over us on a screen—massive, grainy, and mouthing his belief in the world-transforming power of the literary imagination. To be honest, I was flattered that anyone would pay my way to Budapest, a city I knew from the novels of Antal Szerb, Joseph Roth, Dezsö Kosztolányi, and other modernists whose careers ended in alcohol or crematoria. And I was amused by the fact that I counted as a minority voice.

Oliver declined to join us. He hoped one day to visit Budapest, but not without his mother, who would never forgive him, he said, if he traveled to her hometown without her. And yet his mother claimed to have no desire ever to set foot in Budapest again, so maybe it's no surprise that Oliver never did make it to the city of his forebearers. The closest he came to seeing the city where his mother was raised and his grandparents were killed was through our photos. As we said our goodbyes in Hampstead, he slipped us a neatly folded piece of paper with an address penned in his old-world hand. "Don't make the pilgrimage on my account," he said casually. "But if you happen to find yourself in the neighborhood, perhaps you could take some pictures."

We sensed something was amiss when, emerging from the subway, we found ourselves on a boulevard lined with four- and five-story Belle Époque apartment houses, ornate and fanciful, with filigreed balconies and goat's-head pediments. But more disorienting than the general opulence of the street was the ancestral home itself. We had expected to find a dismal block of Communist concrete, straight out of Central Planning. Mel, our designated photographer, made sure the address appeared clearly in her shots. This to underscore what was immediately apparent to us: that no bombs, Soviet or otherwise, had ever touched, much less leveled, Andrássy út 101–111. For we agreed that no Hungarian Communist, freshly installed in power and grimly determined to erect a Socialist state, would squander the People's money on reconstructing a lavish piece of fin-de-siècle decadence.

We were still admiring, or taking in, the building, when a stately woman, roughly of Francizka's age, approached the marble main entrance accompanied by a wire-haired schnauzer. We hurriedly assailed her with a mix of French and German, but made progress only with our native tongue.

"Do you live here?" Mel asked. "In this building?"

The woman, dressed in a trench coat despite the summery warmth, eyed us suspiciously. "Why? Are you looking for someone? What is the name?"

"A family friend once lived here. Many years ago."

"I see."

"Have you lived here a long time?"

"My entire life."

"In this building?"

"Yes. Directly here."

I bent down to pet the dog, but the little beast recoiled. "Villy," remonstrated the woman. "Show some manners!"

"Did you ever know a Sándor Nagy?" I asked.

"Dr. Nagy?" All at once her eyebrows lifted and her eyes brightened.

"Yes, Dr. Sándor Nagy."

"Yes, of course!" she cried; even the dog appeared to swing his attention toward us. "Everyone knew Dr. Nagy. He was a famous man!"

"Really?"

"Yes, of course. All the most wealthy men and women in Budapest came to his practice. And I must say, he was very handsome. All the girls in our building had infatuations. I must tell"—and she mentioned a Hungarian name—"about our meeting here. Oh, yes, we all very much adored Dr. Nagy. From where are you coming?"

"The States."

"America! I would have thought Britain! And how do come to know of Dr. Nagy?"

"We are very close friends with his grandson."

"Ah, Dr. Nagy has a grandson in America. This I did not know. I thought both of Tamás Nagy's children still live in Budapest."

"No, our friend is the son of his daughter, Francizka."

"Whose daughter do you mean?"

"Dr. Nagy's."

The woman wrinkled her brow. "What name do you say?"

"Francizka Nagy."

"Villy, behave! A daughter, you say?"

"Yes."

"No, that's quite impossible. Dr. Nagy has no daughters. He has just one child, Tamás. He, too, is a doctor."

A moment passed as our doubts, each of the other, took hold.

"Are you certain?"

"Quite positive." The woman frowned. The horrible little dog was again pulling on his leash.

"Dr. Nagy died in the war?"

"In the war? Now I am afraid we have a confusion. Dr. Nagy dies only maybe five years ago . . . Yes, Villy, we get you some food."

"That's odd . . . When you were young did you know a girl in the building named Francizka? She would have been maybe about your age."

"Francizka? . . . No, I cannot remember a girl with that name. But it is possible. I really cannot remember. Now you must excuse me."

We watched the woman turn a large ring key in the lock of a heavy wooden door, and disappear into a marble lobby, trailed by the dog, now straining to stay outside.

How long does it take to develop a theory, spin a story? Seconds seem too long. Waiting for a concert to begin, say, I picture a man plunging from a top box in flames, a toy manufacturer facing indictment for a fatally flawed wind-up gorilla, a moment's fantasy extinguished by the raising of the curtain. At an airport baggage claim I notice a young woman astraddle an outsized suitcase held together by duct tape and understand in a flash that a year of teaching in Nigeria ended with a messy affair with an African poet. Now, lingering before this fin-de-siècle extravagance, I didn't have to coax my imagination. Speculations hardened into probabilities and probabilities into certainties. I suppose I'd already framed a picture of Victor Vice. It hadn't escaped my notice that Jules Pascin formed a near anagram of the artist's birth name, Julius Pincas. Bartholomew had placed his father in hell. Oliver placed him nowhere at all. Oliver's utter lack of curiosity about his BF could be read as a desire *not* to know. In London, I'd begun to ask myself why. Maybe the man who'd abandoned his family had dealt in paintings plundered from Jews. A thousand other theories might have fit the scant facts, but this one took hold of my imagination. In the decades after the war, as a shattered continent struggled to reassemble itself, Vice trafficked in art stolen from the exterminated, untraceable art. And made a fortune doing so.

Now there was Francizka's past to contend with. What were we to make of that? I knew the literature on the unreliability of traumatic memory. And yet these studies show the green car in the accident was really blue— not that Soviet bombs might have been a death camp or a firing squad. Francizka was twelve when her parents died, a young teenager, not an infant. Twelve-year-olds are creatures of precise memory and formidable will. I understood something about the impulse to embroider. In my early teens, I began telling strangers and acquaintances that my father was a prominent brain surgeon and that my grandfather had been Einstein's personal physician. In college, I inflated my SAT scores, my high school athletic achievements, and the size of my family's house. I'll never forget the profound embarrassment I felt when a college friend armed with an almanac was able to demonstrate that my mother had never medaled in the Olympics. I wasn't proud of my embellishments, but in my defense they were never designed to extract personal advantage or conceal an unsavory past. If anything, they were immature rehearsals and misplaced foreshadowings of the novelist's craft.

Francizka wasn't a fiction writer, however. What, then, was the purpose behind her lies? A world of possibilities narrowed in my mind to a simple binary. Her parents must have been either Jews or collaborators. If the former, why blame their death on the Soviets? The Soviets liberated Jews; they didn't kill them, at least not in 1944. But they did execute collaborators, thousands of them. Children of collaborators have more incentive to invent, I reckoned, than survivors of genocide. I shared my conclusion with Mel: "Her parents were traitors. That's why she was so upset by Max's sculpture. It hit a raw nerve. The Hungarians, especially the aristocracy, were the worst Nazi sympathizers."

The details of the theory needed work, as did its implications. I needed to secure the links between the family's sordid past and the present generation's Oedipal entanglements, behavioral oddities, and sexual deviances. But surely connections could be found. It was just a matter of finding the right evidence and drawing the proper inferences.

Time, of course, would prove me wrong. Like many other things in my life that I considered solid—my marriage, for one—my conjectures suffered unforeseen vulnerabilities. But these wouldn't surface for some time, not until Oliver had disappeared into the North Atlantic.

Mel continued to click photos of the apartment house. She was prepared to accept the rudiments of my theory but failed to see the connection between familial crimes and Oliver's erotic peculiarities, perhaps because she wasn't fully apprised of the latter. Out of fidelity to my friend, I hadn't told her about the last night in London. At the very least, I thought I ought now to let her know about the nature of Oliver's involvement with Jean.

When I'd finished describing the sexless relationship, Mel exclaimed, "Look, a kestrel!" She trained our palm-sized Olympus on the wrought iron balcony where the little raptor rested, and pressed the shutter.

"You agree that it's strange?" I asked.

"Of course."

She now turned the camera, a marvel of microtech-nology in the days before digital, in the direction of an old orange-and-tan Ikarus bus and clicked away.

Mel often accused me of avoiding her eyes when I was concealing something, but at some early point in our relationship I learned she was speaking of herself.

"I'm not telling you anything new," I said, then waited for a response. "Am I?"

"No."

"Who told you? Jean?"

"Oliver."

"Oliver told you? When did he do that? When you got the hives?"

"Around then . . . maybe a little before."

"And how did he tell you?"

"What do you mean, 'how'?"

"I mean, how did it come up."

"I don't remember. It just did. We were having a con-versation. I don't remember exactly the how."

Briefly I processed. This meant Oliver had told Mel first and, more provocatively, that Mel had chosen not to pass the story on to me. I asked her about this second point.

Melissa riffled through her handbag and took out a pair of sunglasses. "I'm sorry."

"I wasn't asking for an apology. I just want to know why you didn't tell me."

"I don't know . . . I thought maybe he didn't want me to."

"What made you think that? Did Oliver swear you to secrecy?"

"No."

"So then what made you think that?"

"I don't know . . . I thought you already knew."

I drew a deep breath and squinted up at the kestrel. He must have flown off; in his place sat an attentive squirrel. "Excuse me, love, a moment ago you said you didn't tell me because you didn't want to betray a confidence. Now you say you didn't tell me because you thought I already knew. One needn't be a logician to see that—"

"Spare me the lawyer voice. I can stand everything except your lawyer voice."

This struck me as an unnecessary escalation in hostilities. I was hoping to clear up a misunderstanding, not win a debate. But to my surprise Melissa grew only more defensive when I prodded her to explain her concern about betraying his confidence. She'd already admitted that Oliver hadn't asked her *not* to tell me, who, after all, was his closest friend. But even if he had, what right did she grant him to request that she keep a secret from her own husband? And given that he hadn't, why had she unilaterally decided to place his confidence over our intimacy?

I was astonished by Melissa's inability to answer satisfactorily. I had a basic faith in the power of words to settle tensions between persons who'd exchanged vows of love. My faith wasn't naive; it was tempered by the experience of past relationships. I was well aware of the many uses of words, including as tools of efficient laceration. But this wasn't a particularly difficult or ugly matter. I suggested that she might have been flattered by Oliver's confiding in her, and might have wanted to preserve a sphere of communication separate from me. But Melissa didn't reach out to resolve our argument. This refusal to engage, more than the issue itself, disturbed me. In retrospect, I would date it as the first instance in which words failed to disarm a conflict between us.

At the time, though, I gave her the benefit of the doubt. She had gone through an ordeal with the hives. The pregnancy disturbed her sleep, made her groggy, at times irritable. She needed a snack.

The sun had retreated behind a bank of clouds, but she kept her sunglasses on. "Let's walk to Heroes' Square," she said, taking my arm. "And try not to play lawyer, please."

TEN

At times Melissa accused me of being ashamed of my background, but nothing could be further from the truth. My father may not have been a brain surgeon, but it wasn't for any lack of smarts; when he entered the service at eighteen, he scored a stratospheric 152 on the army's IQ test. As a CPA with an accounting firm in the city, he rode the Long Island Railroad into Penn Station every weekday, then walked the twenty blocks to his midtown office. Without traffic, he could do the fourteen-mile drive from home to work in thirty-five minutes, but that's a bit like saying that without gravity he could fly. When I was fifteen, we moved from a two-family house in Little Neck to a split-level ranch in Great Neck. From the window of my new bedroom I could see, when fall came and the trees had cleared of leaves, the needle of the Empire State Building and the towers of the World Trade Center. In the spring, I rode my bike, a ten-speed Peugeot, to high school. At the time, the idea of adding "public" would have struck me as oddly redundant. It wasn't until my first year at Brown that I learned the names Dalton, Riverdale, Fieldston, and Horace Mann (Oliver's alma mater). Until then I believed private schools accommodated delinquents and those with "special needs." The city aroused my pity. I assumed city life was a diminished version of life in the suburbs—Great Neck without lawns and tennis courts.

My mother came from a family of furriers in Flatbush. When she was fifteen, her hopes of studying graphic design ended with her father's improbable, Isadora Duncan–like strangulation by an industrial dryer, which grabbed him by his tie while he was hurrying to close shop for the Sabbath. My father was raised in a Yiddish-speaking house in the Catskills. My grandfather, a kosher butcher, was tiny—a full foot shorter than his son. In my memory he wears a yarmulke like a pharaonic crown, an apron stuccoed with dried blood, and a shy smile that he directs at me in lieu of heavily accented and grammatically mangled words. He nods, and silently I follow him into the back of the shop, where stained and matted sawdust covers a stone floor. I watch him select a chicken from a coop, heft it, and pass something across its neck, like a magician casting a spell with a miniature wand. In the next moment a geyser of blood sprays from the carotid of the thrashing animal. The bird's head hangs grotesquely by a thread as the spray slows to a nauseating pulsing spurt. My grandfather smiles at me tenderly, but then shakes his head when I double over and retch. I refuse to *touch* chicken for over a year, and to this day can still find myself suddenly paralyzed at the prospect of ingesting *dead meat*. (I never told this story to Oliver, and only now as I write am I struck by the strange inverted symmetries between his dream of becoming a butcher and my traumatic exposure to my grandfather's trade, between the confessions of the reluctant vegetarian and the silences of the disgusted carnivore.)

Mel grew up twelve hundred miles to the west, but the story was much the same. Her father sold futures and her mother carpooled. Her great-grandparents, clothing merchants from Landau, Germany, produced a favorable balance sheet and a would-be violinist who died in an asylum. One willowy branch of the family tree claimed an early disciple of Freud's killed off in Auschwitz. Her mother's father had practiced law in Fort Wayne, Indiana, and served as the first commissioner of the city's children's zoo. Having survived a serious heart attack in his early forties, he devoted his practice to pro bono work, patiently filing unsuccessful appellate briefs on behalf of the state's death row inmates. Active in local Democratic politics and a vocal supporter of the ACLU, he was known as a mensch and a Commie, a man who spent his free time arguing with Nixon supporters at luncheon counters. A second heart attack killed him at sixty-three.

Aaron, our firstborn, was named in Red Abe's memory. Matthew, born minutes after his identical-twin brother on a bright morning in the last week of September, took his first initial in memory of Meyer, the kosher butcher.

In a triumph of recessive genes, the twins arrived with locks of golden hair and eyes of sea-foam blue. In a pattern that was to repeat over the years, Matthew beat out his brother in the search after Melissa's breast, clamping himself on her nipple in anticipation of her milk letting down, while Aaron lay on her tummy, arms flailing. The doctors had scheduled Mel for a C-section, but she would have none of it. Holding her hand, I whispered, "There's no right way to do this. Just the way that keeps everybody healthy. Don't be a mule." She answered with a stubborn squeeze of my hand. The doctors predicted a long, difficult labor. Five hours after we arrived at the hospital, the two six-pounders were healthily squalling.

We were resting the next morning when a quiet knock sounded on the door to Mel's hospital room. Oliver entered with tentative steps, bearing a bouquet of asters, the September birth flower. Trailing him into the room, and carrying a pair of Mylar balloons of the Cookie Monster, was Sophia.

"Surprise!" she cried. "I bet you didn't expect to see me!"

The newborns were asleep. I was holding Aaron, and Melissa, Matthew. Or maybe vice versa. The wrist tag was turned away from me, or maybe concealed in the swaddling. I was euphoric with exhaustion, Mel merely exhausted.

"Oh, my God," Sophia exclaimed. "They're absolute little angels. Let's be honest, some babies are total duds. But these two . . . Oh, my goodness, I could eat them up!"

She directed a moist gaze in Oliver's direction.

"How are you ever going to tell them apart?" he asked.

Sophia thrust her arms in my direction, demanding the infant.

"Could you wash your hands first?" Mel said.

Sophia squeezed antibacterial foam from a dispenser, then scooped up Aaron. "My goodness! You're as light as a kitten!" She cradled him gently and played with his nose. Sophia was tanned and extremely thin; the veins on her arms stood out like those of a distance runner. Her jeans were baggy around her previously voluptuous butt and cinched tightly around her waist. Her hair was pulled back in a tight ponytail.

"What happened to San Francisco?" I asked.

"San Francisco was dull," she said in synecdoche. "Very sweet but very dull. And *this* guy wouldn't leave me alone."

Oliver smiled bashfully. But then he frowned and made some vague gesture in Sophia's direction; immediately she corrected her posture.

Balancing Matthew on her lap, Mel held out her hands for Aaron, who'd started to make piteous sounds. Oliver had brought along his camera, and was moving around the room taking photos. Sophia surrendered the baby with a sigh. Mel held the pair like footballs in a first effort at simultaneous nursing.

"Would you please get your lens away from my boobs?" she said sharply to Oliver.

"I brought presents!" Sophia declared, handing me a brown shopping bag. I pulled out two quilted baby blankets patterned with the birds of New England. The first had nuthatches, bluebirds, and goldfinches; the second, cardinals, barn swallows, and cedar waxwings.

"Sophia made them," Oliver said.

"They're absolutely beautiful." I held them up for Melissa.

"Wow." She said, without looking up. She was still struggling to get the hang of nursing two at once.

I was moved by the generosity and artistry of Sophia's gift, but the moment was not altogether right. Having at times felt like a voyeur in Oliver's world, I now felt that he'd intruded upon our newly created happiness. But more than that—how else can I put it?—I perceived an inchoate threat. Though not superstitious, I respected ritual: I secretly tapped the wood that rimmed the feeding table, seeking to ward off some unspecified unpleasantness my friends might inadvertently deposit. They didn't stay long that morning. I ardently wished that Sophia might someday know our good fortune, but something about the mirthless way Oliver held the door open for her, the smile already wilting from his face, as she turned back to blow us and the newborns kisses, told me that it would never be. I was relieved to see them go.

Melissa felt the same way. No sooner had the door shut than she said, "Smell those blankets. Sophia absolutely reeked of cigarettes. I could have screamed. Those quilts aren't touching my babies if they stink of smoke."

"I'll wash them."

She gazed down at our babies and stroked their blond fuzz. "I give birth, and he tries to steal the attention by bringing Sophia here. The bastard."

In those first weeks, as we adapted to our new life, Oliver was the Dear Friend. He shopped for our groceries, cooked us vegetarian meals, and helped clean our house.

While Mattaron (as he called them) slept, swaddled mummylike and kept warm by the freshly washed bird quilts, he would sit in a rocker reading Frege. When they awakened, he'd display and then conceal a ball, apparently in the hope of teaching them something about the continuity of material objects in space and time. He bought them a chess set of soft foamy pieces, evidently designed for the very precocious. True, he was less adept when it came to holding our babies; no sooner did a twin find himself in his stiff nervous arms than a wail of protest would erupt and persist until rescue came from mother or father, to the obvious relief of both baby and holder. But Oliver was the closest our boys ever came to having a godfather. After his disappearance I remember a colleague foolishly saying, "Thank God he never had children." If Oliver had no children to absorb his tragedy, he also had none to prevent it. Certainly a son might have struggled with a father ignorant of the rudiments of baseball and football. On the other hand, I'm convinced Oliver would have asked for no clarification when it came to the meaning of loving a child. He dreamed of one day being a father without the ambivalence that taxed his dream of being a husband. I knew plenty of people who didn't doubt Oliver's suffering, just its significance and warrant; who cast a sidelong glance at his life, envying his freedom to travel, to pamper himself with fine clothes, and to trade up periodically for a younger, more attractive girlfriend. Yet his profoundest ambition was to partake in the humdrum of domesticity. His tragedy, as I've always insisted, was that he wasn't fit for the life he wanted nor able to want the life that fit him.

Sophia moved back to New York and her job at BAM. Oliver spent his weekends with her and his bedridden stepfather, who no longer recognized his own family and who quietly died one afternoon hours after Oliver had left his side to teach a class at Harkness.

"Jacob Epstein, 77, Lit the Stars," ran the headline of the *Times'* brief obit.

Oliver took the news hard. Pick's disease had ravaged the stepfather's brain and erased his identity, had left him incontinent and inert; still, the intrusion of death came as a shock. I hadn't expected to attend the funeral, but Oliver asked me to drive him to New York, and once there, to come to the service. It was the first of three funerals that I was to attend in the family.

Oliver sat in the back seat during the drive down. He'd often mentioned (and Jean later confirmed) his peculiar immunity to insomnia. Even the most severe anxiety or depression failed to ruffle his sleep; rarely did a full *minute* pass from the moment his head touched a pillow until he was *virtually comatose*. The night after his stepfather's death, though, was different. While I drove, he described the night in great detail, obviously fascinated. He said that from midnight until dawn he lay perfectly still on his back, his hands folded behind his head, free of all thoughts and memories. He spent the entire time staring at the ceiling, because, he said, *his eyes refused to close*. He said he felt as if he could have been anybody at all, or more precisely, no one in particular. He surmised that this was how his stepfather had felt at the end of his life, free from any sense of self. The thought comforted him, for the feeling of being unmoored, bereft of memory, thought, and identity, brought no terror; on the contrary, it offered a kind of oceanic calm, a vacant obliterating peace, like napping at the bottom of a deep, warm, still lake.

In the rearview mirror, I could see him intently watching the landscape pass by. It was an autumnal day, gray and chilly. The trees stood bare, and gusts of wind rustled colorless leaves in pointless circles.

At one point, Oliver said, "Have you ever worn the Arpège Pour Homme that I got you last Christmas?"

"No, not yet."

"You really should. I think you'd like it."

I felt very tender toward him, but the terms of our friendship didn't permit saying so. Oliver was not a creature of hugs (I was driving in any case) and emotional demonstrations. I understood, though, that he was grateful for my company; he was glad to have me near.

Later he said, "You're the luckiest man on the planet. I hope you know that."

The funeral took place at a cemetery in Queens in the vibrating shadows of a cloverleaf of the Long Island Expressway. Francizka, in a black hat with a rhinestone broach, raised her veil of flowing black silk ribbons to greet me with three kisses, the Hungarian way. She accepted my condolences matter-of-factly. "I had hoped to see you in happier circumstances. Ollie tells me the twins are precious creatures. I look forward to making their acquaintance. In the meantime, send your charming wife all my love. Jacob was a good man. He had his faults, but don't we all . . ."

Sophia, taut and beautiful in a short mourning dress, pulled me aside. "Mom refuses to acknowledge my existence. I'll never live down those fucking vultures."

Later, though, I saw Francizka hand Sophia a cigarette and cup her hand to extend a light; together they smoked in silence, their veils pinned back.

Dozens of floral displays flanked the casket. The flowers had poured in from the groups and solo artists Epstein had worked with: Aerosmith, Led Zeppelin, Phil Collins, REM, Stevie Wonder, and the Stones.

Epstein's first wife had predeceased him, but his two sons from his first marriage had come to bury their estranged father. Oliver had spoken of his stepbrothers on occasion without mentioning that they were both Lubavitchers. One was tall and dark, the other fair and short, but both wore heavy beards, sidelocks, long black kaftans, knee breeches, and incongruously jaunty felt fedoras. The taller one, I learned, worked in the diamond district in midtown; the shorter had recently been named chief rabbi of Vladivostok. The Hasidic duo had lobbied hard for a plain pine casket in accordance with Jewish law. (*For you are dust, and unto dust you shall return*, Genesis 3:19.) Bartholomew had held out for something more "comfortable." An unlined redwood casket was the compromise. On the foot panel was carved a simple Star of David.

Bartholomew looked much the same as at Christmas except for one dreadful change. The unruly walruslike whiskers that had concealed his upper lip and framed his jowls had been trimmed back to a tidy patch of short brown hairs that covered his philtrum, and no more. I'd never seen such a mustache worn by a living man, and this was an unhappy first. I wondered what inner brutalization or fanatical twist of mind had brought Bartholomew to groom his facial hair so catastrophically. He looked dreadfully pale and large. If he rarely ventured from his mother's apartment, it was probably just as well; it was hard to imagine him appearing on the streets of Manhattan without risking physical attack. Fortunately the funeral passed without incident. To their credit, the Hasidim treated the offending bristles as a simple declaration of lunacy and not as the functional equivalent of a stiff-armed salute.

Still, it was a tense service. As the rabbi rent a white dress shirt in ritual mourning, the four brothers stood in an uneven row, separated only by an aisle: on the one side, Oliver, the dispositional agnostic, dwarfed by his enormous, crucifix-fondling twin; and on the other, the two Lubavitchers, davening and robotically shuffling their feet while furiously mumbling the Kaddish. Behind the men were the women: Sophia and Francizka in elegant black, and the Hasidic wives in formless skirts and long loose blouses, unpatterned scarves tied around their heads. Every now and again Francizka would cast her eyes in the direction of the women and their throng of children, a baker's dozen clustered between the ages of two and ten, and her nose would twitch, as if to an olfactory disturbance.

Oliver rose to eulogize his stepfather. He hadn't mentioned a eulogy during the drive down, but he spoke movingly and without notes about the man who'd been far more a father to him than the BF. He described how Epstein loved stand-up comedy, particularly the routines of Buddy Hackett. "Pappy's favorite joke was one of Hackett's classics. A man goes up to his rabbi and says, 'Rabbi, I'm just crazy about golf, I live for golf, so I have to ask you, is there golf in heaven?' The rabbi looks at the man and says, 'I have to be honest, I don't know, but I'll ask God and get back to you next Saturday after services.' So next week after services, the man goes up to the rabbi and says, '*Nu?* What did God say?' And the rabbi says, 'I have some good news and some bad news. The good news is yes, there *is* golf in heaven. The bad news is that you tee off on Monday at ten.'"

Oliver doing shtick, and more astonishing still, he was something of a natural. The mourners erupted in laughter; Francizka smiled and nodded to herself as if to say, "I remember."

"At nights Pappy would pat the couch, indicating that I should sit close beside him while he worked the *Times* crossword puzzle, which he would race through, except on Fridays and Saturdays, when the puzzles were more difficult. But he'd always pretend to be stumped by *precisely* those clues that he knew I'd be able to answer. He'd bite the end of his gold Cross pen and say, 'Seven letters, Lost to Fischer,' and I'd exclaim, 'Spassky!'

"He taught me chess when I was eight, but warned me against playing *too* much, saying it could pose a health hazard. 'Those champions,' he'd say. 'Unbalanced, the whole bunch.' But he never stopped loving the game, particularly speed chess. For years, I'd get five minutes against his two. I remember how triumphant I felt when

I achieved time parity and how proud *he* was when he confessed that now I'd have to find superior competition.

"For my seventeenth birthday, he surprised me with a nineteenth-century ivory set from India. The carvings were fantastically intricate—the knights wore turbans and rode saddled elephants—but the ivory clashed with my newly adopted vegetarianism, and I rejected the present. It was a terrible display of adolescent self-righteousness, but Pappy took the present back without resentment. He respected the strength of my beliefs, though now I wish he hadn't. It was the loveliest chess set I've ever seen."

Oliver said that in college, when he rebelled against his mother's desire that he become a doctor like her late father, it was Epstein who wrote him a short letter on Lime Light stationery urging him to pursue his passion. From the breast pocket of his suit, Oliver produced the letter and lifted his glasses to read: *Remember when your mother and I took you and Bart to the production of* Hamlet *with Alan Bates, and we all laughed at Polonius? Polonius may have been a windbag and a buffoon, but he was a good father to Laertes when he said,* To thine own self be true. *Mind those words, Ollie. I'm not sure I know words that are simpler, truer, and yet harder to follow.*

Murmurs of agreement spread through the gathered.

Finally, Oliver described how, at the very end, his stepfather's eyes would follow light with fascination. "When the disease had taken away everything else, Pappy never lost his wonder at the marvel of illumination."

It was a lovely eulogy, the kind that I now wish I had delivered for Oliver, had I only been able to do so. Yet neither Epstein son thanked Oliver for his words. And the taller Lubavitcher retreated a step when Francizka offered him her hand.

"My God," she whispered to me, "they recoil from my touch!"

"I think it's because you're a woman."

"Surely at my age I'm not too great a threat. Do you think they would behave that way to a Jewish woman?"

"That's just it. I think they would. They only touch their wives."

"Those poor creatures—womb machines!"

A man in a gray suit and a *kippah* with the Yankees' logo embraced Francizka and bestowed clapping hugs on Bartholomew and Oliver. "We lost a good one, there," he said. "They don't make them like that anymore. Ollie, you said it beautifully. You did yourself and Jake proud. Bart, I think you should invest in a razor, I say this as a friend. People will take that mustache the wrong way. Though tell me, what's the right way to take it?"

Bartholomew grunted indistinctly.

"In any case." The man dusted dandruff from the shoulders of his suit jacket. "I need to talk to you boys for a minute, if you don't mind."

"What's this about?" Oliver asked.

"Not here. Come, let's walk."

"I really don't think this is the time," Oliver said.

"Your call," said the man with the Yankees kippah. "But I think your pappy would have wanted this talk to take place right here and now. Come. Let's find a quiet spot. Look at that tree right there, what a beauty. What is it, Ollie, an ash?"

Oliver offered no response.

"Looks like an ash to me, a majestic tree. You're going to have to lose that mustache, Bart, but that's another day's conversation. Come. Let's walk."

He curled his arm around Oliver's shoulder, and, reaching up to touch Bartholomew, led them some steps away from the fresh earth where their stepfather now lay. Oliver was to spend the night at his mother's, and I had to head back to Melissa and our babies, so that's where I left them all—Francizka and Sophia smoking in silence, the Hasidim preparing a wintry picnic, and Oliver and Bartholomew, arms folded, standing by the leafless horse chestnut, talking in low voices with the pale stranger.

We sat in Panda Garden in the Dead Mall. Here Oliver had first turned to me for romantic help. Now he solicited legal advice. The former was never followed; the latter should never have been sought. I reminded him that I had worked for a firm for only a single summer, which I spent jetting around the country filing motions to delay.

"Did you take Trusts and Estates?"

"This was Yale—we read Hegel, his critique of Roman inheritance law."

That was good enough for Oliver, and I agreed to accompany him to a meeting with Epstein's lawyer. I didn't take much convincing: I wanted to meet the shadowy figure at the funeral, the wiry man in the Yankees kippah. In part, this had to do with a second unexpected

discovery I'd made in Budapest, though as a matter of
strict chronology this discovery preceded our trip to
Andrássy út. During the Soros conference, I'd given a
reading from my work in progress, a novel set in much
the same milieu as *Exit 33*. The reading was hosted in
a lovely auditorium recently restored to its full Jugendstil splendor. From the four corners of the high ceiling,
bare-breasted spirits of the humanities gazed down on
me. The audience was not small. I began enthusiasti-
cally, but then almost broke off halfway through. My
work sounded false, tinny and false. The characters were
based on close friends of my parents', a couple whose
marriage came undone amid accusations that the husband had committed incest with his daughter. Reading
aloud, I could *hear* that my protagonists were no more
than a heap of tics and idiosyncrasies slapped together
without any real understanding or sympathetic insight
into their lives and struggles. Everything was contrived;
I had simply succeeded in rewriting my first novel without its excitement, its sense of fresh exploration. Barely
past thirty, I was already repeating myself. All at once I
was reminded of Disturbed, my wayward student, and
of his rebuke from a year before: *Your imagination is
trapped in a world of banality and cliché.* In his mania,
he'd noticed some essential lack in my capacities as an
artist. And I had failed him. I had punished him for his
insight. After the audience thinned, I pulled Mel aside.

"It sucks," I said. "I fucking hate it."

"Don't be ridiculous. There's some wonderful stuff
there. It just needs work."

"You sure?"

"I'm positive. I loved that scene at the golf course. You just need to smooth things out."

"I fucking hate golf," I muttered. "I'm sick of it. I'm going to cut my losses, dump the whole thing."

"Now you're talking crazy." She patted my cheek with the outside of her hand. "You're just upset. Tomorrow you'll see it all differently."

The next day I dragged the file to the trash and emptied it.

Mel was appalled. "What on earth did you do that for? There was so much work, so much strong material and lovely writing. Now what are you going to do?"

It was only after returning from Budapest that I began training my literary attentions more seriously on the Vices, but I didn't turn to Oliver *because* I needed fresh material. Put somewhat differently, if I'd come to think of Oliver's as a family whose story *had* to be told, it wasn't simply because the Vices were exotic and old-world and as far removed as possible from the reform synagogues and suburban afflictions of Great Neck. Just as Oliver's struggles struck me as exemplary, his family—their passions and contradictions, their fabulous art and obscure history, their betrayals and suspected complicity in historic crimes—assumed in my mind an emblematic character, symbols of a larger ramifying *something* that I hadn't yet identified but would, given the proper tenacity and imagination.

Writing about intimates is not without risks—I understood that. I've mentioned that *Exit 33* was based on the family of a close childhood friend. As soon as the book came out, I sent my friend a copy, tenderly inscribed, fully expecting him to be touched. Some weeks later, I got a letter from him. In it, he declared that our friendship was *dead* and that *I had killed it*. He didn't accuse me of having revealed painful family secrets; he recognized that I'd labored to protect the family's privacy, carefully altering details that might have produced embarrassment. Instead, my friend accused me of *plagiarizing his life story*. My friend was not a writer; he was a molecular biologist without literary ambitions, at least none that I knew of. But he declared my novel an act of theft. There was but one person who had the right to the story, he insisted, and that was he. I had *pilfered his existential narrative*. In a passionate response, I angrily accused him of failing to understand the nature of creative work. From a heap of raw data—stuff he'd told me and that I'd witnessed myself—*I* had shaped and distilled a story with structure and form. If he thought writing consisted of simply transcribing the undigested mess of lived experience, I suggested that *he* give it a turn. I never heard back from him. In retrospect, I regret my self-righteousness and indignation. Over the years, I've come better to understand that writing about someone dear is never an innocent gesture, is always part homage, part predation.

To my mind, then, the more interesting question was not why I agreed to play legal adviser to Oliver, but why he asked me. He must have known that I could offer little in the way of expert advice. Maybe he understood that I, perhaps uniquely, appreciated his greatness. I don't mean he intended me to play Boswell to his Johnson. Or that he was already feeding me with the story line of his own posthumous narrative. But as I've said, I believe he wanted me to feel the force of the Wittgensteinian winds he bent against. At the very least, he was well aware that I was a writer and always carried a notebook. So we returned to New York. This time Oliver drove.

We met in the lawyer's cluttered East Side apartment. In my blue chevron suit and Hermès tie (Bartholomew's Christmas present), I felt less like a lawyer and more like an actor in costume. Still, having taken on the part, I wanted a proper stage: a sound-sealed conference room with carefully spaced Aeron chairs and remote-control window shades, freshly sharpened pencils, legal pads, bottles of Evian, and thermoses of coffee neatly flanking hefty legal binders. Instead, we gathered at a cramped dining room table surrounded by accordion files and overgrown spider plants. The lawyer squeezed my hand. "Emmanuel Morgen." Jeans and a University of Michigan sweatshirt hung from a wiry frame. Thick silver hair, gaunt cheeks, and ferret eyes suggested a fitness freak. He eyed my suit dismissively, and snorted at the mention of Yale Law.

"Doesn't Yale always lead the country in the percentage of graduates who fail the bar?"

"That was just one year," I corrected. "But not me. I never took it."

Worst suspicions confirmed, he turned to Oliver. "As you know, your brother has regrettably chosen not to attend this meeting. He says he'll accept whatever decisions you make. I'm worried about that boy, but that's a different discussion. Karen!" A woman, barelegged and in a simple housedress, black hair lazily pinned up, materialized at this bellowing. "Could you please bring these two gentlemen something to drink and sandwiches. How does tuna sound? Ollie, you eat tuna? Karen can fix you some rabbit food, if you'd prefer."

"I eat fish, on occasion. Tuna's fine."

Without asking me, he said, "Okay, make it a couple of tuna sandwiches on rye. Any objections to lettuce and tomato? And Cokes all around."

The woman disappeared into the kitchen. As an afterthought, the man cried, "And how about a plate of those gurkens . . . *Karen!*"

"I'm not deaf! The gurkens!"

"So let's begin with the bad news. Lime Light is worthless. Jacob Epstein was a genius when it came to design and electronics, but lost the fight when the world went digital. We'll put the company on the block, but my guess is there'll be no takers. Six months from now, it'll be history. It had a nice run, but I'm afraid the fat lady has sung and the curtain is about to fall."

Oliver accepted the collision of clichés stoically. "Will it have to declare Chapter 13?"

"You mean Chapter 11, dear boy, and you don't 'declare.' But we will file Chapter 11. Not to reorganize, mind you. To liquidate."

"Pappy worked his whole life building up that company."

"Nothing we can do now. Take some souvenirs. Stationery. Phones. His office door. I'm serious. It'll all go to the creditors."

"And the employees?"

"They've seen the writing on the wall. Most have already found other positions. The rest will land on their feet, don't you worry." He, at the very least, appeared not to. "Now we come to the interesting stuff. Jake's will was filed in New York County Court and unsealed this Tuesday last. By its terms, you and Bart are the sole beneficiaries of Jacob Epstein's estate. Ezra and Reuben Epstein are to receive a handful of personal effects, but Jacob's assets, which include property holdings here and abroad, his apartment, his investment portfolio, and two cash accounts, are assigned exclusively to you and Bart."

Karen carried in a tray of sandwiches cut in quarters, chips, pickles, and sodas. "Thanks, dear. You're golden." She might have been twenty years Morgen's junior. Watching her indolent, bored, sexy movements, I wondered if she was girlfriend or maid or possibly both.

Morgen thrust the food and snacks at us, while he made do with Coke, straight from the can. "I value your stepfather's estate at eighteen million dollars, give or take a couple of mill. Market's up today, so let's say somewhere just south of twenty." He slurped demonstratively to let this information sink in. "Unfortunately, the will"—he took another long slurp, clearly relishing the drama—"is worth about as much as an empty can of Coke. That's to say, *bubkes*."

Oliver did not blink. He patiently awaited Morgen's explanation.

"You see, Ollie,"—he spoke as if I were absent from the room, never so much as glancing in my direction—"this will is of *recent* vintage. I wasn't involved in its drafting. It's dated last spring. You were in London at the time, if memory serves."

"That's right." Had the cold sore already been on Oliver's upper lip, or had it spontaneously flamed up?

"I'm afraid Jake didn't come to this new will on his own initiative. As you and I well know, your pappy was already very ill last spring. Horrible disease, this Pick's, truly awful. Jake fought it gamely. Anyway, while you're in London, your mother decides it's high time to patch her relations with her ex-husband."

Oliver replaced a wedge of tuna sandwich on his plate without taking a bite. He removed his glasses and wiped an eye with the back of his hand. Without glasses he always looked strangely vulnerable, an important line of defense removed.

"Last April, over the course of a single week, she visits him, I don't know, maybe half a dozen times. This I learn straight from the nurse who was living in Jake's apartment. Spring began the round-the-clock medical attention."

"It started even before."

"Could be, certainly possible. Any case, after a few visits from Francizka, Jake signs a new will. It was done in the presence of a lawyer—I don't know where Francizka finds this guy, but I don't need to tell you, this city has lots of sewers. I don't even want to think what he charges her. Non compos mentis—you still up on your Latin?"

"I'm familiar with the term, Manny."

"Well, Jake was a textbook example when he signs this new will. I'll spare you the sight of his signature— it's an embarrassment to all involved. How your mother thought she'd get away with this is anybody's guess. But Ezra and Reuben will challenge the will, and there's no way it stands up. No chance, nada. Zilch."

An exquisitely black cat with toxic green eyes sauntered into the room, its tail twisting like a periscope. "Pussy want some tuna?" exclaimed Morgen, leaping from his seat. Without asking, he took Oliver's unfinished sandwich and placed it on the worn Persian rug. The cat purred ferociously.

"Where does that leave us?" asked Oliver.

"Hear me out," said Morgen. "And don't worry—it gets worse. Jake was a mensch, but even mensches do things they regret, stupid things. After he and your mother divorced, which must have been, what, ten years ago—?"

"Exactly."

"After the divorce, Jake was bitter. Your mother accused him of philandering—silly, if you ask me. Jake was no philanderer. He adored your mother, at least until she divorced him. Anyway, Jake gets stuck on another theory—maybe you've heard it. His health was already starting to go, though this was before the Pick's disease, and he believes, rightly or wrongly, I'm not here to judge, that your mother doesn't relish the prospect of playing nurse. He also has doubts about *her*—with all due respect, we all know that your mother likes to turn heads, and I'm just reporting what he thought. In any case, the divorce settlement gave her, what, I arranged the whole thing, three mill, which she blew on that apartment, a mistake in my mind."

Oliver waved away a fly. He went to extremes to spare all forms of life. I once saw him carry a carpenter ant out of his loft and place it on a sidewalk. It was winter, and the ant must have frozen to death.

"Jake thought the settlement was more than Francizka deserved. He was angry. Angry is not the time to make wills. Angry is the *worst* time to make wills. I told him this. I tell all my clients, 'Sleep on it.' That's the soundest advice I know. But your pappy could be stubborn. Ten years ago he makes a new will, which cuts you and Bart out entirely. By the terms of the will of a decade ago, Reuben and Ezra get everything. And by everything, I mean the whole kit and caboodle."

Morgen rose from the table, hustled into the kitchen, and returned with a fresh Coke, talking all the while. Supple Italian loafers incongruously pampered his small feet.

"It's a mess, an ugly stupid mess. I know how much Jake adored you and that brother of yours. I mean that. He was gaga over you two. I remember when you got that Oxford fellowship; he kvelled, for real. His relations with Reuben and Ezra were never good. You think he approved of what they became? He was embarrassed, disappointed. He'd say, 'My sons have turned into *shvartzes*.' You know from *shvartze*? He said this because of their black coats and hats. For years he wanted to legally adopt you and Bart, but it was your mother who said no. She thought, why is anybody's guess, that if Victor Vice found out that Jake had adopted you, he would cut her off from the Swiss money. But why bother telling you this?—you've heard it all before."

"What Swiss money?" I asked.

Morgen flashed Oliver a look as if to say, Who's the bozo?

"When my biological father abandoned us," Oliver explained, "he set up an account for my mother in Switzerland."

"Why Switzerland?"

"Why Switzerland," repeated the lawyer, as if relishing the stupidity of my question.

"I think for tax purposes," said Oliver, quietly.

The fact that the Swiss money came from the art plunderer and not the Hungarian collaborators struck me as an insignificant challenge to my theory about the family. It still fit with the larger picture.

"And while we're on the topic," said Morgen, "there's bad news on that front, too. Your mother insisted on treating the Swiss account as an annuity. Years ago I told her, 'Withdraw half and invest in the Swiss and German markets, they'll grow like gangbusters'—but did she listen? She treated the account like petty cash. In the early years, it must have seemed like a bottomless pool. Unfortunately you keep drawing down an account over three decades and after a time the pool gets pretty shallow. It's been years since I've advised Francizka, but I've seen the numbers—let's just say that there can't be much more than a hundred, two hundred thou max, left in that account. It's about to run dry."

"I see."

"It sickens me, really, to think of Reuben and Ezra getting Jake's entire estate. He never meant to disinherit you and Bart, I know that as a fact. He did it in a moment of anger over the divorce, and never got around to changing things back. May this be a lesson to us all. For you and Bart, the lesson comes I'm afraid at a great cost."

"How were things originally to be divided? Before he changed his will."

"A quarter for each son. Equitably. Fairly. The way things should be."

Oliver ran a finger across his lips, palpating the cold sore. This mannerism was fast becoming a tic. "I want to make sure I have this right. There were three wills. In the first, everything was split equitably; in the second, we were to receive nothing; and in the third, the one from April, we were to receive everything."

"Very good," said Morgen. "And only number two— the one in which you get nothing—will hold up in court."

"So how do we proceed? I'm more concerned about my mother and brother than about me. I can live without the money, I think. But Bart doesn't have steady work, and my mother is accustomed to a certain standard of living."

With a section of the *Times* Morgen obliterated the fly. He glanced to make sure he hadn't disturbed the napping cat. The apartment was silent. Maybe Karen, in her simple housedress and bare legs, was napping, too.

"Let's deal first with Francizka, though I have to be frank, she's more your concern than mine. No love was lost between your mother and me. I always bent over backward to give her sound, professional advice, not that she ever took it. I'm the last guy to say, 'Told you so,' but in this case . . . enough said. Anyway, to my way of thinking, your mother has two options. Either she can sell the apartment"—Oliver emphatically shook his head to rule this out—"or she can sell some of the art left by her first husband. From what I recall, she has some very nice pieces—what, three or four Pascins, a Dufy, a Felix Nussbaum, a Kokoschka, you know better than me. The market for European modernists is very strong these days. That said, selling those works might not be as easy as it sounds."

I was struck by the lawyer's knowledge of art. The walls of his dining room were covered with attractive but generic prints of owls, lizards, and flowers.

"And why is that?" asked Oliver, fatalistically.

"Provenance, my friend. The big auction houses, Christie's, Sotheby's, Phillips, they're starting to ask difficult questions about provenance. They have no choice. In the last year or two, they've been hammered by one lawsuit after another. Distant niece Beatrice suddenly wants the Klimt back that used to hang in Great Aunt Esther's *Schloss* in Vienna before the Nazis seized it and sold it to the Swiss watchmaker who sold it to a French businessman who auctioned it to a Chicago software executive. In Europe, a good-faith purchaser of illegally acquired art has nothing to worry about, but that's Europe—here it's a different ball game. Here if the original transaction is rotten, all the subsequent sales are tainted. Find yourself a sympathetic judge and boom, anything can happen. I'm not saying Victor Vicc traded in looted art—for all I know, his business was entirely kosher, at least for the times. In the fifties, sixties, even into the seventies—things were different. You just bought and sold; who asked questions? But the fact is the artists he traded top the restitution lists, and he was doing this privately—he wasn't the agent or rep of some large auction house or gallery. So questions will be asked should your mother try to sell. And my guess is the big houses will decide to pass. For them, it's just not worth the headache."

I glanced at Oliver, inwardly satisfied that I'd apprehended the nature of Vice's dubious business dealings.

"And option two?" Oliver asked.

"It's ticklish—I say this in all frankness. For the record, I'm convinced that Jake, stubbornness and all, wanted his estate divided equally among all four of his boys. We just need to convince Reuben and Ezra that that was his intent. Unfortunately, thanks to your mother's brilliant ploy, there's bound to be bad blood between you and the Epsteins. If Francizka had only tried to restore Jake's will to the predivorce terms, the one that divided the estate evenly, that would have been one thing. But she has to go to the opposite extreme—she has to disinherit Reuben and Ezra. Somehow you and Bart have to convince them that you two had nothing to do with that scheme. Which isn't going to be easy, especially with your brother traipsing around with that little Führer mustache."

"Bart says he's not trying to imitate anyone, he just likes the way it looks."

"It's a distraction, Ollie. Certainly you can see that."

"And what exactly is our bargaining position? Should I tell the Epstein brothers that we're willing to ignore a legally worthless will drafted by my mother when Pappy was no longer competent, if they're willing to ignore a

perfectly legal will drafted by Pappy several years before? Is *that* our position?"

"Good! I like this spirit! You're thinking like a lawyer!"
Morgen drained his Coke and folded his arms on the
table. His leg was shaking furiously, as if in preparation
for a road race. "Because obviously that's completely
harebrained. I recently had a client whose mother died.
The mother unexpectedly leaves all her money to her
daughter—my client—and none to her son. My client
is so upset with this arrangement that she gives half the
money to her brother and has me work things so the
brother will never find out that his mother disinherited
him. This client of mine, she's one in a million, she's
golden, but the law wasn't created for saints. You know
how the law works—?" All at once Morgen turned to
me, demanding an answer.

"The law?" I repeated.

"Yes, tell Ollie here how the law works. Quickly,
though. Life is short."

"By sanctions?" Inwardly I cursed for letting myself
get drawn into this silly law school game.

"Sanctions," Morgen snorted. "Is that what they teach
at Yale? By *incentives! Karen!*"

He didn't wait for a response, but hurried into the
kitchen for more beverages. I was relieved to see him
return without another Coke. He was already quite
overwrought. He poured us seltzer without asking if we
wanted any.

"So let's talk incentives. Reuben is trying to revive
the Jewish community in Vladivostok. Whether there's
even a Jewish community there to be revived, God only

knows, but all the power to him. I wish him every success. But from what I hear, reviving lost communities
doesn't come on the cheap. Ezra's made a handsome
living in the diamond market, and he's been underwrit-
ing all of Reuben's endeavors—the renovation of the
shul, the construction of a cultural center, a library, a
Jewish day school, the whole *geschrei*. As I say, all this
costs money. My sources tell me that Ezra and Reuben's
dealings haven't been entirely aboveboard. The diamond
trade is poison, a real waste dump. You find yourself in
bed with the Charles Taylors and the Foday Sankohs of
the world, thugs whose business model includes chop-
ping the hands off children. And that's just the tip of
the proverbial iceberg. Ezra has shifted profits overseas,
set up dummy accounts. I can't go into more detail—
let's just say people go to the slammer for these kinds
of things, potentially for a *long* time. The IRS would
be very interested in these business dealings. Very, *very*
interested. If Reuben and Ezra were to learn that you
know about their dealings, they might be more receptive
to renegotiating the terms of the will."

Oliver looked visibly astonished. "Isn't there a word
for this?" he said. "Couldn't you be disbarred just for
proposing this?"

All at once Morgen's face turned as gray as his
eyes. His voice, though, was menacingly controlled.
"I haven't proposed a *thing*. If you heard me make an
unethical proposal—if you heard me breathe *one word*
that sounded suspect—then I suggest you get your ears
checked. The idea that I would do such a thing, and with
a stranger present!" He shook his head and glowered at

me. "I made an observation about how persons might be brought to the table to talk. No more, no less."

"And how exactly would that work?" Oliver waved at the air, but this time I saw no fly. "I write an e-mail, 'Dear Ezra, I know you're up to your neck in illegal business transactions. I promise not to tell the IRS if you promise to divide my stepfather's inheritance with my brother and me.'"

"Don't be ridiculous," cried the lawyer, suddenly in better humor. "First rule: nothing in writing. Leave no paper trail."

"I call?"

"Phone—also out of the question. Conversation might be recorded, you never know. This kind of thing has to be done face to face, mano a mano, in a public place, like a restaurant. Over lunch, say. You treat. Hypothetically speaking."

"What if they arrive wired?"

"Unlikely. Especially if you've just asked them to lunch. They have no idea what's coming."

"Manny, I was *kidding*," said Oliver. "I think you've been watching too many episodes of *Law & Order*."

The lawyer's eyes seemed to draw closer together in his skull, which itself appeared to constrict, as if in a vise. He was obviously quite volatile.

"Sweet boy," he said, "one of us works in the real world. One of us *lives* and *breathes* in the real world. I'm not giving academia a knock, I've never been one to pooh-pooh the life of the mind, but let's just say I also know a thing or two. I've been around the block and more than once. And something I've learned, and it

wasn't at Columbia Law where I went on the GI Bill"—
and he directed an odd, malicious, challenging smile my
direction—"is how to bring people to the table. I know
how to make them agree to do things they swore never
to do. And the simple truth is that people will part with
money for security. Give someone the choice between
having more money and living in fear of losing it, or having less and living in security, it's a no-brainer. Only high
rollers and nut-jobs take the money. So *if* you believe
that you and Bart are entitled to a share of the estate
of a man who loved you two dearly, and who, in a fit of
rage against your mother, did a stupid thing, then you
have to create incentives for the Epstein brothers to ne-
gotiate. And they *will* trade dollars for security. Those
boys, whatever their shortcomings, are rational actors.
I'm certain of this."

When we rose to leave, Morgen trained his closely
bunched eyes on me. "So how is it that you're also a professor? Harkness doesn't have a law school . . ."

"Actually, I'm a writer. A novelist. I teach creative
writing."

I expected this to occasion a fresh orgy of derision,
but the lawyer's bipolar face brightened. "You don't say.
I've been working on a novel, you know, a three-in-the-
morning project, for a couple of years. It's sort of a legal
thriller with a fall of the Berlin Wall angle. Based on a
true case of a Stasi double agent. Maybe I could send
you a few pages, tell me what you think."

"Sure, I'd be delighted."

After we had left the lawyer's apartment, Oliver said,
"You don't have to read his manuscript."

"No, that's fine. Maybe it's good. Who knows."

"I like Manny." Oliver said this as if surprised by his own words.

"He's a character."

"So what do you think?"

"I guess I don't see the wisdom of blackmailing your stepbrothers."

"No."

"And I do wonder about him. I mean, you and Bart aren't his clients. What does he stand to gain from all this?"

"Manny? Nothing, I suppose. I think he's just trying to be loyal to what he believes were my father's intentions. I'm sure that Manny can be completely unscrupulous and unethical, but I do think he's loyal."

As, of course, was Oliver. It wasn't a surprise that Oliver would value in others the trait he most cultivated in himself. He walked me to Penn Station; he would stay the night at Sophia's. Cold seeped into the shadowed canyons of Manhattan. December light flamed in the windows of the upper stories. I turned up my suit collar and tightened my scarf as a rogue gust off the Hudson lacerated us. Oliver took no notice.

"You realize, this is a catastrophe for my mother," he said. "It will kill her. And there's Mew to think about. What a fucking disaster."

"What about the art?"

"You heard Manny. That's also a mess."

"He said it *might* be. How much do you know about your father's art business?"

"My father wasn't in the art business, he was in the lighting business. But I suppose you're talking about my biological father. Who you love asking questions about."

"I was asking about the *art*, Oliver. It was your father's lawyer who suggested that selling it might be a way out of this crisis."

"No, you just want to know about Victor Vice."

As I've acknowledged, in recent months my interest in Oliver's family history had grown, become more substantial and focused. At the same time, I'd been struck and puzzled by the persistent lack of curiosity Oliver mustered for the subject. When Mel and I told him about our visit to Andrássy út 101 and showed him pictures of the improbable Art Deco confection, he simply said, "There must be an explanation. My mother wouldn't lie." Baffled by his muted response, I'd noted the irony that a philosopher of identity should show such indifference about who he is. At the time, Oliver had gazed at me in implacable silence, but now, without my uttering another word, he suddenly cried, "Oh, yes! Think of the irony! The philosopher of identity who has no idea who he is! Think of it!"

We arrived at Penn Station. Oliver stepped out of the way of a dazed pigeon. "This whole thing," he said, "it's going to kill my mother. Mark my words."

Several days later, he arrived in my office with a thick sheaf of papers. It was the completed manuscript of *Paradoxes of Self.* "You might want to read this," he said. "Or not. At the very least, it might resolve some confusions in your mind about what it is that I do." When it came to writing, we were hardly each other's strongest advocates. After consigning *Exit 33* to his mother's trash bin, he never spoke any further about my novel, except once to ask, "Did your father really do that thing with the mouse trap?" and sometime later, "Where exactly *is* Great Neck?" a remarkable question from a person who'd spent most of his life in Manhattan. On another occasion I gave him the draft of a story I was working on about a sexually ambivalent young attorney; he returned it without comment or editorial markings, except to encircle the word "penis," which appeared once, halfway through the draft. Another story, about an insomniac, moved him to an excess of enthusiasm: "I thought that was pretty good." He was incapable of false flattery. His mute responses never irritated me; if anything, I felt guilty for having thrust him in the obviously uncomfortable position of demanding from him something he could not give.

As for his writing, I had tried to read a couple of his philosophical articles when we were in London, but never got very far. One had the intriguing title "The Box Might Be Empty," but the piece itself was a highly technical "objectivist" explication of a quotation from Wittgenstein: *The thing in the box has no place in the language-game at all; not even as* something; *for the box might even be empty.* A second essay, a study of the phenomenon of trust, left me stranded at this patch of opacity:

> *If the cuckolded husband were able to accept pragmatic doxastic norms that licensed believing that his wife is faithful, he would still be unable to conclude deliberation until he had discovered (by his lights)*

*whether it is true that his wife is faithful; he thus
would be in the unfortunate position of accepting
doxastic norms that he was unable to implement in
his doxastic deliberations.*

I couldn't square this arid analytic work with Oliver's lively and passionate journalistic pieces; it was as if they had been written by a different person altogether. I picked up *Paradoxes of Self* expecting to have my patience quickly exhausted. The book—no more than two hundred manuscript pages—addressed a pair of questions that had gripped philosophers from Hume and Leibniz to Frege and Bernard Williams: Is our identity stable over time and does it exist independent of our memories and perceptions? But instead of claiming to find a new way to split the split hairs of the problem, Oliver presented no definitive answers. His ambition, which was never explicitly stated, as the book had no introduction or conclusion, evidently was to expound a style of inquiry—organized as narrative and not as argument, and drawn from a broad range of literary, anthropological, and historical texts. Two warring epigraphs framed his project: the first, the ancient Greek adage, variously attributed to Heraclitus, Pythagoras, and Socrates: *Know thyself*; and the second, from *Oedipus the King*: *God keep you from the knowledge of who you are!* Quite ingeniously, Oliver managed to sustain this spirit of contradiction throughout, as the book's form—its discretely numbered assemblage of debates, stories, readings, and reflections—came to complement, echo, and refract its subject. Only after Oliver's disappearance, when I read

Wittgenstein's *Philosophical Investigations*, did I come to appreciate the debt that *Paradoxes of Self* owed to this work; but even if derivative, Oliver's book gripped me, particularly its remarkable opening pages, which I offer here from the original manuscript that my friend thrust in my hands:

1. During my graduate studies at Harvard, I became acquainted with a fellow student in my department, whom I'll call Thomas Trapp (the name, but not its cadence, is my invention). Persons often treated us as a pair; Quine liked to quip, *Thomas Trapp and Oliver Vice, the Dickensian duo.* Trapp had practiced law for several years before returning to Harvard to do philosophy. Although his face was nondescript, he had an extraordinary build, the product of years of dawn trips to the gym. Trapp exercised vigilant control over *every* aspect of his life. He never ate for pleasure—every morsel of food had to be screened for its caloric and nutritional suitability; he kept a diary in which he meticulously recorded his daily intake of food. *May 14, 1993. Two eggs, scrambled; one glass orange juice, fresh-squeezed; two slices of organic sunflower seed bread . . .* He never raised his voice—not in anger, not in excitement, not even to make himself heard. He laughed, but never spontaneously. Even his breathing was controlled, as he'd devoted years to studying Qigong techniques of breathing. He always

looked me straight in the eye, but I felt that
he was actually staring at the tiny reflection of
himself in my cornea. I once found him in Wid-
ener Library, taking copious notes from a book
on the philosophy of humor. When I asked him
what he was doing, he said, *I'm learning how to
be funny.* And yet he couldn't understand why
his answer made me laugh.

2. In the *Blue and Brown Notebooks*, Wittgenstein
wonders, *Now were Dr. Jekyll and Mr. Hyde
two persons or were they the same person merely
changed,* only to add, *We can say whichever we
like.* I believe this is one of the most terrifying
lines in all philosophy. *We can say whichever we
like.* Whether we believe the self to be single or
multiple, whether we believe in continuity or
discontinuity, is, Wittgenstein insists, a matter
of *no philosophical consequence.*

3. To my knowledge, Thomas Trapp had no
friends or romantic attachments. He was not
shy; in fact, he had a habit of subjecting his
conversational partners to the most relentless
questioning, without ever revealing anything
about himself. If asked, *Which flavor do you
prefer?* he would answer, *And you?* Once, at
a departmental reception, Trapp approached
me and suddenly launched into a monologue
about his childhood. He told me that he had
grown up in Kansas, the only boy in a family

of four children. He had a pair of twin sisters who were two years younger and severely handicapped, and a healthy baby sister who was five years his junior. (He called her the *baby*, though at the telling this sister must have been in her early twenties.) As the eldest child, he often had to care for his disabled sisters, who were confined to wheelchairs and whose speech was unintelligible to those outside the immediate family. The *baby*, by contrast, had no such responsibilities, in part because of her age, in part because she was a singing prodigy whom Trapp's mother (he never mentioned a father) indulged at every turn, driving her miles to voice lessons while he minded the disabled twins. On his tenth birthday, he knifed the *baby* in the head. He offered no explanation of the knifing; maybe he didn't remember the reason or no longer found the antecedent relevant. The blow, which struck the crown of the *baby*'s head, left the weapon, a Boy Scout knife, embedded in her cranium. When his mother saw what had happened, she didn't scream, she didn't shriek. She simply carried the dazed but conscious child to the family car and drove off to the emergency room, leaving Trapp alone with his two handicapped sisters, who, having seen the weapon sticking from their sister's head, were howling inconsolably. Alone with the twins, Trapp hatched a *terrible plan*. He would strangle one with twine, which he had learned to tie with murderous precision as a Boy Scout, and would hurl the other down the basement stairs from her wheelchair. As the plan presented itself to him, he felt an unusual feeling: *calm*. He said he didn't know why he failed to go through with it: he had felt no tugs of conscience or worries about getting caught. But from that moment on, he realized that the only way he could possibly avoid committing heinous acts was by subjecting his every impulse and inclination to the most exacting self-scrutiny. He said it was absolutely imperative that he *constantly keep an eye on himself*.

4. Shortly thereafter Trapp disappeared from Harvard. Over the years, he became the subject of conflicting stories and outlandish rumors. I heard that he became a subsistence farmer in Anchorage; that he lit himself on fire on the Amherst town common in protest of Operation Desert Storm; that he took his vows and now worked as a priest with AIDS patients in Somalia; that he resumed his legal practice, married an attorney, and had three attractive children.

5. What do the words *I must always keep an eye on myself* mean?

6. Where is this eye?

7. What does it watch?

8. Some time ago, out of the blue, I received a letter from Trapp. In it he wrote, as if privy to the thoughts that had turned into my professional obsession, *Past experience—traumatic or not—cannot be understood as a* cause *of changes to one's identity, but rather, as an occasion for such changes. Experience is no more than the post hoc explanation we offer to make sense of what a person has become. It is not a trigger that sends a bullet on a clear path. It is a lit match whose smoke unfurls and twists and obscures.*

9. Recently I met someone who knew Trapp from his childhood days in Kansas. He swore that Trapp came from a well-to-do family and had only two siblings: a brother, now a doctor, and a sister, who teaches cello. He said that in high school Trapp had been an excellent student but something of a wiseacre. He'd been a good wrestler.

10. The letter from Thomas was postmarked Mogadishu.

Paradoxes of Self was later named a *Choice* Outstanding Academic Title and a *Times* Notable Book. Writing in *The Nation*, Carlin Romano called it "the most gripping, the most provocative, the most stimulating, the most querulous, the most *playful* book of philosophy to appear since Rorty's *Philosophy and the Mirror of*

Nature." Predictably, Oliver took little pleasure in this praise and even less in the criticism. "Vice's method of numerically interleaving observation, anecdote, and reflection," argued Martha Nussbaum in four dense columns of the *New Republic*, "although intended as a form of homage to his intellectual mentor, ultimately falls short of its ambition of creating a rich density of accumulated meaning and philosophical probity." Others accused Oliver of abandoning Anglo-American analytics for post-structuralist antics, a claim strengthened by the suspicion that Oliver had simply embroidered the entire story about Thomas Trapp, something he refused to confirm or deny, insisting it was a "moot point." He likewise refused to answer his critics in writing, not because the matters they raised failed to interest him, but because he felt the book provided its own best defense. Certainly the question of identity never ceased to fascinate him. Years later, when, unbeknownst to me, he was nearing the completion of his own incomplete excavations into the history of Vice, he returned to the topic, albeit obliquely, in the last letter he ever wrote me, sent from northern Portugal in the days before he boarded the *QM*2.

It strikes me that a crucial difference between us is that you believe in poetic justice and I do not. For years you have labored under the belief that because the Vices committed distant crimes, the exact scope and nature of which remain unknown—but which presumably, drawn as you are to stereotypical Jewish lines of narrative, involve the taint, if not the

*handiwork of the Nazis—Sophia had to die, my
mother had to become a felon, my brother had to
become depressive, etc. Whether you have the facts
right about my family's history—which you don't—is
not my concern. I'm more interested in your sentimental belief in the idea of balance in the long run.
You claim to share my basic agnosticism, but I can
see no difference between a belief in poetic justice
and a belief in God. Both posit a time of ultimate
reckoning. If anything, the belief in poetic justice
is the more unsupportable. At least in the case of
divine judgment, one can appeal to the existence
of a judge—viz. God—who directs the system. In
the case of poetic justice, who or what drives the
system to balance? The mind of the observer? The
artist? But that is to admit that the whole thing is
as artificial as the worst stuff of Hollywood. I don't
mean this as an insult; perhaps your belief in poetic
justice is a sign not of an impoverished imagination
but of basic mental health. In any case, I'm too exhausted to explain this at greater length. After days
of unimaginative sunshine, there is finally a textured
blanketing of cloud overhead, so I'm going to take
the opportunity to walk on the beach, where the
heather, now in summer bloom, grows directly to the
ocean's edge. I commend northern Portugal to you. I
feel certain you will visit here one day.*

O

ELEVEN

After Jacob Epstein's death, Francizka decided to put off the Christmas festivities until Easter. By then, our twins were just past their half birthday. The tufts of blond that had crowned their heads at birth had thinned. They'd grown rapidly, more in girth than length, and were now jolly fat creatures, with abundant creases of flesh far removed from any joint. Matthew remained the more aggressive of the two, having recently discovered pleasure in yanking his brother's ears. Aaron calmly absorbed the fraternal violence, while Matthew wailed at his own acts of abuse. It would be their first trip to New York.

Francizka couldn't get over the babies. "Truly, they are too darling for words. I am not just saying this. And dare I add—they remind me of my two boys at that age. Positively princely. But let me give you one piece of advice. You must never dress them the same. It is critical that they each have their own identity. I was lucky because my boys were not identical. You could tell them apart from day one. These two, though—my goodness!"

But if she'd ever held a baby, she'd long since lost the knack. A look of helpless distress took hold of her features as she fumbled Matthew in her arms and tried to fend off his tugs at her pearls and the twin Phi Beta

Kappa keys. She wasted no time in thrusting him back toward Melissa with the words "Truly, too precious . . ."

The natural with the twins was Sophia. We had no idea that she would even be there. She had done something enlarging to her hair—it was bigger, looser, more abundant, like a bird's feathers in winter. She proudly announced that she'd quit smoking, and accepted our congratulations while Francizka retreated to the kitchen to light up. And yet Sophia didn't look healthy. She had lost even more weight, and her eyes had the drawn, pinched, excitable look of the chronically sleep-deprived. She wore a short black skirt that she made no effort to keep modestly in place as she lay on her back on the living room rug and took turns balancing the babies on her scrawny stockinged legs. They cried with silent delight, small aircraft buffeted by turbulent skies. I saw her glancing in Oliver's direction, seeking approval of her maternal instincts, but he offered no confirmation or smile in return and only fingered the cold sore that had all but permanently installed itself on his upper lip. I knew things were not going well between them. No sooner had Sophia moved back East than Oliver again found himself wracked with misgivings, doubts, and ambivalence. He suspected—no, was convinced—that he'd made a colossal mistake in breaking up with Jean years ago, and chastised himself for lacking the will to forgo a sexual relationship to be with his "soul mate." He refused Sophia's demand that he cancel that year's trip to Switzerland to meet Jean; Sophia used the occasion of New Year's Eve to drink herself into a stupor and to harass Oliver with calls to his hotel in Bad Ragaz. More recently, Oliver had complained that Sophia was trying to poison him. The allegation, more figurative than literal and lacking hard evidence, claimed that she was lacing his vegetarian meals with chicken stock and beef bouillon. Bizarre if true; more bizarre if not.

Francizka's apartment looked grandly unchanged. Now, however, I saw it through fresh, or rather, suspecting eyes. The Pascins and the Liebermanns, the Dufy and the Kokoschka: I imagined the coarse exchanges and unconscionable bargains they had silently endured.

Bernie, Francizka's friend, was stationed in the recliner where we'd last seen him. He was awakening from a nap that might have been the end stages of a sixteen-month hibernation. He offered me a moist hand by way of greeting, and when reminded that I was a writer, said, "Tell me again the name of your titles."

Then there was Bartholomew. He was clearly unwell. Gone was the Churchillian bluster of the year before, and in its place the tidily groomed declaration of insanity on his upper lip. He shuffled from room to room in slippers of forest green boiled wool, blinking dully. The exchange of presents, a low-key affair—it was, after all, Easter—passed without a repeat of the vulture catastrophe; Sophia gave Francizka a bracelet, which the mother accepted graciously, if not warmly. Still, it didn't come off altogether without incident. Bartholomew gave Sophia a banana stuffed into a tennis sock. Even Francizka acknowledged a problem.

"Mew has not been himself. The work as a substitute teacher was not good for him. Do you know what these schools are like? The girls claw each other like animals

and the boys have guns. They kill at the slightest provoca-
tion, the wrong look and it's bang! Honestly, I sometimes
wonder if we've progressed out of the jungle. I can't tell
you how relieved I am that he has quit. Forgive me if
I'm repeating myself, but Mew was an unusually talented
child. He sang like an angel, was devilishly handsome,
and had the most lovely strokes in tennis. I hope it does
not pain Ollie to hear me say so, but it was Mew who
stood out as a boy. Ollie had the good fortune to find his
niche without difficulty. Now Mew must find his. For
some persons, especially those with sensitivities, it can
take time. But Mew will find his niche, won't you dear?"

During this monologue, Bartholomew had risen
from his armchair and, to our alarm, disappeared into
the room where we'd set up the portable playpen for
the twins, quietly shutting the door behind him. With
feeding time as a pretext, Melissa anxiously hustled
after him. There she found Bartholomew, sitting cross-
legged on the floor, playing peekaboo with the delighted
babies . . .

Later, we gathered at the dinner table and Bartholomew commanded us to join hands.

"This is new," said Oliver, skeptically.

"We've been doing it ever since Mew joined St.
Agnes," said Francizka. "It's a lovely way to start a meal."

Bartholomew intoned the dinner prayer in Latin.

"Amen," we said.

Oliver sat in stony silence. "I thought Latin went out
with Vatican II," he muttered.

"Miscreant!" bellowed Bartholomew. "The Second
Vatican was the work of Satan!"

"Enough," cried Francizka, "I will not have my sons fighting like alley cats."

We dined copiously on goulash (made with turkey bacon this time), stewed fruit, and freshly baked potato bread. Oliver made do with the salad of boiled spinach. The memories of the Christmas pork disaster appeared successfully exorcised.

"And the spoon!" Francizka proudly displayed the restored cutlery. "Doesn't it look magnificent? I must thank you again. I would not have believed such craftsmen still exist."

"We found him in Pennsylvania," said Melissa.

"Remarkable. I would have thought only in Hungary."

"You know we were in Budapest last summer," I said. I could sense Oliver's eyes pivot in my direction.

"Yes, I heard! After your visit with Oliver and Jean. Such a lovely girl. I always look forward to our rendez-vous in Switzerland. A good soul, and so intelligent, too."

Sophia's fork clattered on her plate. She made off to the bathroom.

"Did I give offense?" asked Francizka, scrutinizing us with frank bewilderment. I might have expected Oliver to come to Sophia's defense, but he remained silent. "Such ill manners . . ."

"Did Oliver tell you that we went to your parents' apartment building?" I glanced in his direction. His gaze had settled sadly on the tablecloth.

"Did you? I must tell you, I haven't been back. Even now, I have no desire to return, even for a visit."

"It's a beautiful Art Deco building. Really magnificent."

"But of course. My parents adored Jugendstil. We had such a wonderful apartment, far more splendid than this. Twenty-foot ceilings, such buildings are no longer made."

"That's where your father also had his medical practice?"

"His surgery, yes, you remembered! Did I tell you that my father delivered my mother? You must think I mean he assisted when she was pregnant with me. But no, I mean he delivered my mother when *she* was born. My father was already fifty when he married my mother, who was just a girl of nineteen. How many men can say that they married the girl they delivered? Mother later lived in the very apartment where she was born."

"I don't mean to pry, but isn't that the building that you said was bombed?"

Oliver rose from the table, folded his napkin on his chair, and silently shuffled toward the bathroom, perhaps to check on Sophia.

"Bombed? Why, no."

"I'm sorry, I thought you said your parents died in a bombing of their building."

"In a *shooting*, my dear. In the fall of 1944 Budapest experienced civil war, total chaos. My parents and sister were caught in a terrible gunfight crossing a city square."

"You had a sister?" I recalled the Hungarian woman's insistence that Dr. Sándor Nagy had only a single son.

"Yes, two years younger and infinitely more beautiful."

Just then Bernie sneezed.

"The truth has been spoken," Francizka said. "But perhaps we could talk about happier subjects during dinner."

"I'm sorry. It must be very painful."

"It is what it is."

Sophia returned to the table, steered by Oliver, who waited for her to take her seat before taking his own.

"Everything copacetic?" asked Francizka, disdainfully.

"Oh, just peachy," said Sophia. In two long pulls, she drained a glass of Bull's Blood. "Hey, pass me that bottle. This stuff isn't half bad."

Francizka released a sigh and castigated Oliver with her eyes. Timidly Oliver passed the bottle.

Melissa nursed the babies and retired early. Sophia disappeared to her room, and Bartholomew lumbered off to his study. Francizka lit a cigarette and, squinting into the curlicues of smoke, served apricot schnapps and freshly baked strudel. Bernie settled into the recliner, while Oliver worked out a chess puzzle on a small magnetic travel set. He loved these puzzles as much as the game itself; after his disappearance, I learned that he had long subscribed to *Retrograde Analysis Corner*, the leading magazine of chess puzzles. He even had contributed three original compositions.

"I must apologize if I have not been the most satisfactory conversationalist," said Francizka. "I've been in a terrible state, and simply cannot concentrate given my nerves."

Her words surprised me. During dinner—while Bartholomew mechanically devoured a vast plateful of meat, Sophia downed glass after glass of wine, and Oliver silently picked at his boiled spinach sprinkled with tempeh bacon chips—Francizka had single-handedly and indefatigably sustained the table talk.

"Truly, I have not been able to sleep. Insomnia is a terrible curse. I toss and turn, and in the middle of the night I make myself a cup of warm milk, but even this does nothing. It is truly an unforgivable thing what those brothers did—"

I thought she might have been lamenting the deteriorating relations between her sons, but then it became clear that other matters were on her mind.

"They didn't do a thing," said Oliver, without looking up from the board. "It was you."

"Don't say foolish things, Ollie. For all your intelligence, you say some very foolish things. I knew those boys were not to be trusted from the day I met them. Of course they were still quite young when Jacob and I married. But even then, they were already spoiled rotten by their mother, a dreadful beast, that woman. I made every effort to be kind to them, but that woman never tired of making me out to be the evil stepmother from the Brothers Grimm. To my face she called me a gold digger. Can you imagine? She was terribly jealous, of course, and I can hardly blame her with that terrible behind and those fat breasts."

Oliver moved a knight forward, deliberated for a moment, then moved it back. "Impossible," he muttered.

"Don't tell me. She knew her boys could not hold a candle to minc. And Jacob knew it, too. They were a source of terrible disappointment to him, even before they joined that cult."

"The Lubavitchers are not a cult," said Oliver.

"Look how they dress, those unkempt beards and side curls. And those long, awful coats that they wear even in the heat of the summer! Did the Middle Ages never end? Not to mention the poor women, my heart goes out to them, it is no better than Saudi Arabia."

A dry rattle issued from Bernie on the recliner. Hands folded across his beige cardigan, swollen ankles resting on the ottoman, he'd retreated to his vernal sleep.

"I happen to be a very forgiving person. It is not in my nature to hold grudges. Of course, when Jacob's philandering became intolerable, I did what any self-respecting woman would do. But even after the divorce, I remained terribly fond of him. Floozies were his weakness, but who of us does not have a weakness, I ask you? He was a good man and a good father to my boys. That is why I cannot forgive, I will not accept, what that pair are trying to do to Jacob's estate. Ollie told you the disgraceful thing they did to the will?"

"Yes, I've heard."

"Beloved mother, that was you." Oliver examined the board without his glasses, a sign of escalating vexation.

"Truly, the things that come out of your mouth." Francizka lit a fresh cigarette and turned to me, crossing her shapely legs and adjusting the necklaces that Matthew had pawed at earlier. "I know my husband. He loved Ollie and Mew as his own—more! It made them terribly jealous, don't think I wasn't aware. I even warned Jacob. 'You must not neglect your other sons,' I said. 'We cannot choose our children.' And now this is their revenge. Unconscionable. All I did was to ask Jacob to repair the damage that those two did. Of course he was not well when we spoke, but don't tell me he did not understand what he was doing. Where is the crime in that?"

"Mami, I've told you a million times. Pappy changed the will in 1985. Not because he was tricked by Reuben and Ezra. Because *you* divorced him."

"I was to sit idly by while he brought a parade of floozies back to *my* bed?"

"I didn't say that."

"Then think before you open that sharp mouth of yours. Save your tongue for Bill Clinton, not your mother. As soon as we separated, those two were all over him like a pair of thieves, bad-mouthing you and your brother. Out of the blue, they suddenly invite their dear father to their special Friday dinners, this after years of ignoring him! Sadly, Jacob was not a strong man."

"That doesn't change anything," said Oliver. He set the pieces back in the original puzzle position, and started afresh. "The fact is, that will was made when Pappy was fully competent."

"It changes everything," declared Francizka with great finality. She stubbed out her cigarette for emphasis. "It shows that those two greedy *thieves* do not deserve Jacob's estate. Certainly not *all*. That is absolutely unacceptable. You and your brother must have your fair share, that is all I ask."

She turned to me. "I'm asking you, isn't that fair?"

"What on earth is he supposed to say?" said Oliver, turning me into the proverbial third person.

"He's a family friend. He has a mind of his own. I don't control him." Then to me: "Fair is fair, wouldn't you agree?"

"It does seem unfortunate that Oliver and Bartholomew were disinherited."

"There, you see?" The mother threw up her hands.

"I'm not going to blackmail them," said Oliver.

"Don't use silly words. No one is talking about blackmail."

"Extortion."

"Words."

"Not words, Mother. Crimes! You know that's *exactly* what Manny Morgen suggested. That I threaten them with going to the IRS about Vladivostok. I'm not going to do that. I simply won't."

"I, I, I." Francizka's voice growled with anger. "That's all I ever hear. Do you ever think about your brother? Mew is not well. You don't live with him day in and day out. You barely call him. Even on weekends when you come to the city, it's not to see your family—it's to be with that friend of yours. I will not live forever. Who will provide for him when I'm gone? Have you ever for a moment thought about that? Well?"

"There's the art."

"The *art*? Have you lost your mind? The art is my legacy to you two. I had to fight Victor for that art. It is unimaginable that we would part with it. You take it to Sotheby's and they cheat you out of half your money. It can't be done—you would get a pittance. I would rather die than sell off the collection. Maybe that's what you'd prefer. Maybe I should poison myself and your brother before my time comes."

"Please don't start with the melodrama."

"*Melodrama?* You think losing your parents before your

twelfth birthday is melodrama? You think walking half-way across Europe as a young girl is melodrama, serving soup in a displaced persons camp, having your husband abandon you and your children is melodrama? I have something to tell you, Ollie, and I want you to listen. I have sacrificed *everything* for you and your brother, everything. I have done all I could to make life for you and Mew better, easier, happier. But what would you know? Maybe I've made things *too* easy. Maybe you'd be a little more appreciative if you hadn't grown up with everything handed to you on a Zsolnay tray. And that friend of yours dares to call me a vulture!"

"Won't you EVER shut that *fucking* mouth of yours?" We all turned to see Sophia standing akimbo in the archway to the living room, head straining forward as if to bring Francizka into sharper focus. "I could just *puke* listening to all the bullshit that comes out of your mouth. Really."

Oliver and I were too astonished to say anything, but not Francizka. "The girl appears out of kilter," she dryly observed.

"Soap," said Oliver, taking a protective, tentative step toward her. "Let's just—"

"Shut the fuck up, Ollie. You're no better. All of you belong in a NUTHOUSE. I could *scream.*"

Which she did. A sudden piercing scream that turned kinetic and illustrative. Sophia spun with her arms outstretched, like one of the whirling dervishes who'd recently performed at BAM. She bumped into a side table, upsetting an enameled dinner bell and an antique inkstand. After a collision with an armchair, she slowed, arms descending, until only her head remained in motion, wobbling on her neck like a top, and then, with a final moan, she went down.

For four nights Sophia was kept at New York-Presbyterian. She insisted the overdose was an accident. She'd been prescribed Flexeril, a muscle relaxant, for back spasms; tipsy from dinner, she'd overlooked the label that warned of the dangers of mixing the medication and alcohol. She said that she'd taken only two tablets, but the ER doctor thought six to eight was more like it. In the ambulance she slipped into a deep sleep and didn't come to until the next morning. The doctors called her lucky: she could easily have gone into a coma. She was perfectly lucid by the next day and complained about all the fuss; still, it was decided to hold her "for observation." Oliver told the doctors that in recent months Sophia had developed a habit of mixing pills: Sominex, Valium, Extra Strength Tylenol, Dramamine—for her headaches, insomnia, vertigo, cramps. She often sampled her friends' medications: Xanax, Zoloft, Clonazapine, Demerol, Percocet, Oxy-Contin, Ativan, Neurontin—she'd tried them all, often in colorful combinations. He said she reacted to an unknown bottle of prescription tablets like a child to a new flavor of jelly bean. Her drinking was also increasingly out of control. She could go weeks without a drink, only to binge fiercely for a night. She could consume Olympian quantities of alcohol without becoming physically ill or suffering a hangover. Recently she'd filled a water bottle with vodka and taken it to work. To Oliver, the fact that the overdose was accidental made it all the worse. "She almost killed herself without trying, what's going to happen when she puts her mind to it?" He was determined to send her to a psychiatric/rehab clinic for a two-week program, a move the doctors supported. Sophia was equally determined not to go. In a wild tirade, witnessed by Mel, two nurses, and me, she accused Oliver of trying to commit her in order to avoid committing to their relationship. "*Of course*, you want to lock me up, you bastard! It's the perfect excuse. 'How can I *possibly* spend my life with a crazy boozer?' I'm obviously to blame for all your *sick* temporizing. You come off as Mr. Prudent and I'm the Poor Sick Fuck! *Fantastic!*"

Oliver made the mistake of seeking support from Sophia's family, a profoundly troubled unit. Her mother, we learned, had abandoned the family when Sophia was ten. She became a disciple of Bhagwan Shree Rajneesh and one of his favorite "vaginas." Later, after the ashram disbanded, she moved to Oakland, but never repudiated the teachings of her master and continued to use her Indian name. When Oliver contacted her about Sophia, she tranquilly blathered, "I truly believe that Sophia has to find her own path, and that can't be forced upon her, it has to come organically from within her own spirit. But clearly you care a great deal about her, and I'm certain that your love will facilitate the healing process."

Sophia's father, whom Oliver described as a well-meaning, emotionally uncomplicated man who'd never fully recovered from his wife's flight and sexual enslavement, voiced vague support for Oliver's plan, as if fearful that any more active intervention on his behalf would again unleash those terrifying and arbitrary forces that had brought ruin upon him and his family.

Curiously, the fact that her parents refused to side with Oliver weakened Sophia's opposition. It was as if their lack of support supplied the surest indication of the wisdom of the proposed treatment. And so five days after her potentially fatal collapse, she was transferred from New York-Presbyterian to the Octagon, a clinic nestled in the bucolic foothills of the Berkshires and famous for its treatment of "addictive-personality disorder." The cost was appalling and only partly covered by Sophia's insurance, the remainder coming directly out of Oliver's pocket.

Sophia had been at the Octagon for a week of the two-week program when I asked Oliver if I could accompany him on a visit. It was one of those clumsy spring days of shifting winds and clouds that race back and forth in the sky like dumb sheep. Joining us in Oliver's car was the artist of dictionaries and vultures. I hadn't seen Max since Oliver's party, and he appeared to have no recollection of having met me. During the hour's trip through a hilly countryside of antique stores, Indian trading posts, and abandoned mills turned factory outlets, the artist told us about his own stay at the Octagon. "I had a great time—it was like summer camp. Every afternoon we did arts and crafts. They gave us a box of tongue depressors and Elmer's glue. I made a pretty precise scale model of the Eiffel Tower. I remember a nurse said to me, 'Max, this is wonderful. I think crafts could be a powerful outlet for you.' She was so sweet and cute, I sent her an invitation to my show at the Guggenheim."

"You had the good sense to seek help," said Oliver. "You weren't in denial."

"It really wasn't a matter of choice. I'd turn on the television and my heart would pound uncontrollably. I'd open the fridge and break into a cold sweat. NPR would come on and I'd start to hyperventilate. It was no way to live."

"How long were you there?" I asked.

"A month, but I definitely would have stayed longer if I could have afforded it. Everyone should go to the Octagon, if you can get in. The food's the best I've ever had in my life. They bake their own bread and muffins. The gym's amazing."

A long, curving driveway brought us to what looked like an elite boarding school spread over many wooded, manicured acres. The Octagon took its name from its central and most distinctive building, a three-story, granite structure designed by Lyman Beecher or some such nineteenth-century polymath. The Octagon served the facility's "most distressed clients." Other patients were housed on the Quad, a collection of sturdy utilitarian brickworks that formerly served as the dorms and classrooms of the Eastfield Seminary, the Octagon's original incarnation.

The buildings bore the names of New England trees, and we found Sophia in the lounge area of The Elms, flipping through a magazine. She wore an untucked flannel shirt over loose jeans; her bangs were parted to show the smooth intelligence of her forehead, and for the first time I noticed that her eyes, which I could have sworn were brown, were actually hazel. She gave us each a kiss in greeting, "Three hot men, all here to see me. The other patients are going to be jeal-ous!"

I watched her eyes carefully over the next couple of hours: they were all too alive—winking, squinting, opening in trust, narrowing guardedly, changing emotions like an actor in a one-woman Broadway revue switching costumes.

Max wanted to see his old haunts, so Sophia took him and me on a walk, while Oliver stayed behind, planting himself with a book of Hume in her relinquished reading chair. As we strolled around, Sophia introduced us to her new acquaintances with admirable directness: "Dylan, I'd like to you to meet two dear friends of mine. Max here is an artist—he's just visiting now, but was here on the inside a couple of years ago. Dylan is a wonderful singer and a schizophrenic. This is his fourth stay at the Octagon." The patients adored her and the nurses, mindful of the terrific people skills that had made her BAM's most successful fund-raiser, enlisted her to convince them to take their meds. "Now Todd, honey, how do you expect to leave this place if you don't take your Clozaril? I'll get you some strawberry lemonade if you promise to take your pill, deal? And no hiding it under your tongue!"

In a wing called The Larches, Sophia waved at a pretty, freckled girl with a bright, all-American smile. "That's Linda," she said. "She just turned sixteen; we had the sweetest little birthday celebration for her on Thursday. Her parents gave her a brand-new softball mitt. She loves softball, and carried the mitt around the whole day, punching the pocket like a real little jock.

That night, after lights out, she removed all the leather lacing from the mitt and tried to hang herself from the frame of her shower door. The poor dear should have known that all the rods in this place are collapsible—she has bruises all along her side. Now her parents just found out their insurance has expired, so she's going to be transferred to a state hospital, one of those places straight out of *One Flew Over the Cuckoo's Nest*. It breaks my heart, she's so young and pretty and determined to hurt herself."

Max confessed that ever since we'd arrived, he'd been longing for a snack at the facility's organic bakery. He went off on his own.

"Max fits in here well," Sophia said. "He definitely has a diagnosis. Probably Asperger's mixed with a little OCD."

"What about Oliver?" I asked.

Sophia shook her head. "Oliver doesn't belong at the Octagon. His problems aren't chemical."

I had to agree. Or rather, if they were, it was only in a definitional sense. In *Paradoxes of Self*, Oliver had written, *It's all chemical and that resolves nothing*.

"And you?" I asked.

"My psychiatrist—that's him right there. Don't stare! Doesn't he look just like Martin Scorsese?" A diminutive man with eyebrows like coal smudges and an immaculately groomed beard that densely ringed his mouth was examining a medical chart. He did look a great deal like Martin Scorsese. "Dr. Rubin is such a darling little neurotic. He's wound so tight, the poor man. I call him by his first name and he hates it. Hi, Simon!"

The psychiatrist nodded in response, reddening terribly.

"Simon has me down for Addictive Personality Disorder and as Bipolar. Which is ridiculous—I've never been manic in my life."

"What about depression?" Oliver mentioned that in the weeks before her overdose, Sophia had suffered a number of sudden and breathtaking microbursts of anguish, devastating wind shears of emotion, often triggered by heavy drinking.

"Almost never. Though I admit, there are times, and they *are* a bit strange, when I feel a powerful desire to *not be*, at least not in this state. I get this incredible image of us—I mean *all* of us—as broken shards of a single being that used to be whole but was blown apart, at the beginning of time, into billions of tiny pieces all flying off into space. I look around and see the fleshy remains of this very intelligent creator who accidentally blew himself up in his laboratory in the course of a very promising but dangerous experiment. I think that if only we *all* could die, then we would be whole again. Now you're looking at me like I'm crazy."

In fact I wasn't. Her eyes, catching afternoon light, turned agate. They dazzled me with their beauty. Some errant transmission, some electrical discharge jumped across the yard that separated us. All at once, in an inversion of our first meeting at Oliver's party, I pressed a kiss squarely on her lips.

"O-*kay*. What was that for, sweetie?"

"Oliver's my friend, my closest friend," I said, holding her hand. "But you should get out. God knows, I don't mean for me. I just mean, out."

"Oh, sweetie. Ollie's not the big bad wolf."

"I'm not saying he is, Sophia. That's not what I mean at all. I just don't think you're going to get from him what you want. What you deserve. His problems are too big, too refractory, too *too*."

"You sound like you think you know him better than I do."

This brought me up short. I didn't want to insult Sophia, but wasn't it clear that I did? Wasn't the proof that she was still with him?

"I didn't mean for it to sound like that. I know he loves you." Did I, in fact, know that? "I just think you should run, not walk, the other way." It was a message that required the widest circulation. I regretted not having said much the same to Jean in London. Oliver may have been exemplary in his suffering, but not the women around him. They just suffered.

"And you know what I think?" she said. "I think you just want him all to yourself."

She must have sensed my astonishment; before I could formulate a response, she added with a laugh, "Just kidding, sweetie."

She released her hand from mine and placed her palm against my chest. The pressure was gentle, but in the direction of pushing me away, not drawing me close. The pieces of agate mysteriously lost their luster. Her gaze didn't signal distrust, but its onset, a cooling look of self-protection. She patted my chest twice. "Come. You worry too much. I'm a big girl. Let's find the others."

We rejoined Oliver and Max in the recreation room. Oliver was playing Ping-Pong in a King of the Table challenge. It took him a couple of games to find the form that had humbled Keith Richards, but soon he had established his dominion over Sophia's unit. With a wicked slice serve and a crushing forehand smash, he made quick work of an angry man with a terrifying jagged scar that ringed the base of his neck. Sophia quietly explained that the scar was the result of a motor-cycle accident that had shattered the man's larynx and something important in his brain. Oliver next thrashed a friendly talkative guy who, Sophia later told us, had recently beaten his own mother within an inch of her life. Between games Oliver calmly bounced the ball off the *side* of the paddle, a feat of coordination that made me respect him in a new way. A former Marine with a buzz cut played Oliver close, seemingly thanks to coaching advice that issued from a potted plant, but then was called away by a nurse. Max, content in his familiar milieu, napped in a brocaded easy chair. Oliver retired undefeated. Sophia planted a tender kiss on the champion's lips.

Later we followed Sophia down to the indoor pool. Visitors were invited to swim along, but none of us had brought a suit. Sophia appeared to have gained a few much needed pounds since her collapse; she wore a navy blue one-piece, which thrillingly traced the lines of her swayed back and powerful butt, but was otherwise desexed by a no-nonsense cap, nose plugs, and dark gog-gles. In a corner of the pool, an instructor was leading a group of patients in a set of water exercises. Sophia strode over to the side roped off for laps, and without so much as a pause, dove in, entering the water without a splash. She swam a tight confident crawl, coming off the wall with a flip turn and dolphin kick. We watched as if transfixed, unable to take our eyes off her display of strength: the lovely fit body propelled by the young heart that had nearly quit two weeks before. Silently we shared in the moment's poignancy. Sophia was the very picture of health.

TWELVE

Some things must be imagined and this is one: Oliver's arrival at the central office of Credit Suisse on Madison Avenue. He was steeled for disaster, possibly indictment. A month after Sophia had left the Octagon, he received a stiff envelope via courier. He examined its laconic contents. A single sentence on cotton letterhead requested that he set up a meeting with a named bank official. Oliver followed the stern directive. He assumed it had to do with the Victor Vice account, whose cash reserves Francizka had been drawing down and smuggling out of Switzerland for years, decades. Now the account had been shut down for lack of funds, or the family was under investigation for currency violations and tax evasion, possibly both. The *Times* was screaming with headlines about the Justice Department's efforts to pressure Swiss banks to disclose the name of account holders suspected of owing back taxes. Manny Morgen advised him to go to the meeting alone, without a lawyer. Best not to appear adversarial from the outset. If an indictment were unsealed, he would have plenty of time to consult counsel. An elevator whisked Oliver to the twentieth floor. It is there that I see him, alone, adjusting the chessboard-motif cuff links of his pressed Turnbull & Asser shirt. He's met by a senior manager with slicked-back hair and, without any exchange of pleasantries, handed a notification of deposit. He examines it without comprehension. Six million Swiss francs (US$3.7 million) have been transferred to an account set up in his name by Reuben and Ezra Epstein. An identical sum has been placed in an account for Bartholomew Vice. The executive, the deputy director of the Division of Wealth Management, ushers Oliver into a private conference room, where he has him take a seat at a teak conference table. There he hands Oliver specially prepared folders that describe the range of bank products that Credit Suisse makes available to high-net-worth individuals. The executive expresses the belief that a diversified strategy that includes hybrid investments, measured bond positions, and derivative instruments geared to risk transfer and enhanced returns will together optimize all aspects of Oliver's financial situation, maximizing growth while preserving liquidity.

And this, too, I see: Oliver marching the fourteen blocks from Credit Suisse to his mother's apartment on East Sixty-eighth Street. It is a lovely day in late spring, but Oliver only registers the rising heat. His mother has played tennis earlier that morning, her regular game of doubles at the Sutton East Club, and now, after a shower, is preparing herself a salad. His unannounced arrival does not surprise her.

Come, my darling, she said. Join me for a small meal. What on earth did you do?

Sit down, like a civilized person. I won't be spoken to in that tone of voice. Save it for your friends or the president.

Okay. Now tell me.

Only what was necessary. She adds the final garnishes to the salad and begins eating. You look thin. Eat.

You extorted money from them.

I did nothing of the sort. I said that their father would not approve of the present distribution. Jacob was always a fair man who sometimes acted in rash ways. I had to put myself in his position and ask what he would want to happen.

What else did you say?

It was all very civil. For all their strange dress they are reasonable men. Good men. Respectful of the memory of their father.

Go on.

I told them that we wished them every success in their religious activity in the former Soviet Union. I told them that I myself have never been able to find the comforts of faith, but that I can imagine the great good it does for those who can. Jacob was never a devout man, but he liked the harvest festivals in the fall and Hanukkah, of course. I said that I hoped nosy IRS officials wouldn't interfere with their important project.

I cannot believe what I'm hearing.

Sit down, please. The way you pace about, just like Victor! Come, you're unsettling my nerves.

Where did this happen?

Barney Greengrass—Jacob's favorite. It hasn't changed in the least—still a zoo with sawdust on the floor.

You've completely lost your mind.

That is how you talk to your mother? You should be thanking me, my beloved son. It is all for you and Mew. You are used to the fine things in life. The art, the shirts, the fancy shoes. Just look at you. These do not come from a professor's salary. For myself I could not care less. I have done without before and could do without again. But not my sons.

You could go to jail. Who knows how they're going to retaliate.

There will be no retaliation. It was all very polite. They are fair, reasonable, grown men.

She says this with confidence and finality and then utters the remarkable line that stays with Oliver: *You would have never survived.*

"Survived what?" I asked, when Oliver later reconstructed the encounter for me.

"Yes," Oliver said. "Survived what?"

I couldn't help thinking: Oliver already *was* a survivor of her and her endless embroideries.

The summer brought two letters from him, the old-world archaism, *Par avion*, penned in his hand on the envelopes. He was visiting Jean in London and then was to meet Sophia in Iceland for a vacation. He said he would have forgone the trip to England in order to take care of Sophia (he liked to play nurse), but Sophia was back at work, eating and sleeping regularly. Generally she seemed stronger than she had in years. Also, he'd meticulously planned a vacation with her in

Iceland, so she couldn't accuse him of neglecting her for Jean.

The first letter was postmarked Hampstead:

An extraordinary thing has happened & I want to describe it in some detail. You remember that I volunteered to pay for Sophia's stay at the Octagon. The bill was astronomical & I've decided not to touch the money from the Epstein estate; I've put it in escrow until I figure out what to do with it. In any case, I reluctantly decided to auction off the Pascin that I bought at Chapman's last summer. (It was that or another Pascin, and the Chapman's purchase had less sentimental value.) I brought it to Chapman's, NYC, before leaving for London, and several days ago I got a call from the director of the New York office. You remember how upset I was about overbidding; well, it turns out I had good reason, because the Pascin's a fake. The director at Chapman's was incredibly apologetic and offered me a full refund, which, as I'll explain, I declined. The drawing was express-mailed back to London to be fully inspected by Chapman's Department of Authentification, Attribution, and Conservation, and today I met with the senior researcher. I wish you could have met him. He's Iranian by birth; his parents had both been professors of European art history under the Shah, but fled to London after the Islamic revolution. He was also trained for an academic career, but went into the forensics of painting after failing to get a proper university position. (He'd written

*his dissertation on Manet, and everywhere he inter-
viewed he was asked the same question—why had
he written on European painting and not Islamic
art?) He was in his late thirties, I would guess,
dressed in a beige polyester suit. His immaculately
manicured hands had the pinkest fingernails.*

*He said he recently had noticed a problem with
several Pascins that Chapman's had received from
an estate sale. In settling matters of attribution, one
begins, he said, by looking for obvious anachronism.
Does the work use pigments or canvas that were unavailable at the purported time of execution? These
are easy questions, he said, because of advances in
technology. When technology offers no help, one
must resort to the methods of the connoisseur. Here
the expert asks, does this <u>look</u> like a Pascin? In this
case, the recent acquisitions struck the researcher
as odd. Pascin's line, he said, is exceptionally supple
and versatile, defining volume with the slightest
variation of intensity. In these works, the line was
too kinetic, as if charged with nervous energy. It was
clear that whoever had produced these works had
been a superior draftsman; the question was whether
that draftsman had been Pascin. None of the works
appeared in Pascin's catalogue raisonné, but that
wasn't dispositive, as the catalogue hadn't been up-
dated since its original publication in the late 1950s,
and many obviously authentic works had surfaced
since then. The fact that the recently acquired
pieces didn't repeat known images supported their
authenticity, as forgers prefer to copy rather than*

create; on the other hand, two drawings looked as if objects from authentic images had simply been rearranged to produce a seemingly original work.

The researcher then examined the studio stamp that appeared on the verso of each piece. At first glance, the stamp appeared identical to those that appeared on other Pascins. But with the aid of surgical loupes, he noticed subtle differences, which he invited me to consider, handing me a pair of loupes. (He also wore a pair; they made him look like a giant mutant tadpole.) The R in ATELIER had a slight but unmistakable break in the curved bow. And the belly of the S in PASCIN bulged against the adjacent C:

ATELIER PASCIN

The break in the R, he said, might have resulted from a bad inking of the stamp, but that could not explain the bulge in the S; more disturbing still, only those works which connoisseurship suggested were not Pascin's had the broken R and bulging S. The researcher acknowledged the possibility that the artist's studio had used two stamps, though most studios insist on a single stamp precisely in order to avoid such disputes. It was also possible that Pascin's line had evolved or even worsened and coarsened with time. But the fact that the six works in question were not limited to a specific phase in Pascin's career refuted that theory. The idea that Pascin lurched back and forth over the course of decades, from a supple line to an energetic one and back again, reserving a separate, but nearly identical atelier stamp for the works prepared in the energetic style, was too far-fetched to warrant serious consideration. In light of his suspicions, the researcher made an inventory of the Pascins auctioned off by Chapman's over the last decade, and discovered, to his alarm, that at least half bore the line of the forger. When he examined the verso of those pieces held in private collections in the London area, his worst fears were confirmed. He brought his concerns to the attention of Chapman's directors, who, to their credit, acted swiftly and decisively to compensate all clients in full.

When I expressed surprise that so much effort had been expended to falsify the works of a "midlist" artist like Pascin, he said that this was not anomalous in the least. Forgeries on the order of van Meegeren's notorious "Vermeers" were the exception, not the rule, as the work of world-class artists is better known, more rigorously scrutinized, and more difficult to emulate because of the virtuosity of technique. The business of art forgery, he said, works almost exclusively in the dimmer light of the lesser talents. When I asked him if my BF would have known that he was trading in fakes, he said not necessarily. The Pascin forgeries were of a very high order—on a scale of one to ten, he gave them an 8.7 (which he later upgraded, perhaps

*unwittingly, to an 8.9)—and obviously had passed
through Chapman's undetected for years. He added
that the art of forgery had particularly flourished in
the first decades after the war. With so many works
unaccounted for, with so many trained artists drifting around Europe without academic positions or
means of livelihood, it was inevitable that the market would become flooded with fakes. Curiously,
because of the high quality of much of this work,
a healthy secondary market had recently emerged
in the trade and collection of postwar forgeries.
The researcher had been very generous with his
time, and when I got up to leave he made a parting
observation that to my surprise closely echoed an
argument that I'd made in Paradoxes. He said that
in the case of several prominent artists, the market
had become so flooded with forgeries that our very
understanding of what a painting by X looks like
has been shaped by our exposure to undetected
forgeries. He said that today we find it impossible
to believe that canvases by van Meegeren were ever
accepted as Vermeers—more: were praised as Vermeer's greatest masterpieces. At the time, though,
experts thought the van Meegerens looked exactly
like Vermeers for the simple reason that their idea
of what a Vermeer looked like had been formed
by looking at van Meegerens. In the case of other
artists—he was willing to entertain the possibility
that Pascin might fall into this group—this process
of unmasking might never occur. In these cases, the
proper name of the painter may denote less a real*

person than a body of work <u>irretrievably</u> corrupted by mountebanks, forgers, and interlopers.

O

PS. In a strange way, I'm comforted by the notion that if BF ever traded in the works of art seized from Jews, as you insist on believing, then he himself was duped. Poetic justice, as you might say. In any case, I've decided to hold on to my "Pascin." While it's hardly worth what I paid for it, I can always return it to Chapman's, the researcher assured me, should I ever come to tire of it. For now, it establishes a bond with my BF that feels right—one grounded in art, money, and deceit.

And this, sent shortly after his arrival in Reykjavík— perhaps the most hopeful letter I ever received from him:

Sophia's flight is delayed, so I thought I'd write. Today we're scheduled to visit the convention hall where Fischer and Spassky battled in the summer of 1972 and see the tournament set that they played on (now on permanent display in the national museum). We've also set aside plenty of time for hiking. I've long been intrigued by the landscape of Iceland, formed by the violent clash of hot and cold, the collision of volcano and ice, pyroclastic flow against glacial creep (from the observation balcony of this absurdly tiny airport, the entire country looks to be treeless). I would have preferred, of course, to come in the sunless winter, when all manner of

*meteorological violence is unleashed on the dark
island, but the summer's night sun is also a wonder.
I also think that I'll like the people, they're so few
in number. They're said to be the most literate persons on the planet, and yet my guidebook tells me
that a surprising percentage of adults continue to
believe in the existence of elves. The population has
remained inbred since the ninth century, making its
people an extended experiment in the genetics of incest. But most of all, I'm looking forward to seeing the
horses. This may come as something of a surprise, but
I've been interested in the Icelandic horse ever since
my days as a Junior Research Fellow at Oxford, when
I chanced upon a meeting of the Icelandic Horse Society of Great Britain, <u>dedicated to the promotion of,
interest in, and protection of the Icelandic horse</u>. The
horse is famous for traveling in two gaits unknown
to any other breed (I'll forgive your ignorance this
one time): the <u>tölt</u>, or rack; and the <u>skeið</u>, or pace.
Thanks to the British society, I had the chance to see
a handful of these horses up close. They are small of
stature, easily confused with a pony, and yet sturdily
constructed, capable of long hours of work and of
surviving storms that would be the end of their larger,
more elegantly proportioned cousins. Never in my life
have I even been atop a horse, but I've arranged for
Sophia and me to go riding on these lovely animals
in Harkadalor, a wild landscape where Erik the Red
once ruled. And I must say: I can't wait.*

O

THIRTEEN

He stayed with us for exactly two weeks that August, from the day he returned from the funeral in San Francisco until the night I asked him to leave. At first he barely moved. He'd sit for hours on our living room couch, hands pressed between his knees, like a schoolboy waiting for a summons to the principal. He appeared not to sleep. One night I left him on the couch fully dressed, his eyes fixed on the cover of a book about Jan van Eyck that lay closed on the coffee table. The next morning I found him in precisely the same position, still staring at the book's cover. He submitted to a narrow range of commands: *Have a glass of iced tea. Have some water. Eat a piece of toast.* Otherwise, he remained inert.

It was beastly hot, an East Coast drama of relentless heat and humidity, not the harmless London version of the summer before, but he breathed not a word of complaint. The weather satisfied his need to suffer or simply went unnoticed. He refused the offer of a fan. His eyes were puffy and ringed by purplish folds, but I never actually saw him cry—I'm not sure what I would have done if I had. The unwritten terms of our friendship, as I've noted, didn't allow for fraternal hugs or supportive embraces. I hoped the twins, adorably approaching their first birthday, might provide comfort, but Oliver exposed the limits of their power reliably to install a smile on any adult face. Perplexed by this immunity to their charms, the twins avoided him and his grief. Maybe they also associated his arrival with the disappearance of their beloved bird "blankies": Melissa, in a superstitious gesture, quietly removed the quilts from their cribs and packed them off to the attic.

After several such days I found Oliver up early one morning, making himself an egg. He ate morosely, as if resentful of his body and disappointed by his own meek submission to its tyranny of mundane needs and functions. Each subsequent day brought a fresh betrayal. Glumly, he began adding honey to his tea, smearing butter on bread, opening a tin to remove a single peanut, and then, with a sigh, a fistful. He directed a first tender smile at the twins, who continued to regard him warily but soon rewarded him with smiles of their own. And with us, he spoke.

The story emerged in reverse chronology and only gradually, circling back on itself, as gaps were filled, timelines clarified, details added, changed, and redacted. He was at pains to make two things clear: first, that it was an accident, and second, that he was entirely to blame. She had opened the passenger door to their rental car. Instead of stopping, Oliver had tried to lean across to shut the door. Moments before, she had removed her seat belt. As he reached across, he somehow lost control of the car. The sudden swerve to the left catapulted her to the right. They were going twenty-five miles per hour, later it would be twenty, who could say for sure? *Not fast in any case.* He jammed on the brakes and ran to her, but she was already back on her feet, dusting herself off. She had scrapes on her hands and on her chin. Nothing serious. She might have smiled. Then she stood stock-still and reached to the side of her head, as if reminded of some troubling fact. Her mouth opened; she might have said something, but if she did, the sound was swallowed by the stupendous crashing of a nearby waterfall. *The waterfall they had driven to see.* The next moment she collapsed. He knelt beside her and checked her vitals. He examined her for blood and other signs of trauma. There were none. The road was flat and unpaved, littered with volcanic rocks. *It looks like the moon. The rocks look like meteorites.* He had said this minutes before. It was two in the morning, the sun had just risen, and Sophia was dead. How he contacted the police or got back to Reykjavík, he couldn't say.

He had met her at the airport three days before. The police made him reconstruct their time together, but his account remained schematic. *How do two people fill a day?* They'd stayed at a bed-and-breakfast where the furniture was covered by oilcloths. They found a vegetarian cafe in Reykjavík and took all their meals there. They'd seen a famous chess set. On a whale watch they'd seen no whales but plenty of puffins. On the third day, they rented the car in the afternoon and left Reykjavík around eleven p.m. *to experience the light.* The midnight sun dipped in the sky and skipped off the horizon without ever setting. It was a strange luminous dusk; he remembered thinking that maybe this is what the Bible meant by *neither day nor night.* But he couldn't remember if he'd shared the thought with Sophia. The uncertainty gathered around him, left him briefly unable to continue.

I tried to lift this curtain of anguish with questions. It was important that he tell us. I said this for his benefit, not my own. So how long did you drive for? I asked. Two hours? All night? No, around two hours, he said. Maybe a little longer. Did you stop along the way? Once, in Haukadalur Valley to see Geysir, the ur-geyser, the geyser that gave us the word "geyser." (Even in pain, Oliver thought to teach.) There he took the last picture of Sophia, in a Gore-Tex shell, eyes and reflective stitching aglow—Oliver had forgotten to adjust the flash. Then they drove to Althing. Sophia had been reading *Njal's Saga* and wanted to see the craggy towering ring of granite *in whose protective shadows* (Oliver) Icelandic elders gathered to settle disputes a thousand years ago. It had begun to drizzle, and Sophia pulled up the hood of her Gore-Tex jacket. This time he remembered to adjust for red-eye, but the picture never developed. The loss of that final picture—that, too, caused him grief. Then they drove to Gullfoss in the canyon of Hvítá, said to be the most spectacular waterfall in all of Europe. He concentrated hard on the details. He said that Sophia snacked on blueberries that grew wild in wind-stunted bushes, but that must have been back at Althing. The road was unpaved, flat but rough, uneven— *it would have been impossible to drive fast.* The landscape was stunning, lunar, desolate; they had passed only two other vehicles. *Maybe three. I'm guessing.*

They had been fighting, but then they often fought. She had resumed smoking. Not for the first time. It was something of a pattern: she would quit with great fanfare, resolutely avoid cigarettes for a couple of months, and one day he'd find her back at it, waving off any suggestion that she lacked the will to quit for good. She smoked during the drive. She blew smoke out the window but ashes tumbled onto the passenger seat and floorboard. They argued, a stupid argument: he told her not to be such a slob; she said he cared more about a rental car than about her. She remained oblivious to the ashes. He was furious. Her slovenliness encapsulated in his mind every reason why it was impossible for them to remain together—he said something to this effect. In a single motion she released the seatbelt and threw open the passenger door. He reached over; the car swerved hard left.

The question I didn't think of until later: Why didn't he just slam on the brakes? *Why lean over?*

The police in Reykjavík observed that he had nail marks on his cheek. Such violence was not new, he admitted, though it was the first we'd heard of it. He said that typically she directed it against herself. She would call him a loveless arrogant pig and then thunderously ram her forehead against her bedroom wall. He would coldly inform her that he refused to submit to emotional blackmail in the form of demonstrations of instability; she, in turn, would ram her head against the wall even harder. Once he feared she'd cracked her skull. He resorted to violence to prevent worse. On one occasion he slapped her hard across the face; on another, punched her with full force in the arm, a blow that glancingly connected with her chin. The violence left him nauseated; she appeared not to mind. It's better than your coldness, she said. *Your cold cold arrogance.*

That night she'd had three, maybe four drinks. After leaving the Octagon Sophia had gone without alcohol, but then she'd always had the peculiar ability to do without. But she arrived in Reykjavík with a bottle of gin that she'd bought duty-free at JFK before the flight. Oliver had read extensively about addiction, addictive personalities, and alcoholism as a disease. He was well aware that you mustn't blame the alcoholic for her addiction, just as you can't blame the leukemia patient for her cancer. Still, he couldn't shake the suspicion that Sophia suffered less from a disease than from a failure of will. The baffling ease with which she could stop drinking *when she wanted to*, convinced him that her problem was susceptible to acts of *conscious correction*, which she *chose* not to exercise. His disgust and accusations drove her self-abuse.

When he tired of talking, Mel almost physically propelled him from the house. He hadn't been outside for days, and a walk would do him good, she said. But like a cat, he refused to stray from our property. In sunglasses and a straw hat, he circled our lawn, pausing by Mel's garden, where, craning forward, hands clasped behind his back, he examined the lilies and the trumpet vines, the bee balm and the phlox. In an Adirondack chair in the shade of a sycamore tree he intently followed the movement of ants along a blade of grass. With him was a book of Auden poems, which he didn't read, and a plain, clothbound book, his journal, which he then wrote in for an hour or so. Later, when he showered, I took the liberty of flipping through the journal, which he had left on the chair. Ordinarily I would have considered this a gross transgression—in the years we'd been together, I'd never so much as glanced at Mel's journal—but who can blame me under the circumstances? I feared another catastrophe, and this was the surest means available to assess his emotional state, to gauge his despondency.

Like his letters, his entries were penned in a tiny, elegant, barely decipherable script. I was surprised to see, though, that he indulged in private calligraphic flourishes, capital *A*'s with swishing feline tails, *S*'s that looped back on themselves like loose sewing thread, *H*'s that ended in Hancockian filigree. He was scrupulous about noting the location, date, and time of each entry. The entries themselves were reassuringly though oddly speculative, more like notes for a philosophical article than expressions of an interior world. That day, in an hour of writing, he had managed no more than a handful of sentences:

> *When I describe a dream, I say, "I did this and I did that," when the I in my dream bears little semblance to my waking self. For example, last night I dreamt that I was in a bookstore, perusing the shelves for a biography of Marlon Brando. And yet I have never had the slightest interest in Marlon Brando, and rarely read biographies. So who was this mysterious shadow I who shares neither my taste in actors nor in reading? And why do I accept him as identical with myself?*

Entries from earlier in the summer included chess notations and a list of expenditures, presumably from his various trips. There were single words, "inadmissible," "ego-dystonic," "debauchery," "clemency," as well as several definitions copied out from the *OED*:

chuffed, *adj.*
a. pleased, satisfied
b. displeased, disgruntled

Most entries, as I've said, dealt with philosophical questions:

Hampstead, 19.vi.95. noonish
An article in the Times *about a man with complete recall of the days of his life. Point anywhere on a calendar and he can describe with precision what he did on that date. Does such prodigious memory suggest that he is more himself than is a person with a weak memory?*

Hampstead, 22.vi.95. night
Wittgenstein from the Tractatus: *"Language disguises thought. So much so, that from the outward form of the clothing, it is impossible to infer the form of the thought beneath it." A peculiarly self-defeating statement: obviously Wittgenstein's observation about the inexpressibility of thought is expressed in language; how, then, can Wittgenstein possibly claim to know that language disguises thought? More to the point, how can this claim escape contradiction inasmuch as the insistence that language disguises thought belies itself?*

Hampstead, 28.vi.95. morning (rain)
Consider Cavell's question in "Knowing and Ac-
knowledging": "What does it mean to say, 'I know he's
in pain,' and how does this differ from saying, 'I know
I am in pain'?" Cavell rightly points out that the
statement "I know I am in pain" is utterly senseless,
as the experience of one's own pain cannot properly
be said to be an article of knowledge. I can know my
limitations, I can know I should have done better, I
can know that Reykjavík has a wet climate, but I can-
not properly <u>know</u> that I am in pain.

Same, night
I say to myself, <u>Behave, you fool!</u> But why do I ex-
pend words to communicate with myself? Am I only
available to myself through words?

Heathrow (flight delay), 2 July 95
Tomlinson ("Response to Williams") insists that
we come to know our "true" self only in times of
extremis. Nothing could be more absurd. The self
in extremis is simply a different being than the self
under conditions of normality. We can no more
predict how this other self will behave than we can
predict the behavior of a complete stranger.

And this, from the night before Sophia's death:

Reykjavík, 6 July 1995. 11:35 p.m.
By the time one finishes a book, one has virtually no
recollections of it. One can rarely quote a full sentence
from heart, the plot remains only in rough outline.

What lingers is an anecdote or two and one's affective response, whether one liked it or not, whether the reading experience moved, disappointed, provided pleasure. Isn't this much the same as our relationship to our own past? We live our lives like a book.

I gently closed the volume. The notional quality of the writing made me feel less guilty about my act of trespass. And it convinced me: Oliver would be fine.

A thunderstorm rattled the house and sent us dashing to unplug electrical cords. It passed quickly. The wind died down and the rain steadied. We sat in the living room. Melissa cried and took Oliver's hand in hers. The rain tapped against the gutters. Oliver coughed with emotion: Mel's tears appeared to remind him afresh of his loss. The rain took an edge off the heat. Only now did the story of the pregnancy come out in a grief-flattened monotone. The pregnancy hadn't been planned. To the contrary. Oliver told us—in his grief he spoke with remarkable candor— that he'd long insisted on double protection. Sophia had been on the pill since they met, but Oliver always used a condom, an added precaution that, to his knowledge, he had never failed to observe. To our puzzled glances, Oliver explained that years earlier, when he was still living with Jean in England, he had become convinced that he was infected with HIV. Why wasn't clear or important; in any case, he harassed a doctor into ordering a comprehensive battery of blood tests. These found no trace of the AIDS virus but did discover something unexpected: that he was a carrier of Tay-Sachs disease. Sophia was also a carrier, something she had discovered entirely fortuitously when her gynecologist sent routine blood work to the wrong lab. Early in their relationship, talking about their respective afflictions and deformities, they discovered their unusual genetic connection. At the time it seemed a sign of kinship. But given the risks, Oliver thought it prudent to use the greatest caution in having sex. And so the double protection.

"But Tay-Sachs—"

"I know what you're going to say," Oliver said. "You're so utterly predictable. The fact is that it's *predominately* but *not exclusively* carried by Ashkenazi Jews. You can look it up on the Mayo Clinic website."

Which I did, but only later, not wanting to interrupt his story.

He was in London with Jean when Sophia called to say she was pregnant. He tried to hide his alarm, his *suspicions*. Accident couldn't be ruled out. But Oliver was prey to other theories: maybe she'd slept with someone else or had sabotaged their birth control. He knew she wanted a child badly. She often accused him of using damaged genetics to avoid all discussions about starting a family. So maybe she had neglected to take a pill and had run a needle through his condom. It was impossible to talk about such matters on the phone. He would have to wait until Iceland.

In the meantime, Sophia agreed to schedule an amniocentesis. They were both carriers, and so the fetus had a 25 percent chance of inheriting the 100 percent fatal disease. The night of her arrival in Reykjavík, she told Oliver that she'd canceled the amnio. His response was utter disbelief. Why on earth would you do that? he demanded. Because there's still a 75 percent likelihood that everything will be fine, she said. Life is about taking chances. There's no certainty in life. Oliver shouted that was the single most *insane* statement he'd ever heard. Of course life is about chance and randomness, but here was an instance in which chance could be *controlled*. It would be reckless—it would be *criminal*, it would be *criminally insane*—not to do the amnio. Sophia said the test was pointless because even if the fetus tested positive she wouldn't abort. She accused Oliver of being too narcissistic to accept responsibility for a sick child. Here he lost control. *Narcissistic? Selfish?* Tay-Sachs is *not* like Down syndrome, he shouted. It is *not* a disease that permits a happy and fulfilled, if limited, life. It's a cruel disease that deforms its sufferers before killing them, commonly before they turn five. To force such suffering on a child, he yelled, is a crime, *a crime against humanity!*

He said that after this fight, she retreated into a haze of nicotine and alcohol abuse. He felt filthy, disgusted. An excellent demonstration of your fitness for motherhood, he said. Fitness! she shrieked. You arrogant loveless pig! *In that moment, I experienced a flash of panic—an instant of utter psychic chaos that only after the fact did I recognize was a prelude to the feeling of complete derangement that seized me in the moments after her death.* On the night of the accident, she still hadn't agreed to the amnio.

The story kept Melissa in tears but also aroused her anger. She could not understand how a mother could choose to expose a child to the possibility of a brief lifetime of continuous suffering. I don't believe Mel ever cared for Sophia, and like Oliver, saw her instability as a defect of character. She was appalled by Sophia's reckless disregard of common sense.

Like Mel, I felt for Oliver, but the story raised other questions in my mind. If Sophia had agreed to schedule the amnio in their first conversation, what led her to change her mind in the days she spent alone in New York before the flight to Iceland? Oliver said it was a week, by which he meant a relatively brief stretch, but that's not how it sounded to me. I pictured him in that week preparing Jean's toast, walking Ulysses in the Heath, poring over the newspapers, preparing dinner, and checking the clock to make sure that he and Jean wouldn't miss *Benny Hill*. Could this picture accommodate the possibility of great inward suffering, that in the privacy of his mind, he fretted over Sophia and the fetus? Of course. As I've said, Oliver was never less than exquisite in his suffering. Did he confide in Jean? My hunch was no. Their intimacy avoided the Large Topics by some long-standing mutual agreement, itself unavailable for discussion or correction. I imagined Sophia, in her tiny studio, waiting for Oliver to call each night with words of tender solicitude, words that she knew he could not offer without ceasing to be Oliver. So she biked to work, charmed BAM's benefactors, and packed on the morning of the flight. I could imagine how, during those days, a profound obstinacy could take root, an indifference to loveless reason. In the Octagon I had warned her. If only she'd heeded my words!

I also thought about the fatal car ride. Now I saw it quite differently. I could better understand the turn to cigarettes and alcohol, the desperate self-defeating weapons of protest. As for the final act of *reaching over* to close the door: prudence would have suggested braking, and Oliver was a prudent man. I could only understand his act as one of inestimable frustration, a gesture that in no way contemplated or willed the result, but that cried, *Enough!*

The next day the grief hit Oliver again in full, not like a wave breaking over him, but like a swift undertow, pulling him down after it seemed the danger had passed. He stayed indoors, refused food. In the evening, after the twins were asleep, we put on a video. Oliver said he didn't want to watch anything, but Melissa bluntly informed him that wallowing wasn't an option. She made popcorn, and we sat on the couch flanking him. In all the years of our friendship, it was the only time I ever really touched Oliver. I don't recall how his hand found mine, though I remember noticing that Mel had already taken hold of his left hand, holding it protectively between both of hers. So did I take his hand or did he take mine? Odd, the things memory can't retrieve. What remains, though, is the pressure of his curled fingers. His palm was broad but soft; it reminded me less of Melissa's, whose hands were narrow and earth-coarsened from work in the garden, than of one of our twins', for the moist, plump smoothness of it. When our hands finally parted, they were both sticky with sweat.

Next evening he told us about the Icelandic police. He said that a day after her death, he was visited at his B & B by a policeman. The police had already questioned him at length; this one came to report the results of the autopsy. "He asked me with such delicacy if I knew that

Sophia had been pregnant that it brought tears to my eyes. When I nodded he was so visibly relieved that I found myself inadvertently smiling. He seemed to find this strange and wrote something in a little notebook.

"He asked me many questions, but nothing about the drive to Gullfoss. When he learned that I'm a philosopher with published books, he excused himself, dashed out to his car, which was not a police car, but an unmarked white VW, and returned with a copy of a book *he* had written. It turned out that he was a best-selling author of Icelandic thrillers. His most recent book, he said, had sold ten thousand copies—this in a country of three hundred thousand. That would be the equivalent of selling ten million copies in the States, he crooned. He inscribed his book for me and said his dream was to have one of his thrillers translated and for it to become a best seller in the States, like *Smilla's Sense of Snow.* He spoke superb English. He'd spent his final year of high school in California, living with a state trooper's family—he said that's when he became interested in police work. Then he looked at me, smiled sympathetically, and said, 'You realize of course that you're the sole witness to the death of your pregnant girlfriend. That puts you in an odd position.'

"We were in the sitting room of the B & B. The furniture was covered with protective oilcloths as if to be mothballed. All at once I felt immensely fatigued and nauseated; I almost demanded to have a polygraph test on the spot, just to have the satisfaction of failing it. His eyes were incredibly deep set and close together, and he just stared at me with this intelligent, compassionate, skeptical expression. He looked so friendly and distrustful that I said, 'I might have destroyed her emotionally, but I did not kill her. Does that make sense?'

"'Absolutely,' he exclaimed. 'I understand your meaning perfectly.'

"I had the distinct feeling that the line would appear in one of his thrillers."

By the next morning, Oliver was again to be seen circling our house, staring at the flowers, resting in the Adirondack chair, jotting philosophical fragments in his journal. He expressed his first complaints about the weather, a hopeful sign. He played with the twins—not as Sophia had, not on the floor, rough-and-tumble, but in a seated, detached, jiggling-the-keys manner that was answered with smiles less of pleasure than of forbearance. He appeared grateful, settled, with an orphan's sense of found place. When I returned from Bread & Circus, I noticed he was wearing one of my linen shirts.

"I need to wash my clothes," he said. "Mel gave me this. It fits perfectly."

A Ping-Pong prodigy, and something of a tennis and soccer enthusiast, Oliver nevertheless claimed to lack even the most rudimentary knowledge of the rules of baseball, a claim I had to take more seriously when he called runs "points" and an inning a "chance." So after listlessly watching a few minutes of an August showdown between the Yankees and the Red Sox on TV, he wandered into the living room, where, in a reversal of roles from the summer before, Melissa read to him. The twins were asleep. I had the baby monitor and the Yankees a two-run lead. Melissa was reading from Thomas Bernhard's *Woodcutters*, obviously Oliver's choice. I felt good—not happy, but restored and cleansed by the days of sorrow. Grief had drawn us all closer, extended and strengthened our bonds. A pleasing mixture of sound washed over me: the background murmur of the stadium crowd in the Bronx, the chatter of the announcers, the seashore rhythms of the babies' breathing over the monitor, and the soothing sound of Melissa's nasal Midwestern rendition of the Austrian's relentlessly repetitive prose. I was half watching the game, half reading the *Times*, and that back-and-forth, the looping of ambient noise, the comforts of the sonic cushion, invited rest.

I awakened to the sharp sense of something amiss. It wasn't the game; the Yankees now led by five. Had one of the twins cried out? But what troubled me wasn't the excess but the absence of sound. Thomas Bernhard had fallen silent. "Mel?" I said, or maybe whispered. The living room was dark. It had to be crossed to reach the kitchen. My intention was to get a snack, not to prowl. If anything I thought they'd both gone to bed. It's true I padded my steps, but that's a habit of mine in a dark house, why, I don't know. When I saw him, my first thought was Oliver had hurt himself. He was lying on his side, stretched the length of the couch, facing the backrest. Then I saw Mel, seated on the far end, cradling his head in her lap, fingers tangled in his hair. Her head was flung back, lips parted as if to form a silent vowel. His face was buried in her breasts. The uncertainty had to do with her T-shirt, which might have been rolled up, and her bra, which might have been unfastened. When they noticed me, they disentangled but without startle. Their movements had a strange languor, as if slowed by the suspicion that I was a hallucination.

I continued on into the kitchen, where I struggled to pour myself a glass of iced tea. I circled the island following a directionless moth; perhaps the hallucination had been mine. I returned to the living room and switched on a light.

Melissa squinted, her hand held as a visor against the sudden glare. Oliver also squinted as he put on his glasses that lay folded on the coffee table. He stood up and faced me, his expression blank. I've mentioned that we were the same height, but now I considered the possibility that he was a tad taller. His face was flushed, but not with embarrassment.

"I think you should leave," I said.

"Now or tomorrow morning?" he asked tonelessly. "It's already late."

"I think now would be better."

He didn't argue. Nor did he offer a word of apology or excuse, not then, not ever. After he left, Melissa disappeared into the bathroom, and when I came to bed early the next morning, I found her weeping—whether it was for him, me, herself, our marriage, all of the above, I didn't know. Her long bangs were matted with tears and her simple white sleeveless nightgown had coin-sized spots where her breasts had leaked.

"I warned you about him," she wept. "From the very first, I warned you."

FOURTEEN

Several years passed from the morning Sophia was thrown from the car in Gullfoss until the night Oliver disappeared in the North Atlantic. How many exactly isn't important, though now as I work out the chronology I'm stunned by the realization that it must have been close to ten. For life in those years moved in a different register, from the vivid and keenly experienced to the broad and featureless; and time, in its funny way, played tricks of acceleration and contraction. I still remember the name of every student from my first year of teaching at Harkness, while those from the last term have already vanished into oblivion . . .

As for Oliver, he gradually reassembled a life that looked much like the one he'd led before Iceland. He went on to have a string of girlfriends, and if all these relationships proved transient, this was less a consequence of Sophia's death than a signal of the very problems that made her throw open the door of the rental car. Still, Oliver never got over her. The Dead Sophia came to exercise a power over him that she had never enjoyed while alive. Oliver was aware of the irony; he knew that had he been as committed to her in life as he was in death, she might still have been alive, a fact that compounded his sorrow, guilt, and self-loathing.

There were more immediate casualties of Sophia's accident. Oliver never apologized for what happened the night I asked him to leave, and I never asked him to. Grief deforms behavior, and I wasn't about to cut my closest friend out of my life for having sought temporary refuge in my wife's soft inviting breasts. But grief could go only so far in explaining Melissa's conduct. Naturally she felt pity for Oliver, and I could understand how pity, in close quarters, could make for tenderness and intimacy. But pity couldn't explain the expression of tense, escalating rapture on her face. It was an expression I knew well; I never expected or hoped to see it from across a room. Mel was not at her best when it came to apologies, and this time was no different, except that the stakes were higher, and so her inability to say sorry without a codicil or "but" was all the more hurtful. She subtly, or not so subtly, shifted responsibility, as I was the one who'd brought Oliver, a force of disturbance and disruption, into our placid lives. She inventoried a long pattern of transgressions: the *Beggars Banquet* party, when Oliver, the magician, had let his fingers rummage oddly for an AWOL knave in the back pocket of her jeans; the first Christmas at Francizka's, when Oliver had "accidentally" walked in on her in the bathroom; the time in Hampstead, when he volunteered to read to her while she bathed naked in a slurry of oatmeal; and the sundry other occasions when he had peered down her blouse and collided with her in hallways. Melissa's recitation was tendered as proof not against Oliver but against me. Because I'd tolerated such trespasses.

It was the first time I had heard of the incident at Christmas. Was I to be held responsible for actions I never knew occurred?

Melissa acknowledged that would be outlandish.

"So then what *are* you saying, Mel? That *I'm* to blame for *your* taking him in your arms?"

"I never said that."

"Okay, good. That's progress. Then let's try again."

"I said I was sorry."

"No, you didn't. Not really."

"I'm sorry. I'm sorry. What else do you want me to say?"

"Well," I said, my voice quivering with emotion that I hoped to keep in check, "are you in love with him?"

Mel looked at me with stupefaction. "In love with Oliver?" she cried. "Are you out of your mind? With that fucked-up little puppy? *You're* the one in love with him."

"What on earth is that supposed to mean?"

"It's true! You're obsessed with him. Him and his *extraordinariness*. You dress like him, you follow all his interests, you even wear the same cologne!"

"That's a peculiarly self-incriminating statement," I observed.

But Mel wasn't about to be derailed by rational argument. "You're more interested in him than you are in your wife and your children," she shouted.

"That's absurd."

"No, it's not. You're the son of an accountant from Long Island and you have this distorted fantasy of being the descendant of aristrocrats with castles in the Lake District and Transylvania. Oliver doesn't appeal to you because you're a novelist. You're a novelist so you can dream about wealth and titles and exclusive bloodlines. You don't want to write about him, you want to *be* him."

I patiently waited for her to finish before I again reminded her that *she* was the one who had cradled him to her breasts. What feelings, I asked, did her accusations against me screen?

"I'm not in love with him," she screamed. "I felt sorry for him. I got swept up, made a mistake. That's all. I could never fall for someone so totally fucked-up. You're the one who's convinced that he's some magic figure with a great secret. It's all your crazy fantasy!"

As I've said, Mel was a lover of words when organized in quatrains and couplets, when gathered to describe and evoke. She had little faith in the capacity of human beings to argue their way toward understanding, perhaps because she lacked the basic equipment to do so. She had little stomach for conflict, a brittleness I first detected on a street corner in Budapest when I asked her to explain why she hadn't told me about Oliver's sexless relationship with Jean. Silence and withdrawal were her preferred means of dealing with marital discord, as if time healed all and didn't simply provide a breeding ground for more powerful resentments. She insisted my zeal for argument was a vestige of my legal education, a claim that I would have been happy to dispute if doing so hadn't seemed so transparently self-defeating. In a futile attempt to engage Mel in meta-argument, I defended the sapper theory of words: if sensitively chosen, they can defuse conflicts before they turn explosive. She voiced no disagreement; in fact she said nothing at all, a more intractable form of dissent. I became furious, but only because I was terrified. If a couple can't talk about how they might talk about their problems, then everything is lost. My shouting and prognostications of marital doom, drastic rhetoric meant to vex a reaction from her, only brought a desperate look to her eyes. She retreated into silence and from the room.

Apologies were never Oliver's strong suit either, but to his credit, from that night forward his dealings with Melissa were rigorously proper. He didn't sever communication; he simply ducked occasions that would have left the two of them alone. The three of us went back to having meals together; Christmas at Francizka's became a family tradition; but games and flirtations were a thing of the past. Mel accepted the change, though not, I believe, without regret. Just as she reproached me for ushering Oliver into her life, she seemed to hold me responsible for his guardedness toward her—as if I'd made it a condition of our continued friendship, when, in fact, Oliver did it all on his own. I told her this plainly, with a minimum of schadenfreude; her response was to insist that she *preferred* the new arrangement. When I challenged her on this, she threw up her hands and called me insane. She obviously felt more deeply for Oliver than she was ever prepared to admit to herself.

I wish I could say that our marriage quickly extricated itself from this bad patch. But time passed, and soon the bad patch was the marriage itself. I don't blame Oliver. To borrow the terms from *Paradoxes of Self*, he was the *occasion*, not the cause of our troubles. We were both working, had ever more energetic twins to take care of, so it was easy to sweep the unhappiness behind the daily clutter of activities. We told ourselves that the pressures of work and parenting contributed to our problems, when, in fact, they hid them and made them manageable. And I admit that Melissa's first, minor breach of the norms of marital fidelity became a precedent in my mind for reciprocal acts—not that I was interested in retaliation or in evening the scales. But Mel had strayed over a line that, in my mind, had been fixed and inviolate, and which once crossed, no longer defined stable or familiar ground. Or maybe that's not it at all. Maybe we simply discovered, with all the deflating surprise of an unhappy find, that we were not as compatible as we once believed. Maybe ties forged before children proved themselves less durable under the stress of twins. In any case, for several years we battered our marriage only to limp back, like survivors of a hurricane, to assess the damage and see what could be salvaged—until we decided, one fine summer day after my return from North Portugal, to move on.

He gave the money away. Not all at once, but within a year or so of Sophia's death, the millions that he had "inherited" from his stepfather were gone. His first beneficiary was his chess adversary, Sam, the purblind bookseller. Sam's eyesight had steadily deteriorated as the retinopathy advanced, yet he continued to drive himself to work, even after an accident left him with a revoked license. He couldn't afford the costs of a taxi every day; friends and neighbors tried to arrange a carpool, but there were the inevitable breakdowns. Working with a local bank, Oliver set up a yearly annuity to cover the costs of a driver. He also paid for an assistant to help Sam inventory the books whose titles he could now barely read.

He gave to Chess-For-Youth, a program that brought after-school chess instruction to kids in inner-city schools, and to the Best Friends Animal Society, a charitable organization that provided shelter and searched for homes for abandoned pets. He gave to Human Rights Watch and Refugees International and to the National Tay-Sachs and Allied Diseases Association. He bought a sculpture from Max that he donated to Harkness's modest art museum. He established a private trust to help support scholars displaced by war or political repression. When I jokingly asked him whether creative writers in domestic war zones were covered, he shook his head and added a quiet no.

Oliver's philanthropic plans won him widespread but not universal admiration. This, a letter from Francizka:

I plead with you to talk sense to him. I understand his loss. Believe me, I learned when I was still a child what it means to lose loved ones. But he must think of the future. He is still young, my father was fifty when he married. Doesn't he think of having children of his own? Should they not be provided for? And what of his brother? Thank goodness Mew has recovered his spirits from when you saw him last. He has steady work that doesn't insult his intelligence, and he has met a lovely girl at his church. I am not

one for faith but was taught from my earliest years
that charity begins at home. I fear Ollie has a head
only for abstractions. You know I have read every
sentence that he has published, and although much
of it goes straight over my head, there is one line that
I will never forget even if I live to 120! "My moral
obligation to my brother is no stronger than my ob-
ligation to a stranger halfway around the globe." It
shocked me then and shocks me now. Do you know
that after I escaped Hungary and came to Paris, I
briefly studied philosophy? Well, it's true! I took a
wonderful course at the Sorbonne where we read
Descartes and Montaigne and other captivating writ-
ers. I don't remember them expressing such nonsense.

Perhaps I am to blame. Maybe I made life too
easy for my sons. Having suffered what I did, having
watched a whole world turn to dust, my only con-
cern was to protect them and to provide for them.
Maybe I have given them too much security. I fear
Ollie will come to regret terribly what he has done.
So I implore you—reason with him.

Please send my love to your special boys and your
lovely wife.

Most fondly,
Francizka

I never honored Francizka's request. It seemed pointless. The Kantian Oliver, the Oliver of moral choice,
never equivocated once he'd made up his mind. I suppose that is why he aspired, in the last years of his life,
to simplify and loosen his attachments, to live according

to the maxim that outraged his mother. He was drawn to the austere beauty of morality, the luxury it affords of dealing with others at arm's length. Romance offered him no such recuperative space. Romance was about proximity. And in his journal I had once come across the words *Proximity disables.*

Forgoing the inheritance brought a change to his material circumstances, but this downsizing of life appeared to agree with him, as if Sophia's death had made him less deserving of a robust stake in the world. He continued to wear neatly pressed shirts with French cuffs, though no longer from the Jermyn Street haberdasheries he had once favored. He sold his loft and moved into a modest apartment. There he hung his collection of Pascins, all of which turned out to be fakes. He discovered that his mother's four Pascins also bore the bogus atelier stamp, though he couldn't bring himself to tell her—not, he said, because he wanted to protect her, but because he wasn't psychically equipped to deal with her anticipated volley of strident counterclaims: that Oliver had to be mistaken, that the greatest art experts in the world had personally authenticated her priceless collection, that he was at war with all forms of wealth now that he had chosen to live like a pauper.

The experience with the Pascins sparked his philosophic interest. He read widely in aesthetic theory, and began work on a book about authenticity, imitation, and forgery. Having donated an authentic Max to the Harkness art museum, he now approached the museum's director to explore the possibility of mounting a show on "The Authentic and the Fraudulent" that would include his Pascins. The exhibition came to naught, but Oliver did have a two-year affair with the museum's beautiful, Korean-born curator.

She was but one in a long list of love interests. Six months after I asked Oliver to leave our house, I ran into him entering a cafe in the nearby town of Munster. It was a day of wintry sunshine, and he was in the company of a tall woman in a white shearling coat and matching white earmuffs clamped over tiers of shiny blond hair. She was laughing brightly, arm looped in Oliver's.

I'd seen Oliver redden before, but never this brightly. The romance, following close on the heels of Sophia's death, was obviously a source of embarrassment. But more than that, I think we both realized what this chance encounter said about our friendship. In the past, he had always solicited my romantic advice. This time I'd been kept on the outs, not because he feared my judgment, but because he appeared no longer to need or want it. During the ten or so minutes that we chatted on the street, Oliver stamped his feet more than the cold mandated and the woman laughed a great deal. The woman was extremely attractive and I found her accent, lilting and Scandinavian, pleasingly melodic. Only after they ducked into the cafe did it strike me that we'd met before. This was Strindberg's great-granddaughter, the woman in the chartreuse party dress who'd emerged victorious in a staring contest in a dark vault in London.

I met her twice more. The second time she laughed not so much; the third, not at all. Their relationship lasted maybe a year and a half.

Next followed the Korean-born curator, though the verb doesn't do justice to the complex chronologies of Oliver's relationships. Typically his lovers would briefly overlap, like runners sharing a baton in a relay race. When I began work on this book, under the terms later stipulated by Francizka, I sent a query to Oliver's fellow fellows from his years at Oxford, and got this response, hardly atypical: *Of course I remember him. We used to get stoned together and play chess. My wife dated him for a time. (At the time, she wasn't my wife.) He had bad habits with the ladies—his reputation was really quite notorious. I always admired his work, though he never really did much after* Paradoxes, *did he?* So Mary Gwon didn't follow Anna Strindberg as much as run with her until the latter flagged and dropped from sight.

Like all aspects of his life, Oliver's post-Sophia entanglements followed fixed forms. He would tell New Romantic Interest that he wasn't yet prepared for a relationship, as he was presently stuck in one that first had to be cleanly ended, something he couldn't bring himself to do, allegedly out of concern for Incumbent Romantic Interest. This scenario repeated itself over and over. On the surface his lovers shared little in common—some were beautiful, others plain; some were charismatic, others guarded; some were wickedly verbal, others reserved. But they all accepted—no, embraced—the role his pathology scripted for them. Maybe they were helplessly drawn to the romance of the "widower" who had witnessed, and possibly precipitated, the death of his pregnant lover. Maybe they were damaged goods themselves. But they all subscribed to the belief that his love life remained chaotic thanks to a trauma, which, over time and with the proper nurturing, could be mastered and laid to rest. Little did they realize that Sophia's death, far from the ur-catastrophe, was merely the most visible sign of a deeper derangement.

Over the course of months, as he vainly searched for the certitude and will to end things with Incumbent Romantic Interest, New Romantic Interest would grow impatient, make demands of her own; and invariably Oliver would find himself hurting Incumbent in precisely the manner that he had most wanted to avoid, ousting her for New—although technically speaking, it was always Incumbent who finally pulled the plug, as Oliver found it impossible to break up and instead would make circumstances so intolerable as to guarantee being broken up with. The shoddiness of the ouster, though, would leave Oliver resentful toward New—as if her desires rather than his incapacities were to blame for his mistreatment of Incumbent—and so set in motion the process of her own inevitable removal.

For a time the former Incumbent would vanish from Oliver's life, only then to reappear, assuming the mantle of Ex. This process of reintegration was smoothed by Oliver's loyalty, a quality not to be confused with fidelity. In fact, it was only after the breakup, after Incumbent turned Ex, that she came to enjoy the full benefits of Oliver's solicitousness. He never forgot a birthday or a special occasion. If a new book appeared on, say, the history of Swedish drama, you could bet that a package had already arrived at Ms. Strindberg's doorstep. These displays of loyalty and flourishes of thoughtfulness gradually convinced Ex not to take her removal from the center of Oliver's romantic life personally—in fact, to feel *lucky* for having been released from the withering exposure to Oliver's pathologies, which he would continue to avow and describe in despondent e-mails. Ex would then emerge as a trusted confidante, offering advice designed less to solve his romantic problems than to help him deal with the despair that gripped him when he apprehended the impossibility of a solution. It was a bit like watching the political workings of some small, vaguely corrupt, but insufficiently ruthless monarchy, in which advisers would be endlessly promoted and purged, but in which no one ever quite disappeared from the political scene.

And, of course, there was still Jean. Even after the closing of the Vice account, Oliver and Jean still met every winter in Zurich and every summer in London. Acceptance or at least forbearance of the *arrangement* served as something of a litmus test for all of Oliver's romances.

As far as I know, Mary Gwon was the only one to launch a meaningful challenge to Jean. What made her resistance powerful was its gradual escalation. At first, like her predecessors, Gwon raised no voice of protest. Far be it from her to come between him and a long-standing friendship. Gwon had grown up in Seoul, had studied in England, and had done her graduate work at the Courtauld Institute in London, writing a dissertation on Lucian Freud. She became the director of Harkness's museum and Oliver's lover at the ripe age of twenty-five; Oliver was by then nearly a decade older. She was small, exquisitely proportioned, and spoke in a formal, self-protective manner. Her eyes, which, Oliver never failed to point out, were, in contrast to most Asians, *fully lidded*, expressed fierce will and determination. Six months after supplanting Ms. Strindberg, Gwon set her sights on Jean. Her campaign began with quiet complaints, ramped its way up to forceful expressions of displeasure, and, as England loomed, ballooned into an ultimatum. Oliver appeared to be truly in love with Gwon; he said he had never before felt so intellectually stimulated and erotically enthralled by the same woman. For her part, Gwon believed that the *arrangement*, even if nonsexual, had to be brought to an end.

I never got to know Gwon well. We had little contact outside of a handful of phone calls, when she appealed to me for advice. The calls always began with apologies. "I'm sorry to trouble you—I know you're Oliver's closest friend and I'm worried about him. I'm thinking seriously of leaving him, but I don't want to hurt him, especially in light of what he's been through. He's about to go to Britain, and I was wondering if you could tell me what you thought about these visits."

"I'm not sure what you want to know . . ."

She was crying. She cried through all our phone conversations. But even then she never lost her formality or sense of high purpose. "Don't you think it's . . . *wrong?*"

"I think I'm beyond judging Oliver."

Gwon sniffled and her voice turned hard. "But those trips—they fall on *my* weeks off. Don't you think Oliver should be traveling with me, not visiting his old girlfriend?"

"You could always go along . . ." Why did I say this? Not to be cruel. Maybe I was thinking of the words of Spinoza that Oliver liked to quote, *Persons persist in being themselves.*

"That's ridiculous!" She was arguing with me as she would with Oliver. Clearly I wasn't the ally she'd hoped for.

Notwithstanding Gwon's ultimatum, Oliver left for London. There he sent me a short letter. *You remember, of course, Ulysses, Jean's dog. As we were returning from his walk the other night, he bolted from his lead and dashed into the street, where he was struck by a car. We saw the whole thing. He lay on his side paralyzed; only his eyes could move, and they looked at us as if to apologize for his carelessness. The driver was very sorry and drove us to an animal hospital where we held Ulysses as he was put down. He was in no pain. Jean has taken this particularly hard. I'm sure she would appreciate a note of condolence from you.*

After another year of tears, harangues, and breakups threatened and rescinded, Gwon ended things for good. She met a painter in New York; they married three months later.

Next came Caroline Dworkin, though, again, "next" might be something of an exaggeration. Dworkin worked in a local bookstore; she and Oliver became friendly discussing his special orders: monographs on Hume and Wittgenstein, pamphlets on retroanalysis in chess, and the latest political tracts by Chomsky. Dworkin was younger than Gwon; if something less than a decade had separated Oliver and Mary, nearly fifteen years divided him from Dworkin. She'd graduated from Harkness only the year before. She hadn't been Oliver's student, but that didn't stop people from talking. I never got to know Dworkin any better than Gwon. She had oily skin, large eyes seeking direction, and spoke nostalgically about high school. A year later, when she turned to me for counsel about her deteriorating relationship with Oliver, my advice was lapidary.

"Get out now."

"Why?"

"Oliver's the why. Just get out. You're in *way* over your head."

I had said much the same to Sophia, but in Dworkin's case I felt no impulse to imprint my advice on her lips. I was fatigued by Oliver's love life, by its inexorable repetitions. I didn't expect Dworkin to listen and she didn't. She was twenty-three, infatuated, and the object of the affections of a prominent professor. She hung on for two more punishing years before being replaced by a more recent Harkness graduate who *was* Oliver's former student.

All the while, he remained haunted by the loss of Sophia. In death, Sophia attained the perfection of myth. That is why, he came to believe, he'd had to destroy her. She had posed too great a threat to the elaborate ramparts and fortifications erected around his infirm life. In e-mails, Oliver would conjure, grieve, and speculate:

> I woke up in the middle of the night, having dreamt
> about her, only it was more like a visitation, as if
> she had just gotten out of our bed, her warmth and
> contours still in the comforter. As I waited for her to

return, I happily fell back asleep. I awakened several hours later, sick to my stomach. The feeling from the dream was gone. I kept expecting a random object, a teakettle, a balled sock, a bottle of perfume in a store window, to bring the feeling back, but nothing. I've never felt so cheated. It's as if I'd lost her a second time.

And this:

Have I ever told you that she was a wonderful nurse? Shortly after we met, I came down with the flu. My temperature spiked to 104 & I became delirious, saw spiders in corners. She placed a cold compress on my forehead & sat in a chair next to my bed; I must have woken up a dozen times in the middle of the night & every time, she was still sitting there, smiling, warding off the spiders. The next morning I asked when she'd slept. "Slept? I had to make sure my little beast didn't stop breathing."

And:

Sometimes I wonder if the baby would have been born healthy. At the time I could only fixate on the 25% chance of disease. Now I'll never know. It comforts me that they're buried together.

And:

God I miss her.

• • •

I had arrived at Harkness with a three-year contract. At the time, that sounded like a short eternity. There seemed little need to plan for the future: my next book would be out, some other opportunity would come our way, and we'd leave the gentle hills and townships of western Massachusetts for someplace else. But three years passed and though I'd published a couple of stories and essays, I'd jettisoned the novel about incest in Great Neck. When Harkness offered to extend my contract, I gratefully accepted. I liked my department, and the department liked me. I taught satisfactory workshops in fiction and "creative nonfiction," and had introduced a popular course called Misreadings, which studied novels about characters who fail to make sense of the signals and codes that control the world they inhabit; and another called Unreliable Narrators, the original idea coming from something Oliver had said about Nabokov's *The Real Life of Sebastian Knight*: "Certainly the main character might be no more than an invention of the narrator. But imagine a book that does the reverse, in which the narrator turns out to be the invention of the main character. The only way the character can tell his story is through an act of radical alienation, projecting his life onto an imaginary storyteller who then, in a sense, becomes the vanished character. Now *that* would be truly remarkable." Oliver struggled to name a novel that fit this obscure and remarkable vision, but I found more than enough treacherous narrators to attract the college's theory heads. Somewhat to my surprise, I liked teaching, and was generally happy with my students. A fellow writer once warned, "Watch out, or you'll end up a lifer," and I remember thinking, "I certainly *hope* so." When my second contract was due to expire, I was offered a "senior lectureship." Although not a tenured position, this offered basic job security. By then, Mel had moved from the classroom to the administration of the Inverness Academy, where she was an associate dean and where the boys would be able one day to attend tuition-free. We had our sinecures.

Oliver during this period went into premature eclipse. Formerly the young star of the Harkness faculty, he faded from prominence, largely by choice. By the standards of a small liberal arts college, even a first-tier one, he still boasted an impressive record. His book on free will, written during his Oxford days, came out in a second edition, and *Paradoxes of Self* remained widely cited, admired, and even read. But as the years passed and no further works appeared, *Paradoxes of Self* no longer marked the rapid ascent of an original thinker to the elite in his field, but instead came to signal the apogee of a philosophical talent that peaked prematurely and then slipped from the scene. After Oliver's disappearance, I learned that some philosophers were under the impression that he'd been researching a book about miracles and magic—they called it *Hume and Houdini*—but no drafts had ever been circulated and no conference papers presented. As far as I knew, he'd been at work on the book about authenticity and fraudulence, but here again no articles ever appeared, and I never was able to discover any drafts. He continued to write the occasional book review and commentary, but whereas these once supplemented his philosophical output, they now represented the full extent of his publishing.

His reputation in the classroom also suffered. In his early years, particularly after his confrontation with Clinton, Oliver had enjoyed a cultlike status among students. His aloof lecture style, his dry wit, his thick hair and pressed English shirts attracted a coterie of fiercely devoted students who located in Oliver the very embodiment of intellectual commitment and chic. He was a campus celebrity; and his courses, events. Over time though, the buzz faded, enrollments fell, and students clamored after newer, younger hires. In an age of grade inflation, he gave out more than a symbolic sprinkling of C's, refused to accept late papers, and downgraded in draconian fashion for errors of spelling and syntax. On RateMyProfessor.com he was called a *stickler*, a *curmudgeon*, and an *uncaring professor*.

Granted, in a handful of chat rooms and blogs sustained by the college's hard-core philosophy geeks, Oliver remained popular, or rather, became the stuff of persistent rumor. Following these cybertrails, I learned that he'd been implicated in the death of a Finnish girlfriend; had dated Derrida's daughter; had written *Paradoxes of Self* in a psychiatric hospital; had called Tony Blair a war criminal to his face; and had inherited a vast fortune but, in the tradition of Diogenes and Wittgenstein, had given it all away.

Among this small dedicated group, the myth of Oliver continued to grow and flourish, reaching its grandest proportions after his death, thanks in large part to his last CIA vigil and his "resignation" from the college. I've mentioned that every year Oliver would mount a one-man protest against the CIA's practice of recruiting at Harkness. His first protest was staged barely two months after his arrival on campus, and every October since, on the day of the agency's interviews, Oliver could be seen outside the college's white clapboard career center holding a neatly hand-printed placard: THE CIA TORTURES. What was most remarkable about this private act of conscience was how little reaction it stirred. If not ignored entirely, it was dismissed as a quaint rehashing of the controversies of a bygone era, when Henry Kissinger made sure that fledgling South American democracies didn't elect foes of free enterprise.

In 2001, the CIA arrived on campus a month to the day after 9/11. Brilliant sunshine flooded the campus as on the morning of the attacks, and a line of patriotic students queued before the career center. Oliver was there to greet them. He uttered no chants, blocked nobody's way; he simply stood in silent admonition with his hand-printed words. Few students recognized him, and most contented themselves with hostile stares. One student, though, a cocaptain of the hockey team, stepped out of the line and bumped Oliver squarely with his shoulder, knocking him flat on his back. "Hey, dude," the student said, standing over the dazed protester. "You gotta watch where you're going." The hockey player didn't offer him a hand up, nor did anyone else. Oliver brushed himself off, picked up his sign, and resumed his silent vigil. Later, an egg hurled from the Quad narrowly missed him, splattering the sidewalk and his shoes.

In the wake of this episode, a small group of students and faculty objected to the college's failure to reprimand the hockey player (the act was grounds for expulsion, but the college said it couldn't prove it wasn't an accident) or to identify the egg thrower. But given the general mood of the moment, sentiment ran against Oliver. Harkness's president, who hadn't forgotten Oliver's encounter with Clinton, a major headache in his first year at the college's helm, issued a terse statement: *While the College seeks to protect the expression of unpopular views, it is also important for speakers, particularly within a collegiate setting, to respect and remain mindful of the sensitivities and values of their audience.*

The CIA incident received little press coverage compared to the Clinton episode, but it circulated on the Web, ricocheting through cyberspace along unpredictable pathways. One day, out of the blue, Oliver received an invitation to participate in an international conference on "The United States and Global Terror: Who's the Real Sponsor?"—to be held in Teheran. Never one to be displeased by irony, Oliver posted the invitation on his office door. No sooner had the college newspaper run a short piece about Professor Vice's apparent popularity among the ruling clerics in Iran, than the administration found itself inundated with letters from angry alums wondering why the college insisted on tenuring sworn enemies of America. As the controversy intensified, Oliver did what no one expected: he tendered his resignation. Or rather, he met privately with the president and expressed his intention to resign. He said his decision had nothing to do with the CIA incident. After a decade he'd simply grown tired of teaching at the collegiate level and now wanted to try something different. He said he'd become interested in the pedagogic theories of Rudolph Steiner, and had decided to teach at a local Waldorf school.

The plan left me stunned. Melancholic, judgmental, increasingly withdrawn, Oliver hardly seemed temperamentally suited to being in a classroom with young children. And I'd never heard him so much as mention Steiner. How Steiner's teaching, which, among other things, posited the existence of astral bodies and *hitherto undiscovered whole numbers*, could appeal to Oliver's skeptical mind was beyond me. Oliver acknowledged that he found much of Steiner *problematic*, but not the pedagogy, which he said was progressive—this despite the fact that Steiner himself insisted that his pedagogy was entirely derived from his philosophy and unintelligible without it. Maybe Oliver was inspired by the example of Wittgenstein, who, tired of the contrivances of Cambridge, went off to teach in a boys' grammar school in the foothills of the Austrian Alps. Oliver might have recalled that Wittgenstein's experiment ended prematurely with his suspension for thrashing his pupils.

In any case, his plan put the administration in a bind. No doubt the president relished the prospect of having Oliver out of his thinning hair. Still, Oliver was one of Harkness's few professors with an international reputation, and his departure would be bad publicity, particularly if, notwithstanding his own disclaimers, it appeared the result of political pressure. So the president found himself in the odd position of trying to talk Oliver out of his decision. For his part, Oliver remained quietly adamant, until he learned that the Waldorf system required a two-year certification that could only be completed in a handful of pedagogical centers, mostly in Germany. So Oliver agreed to withdraw a resignation that had never been tendered in the first place, and the president agreed to let him extend his next leave for a second year to complete the Waldorf training—assuming it still held his interest.

Oliver boarded the *QM2* before that sabbatical, so the whole issue became moot. After his disappearance, he was remembered for his dedication to Harkness, not his desire to leave. The president emerged as his strongest defender. This was after Abu Ghraib and just as headlines became cluttered with stories of extraordinary rendition, enhanced interrogation, and Black Site prisons. To memorialize one of its own, the college held a service in venerable Marsh Chapel, a colonial structure of red brick planted on a hilly rise where minutemen had once squared off against red-coats. Surrounded by heavily varnished portraits of two centuries of lantern-jawed predecessors, Harkness's president lauded Oliver as "a true patriot":

> *In the best traditions of Harkness men and women, Vice was a scholar and moral beacon of prescience and courage. Like the great philosophers over the ages, he was a gadfly, not afraid to talk truth to power. His quiet solitary voice called us back to our better selves at a moment when our leaders invited fear and zealotry to command the day. And today we honor with pride the memory of a scholar and teacher who taught us all how the life of the mind must test its mettle in the crucible of worldly commitment.*

. . .

Oliver's last months stand out in another respect. He trawled in his past.

He'd never shown any interest in such explorations, and I'm still not clear what spurred the change. Maybe the inspiration came from his friend Max, who mounted a powerful show at Gagosian about his origins. Oliver had once told me that Max, an adoptee, had never shown any interest in the circumstances of his birth. This was only partially true. I learned that Max had been shuttled from one foster home to another before being adopted at the relatively advanced age of five. As the result of those early dislocations, he'd long harbored the belief—though "belief" might be too strong a word—that he came from outer space and had been deposited by extraterrestrials on earth for safekeeping. One day he would be picked up and returned to the galaxy where he'd been born. These thoughts had begun to preoccupy Max's work, the dimensions of which had shifted from the minuscule to the gigantic: space as conceived by astrophysicists and cosmologists. Staggeringly large canvases of supernovas and spaceships figured prominently. After installing a sculpture of a flying saucer, fifty feet across and made of concentric rings of colored steel and high-density plastic resin, over a cornfield in Iowa, Max received a call from a physicist at Grinnell College, who claimed, or at least strongly suspected, that he was Max's birth father. The story was easy enough to confirm and Max arranged to meet the Grinnell professor. The story behind the adoption was not unusual—too young, too poor, hardest decision ever—and the mother had died long ago. Uncannily, Max and the physicist shared mannerisms, patterns of speech, and a specific interest in the science fiction of Harlan Ellison. For the Gagosian show, they collaborated in the creation of a set of humongous photographs of father and son pixilated into abstraction, as if a wonderful cataclysm had transformed them into points of light in a brilliant night sky.

Oliver's search was modest by comparison. He didn't search for the living, only for the dead. Even this proved impossible in the case of his mother's family. A genealogical researcher in Budapest confirmed what we'd told him long ago—that Dr. Sándor Nagy of Andrássy út 101 had lived to a ripe old age without ever fathering a daughter named Francizka. There the genealogical trail went cold. It might seem odd that he never directly asked his mother, but that is to betray a misunderstanding of how communication worked in that family. Relations between them remained strained after his summons to Credit Suisse, but even that misses the point. Even their fights confirmed Francizka's power over her son. Oliver was prepared to reject his mother but not to cross her. So he turned his attentions to Victor Vice.

What he hoped to find wasn't clear. In the last years of his life, Melissa and I rarely discussed Oliver; in fact, we rarely spoke about much of anything, but once, out of the blue, Mel said, "He's Jewish, isn't he?" The same thought had often crossed my mind. Oliver was right, not all Tay-Sachs carriers are Jewish—two other demographics make up about 5 percent of carriers: French Canadians living near the Saint Lawrence River and Cajuns in Louisiana.

Since Oliver had never spoken of a secret French or Cajun connection, it seemed more likely that the family had Jewish blood. Presumably it came from Francizka's side—it was hard to imagine the fifteenth-century British lords who founded the House of Vice belonging to a secret rabbinic cult. In any case, the likelihood of Jewish ancestry only added a layer of rich irony to my theory of the family: the collaborators and art thieves had themselves once included Jews in their ranks.

Oliver had not embarked on a religious quest, but rather on a "fact-finding" mission, a phrase I heard not from him but from Francizka after his disappearance. I'd told her about my writing project, and though she expressed skepticism, she didn't fight me. "I am beyond that," she said. "Every time I fought Oliver, it just made him harder. He was so hard at the end. He became so much like Victor, his father." I listened patiently as she looped through the familiar litany of remorse. "He never got over the loss of that poor girl. From the instant that we were introduced, I knew that girl would bring no good. I tried to warn Ollie, but that only turned him against me. I hope, my dear, that you learn from my mistakes. Your boys are still so preciously young. The worst thing about being a parent is seeing your child set off on a path of ruin and not being able to do a thing about it, not a thing. Because they will only resent you for knowing better. Jacob had four sons—do you think he meant to choose who was more deserving? He was a generous man, not a Lear! Yet Ollie carried on so. Do you know what he said—he said the money was *tainted*. Have you ever heard of such a thing? As if money could be *clean*? My dear, I've lived a long time. Ollie could be so terribly naive. My childhood made me grow up fast, too fast—I wish that on no one."

Francizka lit a cigarette with a steady boney hand. She tossed the still burning match into an ashtray from the Hassler Rome. We were sitting in the dining room of her apartment; I was sipping tea and nibbling on tangerines piled in a hand-painted Italian bowl. The striking sixty-year-old who had served me my first true Christmas dinner was now two years past seventy. Thin when we first met, she had grown over the years thinner still. She wore a plain knit turtleneck over a woolen skirt that ended at her knees. The shapely legs that I had once eyed with desire now looked like those of a marsh bird; tan stockings hung like loose skin. She fingered the pair of Phi Beta Kappa keys that dangled from a gold chain around her neck. Crimson lipstick bled into the fissures around her mouth. Through an open window, she blew smoke into the building's airshaft. It was a spring day of windless, steady rain that pattered on a tarp below.

I remained silent, but all at once she volunteered, "We met in London. A car brought us to the Cunard dock in Southampton. Ollie had arrived some days earlier to attend Jean's wedding. That, too, was a blow."

Oliver had told me that Jean had met a man in a speed-dating event staged in the lobby of an Edwardian hotel in Bloomsbury. The pair was involved for six months before deciding to wed. The fiancé worked as a curator at the Courtauld, and, in one of those strange coincidences that is often mistaken for irony, was a former instructor of Mary Gwon, the Harkness museum director who tumultuously broke off her relationship with Oliver because of his with Jean. Oliver said that he was very happy for Jean, which I'm certain was true. But happiness *for* someone isn't the same as happiness. Oliver had come to think of the *arrangement* as a fixed point, both shoal and beacon, around which his romantic life had to steer. Just as he'd declared himself off limits to any woman if it meant sacrificing Jean, he'd likewise assumed that Jean would prefer a sexless intimacy with him to a full relationship with anyone else. Now he learned that this assumption had been false. I suspect he felt betrayed—not by Jean, but by his own failure accurately to measure what he meant to her. Maybe all along he had sensed the weakness of his guiding axiom, only to ignore questioning it too closely lest he realize it was all pretext—an excuse designed less to protect Jean than himself from the exactions of love.

I mentioned to Francizka that Oliver had written me a letter (the remarkable one in which he attacked the idea of poetic justice) from northern Portugal a week or so before boarding the *QM*2. "He once told me that's where his father lived at the end of his life. I assume he was visiting Victor Vice's second wife . . ."

"During the cruise we spoke very little," Francizka continued. "He was still angry about . . . *everything*. You know, he would not let me pay his way? And this sudden desire to meet Victor's second wife, why? She is not family. A stranger!"

"Oliver once told me that she waited a decade before telling you about your first husband's death."

"I don't recall the specifics. Suffice to say, it was an unconscionable delay. But what does it matter? Let sleeping dogs lie, is what I say. What good can possibly come from dredging up ancient history? What did Ollie hope to learn? That his father was a glamorous art dealer with little stomach for the responsibilities of family life? He knew that already. I'm afraid I never had great success with men, maybe because I had *too* much success, if you understand me. So why the sudden interest? If a man doesn't know who he is by the age of forty, he is lost anyway."

Francizka crushed the butt of her cigarette into a porcelain ashtray. She stared at me hard, her eyes dark and lusterless. Her lower lip betrayed a tremor, though not as a prelude to tears. I realized that Oliver's death had not simply devastated this formidable woman; it had left her furious. "And now you want to do what—follow Ollie's steps? Continue the search for the Holy Grail? By all means, be my guest."

She tamped a fresh cigarette on the dining room table, tucked it, unlit, between her painted lips, and then, all at once, retrieved a pad from the kitchen counter and scribbled down a name. "Here, the address, too." In the next moment she was seized with a fit of coughing, a hoarse dry bark that brought tears to her eyes and left her wiping her mouth on a monogrammed handkerchief that she pulled from the sleeve of her turtleneck.

"I am through," she said, her voice cluttered with phlegm. "I'll tell you honestly. Life has taken advantage of me. I wish you better luck, my friend. May your lovely boys bring you nothing but happiness. The pain of losing a child—it is unimaginable. And you know what? They have the *gall* to blame the mother. I have seen the looks on the faces of some of my so-called friends. Even Bernie. On top of it all, on top of *all* I must bear, I am also made to feel like a villain."

I reached across the table and took her hand. Her long fingers folded into mine and held tight. "Write what you will, my dear friend. But please—do not publish until after I am gone."

"Pooh, pooh, pooh," I said, a gesture of warding off the evil eye I'd learned from my mother. But I gave her my word.

We continued to hold hands. Afternoon had settled on the apartment like a mist. A truck rumbling in the street tacky with rain set the dining room chandelier atremble. An occasional horn blared. Around us hung the "Pascins" peddled by the man who abandoned his orphaned wife and sons, one now dead, the other on his knees in a pew at St. Agnes Church, responsively intoning a Lenten service in Latin. Francizka said what I'd often heard her say before, that she was grateful Bartholomew enjoyed the comforts of faith; she and Oliver had never managed the byways to belief.

"I haven't cried or prayed in decades." Her voice dropped to a whisper and her dark Hungarian eyes opened and drew me in. Her lips curled down, not in a frown but in a weary ironic confiding smile. "I must be honest. Sometimes when I hear a friend or even Mew pray to God, I want to laugh out loud. Or spit."

FIFTEEN

"Oh my God, you look just like Oliver!"

It had been years since I'd heard this implausible claim, and I suppose it was a response to my dark jeans and tailored shirt, by now thoroughly rumpled from a day of travel. Penelope Stiller reached for my suitcase and ushered me into Casa do Mar. I'd arrived at the Stillers' doorstep after a thunderstorm-delayed overnight flight from Logan to Lisbon, a stomach-churning jumper to Oporto, and a harrowing, high-speed, death-courting, vertebrae-crunching taxi ride along narrow ill-paved country roads to the tiny town of Afife. I followed Penelope up a staircase and into the guest room, where a set of yellow towels had been laid out for me on a bed with a simple wicker headboard.

"Would you like a small bite or maybe a short rest first?" She was a Brit, like her deceased first husband, her English pleasingly homey.

Maybe because questions about the purpose and goals of the trip had begun to assail me, I opted for rest. Fully dressed, I stretched myself on the bed and did not awake until Penelope knocked gently on the door and asked whether I would like some dinner.

Unshaven and unshowered, discombobulated by not enough and then too much sleep, I followed her down the stairs and into the dining room. Working a corkscrew into a bottle of red was her husband, Horst. He proffered a tentative handshake. We sat down to a dinner of hard peppercorn salami, sour gherkins, pickled onions, fresh Portuguese rolls, and kippered sardines that Penelope and Horst ate in their entirety, head, tail, and all. Conversation failed to materialize. I blamed my discursive paralysis on jet lag, but they waved this off. They appeared content with silence.

Table cleared, I returned to my room and promptly fell back asleep—only to be awoken by a church bell tolling a flat two. Venturing from the guest room, I noticed light seeping from a room at the far end of the hallway. Padding on the uncarpeted pine floor, I found Horst sitting at a desk, busy at work. He waved me in.

"Please. Close the door behind you. Penelope wakes up with every noise." His English plodded heavily through a German accent. "So you are not sleeping well after the flight. That is not unusual."

On a workbench in his room stood an exquisite model of an old sailing ship. I asked him where he had gotten it.

"Oh, this? I made it."

"Really? Wow, it's incredible. Is it from a kit?"

"No. No kit." The suggestion appeared to have given mild offense. "I built it maybe twenty years ago. Every now and again it is needing restorations. Do you also build?"

"No, not at all, but I've always admired people who can."

He showed me where the rigging had loosened, frayed, and in a couple of places come undone.

"This is a model of James Cook's ship," he explained, "the HM Bark *Endeavour*. During his time on the *Endeavour*, Cook is making the first mathematical algorithm for plotting a longitudinal position on the open sea."

"I didn't know that."

"Yes, this Cook was a brilliant man, a genius."

An Audenesque pattern of wrinkles striated Horst's gentle face. He appeared to be seventy or so, fit and trim like a seasoned runner. He twisted the neck of a high-intensity lamp to a spot on the rigging, cleaned his glasses, and set about tying a series of minuscule knots.

"Please, can you pick up the scissors there? Yes, that one, and now very carefully, cut the string just here? . . . Very good! Thank you!"

I assisted him for perhaps an hour, working in close quarters, until he said, "I fear I am tiring. But our progress is good. You make an excellent—"

"Assistant."

"Apprentice. Good night."

The next morning we breakfasted in a sunny alcove that adjoined the living room. "You look fresh and rested," said Penelope to me. "I hope that stray dog didn't disturb you."

"*Ach, dieser Scheißhund,*" muttered Horst.

"I didn't hear a thing," I said.

On the breakfast table stood a pot of coffee, a wicker basket of fresh rolls covered with a linen cloth, and a plate of butter and cheese. A sugar bowl rested in a shallow trough of water. "Ants," Penelope explained. "They're quite a nuisance." A decade or so younger than her husband, Penelope was the anti-Francizka: pillowy, abundant; without angles, tone, or sharpness, bodily or otherwise. She hurried to the kitchen to answer the phone and returned vaguely winded.

"That was my daughter," she announced. "She's coming for a few days!"

"*Ach Gott, ach Gott,*" cried Horst.

"Don't pull such a face." To me she said, "Horst doesn't enjoy surprises."

"I hope I'm not getting in the way," I said.

"Don't be silly. Horst and I will do a bit of shopping this morning. Maybe you'd like to take a walk to the beach. It's really quite lovely, particularly before the afternoon crowds. Now Horst, please behave."

"Yes, of course, of course . . ." he grumbled.

In the ten days that I spent with the Stillers—that is, a week longer than I had planned and arranged with Penelope—I came to learn that Horst's temper followed strict circadian rhythms. Mornings invariably found him in a foul mood: truculent, aggrieved, prone to self-pity and pointless aggression as he contemplated the long list of pressing domestic chores that required his immediate attention. By his third cup of heavily sugared coffee, he became less visibly aggravated with the world; come late afternoon, chores complete, and after two more cups of coffee and his daily swim in the pool of aquamarine hand-painted Portuguese tile, which I learned he had built himself, he would toil contentedly in the garden in his sandals, nylon briefs, and a broad straw hat. But it was only at midnight—after a late dinner of cold cuts, a shot or two of schnapps, and an hour of improvising Bach or Telemann on the harpsichord—when he moved into his study, took out his ship-building tools, and turned his attention to the *Endeavour*, that he was happy.

For Penelope, the quotidian mood swings ran in reverse. A late riser, she'd dawdle down the steps in her terry cloth zippered robe after Horst had finished grinding and brewing the coffee and setting the table in the breakfast alcove, greeting us with a cheerful, lilting "Good morning! *Guten Morgen!*" She'd survey the breakfast spread and say, as if the meal couldn't proceed without her orchestration, "So, who would like what?"— despite the fact that Horst had already placed a fresh roll with a wedge of butter and a dollop of apricot or raspberry jam on everyone's plate. Her high spirits lasted until the arrival of the mail after lunch. This was an eagerly anticipated moment—the punctual snarl of the postman's smoke-belching underpowered scooter—and invariably one that brought crushing disappointment. She appeared to expect a letter that stubbornly refused to materialize. Absorbing this setback, she'd lie in a hammock between a pair of chestnut trees and make her way through *The Guardian*, the *Süddeutsche Zeitung*, and the *Herald Tribune* in reverse order, beginning with the cultural pages at the back, which usually weren't too dispiriting, then working her way forward, through the national stories about political corruption and budget irresponsibility, and concluding with the disasters and calamities of the front page. By the time she'd let the last page of newspaper fall to the grass, she was crippled with depression. She'd withdraw to her bedroom for a nap, emerging only after Horst had set the table for dinner, or—as was the case on two occasions—not until breakfast the next morning.

That first day, after my hosts left to go shopping, I walked to the beach. The tiny village where Horst came to retire and met the widowed Penelope lay nestled in a crook of rugged granite hills and yellow cliffs, happily bypassed by a new highway that carried truckers from Lisbon to Santiago de Compostella. A hundred or so houses lay scattered along a loose spool of cobblestone streets. Casa do Mar, the Stillers' mission-style house, looked out over a Teutonically tended vegetable garden, an English flower garden, a terraced vineyard, a tiled fountain, and the swimming pool Horst had built. A whitewashed stone wall ringed the property.

I reached the empty beach via a dirt road. The sun stood in a purplish sky so clear that my retinas felt under assault, unable to process the sharp reality of objects. On a stretch of sand that skirted a field of heather, I sat, arms clasped around my knees, and watched the ocean lazily massage the shore. It was my first glimpse of the eastern Atlantic. In his last letter to me, Oliver had described beach heather—had he written about this very spot? I'd brought along copies of Oliver's correspondence to read over, but jet lag and sunlight sapped my sense of immediate purpose. I'd written to Penelope Stiller several months earlier, informing her of Oliver's death (which for simplicity's sake, I left as a car accident) and asking her if I could come and interview her for a book project. Her response arrived promptly, not what I'd expected from a woman who'd dallied a decade before notifying Francizka and her sons about Victor Vice's death.

I am stunned and extremely saddened to hear of Oliver's death. He was such a delightful guest and we had such a nice visit last summer. We would have liked him to stay even longer. Such a tragedy! I'd be happy to offer whatever assistance I can for your book. I must confess, I had no idea that Victor's son was so famous; he was so modest and quiet when he was here. I must additionally confess that I don't know a great deal of value. I don't mean to discourage you; I just don't want you to feel that you have traveled a great distance in vain. I'm certain you would have a lovely time here in any case. (The weather in July is splendid, and the area is still quite pristine compared to the dreadfully overdeveloped Algarve.) It goes without saying that you shall stay with us. We have a guest room that is very comfortable and the hotels in the area are rather drab. So do come.

As I prepared for the trip, I often asked myself the same question that Francizka had posed to Oliver: *What do you hope to learn?* It was Oliver who had first described Victor Vice as like the planet Pluto (it was still a planet at the time): an unseen entity that tugged on distant bodies, altering their course, catapulting them into otherwise inexplicable orbits. If possible,

I wanted to get a measure of this elusive entity, this formidable absence. More: if my project were to be a success, I felt I had to retrace Oliver's journey of the summer before. Was it possible that he had learned some small yet ramifying fact that made it *more likely than not* that he would straddle the guardrail of the *QM2* two weeks later? Or what if Oliver had learned *nothing*, and this frustration of expectation, this failure of anticipated revelation, had itself propelled him toward the windswept deck? In either case, I would have learned a great deal.

Only now the relentless sunshine shriveled my resolve and burned holes through my logic. I inventoried the questions I'd prepared before my departure: suddenly they seemed few in number, lacking necessary sequence, and either banal, ill considered, or offensive, promising to leave me no better informed than before. I had the powerful feeling that Oliver had been seized by similar if not identical doubts as he idled on the heather-clad beach. *I have come this far. Why?* Oliver had always ridiculed the idea that a person could be treated like a jigsaw puzzle. As if a person's identity could suffer from missing pieces! It was no more than a sentimental attachment, a contrivance of novelists, he'd said—not once, but dozens of times! And yet why else had he come, if not to find out about himself? And what of the sentence he'd written in *Paradoxes of Self*, the book he once cryptically insisted "was not a mere anagram for Oliver Vice": *The nonbeliever who mumbles prayers in a moment of mortal danger offers no refutation of atheism* (p. 73)—how was this to be parsed in light of his own conduct? Was his trip to Portugal the functional equivalent of "mumbled prayers"?

The sun addled my thoughts. Dreamy apparitions, a butterfly and a motor scooter, traipsed across my closed eyes. But I fought off sleep. Like Oliver, I burned easily.

The terrace of Casa do Mar could be entered through the garden or from the living room through a pair of glass doors. A rosewood pergola offered shade and a checkerboard trellis woven with grape vines and ivy scattered the breeze. The table was set with a simple white tablecloth with red border stitching and bright yellow napkins. Lunch was grilled cod, boiled potatoes, and string beans from the garden.

"It's delicious," I said. It seemed the Stillers had mastered a vital lesson, that life can be lived most contentedly in circumstances of tasteful simplicity. Perfect weather and ocean views helped, of course.

"It's lovely here, isn't it?" said Penelope.

"Gorgeous."

A pair of domestics also didn't hurt. Rosa, their cook, had prepared lunch. Arturo landscaped and helped Horst with his various building projects. They both worked half-days.

"Do help yourself to more," said Penelope.

Paradise was disturbed only by several obnoxious yellow jackets. Horst spent most of the meal swatting at them ineffectually until Penelope cried out, "Just ignore them! *Mann!*"

"When does your daughter arrive?" I asked.

"*Ach Gott, ach Gott,*" Horst muttered.

"Her plans are often liable to change," sighed Penelope.

"Is that because of her work?"

Horst laughed, though by the sound of it not because he had heard anything funny.

"She's a student," Penelope said, "of linguistics, at work on her doctoral degree. Her progress has been rather *slow*. She's a wonderfully talented girl, artistic and athletic, but she follows her own schedule."

After lunch I called Melissa and the boys. They were finishing breakfast; Melissa was less than conversational. She appeared not to care that I hadn't decided on my return date; all that mattered was that I be back by the time she left on *her* summer vacation. I asked if she was traveling alone or with a friend; this question apparently did not warrant a response. For all practical purposes we were separated. Or rather, for all practical purposes we still shared the same house; only in all those nonpractical, deeply emotional ways did we live bewilderingly apart. The call left me depressed. I wanted to plunge into the pool and swim underwater until my lungs burned, but Horst and Arturo were tinkering with the filter. I offered to help, but Horst waved this off. Not that I would have known what to do.

Then came afternoon tea. Rosa had baked a plum pie and Penelope made a bowlful of fresh whipped cream. We sat at a fruitwood table in the classically English living room. Above a worn leather couch hung two portraits, one of a young girl and the other of a younger Penelope.

"The portraits are quite wonderful," I said.

"Yes, Victor did those," Penelope said.

Had I known that Vice could paint? I couldn't remember whether Oliver had told me or not—perhaps he himself hadn't known. The eyes, oversized and glassy, and the obsessive detailing of hair, skin, and incidentals—a patterned scarf in the girl's portrait and a potted plant in Penelope's—reminded me of the early work of Lucian Freud.

I asked to see more of Vice's work and Penelope directed me to two landscapes—equally impressive but seemingly not by the same person. These were Kokoschka-like outbursts: vortices of color and unstable shapes, a valley in the throes of violent creation by a God strong on improvisation.

"This is very different," I observed.

"Later work," said Penelope ruefully. "Victor never quite found his own style."

Horst scooped the last of the sugary coffee from the bottom of his cup, then looked up and smiled. Penelope was gazing down at a worn Persian rug, as if just then reminded of some melancholy fact. Like a graph of supply and demand, afternoon tea charted the moment in each day that Horst's improving temper momentarily intersected with Penelope's deteriorating emotional state. By the time we cleared the plates and cups, their moods were quickly traveling in opposite directions.

The next morning I was awakened by the sound of splashing. From the window I saw Horst afloat on his back in the pool, naked, kicking up a storm. I waited for him to leave the pool area before taking an early morning dip of my own.

As I did laps, I resolved to interview Penelope without further delay. The first couple of days had been devoted to settling in. Now it was time to get to work. Morning was the best time, before the mood-altering newspapers arrived.

And yet it was Penelope who asked the first questions.

"So, tell us about your book about Oliver," she said as we sat down for breakfast. "Are you making progress?"

"Definitely. It's really coming along."

"I'm delighted to hear that. What exactly prompted you to write about Oliver? I understand he was a close friend of yours. But was he famous? Was he an important figure in his field? He never gave any hint of this."

"Not exactly famous," I said. "More emblematic."

"*Emblematisch . . .*" Horst weighed the word with a frown.

"He *was* pretty well known as a philosopher," I added. "But there was something more about him. Something quite . . . extraordinary."

Penelope's dry, frank eyes waited for me to elaborate, but I was at a loss for what to say. It was as if I'd been asked to explain what makes Kafka a remarkable writer. Either one sees it or one doesn't.

"Well, then," she said. "I do hope I can be of help. You have traveled a long way." She again waited for me to say something, but I remained silent.

"In any case, it's another glorious day," she said. "Maybe you'd like to join me for a walk?"

"Thanks, but I think I'll head down to the beach."

"Well, it's a bit blowy. Do take a sweater."

Penelope clearly found my behavior odd, and so did I.

I felt as if some residue of Oliver, some viral aftermath, had taken hold of me, leaving me helplessly in the grips of the misgivings that I imagined had seized *him* as he confronted the same task. These feelings made for a vaguely psychotic state of mind, and I labored to shove them aside by tossing rocks into the surf.

I returned from the beach at midday to find an unknown car parked before the gate to Casa do Mar. I went down to the pool, where I came upon a young woman curled on a chaise, reading *Word and Object* by Willard Van Orman Quine. Without rising, she extended a sturdy tanned limb and shook my hand. "I'm Olivia Vice. You must be the writer doing a book on my half brother."

"Yes, that's right."

"Well, *do* sit."

I pulled up a garden chair. The woman placed *Word and Object* face down on the chaise, clasped her arms around a pair of smooth tanned knees, and regarded me through her sunglasses.

"So, tell me. Have you learned any fascinating new tidbits about Oliver Vice since you've arrived here?" She wore a loose white T-shirt, sleeves pushed up to her shoulders, and a woven sunhat. Large oval sunglasses, resting on high, sculpted cheeks, appeared designed to blunt the glare of paparazzi.

"Yes, in fact, I have."

"Really? Do tell—oh, hi, Mum!"

"Hello, sweetheart." Freshly returned from her walk, Penelope proffered a sweaty cheek that her daughter kissed. "How was the drive? I do hope you didn't speed."

"Mum, please."

Just then a gust of wind sent Olivia's sunhat somersaulting into the pool. Gallantly I retrieved it. Why had I assumed the child to be Horst and Penelope's? Penelope had spoken of "my daughter," and yet I'd never considered that she might have been referring to Oliver's half sister. What other connections, I wondered, was I failing to make? I felt blockheaded and elated, like an investigator who stumbles on crucial evidence despite overlooking every lead.

At lunch, Rosa held Olivia at arm's length, beaming at her while the two chattered away in Portuguese.

Horst managed a stiff hug. "If you had called I could shop properly. Now I'll have to shop again after lunch."

"Oh, Horst, stop," said Penelope.

"And remove those *scheußliche Sonnenbrille*. Why is she always hiding behind sunglasses?"

Horst made circles of his thumbs and forefingers, and frowning like a clown, gazed at us through his mock glasses. Penelope laughed merrily. Olivia removed her sunglasses with a sigh. I stared at her eyes, dumbfounded. Oversized, thoughtfully spaced, suggestively Asiatic, as dark as brazilwood, so dark that pupil and iris merged, they were the eyes of her half brother. The similarity—the identity—was astonishing. My stare must have betrayed me. Olivia gave me a look, part puzzled, part irritated, as if to say, *What?*

The day after her arrival, Olivia and I were reading by the pool when all at once she closed her Quine, stepped out of her Madras shorts, moved swiftly to the diving board, and plunged into the water. Climbing from the pool, she fished a thumb around a band of suit that had ridden up her hip and shook water from a mass of hair twisted and pinned over her head. She returned to the diving board, turned on her tippy toes, and with her body cantilevered over the pool, lifted her arms over her head like a genie about to dematerialize, sprang, her body twisting in a shape that was too complex for me to follow visually, and then magically disappeared into the water as if through a secret entrance. She surfaced to my applause, and in one continuous motion turned onto her back, spouting water from her puckered mouth.

"Did you ever compete?" I asked.

"Briefly. I found it a bore. How about you? Are you an athlete?"

"Not really. I used to be very good at Ping-Pong, but that was years ago."

"Really? Me, too."

For teatime, Rosa made a plum cake. Horst piled whipped cream on a wedge of pie and hustled upstairs to review the blueprints to Casa do Mar's water heater, which over the last day had failed dependably to produce hot water. He appeared to hold Olivia responsible for this. At breakfast, Penelope had appeared oblivious to Horst's hostility toward Olivia, but by teatime, having absorbed the day's toxic headlines, the domestic tensions wore on her, and after several nibbles, she declared, "Nothing has any flavor today," and retired to her bedroom.

"And they wonder why I hate coming here," Olivia said, helping herself to a second slice.

Olivia's bedroom was adjacent to mine and we shared the same bathroom. To bed she wore flannel boxer shorts and a plain white T-shirt. She liked to read on her bed, legs crossed, tugging on split ends between sentences of Quine. Later at night, she'd curl on the living room floor in front of the television, cover her legs with an alpaca throw, and watch *Seinfeld* reruns in Portuguese.

Next morning, Olivia was up early. When I came down, a Ping-Pong table stood in the center of the terrace. Olivia was clamping the net taut.

"Where did that come from?" I asked, inwardly grimacing.

"It was my father's. Horst keeps it in the storage shed. Come. Let's play. I can't remember the last time I held one of these."

She handed me a paddle, one side smooth, the other stippled. She placed the ball on the table and gyrated it with her paddle; this appeared to be a test of sorts.

"I used to love table tennis," she said. "My father was a local champion. We played all the time."

I was moved by the fact that the half siblings should share identical proficiencies. Had Oliver also learned the game from the BF?

We rallied briefly. I blamed my ineptitude on the gusting wind and rustiness.

"I always play better in games," Olivia said. "Twenty-one to win. You can serve."

"No, you start."

I took over the serve trailing 0–5. She resumed at 10–0.

"Didn't you say you used to be pretty good?"

"At *tennis*," I said. "Not *table* tennis."

"Oh. I must have misheard. Well, let's continue, anyway."

"But my mother was the real tennis player in the family," I continued. "She made it to Junior Wimbledon."

Olivia crushed a smash down the middle of the table that ricocheted off my chest. "Sorry. Twelve serving nil. My father also played tennis, but not competitively."

"Your father was quite talented," I said. "Did you also inherit his artistic abilities?"

"There! Your point! Thirteen serving one. He tried to get me to paint. I did for a while. It didn't take."

"He worked as an art dealer?"

"He gave that up when I was quite young, when we still lived in London. At the time, this was our summerhouse. When he couldn't work anymore, he and my mother moved here year round."

"He was quite young when he died, wasn't he?"

"Fifty-four. I was twelve. That's another point for you. Two serving fifteen."

"I'm sorry to hear that. He'd been ill for some time?"

"Let's finish our game, shall we? Then we can play interview all we want."

All at once, I felt gripped by a sense of renewed purpose, my faith in self and Oliver restored. Questions suddenly crowded my mind, resisting an orderly queue.

Olivia had lightning reflexes and could command the ball with a variety of spins and slices. Dropping all that from her repertoire, she coaxed me to win several more points.

"What about chess," I said. "Did your father play?"

The question was minor, but who could say where the answer would lead? The obscure but richly symbolic connections between Oliver's sufferings and the Vices' notorious past—if they were to be divulged, they would come from this beautiful master of topspin. This realization struck me with force.

"Come, stay focused, you're doing better. Interview later."

We stopped keeping score. Olivia encouraged me to raise the level of my play, and we managed several extended rallies.

"See? That was fun!" Through a curled bottom lip, she blew a lock of errant hair off her sweaty forehead. Seashells of sweat darkened the underarms of her T-shirt. "Come, I could use a dip."

She surfaced from the pool just in time to hear Horst bellowing, as if to a child: "Olivia, you left all the *Tischtennis Zeug* on the terrace!"

Olivia made a point of taking as leisurely a swim as possible. I toweled off and headed to the terrace. The Ping-Pong table had already been folded, covered with its tarp, and wheeled behind the trellis.

I sought Horst out. "I'm sorry if we left something of a mess . . ."

He raised a hand to wave off my apology, then brightened at the news that Olivia and I planned to spend the afternoon at the beach. He generously offered to pay should we decide to stay for dinner at the village's single restaurant.

We extricated two old bicycles from the tool shed and set off. Olivia rode no-handed, occasionally steadying the bike around a curve or over the bumpy cobblestones. A single orphan cloud briefly dulled the sun. I scanned the skies—completely clear except for this rogue. It occurred to me that it was the first cloud I'd seen since I'd arrived. Olivia let me guide her to my favorite spot on the beach, where the sand skirted the heather. Sitting on her beach towel, she massaged sunscreen into her legs, arms, and shoulders, and even into the lobes of her lovely ears.

"If you do my back," she said, handing me the tube of lotion, "I'll do yours"—as if incentive were required.

She worked the sunscreen into my back with a few broad, businesslike strokes. Glistening with lotion, she lay back on her towel, offering her body to the sun. "So, tell me," she said, "what was Oliver Vice like?"

"You never met?"

"I was supposed to come last summer on holidays when he was here, but somehow never made it. I can't remember why. Were you his lover?"

"No. What gave you that idea?"

"I don't know. He always struck me as sort of . . . fey."

"You just said you'd never met."

"Not in person, but we used to exchange quite a number of e-mails. We had a nice back-and-forth when I was still reading for my B.A."

"So he knew of your existence."

"Yes, of course. He wrote me first. I knew that my father had sons from his first marriage, but there was no contact between the families. And then, out of the blue, he wrote me. I remember it was a very odd coincidence—I had just read one of his articles in a philosophy tutorial. We made plans to meet in London, but it never happened. Again, I don't remember why."

"And then what?"

"The e-mail kind of ran its course. I have to confess, I'm not a brilliant correspondent. I googled him a few times, but that's all."

"What about Bartholomew?"

"No, we've never been in contact."

So Oliver had long known of his half sister. Did it matter that he'd never spoken to me about her? Something told me that it did, but I'm not sure I trusted that something. I felt vaguely perplexed and resentful, as if anything not shared were an article concealed, as if this belated revelation supplied a referendum on our closeness. At the same time I wondered why Oliver hadn't tried to look up his half sister, given that he spent part of every summer in London. Then again, I've never tried to contact my first cousin, the son of my father's estranged sister, whom I met for the first and last time at my grandfather's funeral when I was ten. And yet this cousin lives no more than an hour's drive from Harkness.

"It's odd that your father gave you a name almost identical to your half brother's."

Olivia turned onto her stomach and repositioned her sunhat.

"My father did lots of odd things," she said. "He was ill for so much of my life. It made everything . . . difficult."

"You know Oliver never learned of your—and his—father's death until some years later."

"How can that be?"

"Evidently your mother waited several years before notifying them."

"That's absurd."

"I heard this straight from Oliver's mother."

"Well, it's still absurd. Of course Mum contacted them when Father died. Why wouldn't she? That's total nonsense."

"Maybe she misremembered—Oliver's mother, I mean. I hope it's okay to say, but she's still quite bitter about being left by your father."

"Left by Father?"

Her outraged tone made it clear we were in the world of contested narrative.

"Yes."

"Excuse me, but it was that woman who walked out on Father after he fell ill. For his friend in the lighting business. You know, it doesn't really matter greatly to me, but you might as well get your story straight."

"Your father knew Jacob Epstein?"

"I believe they were quite friendly. For a time."

"Was this when your father developed his heart condition?"

"Heart condition," she repeated. Olivia sat up with a swing of her long legs, and peered at me over the tops of her sunglasses, a theatrical gesture. Her expression condescended, doubted, and probed, as if unsure whether I was feigning naïveté or, perhaps just as bad, displaying bona fide ignorance. Her lovely dark eyes silently castigated.

"No heart condition," I said.

"No."

It was Oliver who had told me the cause of his father's death, but his source must have been Francizka, the source of most of what passed as knowledge of his family.

"Father parked his car on a beach about twenty kilometers from here. He kept the engine running. The day before, he had bought a piece of rubber tubing. You get the idea . . ."

"I'm very sorry to hear that."

"It's ancient history now. You know, I have so few memories of him being healthy. Those that I have are very nice. He had a wonderful sense of humor and was a natural teacher, like when he taught me to play table tennis. I used to love to watch him draw—he had so little control over his life, but the pencil always effortlessly followed his commands. But mainly I have memories of those days when he would sleep fourteen hours and lie in bed, unshaven, sometimes with the sheet drawn over his head. For years, Mother kept a stockpile of cheese sandwiches in plastic wrap in the fridge, and that's all he ever ate. My God, how I hated those cheese sandwiches."

A sand fly landed on her forearm. I wanted to reach out and brush it away, but worried that a touch might be misinterpreted. It flew off.

"Here's a good story for you. When I turned eight, I had my friends over for a party. At the time we were living in Hampstead, in north London, in this lovely flat, all very shabby but nice. We were playing Pass the Parcel—it's like your Musical Chairs, only instead of running around chairs, you pass an elaborately wrapped gift quickly around in a circle, and whoever is holding the gift when the music stops gets to unwrap a layer . . . Anyway, the music was playing, and we were all excitedly passing the parcel, and then Father appeared on the threshold to the living room. He hadn't shaven and was still in his pajamas—they weren't exactly filthy, just all gray and soiled. Worst of all—it's really almost too horrible to mention; even now, twenty years later, it makes me shudder—the fly of his pajama bottoms wasn't properly snapped.

"I spotted him first, but then my friends noticed him, too, and the game came to a standstill. The music kept going—it was bright and cheerful, upbeat party music—and a character named Jack the Mouse—Jack the Mouse was famous all over Britain at the time; every child of that age knows him—was urging us in his squeaky cockney voice to keep the parcel moving, *'urry now boys 'n' gells*, but the parcel wasn't moving at all. My friends were just watching Father in silence, just as he was watching us. At last he shuffled off and headed back up the stairs. Once he disappeared, we all burst out laughing. I laughed the hardest, but inwardly I *hated* my friends for laughing at him. To this day, I pray that no one saw those open pajamas. *That* was my eighth birthday."

"Sounds truly, truly awful."

"You know what's the worst thing about having a mentally ill parent?" Olivia was now sitting with bent legs, one arm wrapped around her knees, scooping up fistfuls of sand with her free hand and letting the grains filter through her fingers. A seagull landed just steps away and stood in curious profile, as if hoping to overhear her answer. "You grow up thinking that their behavior is *normal*. You go to a friend's house and you think: Susie's father is jolly and likes to watch football matches and Mary's father is quiet and likes to wash his car and my father's sad and likes to stay in bed. You just accept it as the way things are. Mum tried to explain to me that Father had lived through something terrible, but it's hard to explain to a child the meaning of survivors' guilt. I remember thinking, well, if Dad survived, shouldn't he feel happy and *relieved*? What's there to feel guilty about? Of course, since then I've read a great deal about survivors who later took their lives."

Another rogue cloud had mysteriously materialized in the periwinkle sky. "I'm not sure I understand," I said. "A survivor of what?"

"Don't you know that term?"

I mentioned that I was familiar with two standard references: to a television show and to the Holocaust.

"Well, right. The latter, not the former."

"Now I'm really confused. How did a British boy come to be a Holocaust survivor?"

"British? My father came from Berlin. He was a German Jew."

There was no reason to hide my stupefaction. Mel and I had suspected "Jewish blood" in the family, but we assumed it came from Francizka, not from the venerable house of Vice. "I was under the impression that your father came from some noble family in Sussex." And yet it wasn't an impression—it was a presumed fact. I recalled Oliver's confident assertion that the Vices could trace their ancestry back to the fourteenth century. I could clearly visualize Oliver's set of coasters enameled with the family coat of arms: the silver shield embossed with a buck's head, a black cross fixed between its antlers. *The Ancient Arms of Vice.* The lineaments of a project of deceit, mythmaking, and familial self-fashioning even more audacious than anything I had contemplated began to take shape in my mind.

"Sussex?" Olivia laughed. "I don't think so."

"What about the family name?"

"That story is quite rich," she said. "Are you by any chance Jewish?"

"I am."

"Just curious. Anyway, my father was born Viktor *W-e-i-s-s*"—she spelled this out. "It's German for 'white,' a typical German Jewish surname. In German, 'Weiss' is pronounced—"

"Yes, I get it."

"So, after the war, my father was kept in a DP camp, waiting to emigrate to England. A very literal-minded British official anglicized the German."

Ellis Island officials had of course committed hundreds of thousands of similar acts of phonetic transubstantiation, but perhaps few with such remarkable results.

"Do you know anything about his family?"

"They were originally tanners from a shtetl in Poland. His grandfather moved the family to the Scheuenviertel in Berlin, that's where most of the poor Jews from the East lived. His father was excellent at math. He worked as a bookkeeper and later taught at a *Gymnasium*. His mother was a passionate reader and named him after Victor Hugo. It was one of those classic stories of a family eager to assimilate as quickly as possible. Father studied art, his older brother became a journalist, and his younger sister was apparently a very gifted singer."

"Did they all survive?"

"But that's just it, isn't it? In a sense not even he did. Think of Primo Levi and Jean Améry and Paul Celan and Tadeusz Borowski and Jerzy Kosiński. Can you really call them *survivors*? It's more like they were *delayed* victims . . . Anyway the family managed to stay together until 1942. The first to be deported was Father's father, and six months later his mother and older brother. I don't know how he and his sister survived this period—he was barely a teenager, but I think he was able to sell some of his drawings to his German neighbors. Then he and his sister were deported, too. He was the only one to make it."

"After the war he became an art dealer?"

"He was still very young. He must have started his business in London, then moved to New York when he married Oliver's mother. After she left him and he returned to Europe, he more or less gave up dealing. He tried to make it on his own as a painter, not very successfully, poor Father. Of course, his illness made everything difficult."

"In your e-mails with Oliver, did you ever discuss your father?"

"It was a while back. I suppose I could check, though I doubt I still have his messages. I'm not one for saving much . . ."

"Because I don't believe that Oliver knew his father was German or a Jew or a survivor. I don't think he knew the Weiss story. If anything, he believed his father was a wheeler-dealer who traded in plundered Jewish art."

I expected the irony of this to resonate forcefully in Olivia, but she fell silent. Her gaze fixed on a distant point of the ocean. A tanker, seemingly unmoving, quivered on the horizon. Closer to shore, gulls bobbed on the water. I watched her profile, but she didn't return my stare: her concentration expended itself on other tasks. The distant tanker trembled in the sun. A sob escaped her lips.

I reached out, her hand found mine, our fingers interlocked. Her squeeze answered mine, and then squeezed again.

"I'm sorry if I've upset you."

"I like your questions," she insisted between hiccuped sobs. "It's so *rare* I get to talk about this. Your friends find out that your father killed himself and they head off to the hills. They just don't know *what* to say."

"I know what you mean."

"You do?"

"I just meant, I can imagine. That's all."

She was beautiful to begin with, and my inadvertent trespass on some inner sanctum of self, the communion of our fingers, overwhelmed me with the desire to comfort, hold, and do more. I imagined this is what Mel must have felt sitting on the couch with the grief-stricken half brother of the woman beside me. In that moment, as I reached for Olivia, I felt I better understood my wife.

But Olivia had already released my hand and sprung to her feet. The last of her tears vanished in a swipe of her palm. "Now it's time for me to ask you a question," she said, giving her nose a vigorous blow. "Why does one lie about something like one's table tennis ability?"

I held my hand as a visor and squinted up at her. Her eyes expressed curiosity without judgment. Was it worth explaining that I'd asked myself the same question countless times over the years? That several intelligent and well-meaning therapists had hazarded tentative answers? That Mel speculated it was a compensatory mechanism, a need to make myself larger, grander, possibly more worthy of love, in order to cover some presumed early trauma or deficit—my mother's breakdown, my father's bankruptcy, the absence of siblings, facts with strong explanatory purchase had they only been true?

"I don't know. Maybe because it's such a stupid thing to make up. I'm sorry."

"What else do you lie about?"

"Just the little stuff, honestly. I used to be much worse."

"That's comforting, I guess." She stashed her sunhat

and glasses in her beach bag, and jogged to the shore-
line. "I'm going in. Are you coming?"

"In in a sec," I said.

"Watch out for the jellyfish!" And then as she splashed
forward, "It's *freezing*! Come on, don't be a Larry
Lightweight!"

The tide had rolled in and with it a wilder surf. Olivia
launched herself into the water and swam, head above
the waves, parallel to the beach. She rode a wave, then
dove like a torpedo into a cresting swell, emerging on
the calmer side, buffeted, gleeful, triumphant. It was
hard to resist the pull of metaphor. She waved at me,
a gesture of beckoning; the second time, she simply
waved, then turned and plunged.

ALIBABA TOMATO PASTE was printed on the side of the
corrugated cardboard. The tins had long been used up.
Now the box, barely half full, held the artifacts of a
man. After dinner, after Olivia had retreated to Quine
and Horst had settled himself before the harpsichord,
Penelope had knocked at my door. She carried the box
with care, as if it contained a gerbil or guinea pig, something small and living.

"Olivia said you had a conversation today."

"Yes, it was very helpful."

"I'm so glad to hear that. It's rather a relief knowing
that you haven't traveled all this way for naught. I'd be
happy to answer any more of your questions, though
Olivia probably told you most everything. I thought
you might want to see these. They're Victor's personal

effects, though I fear there's very little of value here. After my husband's death, I *needed* to clean house. The clothing—why keep it? It went mostly to charity. I'm afraid I got rid of many of the paintings, too. Of course, I gave several to Olivia as mementos, but most of the art—why would I want to continue to surround myself with Victor's work? To be perfectly honest, I wanted as *few* reminders of Victor as possible. I'm sure you can understand. There were some items that I had hoped his sons might want, but their mother never answered any of my letters. And for no good reason, I couldn't bring myself to throw this stuff out . . ."

She placed the carton gently on my bed, then left the room, closing the door behind her.

For all her care in handling the box, its contents were completely disordered, as if a random drawer from her dead husband's dresser had been unceremoniously dumped out. A small drawer. The worldly remains of Victor Vice amounted to little. There was a felt-covered box that contained a pair of elliptical cuff links, silver and blue enamel—the enamel chipped, the silver tarnished. There was a wrinkled purple-and-yellow bow tie from Aquascutum, mottled with mildew. A deck of Barclay's bridge cards, held together by a desiccated rubber band that crumbled at the first touch. The deck: short one card. I ran my thumb over the blunt blade of an X-Acto knife. There were several green Faber-Castell drawing pencils: one 6B, three 4Bs (one no more than a nub), two 2Bs, two HBs, three 2Hs, and one 4H, all in need of a sharpening. There was a box of Conté crayons, most of the sticks broken. A mahl stick. An eyeglass case without eyeglasses. A pocket square, lightly mildewed. A keychain with keys to who-knows-what. A worn leather wallet, tri-fold with ID window, but empty of everything. A kneaded eraser. An empty bottle of Winsor Newton matte varnish. Another empty Winsor Newton bottle, this one Dammar varnish. A paintbrush. Another pair of cuff links.

My heart went out to the poor man. Photos, letters, postcards, ticket stubs, driver's licenses, fortune cookie fortunes; anything that might conjure a living presence, that might aid in the reconstruction of a history or an identity—gone. The pencils and erasers, the collar stays and the cuff links: these were all that remained, the leftovers of an efficient and discriminating purge. It was as if the two wives of Victor Vice shared but one similarity: a determination to leave no more than token vestiges of the man who had been their husband. This appeared to be his most notable legacy: the intensity of his ex-wives' efforts to eliminate traces of his existence.

And so an examination that began with great care— each artifact exhumed from its haphazard resting place and carefully displayed on my bed for archaeological assessment and mental inventory—quickly succumbed to disappointment. I confess: I shook the box. I was bored, and had given up hope in finding anything of interest. The shaking was a gesture of impatience—let's mix things up and see what surfaces. That's how the rubber stamp first came to my notice: a half-inch across and maybe one and a half inches in length, a tidy rectangle with a grooved wooden back permanently ink-darkened. It, too, seemed like just another piece of detritus. I paid it no further attention until another shake flipped it stamp-side up. Then I saw the two words. These, of course, were reversed, but in this case fittingly so, as they signified reversals of things larger. The Palatino capitals were easy to read—the difficulty lay in grasping their significance.

ATELIER PASCIN

Understanding started with my fingertips. Clusters of nerve endings picked up the excited buzz, synapses lit up like an overused power grid, but even then my brain required a moment to make sense of what my hand had pulled from the box. But only a moment.

I tapped on the door to Penelope's room. Propped up in her four-poster bed, she was reading a biography of Iris Murdoch. She wore her zippered terry cloth bathrobe. A mug of tea steamed on the nightstand.

"Not terribly much of interest, I fear," she said.

"There's one thing, though . . ." I held the ATELIER PASCIN stamp for her bifocaled inspection. "Do you by any chance know what this is?"

"How remarkable!" she exclaimed. "Oliver asked *precisely* the same question last summer. I'm afraid I can't give you any better answer than I gave him. I assumed it was just a piece of Victor's studio equipment. But now you've made me terribly curious. Is it of value? I told Oliver that he was of course free to keep it. I said he could have the entire box. I don't believe he took a single thing, though."

She stared at me with curious dry blue eyes. It was clear that Victor Vice never told his second wife how a penniless orphaned refugee in a new country came to trade in the works of second-tier masters of European modernism.

"No, I don't believe it's particularly valuable . . . It just, well, stuck out, that's all."

"Pascin—he was an artist, wasn't he? Victor must have admired his works."

"I guess so . . ."

"Would you care to keep the stamp? I have no use for it."

"May I? I mean, if it's okay with Olivia."

"She's been over that stuff many times, believe me. I'm sure she wouldn't mind."

"Well, okay, thanks."

From outside came the sound of a dog barking. "Oh my goodness," Penelope exclaimed. "Now I'll never be able to sleep. Horst! The dog!"

"Yes, I hear," Horst shouted from his study.

"May I ask you a few more questions?" I said.

"Please. But don't just stand there. Do sit." She drew her legs to the side, making room for me on the bed. "Now then."

"When Oliver was here last summer, did he ask you much about his father?"

"Well, of course we spoke . . . That dog will be the end of me."

"I mean, I learned a lot today. That Victor Vice was Jewish, was a Holocaust survivor, took his own life. I don't believe that Oliver knew any of this. I was just wondering if you discussed this with him, too."

"Well, of course, *I* didn't discuss it with you. It was Olivia—"

"I just meant, did you have a similar conversation with Oliver?"

Her lips pursed in concentration, but her eyes wandered to the window closest to the sound of the barking. "What *truly* drives me to distraction is how he stops and then starts in again! What on earth provokes him so?"

"Maybe chickens," I said, idiotically.

"I dislike *all* dogs. Do you as well?"

"I have to admit, this one *is* awfully annoying."

"It should be a crime. But the Portuguese, they're crazy about their dogs."

"*Scheißhund!*" shouted Horst from his study.

"You're making a bigger racket than the stupid dog," cried Olivia from her bedroom. "All of you."

"Quiet!" commanded Horst.

"So did Oliver ask you about—?"

"Well, it's a bit difficult to remember exactly *what* we discussed. For an emblematic man, he was quite shy, you know. I suppose many great thinkers are socially awkward."

"Did he ask you about his father's suicide?"

"Well, I'm asking myself precisely the same question. I certainly can't remember him looking at me all agape, as if the scales had just fallen from his eyes. On the other hand . . . I just *don't* know. Some years ago, I had a conversation with a friend about a mutual acquaintance.

My friend kept saying things about the acquaintance that I found odd, and I said things about our acquaintance that my friend clearly found most extraordinary. It was only hours later, after I had myself a cup of tea that it suddenly dawned on me that we must have been talking about different acquaintances! That might have happened with Oliver. We both were talking about Victor, but we might have been talking about different men, if you see what I mean. Because I simply *assumed* that he knew about his father. I had no idea that his mother had been lying to him and his brother their whole lives. What a terrible thing to do to a child."

"Maybe she thought she was protecting them."

"But to lie about *everything*! Olivia told me this business about Francizka claiming that I waited years before notifying the family of Victor's death. Why, that's simply not true!"

"You told Francizka at the time."

"But of course! I called! We spoke on the phone, she and I. I said that they would be welcome at the funeral. We are, after all, talking about Victor's children. There he goes again, that dog! Horst!"

"Tomorrow, poison!"

"You're all insane," shouted Olivia.

"What I *do* remember most vividly about Oliver's stay last summer was his desire to visit his father's grave."

"It's here in town?"

"A bit up the coast. I must admit, I don't go all that frequently, but I offered to have Horst drive him there. He wanted to see it alone, so we lent him our car. He was gone for several hours—I remember because Horst began to worry that he'd had an accident. It was the last day of his visit; the next day he left for England. That *bestial* dog!"

Olivia wove her old yellow Opel between donkey-drawn carts and smog-belching trucks. In her knee-length shorts, red hoodie, and outsized sunglasses, she looked like a carefree northern Californian wheeling toward some good surf.

"You were talking to my mother last night. I heard her say how awful she found it that Francizka Vice lied to her children about Father's death. Well, the fact is, *I* didn't find out about Father's suicide for nearly two years. Mum first told me that he died in an auto accident and of course I believed it. The Portuguese drive like complete maniacs. I read somewhere they have the highest auto fatality rate in the world. Which reminds me, how did my half brother really die?"

She held the steering wheel with one hand and ran the fingers of her free hand through her wind-fluffed hair. She was smiling, seemingly at peace with the world.

"He jumped off the *Queen Mary 2*."

"The ship?"

"Yes."

"For real?"

I explained the ambiguity surrounding his disappearance, that an accident couldn't be entirely ruled out, but that it probably had been an intentional act.

"You didn't know?" I asked.

"Of course I did. I googled. You're lucky that my mother and Horst are so incurious and rarely touch the computer. See, everybody lies when it comes to suicide."

"It didn't seem like lying," I said. "It just seemed pointless to go into it. It's not as if your mother knew Oliver well. At the time, I had no idea about your father, not that that changes anything."

"I'm not accusing you, I'm just making an observation. Of course, it came to me as something of a shock when I found out—about Oliver, I mean. I like to think that if Father hadn't lived through the extermination of his entire family, he might have been a normal functioning man. But when I hear about Oliver, I start to think maybe bad plumbing runs in the family."

"Maybe it isn't as simple as either-or."

She glanced in the rearview mirror. I'd already noticed that she had a habit of not acknowledging statements she had little use for. Hadn't Oliver had the same trait?

"You know, I never had a burning desire to meet him. I saw a couple of photos, and he always looked attractive in a gay kind of way. I've read a couple of his papers, which I thought were quite smart, though not the book that made a big splash. But now—it feels like a terrible loss. Even if I never met him, the idea that I had this half brother out there, this man who shared with me the same unusual fate of having Victor Vice as a father—it was somehow comforting."

"There's still Bartholomew."

"True. Somehow he never factors. What's he like?"

"I don't know him well. He teaches middle school history. Very knowledgeable about Churchill." I couldn't bring myself to mention the chronic depression, the Tridentism, the mustache. Not lies, just omissions.

Once we turned off the main road, I took Olivia's hand. Her fingers closed around mine.

We parked on a grassy bluff. The drive had been no more than thirty miles, but had brought us to a chillier clime, an Irish-like coast of skin-stippling wind. Olivia pulled up the hood of her sweatshirt. A path of packed dirt brought us to a small stone church, its door ajar, giving view onto a table of lit votives and rows of wooden pews. In the churchyard, colorful laundry flapped stiffly on a pair of clotheslines. The yard fronted a bluff; below a vexed ocean pummeled the coast. A handful of goats and a lone cow supplied a grassy field with local fauna. Beyond the field, enclosed by a stone wall, was the cemetery.

The distant crash of waves, the hollow clink of goat bells, and the flap of the wind through the taut laundry offered a soothing collage of sound. The gravestones— Portuguese crosses—stood higgledy-piggledy, like a gathering of neighborly acquaintances. The outcast, the loner, stood some distance off. The single tablet was shaped like half the Mosaic commandments. Engraved above the name, restored to the original German, was a simple Star of David.

"Did the church raise any objections?"

Olivia shrugged. "You'd have to ask Mum, but I don't think so, unless it had to do with medieval rules about burying suicides. Generally speaking, the Portuguese are a pretty tolerant lot."

Shoulders pressed together, we stood backs to the wind, staring at the same thing.

On the flat top of the tablet stood a stack of five stones retrieved from the beach below or brought along in an exercise of forethought. It was clear they had been chosen for uniformity of color, symmetry of form, and gradually diminishing size.

"Presumably not your mother's work."

Olivia shook her head. "For a guy raised as a Catholic, at least he knew the ritual."

That night the gods of equilibrium made amends for the monotony of lovely weather. The storm began with lightning thoughtlessly discharged over the ocean and advanced with relentless sweep, like a vast seafaring expeditionary force. The wind picked up abruptly; swirling gusts scattered birds and silenced the satanic dog. Communications went first; out of curiosity, I lifted the receiver of the phone and was greeted by the curiously unnerving silence of a dead landline. The garden lit up under a brilliant flare as window-rattling thunder detonated on both sides of the house simultaneously. The rain came, first in thick heavy drops, then in torrential sheets. Next the power failed. Like a demented ship captain, Horst dashed from room to room with a flashlight, hysterically commanding, *No candles!*, lest we burn down the house. I was reminded of one of Oliver's favorite jokes, evidently also a favorite of Wittgenstein's. A man is so terrified of dying in a fire in his bed that he sleeps surrounded by buckets of water. One morning, he climbs out of bed, stumbles into a bucket, and drowns.

Horst had additional flashlights, but refused to distribute them, as these were to be used only in case of an emergency. When it was suggested by his stepdaughter that this was exactly what we were experiencing, he shouted, *Flashlights are not to be mishandled as ersatz reading lamps!* Olivia threatened mutiny, but I was touched by the pitiable depths of his terror. I watched the storm with awe, and when the ferocity subsided, went to bed.

I awoke to utter blackness—the power was still out. Rain fell steadily, accompanied by the murmur of retreating thunder. The air was damp and cool, but the breath on my cheek, the nuzzling pressure along my flank, brought warmth.

"Hello," I said.

"Uh, hullo."

"Did the storm scare you?"

"No."

I liked this frankness. Olivia pressed her nose, like a butting goat, into my throat.

"May I ask you a question?" she said. "Are you really separated from your wife?"

"Yes. Alas."

"Truly?"

"Truly."

"Why should I trust you? You've already confessed that you're a pathological liar."

"Not pathological. I told you, I only lie about small stuff. I'm pretty honest when it comes to the big picture. Really. And I'm not a sleaze."

"Okay, I believe you. I'm sorry about your separation, but now I'm just a little bit happy, too. You smell good, like cherry licorice."

Later I said, "Do you think we're both just enacting some sick fantasy—you standing in for Oliver for me, and me standing in for Oliver for you?"

"Oh, I'm quite certain of it. On the level of fantasy, the idea of fucking my unknown half brother, it's rather powerful stuff. Which isn't to say I don't find you attractive. I do. Very."

"Thank you. I do, too. You, I mean."

Still later she said, "Did he wrong you in some way?"

"What do you mean?"

"I don't know . . . Tell me, is writing about a dear friend an act of love or an act of hostility? I'm sorry. Sex makes me all very talky. Keep doing whatever it is you were just doing. It feels nice."

By the next morning the birds were happily chirping and the sky was clear, as if in a state of complete denial about its nocturnal insanity. The sun cooperated in the destruction of evidence, vaporizing puddles and drying rain-slicked cobblestones. By noon Horst and I had collected all the downed limbs and dragged them to the head of the driveway. Olivia thrashed me at Ping-Pong and later in the day we walked to the beach. There I showed her the atelier stamp. She pressed it against her palm, leaving a faint trace of the artist's name. She'd never heard of Pascin, and struggled to gauge the proper emotional response. After some reflection she said, "I suppose it's nice to know that Father *was* a successful painter, in a manner of speaking." She wanted to keep the stamp, but agreed to let me borrow it for a short while. She shed some tears, then broke free of my embrace and dashed into the water still roiled from the storm. As she dove into a thunderous wave, I almost called a word of caution, but there was no need. Olivia knew what she was doing.

When we returned to Casa do Mar, Penelope was reading the papers and Horst, nerves quieted, was examining the whaler *Elizabeth* for possible repairs. At night Olivia came to me. This went on for two more happy days. Then I left.

SIXTEEN

The elegant old-world bedroom had undergone an unhappy redecoration. Gone was the bed fit for a queen with its plump mattress, quilted sham, and headboard of carved nightingales. In its place stood a hospital gurney. Cantilevered over the bed was a tray with a bowl of yogurt and another of lurid green Jell-O. The sickly woman propped up in the bed was Francizka Nagy. I issued a stern command to myself to hide my shock.

"What's this all about?"

"They call it esophageal cancer," she said. "I guess they have to call it something."

Her appearance had undergone a dreadful change, but it took me several moments to locate it in her hair. I'd only ever seen Francizka beautifully and imperiously coiffed. Now lank lusterless strands of gray clung to a translucent scalp. Her head was improbably small. The odor in the room was not wholesome.

"You should have contacted me," I protested.

"My dear, you were off on your fact-finding mission."

"I've been back a month. More."

"And I've been here the entire time."

Her eyes, incongruously, were made up. Blessed, which was the name of the African nurse who'd ushered me into the apartment, must have applied eyeliner and shadow in anticipation of my visit. And I was the malingering son, trying to deflect blame for his prolonged neglectful absence. The substitution was complete.

"And the treatment?"

"My doctor, a very kind gentleman, gave me three options: surgery, chemo, or radiation. I chose None of the Above."

"But why—"

She raised a bony wrist, from which hung a thin gold bracelet, ending the discussion. "He also tried to sign me up for a clinical trial, something involving lasers. I said, 'Find yourself another guinea pig.' Now, please. Tell me about your trip. And don't stand there like this is my wake. You're making me terribly nervous."

I pulled up a chair. Draped across its back was a colorful kerchief that must have belonged to the nurse. Francizka was propped up in bed. She wore a silken robe over a dressing gown; the robe, sadly, had come undone, and through her gown I couldn't avoid seeing the outlines of her breasts, hanging like two old athletic socks pinned to her chest. I remembered the story that Olivia had told me about her eighth birthday, when Victor Vice had disrupted her party in his pajamas. Did anything connect these stories other than the embarrassment of bodies in decay? I'd come to the city to interview Francizka, but now I balked before the prospect of pressing a dying woman for information she'd spent decades concealing. But to my surprise, Francizka appeared genuinely curious about my trip. I found myself answering *her* questions, even if these promised to expose a life project of outrageous fabrications.

"Did you find Penelope copacetic?" she asked.

"She was very pleasant, but also rather moody." I described how she would become withdrawn every afternoon after reading the newspapers.

"Then why doesn't she stop?" The logic was irresistible, yet somehow failed to do justice to the drama of Penelope's daily ritual of expectation and crashing disappointment. Francizka frowned. "She sounds too labile for my tastes. I like steadier types."

"I also met Olivia Vice," I said.

"A nice girl?"

"Yes, very nice and attractive. She's finishing a doctorate in linguistics."

Francizka's eyes wandered to the mute TV. A chef was demonstrating how to prepare a soufflé. He whisked eggs in silence and wiped his hands on a black-and-white pin-striped apron. I felt she was challenging me to break the silence.

"So your first husband was Jewish. I hope you don't mind talking about this . . ."

"Why on earth should I mind?" she cried, summoning a hidden reserve of energy. "Jacob Epstein was a Jew, wasn't he? If you go back to Adam, isn't everyone Jewish?"

I accepted this lapidary bon mot only in the next moment to recognize its basic flaw—that she had confused Adam with Abraham.

"And yet Oliver only found out last summer. That must have been quite a surprise."

Francizka's face collapsed into a frown. "Of what relevance is this comment? You think a grown man leaps from a ship because he learns his father was a Jew? I've never heard such foolishness."

"That's not what I meant, Francizka. I didn't mean anything of the sort."

"This whole fixation with the past is morbid, a waste! Let sleeping dogs lie, is what I say."

"I only meant that he must have been surprised to learn something new about his father."

"Oliver knew."

"Before he went to Portugal? You'd told him?"

"He was curious. He had learned about certain genetic predispositions."

"The Tay-Sachs?"

"You see? Of course, I told you."

Perhaps I had misheard or maybe she had misspoken. She glared at me, her eyes defiant, angry, challenging. They betrayed no confusion or disorientation. But what exactly did she see? Her lips were dry and cracked. Why had the nurse applied eyeliner but not lip balm? I handed her a glass of water but she pushed it away.

"Are you in pain?"

"What do you mean?" she asked sharply.

"The cancer . . ."

"Ach, *that*. I've known worse."

Her expression turned impatient, as if awaiting my next question. I asked her if Oliver had known that his father was a survivor.

"Survivor," she repeated, as if weighing a tool to see its strengths. "That is a term of recent invention. It was never used until . . . I don't know when. We never used it back then."

"What do you mean by 'we'?"

"This is not a complicated word."

"I mean, are you also a survivor?"

"My friend, who of us is not a survivor?"

Just then Blessed shuffled into the room carrying a mug. She wore a white nurse's uniform, flip-flops, and a brightly colored African kerchief around her hair. A big woman, she moved with lugubrious economy, her every step geared toward conserving energy. "Mrs. Francizka, you drink nice tea now?"

"No, Blessed, but thank you."

The nurse nonetheless placed a mug on the tray table and wheeled it to the bed. "It hot and sweet like she like it. Doctor say it nice for you."

"Okay, thank you, my dear."

"Now shame! You no eating the nice yogurt and Jell-O. How she getting back to strong when she no eating the nice food?" The nurse stood feet apart, hands sternly pinned to her formidable hips.

"Take the Jell-O, Blessed. I'll have the yogurt, I promise."

"And mister want hot tea?"

"Thanks, I'm fine."

The nurse shuffled from the room, nibbling spoonfuls of Jell-O.

"She's an angel in human form, that Blessed," said Francizka. "An absolute saint. But you were asking your questions."

"When I was in Portugal, I saw some paintings by your first husband. I didn't know he was an artist."

"Victor was a draftsman. He fancied himself an artist. Sadly he had no real ability."

"Do you have any of his work?"

"Not to speak of." I wondered if this peculiar illocution contained deeper significances.

"You worked together in his gallery business."

"He was a trader, not a gallerist. I was his assistant."

Francizka looked bored, tired, disappointed that my questions should chase fruitless tangents. The pocket of my sports jacket held the Pascin stamp. I grasped it in my palm like the lawyer I wasn't, running my fingers along my secret piece of evidence, the proverbial smoking gun. During the trip down, I had pictured the moment of drama as I nonchalantly took it from my pocket and placed it before her. But I was never suited for a legal career or the theatrics of the courtroom. What would have Exhibit A proved? That she knew the Pascins and probably the Kokoschka were no more authentic than her Christmas cutlery? What more confirmation did I need? Everything I knew about Francizka suggested that far from merely knowing, she had probably masterminded the scheme and orchestrated its success. Did I need to see the expression on her face when I gently placed the atelier stamp on the table? What reaction did I imagine? *Ah, the Pascin stamp. It's been years since I've seen that. I wonder why Victor kept it. Now please, there's a trash in the corner. Place it where it belongs.* And if, by some chance, she displayed complete incomprehension, feigned or genuine—what then? Was I now going to inform her that the gouache that hung over her bed, a seated female nude, was a fake? As I glanced at the work, I realized why the picture had reminded me of Francizka, from the very first time Oliver gave me a tour of the apartment: *she had posed for it.* She knew. The stamp remained in my jacket pocket. The next day I would mail it to Olivia. Or would deliver it by hand when I visited her in London after New Year's.

"Victor suffered depression," I said.

"Among his many problems, I'm afraid. I tried to spare the boys the brunt of his disease. I'll be truthful, when he left, I did not try to stop him. I thought, just as well that the twins not grow up with such a father— for a boy to see his father crying for no reason, it is not a recipe for health. So I tried to shield my boys, but I'm afraid that nature has had the last laugh on me. You know, Ollie was born with a caul—it's supposed to be a sign of good luck. He was always such a happy child, always skipping on the way to school. But then things changed. It started with that poor girl. Mew has also had his spells, but thank God he's much better now. Have I told you—he's dating a lovely woman, a member of his church?"

Francizka had always insisted that Oliver's disappearance was an accident. I wondered if her comments marked a change in her thinking. Or maybe she enjoyed the enviable gift of holding contradictory beliefs without any experience of dissonance.

"Did Oliver ever learn how his father died?"

She appeared not to understand my interest in the question. But certainly one would want to know whether Oliver had first learned of his father's suicide only days before he took his own life. Maybe the knowledge weighed him down; maybe it liberated him. In either case, the question *had* to be relevant. Her eyes narrowed, as if she sensed a trap but not the direction it would spring from.

"I honestly do not know what that woman told him. If she did, he and I did not discuss it. Not on that ship."

I asked myself what it meant if Oliver hadn't known. He plunged into the Atlantic almost twenty years to the day that his father ran the rubber tube from the exhaust pipe into the passenger compartment of his Opel—almost, not exactly. So it might simply have been a grand coincidence, or rather, that form of coincidence tailored by rough genetics or gods strong on irony. On the other hand, what would it mean if he had known, but not about his father's wartime trauma? What if he saw himself as simply succumbing to what Olivia had called the family's "bad plumbing"; what if he leaped to fulfill his destiny without knowing that his father had been broken by forces stronger than even DNA? I realized that I would never have these answers. This uncertainty, this absence of certain knowledge, more than any other gap in the Vices' story, filled me with nagging regret, a sense of material loss. I remembered the anguish that would grip Oliver whenever he thought about the night of Sophia's death—how he'd failed to share some consequent thought or observation with her. A similar feeling took hold of me. I wanted to chase after Oliver to make sure he had his facts straight, and, if not, to provide him this vital addendum—not because it would necessarily change the outcome, but because I felt he would very much want to know.

Francizka coughed and the cough turned into a dry search for air. I realized with dismay that the odor of ammonia and sour pickles in the room came from inside her. I encouraged her to sip some water; this time, she did.

"Maybe that's enough for today," I said.

"My dear, may I make a recommendation? If you have something more you want to ask, I suggest you do it right here and now."

Her dark exhausted eyes showed no fear, not of death, certainly not of me. Questions competed in my mind—particularly those left unanswered by the Jugendstil apartment house of Dr. Sándor Nagy. But why should I now be privy to information denied her own son? By what prerogative could I claim the right to ask and, more crucially, to know? If she had found a name and a narrative that made the past bearable to herself and plausible to her children, far be it from me to insist on a belated correction that could neither help the living nor recover the dead. It was a shibboleth of self-help gurus and talk-show hosts that the truth was the necessary and adequate answer to an unmastered past. But who was to say that myth and invention delivered a means of reconciliation, accommodation, and perseverance any less potent? *The Truth will set you free*—why did people place such stock in this belief? Free from what? From Untruth? If that is the answer, then the statement

collapses into tautology, I could hear Oliver sternly de-
claim in his professor's voice. If the answer is misery, then
it states a hope, an article of faith. And it certainly does
not follow that the truth *alone* will set you free. Stories,
lies, fiction might do just as neat a job. Possibly better.

From somewhere in the apartment came the sound of
Blessed singing a lovely lilting tune of biblical lament.
The nightstand next to Francizka's gurney was cluttered with photos from happier, or at least less ruinous,
times: Oliver and Bartholomew against the backdrop of
the Swiss alps, Bart at Princeton, Oliver with Jean in
Oxford.

It was time to say goodbye, but then Francizka said,
"I want to tell you about my last visit with Jacob." With
dread, I realized that she was circling back to the matter
of the contested will.

"You know, Jacob had his shortcomings but he was a
wonderful father to my sons. He came into a difficult
situation, two young boys, distrustful of this new man,
and yet he won them over effortlessly. His secret was the
stories of Kipling. Jacob had a splendid deep voice, a true
New Yorker's voice, and he loved to read aloud to them,
always Kipling. Kipling, Kipling, Kipling! 'The Man Who
Would Be King'—the boys never tired of that story!

"Toward the end, when he was ill with that terrible
disease, I went to his apartment. Not to talk money—
please, nothing could have been further from my mind.
I went with the thought that I might read aloud to him,
but then it occurred to me that his first love was always
music. So I arrived at his apartment—he would not
stand for being in a hospital; you see, he and I had much

in common—and noticed to my *horror* that *Camelot* was playing in his bedroom. After rock and roll, Jacob most despised show tunes. I asked his nurse, 'Whose idea is this?' and she said that Jacob's sons had brought a number of CDs for their father. Well, the very first thing I did was to remove that awful music. I marched straight to Orchard Records on Third Avenue—sadly, it has gone under, like all the fine book and music stores we used to have—and returned with a dozen CDs for Jacob. Then we sat together listening to his beloved Mahler. We sat in each other's company, he in bed and I in a chair, just listening. When the Fifth Symphony's Adagietto for harp and strings played, Jacob looked at me, and I swear, a tear fell onto his cheek. A single tear! I squeezed his hand and he squeezed back. The doctors said that Jacob could no longer follow things at this point but what do they know? Had they shared the same bed with this man for two decades? It's true, he did not speak, but he *understood*. He wanted to help *all* his children. Believe me. I knew my husband."

"You did everything for your sons."

"I did. Yes."

It was her summation and valedictory. The room darkened, maybe clouds had gathered outside. The cool light indulged and revived Francizka, made her look younger, ready to rise from her bed and prepare a Christmas dinner.

I collected the dying woman into a farewell embrace. "I know you and Oliver argued toward the end," I said. "But I know that he loved you as dearly as any son has ever loved his mother."

She hugged me with a strength I would not have considered possible, and pressed three kisses on my cheeks, the Hungarian way. "Ollie was lucky to have you as a friend. Now go. Give my love to your wife and your precious children."

I hadn't told her about my separation. "I will. Goodbye, Francizka."

As I was leaving the apartment, I again heard Blessed singing. Accompaning her was a strange mechanical whine, like a kitchen blender. But the sound of singing and machine came from the study. There I caught a glimpse of Manny Morgen, the lawyer, bent over Francizka's desk, handing stacks of files to Blessed. Humming a Creole spiritual, Blessed dreamily fed the documents into a paper shredder.

SEVENTEEN

Two weeks later Francizka died. I'm certain that she could have willed herself to live for however long she wanted. But she was tired and out of fight. She went in her sleep.

Word came from Bartholomew. I assumed her death would leave him undone, but Bart had undergone a remarkable change since I'd last seen him. At the funeral he carried himself with strength. He was still large, but had shed whole layers of bulk: he looked imposing, not obese. He was clean-shaven, his upper lip free of the demented whiskers. Despite the years of smoking, overeating, and depression, his face remained unlined, his skin as supple as a child's. As the assembly sang the three acclamations of the Eucharist, Bartholomew's lovely tenor carried over all other voices. At his side, holding his arm, was a woman: handsome, if not beautiful; impressively broad-hipped; and perhaps ten years his senior. They wore matching crucifixes.

In accord with Francizka's wishes, the service was held at St. Agnes, Bartholomew's Tridentine parish. A lanky priest in a black cope stretched out his hands. "Today we gather to illumine the mystery of Christian death in the light of the risen Christ!" He delivered the requiem in Latin, in accord with St. Agnes's repudiation of Vatican II. His homily conjured the coming Days of Wrath, when trumpets will summon the saved to the throne of God and the damned will be cast into eternal flames. Then Bartholomew rose to eulogize the mother he still called "Twigs." The bier was in the middle of the small church. He flung his arms around it in a final embrace, but otherwise maintained his composure.

I recognized faces from Christmases past—Bernie, and Nora and Jeffrey Ferris—as well as a handful of others who had been in the family's employ—Manny Morgen, and Blessed, who, alone among the gathered, wept silently through the entire service.

After the service, Manny Morgen took me by the elbow. "Hello, Mr. Novelist."

"Hello, Esquire."

"It's good of you to come. Can you believe it, first Jacob, then Ollie, now Francizka. A lot of suffering in that family. Too much." One could have added Victor Vice and Sophia to the unhappy enumeration. "And yet she bore it all."

"She was a remarkable woman," I said.

"Remarkable. That's *exactly* what she was. We had our differences, God knows, but she deserved better. Even now I can think of a dozen people who should have been here today. More. I keep asking myself, where's so-and-so and so-and-so."

"It was an intimate service."

"That it was. I only wish she could have been here to see her boy Bart. He insisted on the eulogy, usually Catholics do without. Who knew he had it in him? When he first got up, I frankly didn't know what to expect. But he did himself proud."

"He spoke very well," I said. Not intending to diminish the emotional power and sincerity of his words, I observed that everything he said about his mother was almost certainly false.

"Oh, really? What, for instance?"

I had a strong suspicion that Morgen could better answer his own question than I could. Still, I enumerated several of the presumable falsehoods unwittingly repeated by Francizka's surviving son: the aristocratic Hungarian forebearers, the abandonment by a pair of husbands—not to mention the obvious omissions, such as the fact that Bart's own father was a Jew and a Holocaust survivor.

"You have a very vivid imagination," said Morgen. "As a novelist, it must come in handy."

"I suppose."

"But at least you have the good sense not to share your novelist's speculations with Bart. Who happens now to be quite a wealthy man. His stepfather left him well provided for."

"So I've gathered."

"Even Francizka left him a nice little nest egg with that apartment."

"I can imagine. Her art collection alone must be worth a fortune."

Morgen looked at me through canny vulpine eyes. "A novelist with a sense of humor. Even better."

"Thank you."

"You know, your alma mater also stands to get a considerable gift from Francizka."

I had heard about Francizka's bequest to the college. "I'm not a Harkness graduate."

"Your employer, I meant. You understood me."

"Yes."

"So how's the book coming?" He must have learned about it from Francizka. He dusted flakes of dandruff from his charcoal suit.

"Well, there are some large gaps. It would be nice to interview someone who could offer some of the missing pieces. Assuming that such a person exists."

Morgen smiled, but his eyes, small and gray to begin with, shrank to something wintry and unreflective. "What missing pieces are we talking about?"

"Francizka's family remains a mystery. She said her parents and sister were killed in an air raid in the summer of 1944, later she said they were shot. She never even tried to keep her story straight. It was always something new. At times I've wondered if her parents were collaborators. On the other hand, her parents were killed during the time when the entire Jewish population of Hungary was liquidated."

"Not quite," he said. "Most of the 1944 summer liquidations involved Jews in the towns and provinces. Deportations from Budapest didn't really swing into gear until October 1944. And don't forget the Nazis' crazy scheme to trade Jews for trucks, a million Jews for a thousand trucks. Don't give me that look, my friend. I'm a history buff, particularly that history. Hilberg, Browning, Friedlander, Bauer—I've read them all."

"Do you have a personal interest?" I asked.

"Are we here to talk about me?"

I accepted his point. I told him that in the year before

his disappearance, Oliver had hired a genealogical researcher in Budapest. "The researcher found a lot of information about the family of Dr. Sándor Nagy—only it wasn't Francizka's family."

"Maybe Oliver hired the wrong guy."

"Oliver said he was quite professional. Anyway, I can corroborate that it wasn't her family."

"*Corroborate?* Is this a criminal investigation?"

I smiled, only he didn't let go. "I asked you a question. Is it?"

"Of course not."

"I'm relieved to hear that. Now, this professional whom Ollie hired. Did it ever occur to you that he might have searched under the wrong name?"

"What do you mean?"

"Just what I said. Maybe he looked under the wrong name. A young girl loses her family during a time of great losses. Maybe she loses her name, too."

"What name might he look under?"

Manny laughed, a quick theatrical burst. "Haven't you ever heard of the attorney-client privilege? Didn't they teach you anything at *the* Yale law school?"

"I didn't realize Francizka was your client."

"Sure! Victor, Jacob, Francizka—I represented them all. And while we're on the subject, please don't write anything that would force a libel suit. I still represent the family. Libel is such a tricky animal—you get before a jury and anything can happen. I say that for your benefit."

"Thanks for the warning."

"You said it best—she was a remarkable woman. But maybe I'd look under a name like 'Bart.' It's German, you know, for 'beard.' Theoretically speaking."

I had no chance to thank him. He had already turned to an usher at the funeral. Manny shook the usher's hand and adjusted his boutonniere. "Not a happy day," I heard him say.

EIGHTEEN

The faculty of Harkness College—less than two hundred professors—meets as a whole three or so times per term to do business. We convene in a windowless amphitheater known as the Red Room, so named in recognition of the carpeting and seat fabric that gradually saturates the retinas of those confined to it. It is here, at an afternoon meeting in early November, that the college's president announces Francizka's bequest. Even before the announcement, Oliver's spirit presides, as our first order of business is a motion, brought jointly by several professors in the history and philosophy departments, calling on the college to bar future CIA recruiting on campus. It is a nonbinding resolution, the final say rests with the Board of Trustees; still, a Sense of the Faculty resolution carries symbolic heft, and the debate is no less vigorous for its lack of practical effect.

The first to speak is a member of the old guard, a professor in the religion department with the fleecy beard of a prophet, who rises slowly and begins by reminding the gathered that he first came to teach at Harkness in the semester before the launch of the Tet offensive. He recalls that two years later, "the spring term vanished in a haze of tear gas and windy rhetoric." It's not clear if he's speaking for or against the resolution, but after five minutes of unfocused reminiscences and dire warnings, he signals his ambivalent support and sits down. Two more professors register support. Professor Hirson in theater and dance labors through her stutter to make the pithy and seemingly irresistible point that it's difficult to reconcile the aims of the liberal arts with the practice of torture. This brings Simon Mullhouse to his feet, a Straussian in political science and a former speechwriter for Dan Quayle. Thumbs hooked in the pockets of the vest of a superannuated three-piece suit, Mullhouse asks whether it is not the height of presumptuousness for the Harkness faculty, far removed from the instruments of power, to install itself as the judge of the executive branch in matters of national security. By what *right*, he asks, do we as educators condemn actions about which we know so little? Is this the lesson we want to teach our students, to judge rashly without benefit of the full record? The record is *transparent*, says Adam Blum, a recent hire in English, backing his insistence with an appeal to Benjamin and Agamen. What of the ticking time bomb? asks Alison Theroux in geology. The ticking time bomb is a bogeyman, insists Dennis Singer in history—a rhetorical trap designed to justify the unjustifiable. The college's president, whose sonorous voice has recently been transformed by polyps on the vocal chords into a vague caricature of Truman Capote's, notes that refusing access to the CIA might lead to the college's loss of federal monies, which presently total in the tens of millions per annum. Eduardo Konwicki in Latino studies answers the president by reminding us that the resolution is nonbinding and that the trustees will do what they want anyway. This brings Simon Mullhouse back to his feet; thumbs in his vest, scanning the room in his best channeling of either Clarence Darrow or Stephen Douglas, he rebukes his colleagues. Is it not the *height of hypocrisy* to vote in favor of a motion precisely *because* it lacks all real-world consequences? What if a senator voted for a reckless law while saying to himself, "Ah, no matter—the Supreme Court will strike it down as unconstitutional"? Is this not the very *nadir* of intellectual laziness? *Apogee*, cries W. M. Prescott, a septuagenarian Frost scholar, *not nadir!* Laughter erupts and the question is called. A member of the psychology department who has been diligently knitting asks for clarification: Does a yea vote signal support or disapproval of the CIA? To my pleasant surprise the final tally isn't even close: yeas, 120; nays, 38; abstentions, 3. The yeas have it. A posthumous victory for Oliver without mention of his name. The president wipes sweat from his brow with a handkerchief. The Red Room lacks proper ventilation; the meetings typically begin cool, only gradually to become more oppressive; still, no one wants to repair the defective thermostat, as it is believed that the heat creates incentives for efficiency. But the president clearly suffers. He's a born sweater.

Later he announces the creation of the new Oliver Vice Memorial Professorship in Ethics. The chair will be established through a major bequest from the estate of Francizka Nagy, Oliver's recently deceased mother, and from Oliver's surviving brother, Bartholomew Vice.

In addition, Ms. Nagy has donated a painting from her estate, an oil by the Austrian expressionist Oskar Kokoschka, to Harkness's Museum of Fine Arts. A search to fill the new chair will begin next year; it is the college's hope and expectation that the search will attract a strong international field of candidates, and that Harkness will be able to appoint a scholar who exemplifies Oliver Vice's dedication to a life of philosophical rigor and political engagement. A healthy round of applause greets this announcement. Then the president muses on the oxymoronic quality of the name, the *Vice Professor in Ethics*; easy heat-abbreviated laughter ripples through the faculty. A formal press release announcing the new professorship will be issued in the coming days. The Kokoschka can already be viewed in the museum.

Other orders of business follow, but my thoughts remain with Oliver. On a finance committee report, I draft sample language for the press release.

The Vice Professorship has been made possible by a generous bequest from Francizka Nagy (sic), née or rather aka Bart. The daughter of a Hungarian dentist, Dr. Sándor Bart, Nagy lost her parents and sister in the Holocaust. For obscure reasons (shame, a longing for an intact life, a desire to shield her sons from the calamity of being Jewish, etc.) Nagy concealed her real name and her religious identity from her children. Together with her first husband, Victor Vice (Weiss), also a Holocaust survivor and an accomplished art forger, Nagy established a lucrative trade in Vice's forged paintings. This marriage ended

*in divorce; a second marriage, to Jacob Epstein, a
lighting entrepreneur, also ended in divorce.*

*The professorship is named in memory if Nagy's
son, Oliver Vice, a Harkness philosophy professor
who "fell" from the QM2 during an Atlantic crossing. Untaxed proceeds from the sale of forged art,
along with monies extorted from the estate of Jacob
Epstein and received from Cunard, Carnival Corpo-
ration & PLC, have made possible the Vice Professorship in Ethics.*

The language needs brushing up, but touches most of
the essentials. Does every endowed professorship hide
a similar provenance? I doubt it. After all, Oliver was
nothing if not extraordinary. Though maybe not quite in
all the ways once imagined.

A gavel rap adjourns the meeting. As I leave the Red
Room, I deposit the press release into the bin for re-
cycled paper.

It is already late afternoon, a November day that
would meet with Oliver's approval. The clouds look like
bowed sheet metal; off to the horizon, where they break,
the sky is colored luridly. Sudden winds materialize and
shift. A loose page from the student newspaper wraps
around a lamppost and just as suddenly breaks free.
Piles of leaves eddy to and fro, shifting alliances and
direction.

The Florentine-style art museum, a McKim, Mead,
and White design, sits uncomfortably on Harkness's
neatly ordered colonial campus. A student monitor,
hunched over a chemistry textbook and listening to her

iPod, barely glances at my ID. The museum is nearly empty. The newest bequest hangs alone on a wall, across from several other recent acquisitions. A provisional label identifies the painting as a portrait of Alma Mahler, the composer's widow and Kokoschka's lover for two tumultuous years. I study the painting. It's certainly possible that the Vices acquired it through the sale of other works. The energy of the brushstrokes, the vertiginous background—it all looks very Kokoschka. And yet Alma's carriage, the tilt of her head, the cast of her eyes—why do they remind me of Francizka? Is my imagination playing tricks on me? I'm not an art historian. It's not for me to judge.

North and South Pleasant Streets, known in Harkness as No Pleasant and So Pleasant, bisect the town. I steer my car down So Pleasant, pass a Starbucks, a used CD store, a cafe with fair-trade coffee, a handful of restaurants, a CVS, and a Bank of America that recently burned to the ground. Quickly the town is behind me. So Pleasant narrows and wends past Sugarstack Dairy, a bicentennial farm that supplies the cream for an award-winning sharp cheddar; and Wildwood Elementary, where Matt and Aaron recently started fifth grade. Today is not my day to pick them up. Melissa and I have joint custody while our lawyers siphon our assets and I try to figure out what I'm doing with Olivia Vice. Passing the school I slow to see if the boys have after-school soccer. The field is empty. It's 4:50—practice would have ended twenty minutes ago.

Another mile and I turn off So Pleasant and pass Pilgrim's Pond. In summer, the pond's pebbled shores are crowded with families escaping heat and humidity; in winter, after a cold snap and before the snow, couples skate on the choppy ice and students play pickup games of hockey.

No sign points the way to Maple Cemetery. Enclosed by a low metal gate, bordering a nature preserve, and shaded by sycamores and sugar maples now past their peak fall colors, the cemetery guards its solitude. Here rest two of the nation's most famous poets, both formerly affiliated with the college, one as a student and the other as a professor. It is here, among Puritans and minute-men and ministers, far from his mother and Pappy, far from Sophia Baum and Victor Weiss, that Oliver once expressed the desire to be buried.

The gravestone, austerely lettered and nondenominational, is, of course, nothing more than a cenotaph. Dig and you will find no dry bones in repose, no bodily remains to direct your prayers or remonstrances or love or curses toward.

Standing before the grave, I play Counterfactual, a tricky game of speculation that reverses time, upsets the order of things, and generally occupies itself with impossible questions of *what if.* The day before, I'd cut from the *Times* a small AP piece describing the arrest of a steward on a Viking Caribbean cruise ship who confessed to robbing a passenger and pushing him overboard. The passenger's death had previously been supposed a suicide, but after the steward was recently accused of stealing cash from a fellow crew member, an inspection of his cabin uncovered the deceased passenger's watch. A confession followed. Now I ask myself, what if this steward had previously been in the employ of Cunard? How would it change things to learn that Oliver, indulging his melancholic affection for inclement weather, had been assaulted on the empty deck, robbed of his IWC watch, a present from his mother from an earlier cash-smuggling trip to Zurich, and pushed overboard? It would change a great deal, I conclude. Whether fairly or not, we see a life through the prism of its end, and when the end is self-willed, the preceding life assembles itself into an elaborate premonition of destruction. Is there any reason to believe that Oliver was murdered? None whatsoever. But the absence of supporting evidence offers no disproof. And if we multiply the probability of an event—no matter how unlikely—by its importance if it *did* occur, then we are left with something small, but not trivial—something that warrants consideration. Like checking the steward's employment history.

There is a second kind of thought experiment. Take the poet Randall Jarrell, killed by a passing car on a country road. Jarrell's death had all the hallmarks of a suicide; he'd left a note of sorts, something that Oliver, for all his scrupulous dedication to courtesy and reasoned justification, most emphatically did not. Yet witnesses to Jarrell's death say that in the crucial moment he lost nerve, or to put it more affirmatively, chose life: he tried to dodge the oncoming vehicle. Might Oliver have been toying with suicide only to have his toy explode, so to speak, in his hand? Might he have learned something important about himself in the very moment that a wild avalanche of ocean swept him off? Again, the possibility cannot be ruled out.

Finally, imagine a fellow passenger, also prone to melancholy and drawn to the comfort of storms; he sees Oliver go overboard and sounds a prompt alarm, effecting an improbable rescue. What then? We tend to think of despair as "chronic," the patient always vulnerable to relapses. But maybe it can also behave like a life-threatening virus, which, if overcome, confers a permanent immunity. Had Oliver been able to get through that *one night*, maybe he would have mastered the danger once and for all. If only.

The speculations loop through my mind, in hamster-like repetitions. All the while, I search. Not for answers but for something more readily at hand. Maple leaves, brown and brittle, litter the ground. Brush them aside and the earth is cool, packed dirt and rocks. Twigs and small sticks can be used as levers, to dig and pry loose. Most rocks must be discarded. Pebbles obviously are too small. Some stones are the right size, but are too rough, too jagged, too *unsuitable*. The principal criterion is that each should fit pleasingly in my palm. Flatness, too—that's also key. After thirty minutes or so, I have my five. The first is perfectly smooth, as if transplanted from a distant beach; the second has veins like a fertilized egg; fissures traverse the third like a wobbly chessboard; the fourth is entirely black; the fifth is gray like the skies he preferred. Together they lie securely atop Oliver's headstone, a neat, even stack that should survive today's wind and tomorrow's snow and the steady erosions of time.

ACKNOWLEDGMENTS

Forbearance, support, and help came variously from Rand Cooper, Owen Fiss, Alex George, Daniel Greenberg, Judith Gurewich, Katie Henderson, Nasser Hussain, John Kleiner, Betsy Kolbert, Brad Leithauser, Eric Sanders, the National Endowment for the Humanities, and, of course, Nancy Pick. My thanks to them all.